CHILLED TO THE BONE

When an elderly shipowner is found dead, tied to a bed in one of Reykjavík's smartest hotels, Sergeant Gunnhildur Gísladóttir of the city police force sees no evidence of foul play, but still suspects that things may not be as simple as they appear. As she investigates the shipowner's untimely and embarrassing demise, she stumbles across a discreet bondage ring whose existence she never suspected, and which someone is exploiting as a blackmail tool to extract cash from the most unlikely people. What begins as a straightforward case for Gunna escalates into a dangerous investigation uncovering secrets that ruthless people are ready to go to violent extremes to keep.

CHILLED TO THE BONE

QUENTIN BATES

LARGE
PRINT

First published in Great Britain 2013
by
C&R Crime
an imprint of Constable & Robinson Ltd.

First Isis Edition
published 2017
by arrangement with
Constable & Robinson Ltd.

A catalogue record for this book is available
from the British Library.

ISBN 978–1–78541–437–4 (hb)
ISBN 978–1–78541–443–5 (pb)

Published by
F. A. Thorpe (Publishing)
Anstey, Leicestershire

Set by Words & Graphics Ltd.
Anstey, Leicestershire
Printed and bound in Great Britain by
T. J. International Ltd., Padstow, Cornwall

This book is printed on acid-free paper

CHAPTER
ONE

Thursday

Gunna stamped the snow from her boots and flinched as the overpowering heat of the hotel's lobby hit her like a slap in the face. The door whispered shut behind her as she looked around, spying a man wearing a grey suit and a worried expression by the reception desk. He immediately hurried over to her.

"You're from the police?" He asked in a voice laden with drama but kept so low as to be almost a murmur.

"That's me. Look like a copper, do I?" Gunna replied brightly, shooting out a hand for the man to grasp and shake limply. "Gunnhildur Gísladóttir. And you are?"

"Yngvi Jónsson, I'm the duty manager. Where are the rest of you?"

"Only me to start with. Can you show me what's happened?"

Yngvi wrung his hands as he scuttled towards the lift, which opened in front of them.

"Of course, we've had guests who've had problems before, and even people who have . . ." he gulped, "passed away on the premises. But never anything like this."

"You know who the man is, I take it?"

"Of course. He's stayed here a good many times in the past and has always been a real gentleman. It's been such a shock . . ."

"And his family? He has a family I presume?"

"I haven't contacted anyone except the police. The staff are in the canteen, waiting for you."

Gunna nodded. Yngvi continued to wring his hands and the lift played muzak until a soft voice warned them the third floor was approaching.

"This way, please," he said needlessly, stepping out of the lift and hurrying along the corridor, with Gunna striding at his heels. He swiped a card through the electronic lock of a door, looked left and right along the corridor and pushed the door open.

"There," he said, and Gunna stepped inside, pulling on a pair of surgical gloves as she did so.

The room was silent and dark. She carefully used the butt of a ballpoint pen to turn on the lights at the switch by the door and surveyed the room in front of her and the naked man stretched across the king-sized bed.

"Who's been in here?" Gunna asked, calling over her shoulder and sensing Yngvi standing in the doorway.

"The cleaner who found him, the supervisor, me and the doctor."

"Which doctor was that?"

"Sveinn Ófeigsson. He's retired, but he's staying here at the moment, and as he was in the bar, I asked him to come up with me. I don't know if that was right or not, but it seemed quicker than calling out an ambulance."

Gunna went along the side of the bed and crouched by the man's head, lolling at an unnatural angle, his mouth blocked by a bright red ball held in place by straps around the back of his neck. The face looked vaguely familiar, a man in late middle age, with eyes half-closed and strands of thin hair in disarray, revealing a gleaming scalp. The pale arm that reached up behind him was tied securely at the wrist to the top of the bed frame. Standing up and retracing her steps, she saw that the man's other hand and both ankles were tied in the same way with dark red scarves that almost matched the burgundy of the rich bedspread.

"Don't touch anything, please," Gunna told Yngvi, who had advanced a few steps into the room.

Gunna looked around, taking in as many details of the room as she could, but nothing appeared to be out of place. A suitcase lay open on a frame in the corner of the room, with rows of shirts and underwear neatly laid out and ready to be plucked for use.

The bathroom light shimmered into life automatically just as she was looking for the switch, to reveal sparkling marble tiles and a vast basin. A small sponge bag sat next to the sink, along with an electric razor. Gunna peered into the sink and spied a long black hair in sharp relief against the pale marble.

She nodded to herself and backed out to where Yngvi was waiting for her.

"That'll do for the moment, thanks. I'll get a forensic team to come and examine the room as soon as possible. Until then, it needs to be sealed."

"But what about . . .?" Yngvi asked, gesturing towards the corpse on the bed.

"Don't worry. He's not going to run away. We'd best go back downstairs and I'll start asking questions. You said the girl who found him is still here?"

Yngvi nodded miserably.

"In that case, I'm going to have to borrow your office, probably for the rest of the day," she said.

"I was wondering how long . . .?"

"How long, what?"

"How long all this will take? He was due to leave today and we'll be needing the room for a guest tonight."

"In that case, I think someone is going to be disappointed. This is going to take a while, so you might have to send your guest to Hotel Borg instead. Come on."

Hekla's new hair had a blonde sheen that gave her an allure and a confidence that she enjoyed. Everything was new, the expensively simple dress, the nails, the shoes, even her minuscule underwear was understatedly elegant and straight from the packet.

She sat in the hotel's lobby and did her best to stay calm, forcing herself to breathe at a measured rate in order to numb the combination of anticipation and anxiety. This wasn't something she could see as a job and detach herself from. It still took its toll and kept her awake at nights, especially since that scare before Christmas, though less often than before. In a small country like Iceland, she reflected, there simply wasn't

4

enough of a clientele. Sooner or later she would run out of men, be recognized on the street or else have to leave the country and maybe take her line of work with her.

Hekla sipped chilled water and delicately replaced the glass on the table in front of her. She could retire, she thought, and smiled at the prospect. The bank balance was piling up nicely. Debts had been paid off. She would be able to take it easy and perhaps get a proper job once the children were at school.

She hardly noticed the florid man in a dark business suit approach and stand looking sideways at her. Hekla looked up and reproached herself for a lack of awareness, giving the man a discreet smile and a nod.

"Sonja?" he asked.

"I'm Sonja. You must be Haraldur?"

"That's me. Call me Halli. Shall we?" he asked, the eagerness in his voice unmistakable.

"Of course. But if you don't mind, I'd like to talk here first for a little while. Think of it as an icebreaker." She smiled. "Would you like a drink?"

Haraldur sat in the chair opposite her, at ease but still tense, although he hid it well. Hekla looked deliberately at the bar and caught the eye of the young man behind it, who quickly came across to them, his steps silent on the hotel's lush carpet.

"Can I offer you anything?" he asked.

"What would you like, Haraldur?"

"Bacardi and Coke for me."

"And I'll have some tea, please. Camomile if you have it."

The barman almost bowed as he backed away.

"So, Haraldur. Are you in Reykjavík on business?"

"Yup. Here for two days, then back home."

"You're in the seafood business?"

"Actually, no. Transport and storage equipment. There isn't much I couldn't tell you about forklift trucks," he said with a sharp bark of humourless laughter.

Hekla could see that he was becoming increasingly nervous; perhaps he was worried that someone would see him with an unfamiliar young woman. The hand that lifted the glass the barman brought him trembled slightly.

The barman placed a small teapot and a delicate china cup in front of her.

"Thank you. Charge to room 406, please," Hekla said to the youth, and smiled warmly at him as he backed away again.

"No offence, but I'd just like to lay down a few ground rules before we go any further," Hekla said, flashing a smile.

"Yeah. Of course."

"I see myself as a professional and I expect to be treated as one. There has to be respect on both sides. I take pride in my work and aim to do a good job, the same as I'm sure you do in your professional life," she said smoothly.

"Absolutely."

"Once we are alone, I'm at work. I expect you to address me as 'mistress' at all times. If at any time you want to stop, all you have to do is say 'terminate' and we stop immediately. You're happy with that?"

"Understood."

"What could you tell me about forklift trucks, then?" she asked, her voice silky, and deliberately uncrossed her legs as slowly as she dared.

"Well, they come in all sizes. Depends what you need to . . ."

His voice faltered as Hekla recrossed her legs the other way, hiding the reason for Haraldur's sudden loss of speech. She poured fragrant tea into her cup and sipped, looking over the rim at him and wanting to laugh as he quickly gulped his drink. "You were saying?"

Jóel Ingi Bragason shrugged on his jacket and picked his way through the toys that his wife's nieces and nephews had left littering the hall to the door of the flat.

"See you at six," he called out, waiting for a second for a reply that didn't come from his wife before closing the front door and cursing the realization that she must have gone back to sleep.

It was cold and damp outside, as well as dark, and Jóel Ingi found it difficult to reconcile himself to Icelandic winters, even in Reykjavík where heavy snow was a rarity. The years of study in America and a delightful sojourn at the Sorbonne had spoiled him, he reflected as he took short steps along the ice-bound but gradually thawing pavement, scared that overconfidence in unsuitable shoes would send him flying. Once in the car, he felt better. It became a bubble around him, safe and warm, its airbags and discreet steel pillars protecting him from the cruel world outside.

He could have walked to work in roughly the same time as it took to walk to the car and drive it to the underground car park beneath the ministry.

Coffee arrived halfway through the morning and it was a relief. A couple of glasses of wine the night before had left him heavier than he should have felt and Jóel Ingi wondered if this was the onset of middle age. In spite of two strong cups of coffee, he struggled to stay awake during a meeting later in the morning, and had to force himself to pay attention to the minutiae of European Union proceedings.

Checking his phone discreetly during the meeting, he saw there were no messages from Agnes, which was a relief as she had taken to shooting him sideways glances and he was beginning to get the feeling that she was checking up on him. Shrugging off his misgivings, he steered his thoughts back to the fine detail of the proposed policy, but not before noticing with pleasure that the most junior person in the room, a newly appointed secretary, had slipped off her shoes under the table opposite him and that she had delightfully shapely calves. The voice of the meeting's chairman became little more than a distant drone as Jóel Ingi's thoughts drifted increasingly towards how those legs might shape up above the knee.

As his thoughts slipped in another direction, he scowled to himself, unconsciously chewing his lip as memories of that damned woman came back to him again, and he wondered if that afternoon would come back to haunt him. He started as he looked up and saw with discomfort that the girl with the delightful calves was looking right at him with concern in her eyes. Jóel Ingi smiled as broadly as he could and hoped that he hadn't looked too bored or stupid.

The city felt different. There was a cautious, watchful feel to Reykjavík, as if the place were waiting for another kicking. Baddó hadn't spent many of his years away following events in Iceland, but the news of the financial crash and then the volcano erupting and stopping air traffic had been the basis of a few ribald comments from prisoners who hadn't got to know him or his reputation, resulting in more that one sore head.

When Baddó had left Iceland for somewhere a man could have space to flex his muscles, it still felt like a quiet backwater, a place where not much happened and, when it did, it wasn't going to happen in too much of a hurry, regardless of how much fuss people made. The occasional visit during the good years before he had fallen foul of the wrong people and found himself behind bars, when it seemed that business had discovered some hidden philosopher's stone had left a sour taste behind. All the same, it had been like a rest cure to come back and see the place once in a while. Although most of his family hadn't wanted a great deal to do with him, there were a few friends who respected a man who could stand his corner and keep his mouth shut.

Now it was different. Baddó had to admit even to himself that he was tired. He had been ready to explode with fury at any moment during the flight over the Baltic with a mustachioed policeman on either side of him, and while they sat and wolfed down pizzas and beer at Kåstrup, their eyes never strayed far from him. The two hulking giants didn't take their eyes off him until the stewardess had closed and locked the pressure-tight door of the aircraft that would take him back to Iceland for the first time in almost a decade.

He unfolded the newspaper he had put under his arm without thinking in the shop at the corner, and was surprised to see that it was in English. He threw it in the bin, lay down on the wine-red sofa, tucking a cushion under his head, and tried to sleep. Ten minutes later he gave up and stood to gaze out at the grey roofs opposite the little flat's bathroom window, watching flakes of snow spiral down and settle. It was going to be a cold day, he thought, wondering when María would be home.

"His name's Jóhannes Karlsson," Helgi said. "Shipowner from Húsavík, retired. Lives in Copenhagen part of the year. Rolling in dosh, if I recall correctly. Used to be in politics years ago, MP for a term or two in the seventies, until he decided business was more important, or lucrative, than politics. Does that tell you what you want to know?"

Gunna and Helgi had retired to a corner of the hotel's bar to confer while the forensic team and the police pathologist examined the room where they had left the late Jóhannes Karlsson still strapped to the bed he had died on.

10

"Independence or Progressive?"

"Independence Party, I think. I wouldn't want to think that he was one of us," Helgi said in a severe tone.

"One of you, you mean. I'd prefer it if you didn't take me for a Progressive Party supporter, thank you very much."

"Sorry. I never saw you as anything but a bleeding heart liberal, Gunna."

"Cause of death?" she asked.

"You're asking me?"

"Sorry, Helgi. No, just thinking out loud. I'm wondering if this was murder or accidental? What do you reckon?"

Helgi snorted. "Doesn't look in the least bit intentional to me. I reckon there was some fun and games going on, our boy got his first stiffy for years and keeled over under the strain. The girlfriend — or boyfriend, or paid companion, or whatever — ran for it. That's what tells me that whoever was with him probably decided he or she wasn't being paid enough to deal with this kind of stuff."

"You know, Helgi, with brains like yours you're wasted on the police. I reckon you've pretty much summed it up. But, unfortunately, that doesn't mean I get to go home."

"And do some knitting?" Helgi asked innocently.

"Don't push it," Gunna growled, signalling to Yngvi, hovering by the bar, with a cup-to-the-lips gesture. "How long has he been staying here? This place must

11

cost a fortune," she said as a waiter approached with a tray of cups and a flask of coffee.

"He's been here for two weeks. His wife was here for the first week, apparently, and went home while Jóhannes was dealing with some business in Reykjavík. He was due to check out at twelve today. When he hadn't showed up at one, the chambermaid knocked, as they always do, to see if he'd already gone, and found him spark out on the bed. She screamed, called the housekeeping manager, and she called us. I called the doctor who was at the bar."

"Fair enough," Gunna said. "Where's Eiríkur?"

"On his way. Won't be long."

"Good," Gunna said, sipping daintily at the coffee the tall, dark-haired young man placed wordlessly on the table. "When he gets here, start him off checking the passenger lists to see when our boy was due to travel and then get him to see if he can track down the man's wife. If she's still in Húsavík, he'd best get the police there to speak to her and break the bad news that she's a widow."

"Right, will do. And me?"

"Talk to the staff, and see what you can find by way of CCTV. We need to speak to whoever tied Jóhannes Karlsson to the bed, even though it looks like he'd probably paid whoever it was handsomely to do just that."

"Yup. And you, chief?"

"Oh, you know. I'll just take a walk around the shops while you and Eiríkur do the hard work."

"Nothing unusual there, then?"

"Get away with you. I'll start with the chambermaid who found our boy and then the duty manager, and hopefully the forensic team will have done their business by then. But first I'm going to have another cup of this rather fine coffee."

"Are we paying for this?" Helgi asked dubiously.

"Good grief, no. It's an integral part of the investigation."

Haraldur sat on the bed in his underwear, breathing heavily. Hekla stood in front of him and unzipped her black dress with one hand behind her. His hands reached forward and his face was flushed.

He groaned. "God, you're gorgeous."

"God, you're gorgeous . . .?"

"Sorry. Mistress."

"That's better," Hekla warned, lifting his hands from her hips and pushing them firmly back. "You're a bad man and now you'll have to wait. If you'll just get yourself in the mood, I'll be right back."

She let the dress fall, turned and stepped towards the bathroom, her heels clicking on the warm tiled floor, knowing that Haraldur's eyes were glued to her buttocks, which he could just see below the hem of her shift.

She washed her face in cold water and dried it with a towel that felt as soft as fur. She could hear Haraldur's breathing in the bedroom and the sound of him moving about on the bed. She pulled on the tight PVC one-piece suit that she had ready in the bathroom and took a deep breath, picking up a handful of scarves and a small leather strap on the way.

Hekla dimmed the lights as far as they would go and sent a slow smile towards Haraldur where he lay on the bed. She added a low chuckle and stepped towards him, standing over the naked man, hands on her hips.

"So, Haraldur, you've been really bad and I'm going to have to teach you a little lesson, aren't I?" She pitched her voice deep and reached forward to tie one of his wrists to the headboard with practised ease. He moaned as she leaned over him, her breasts encased in electric blue plastic and skimming his face as she tied the other wrist back in the same way.

The fingertips of one hand brushed his chest and down to his belly. A reasonably attractive man and in good condition for his age, she thought. Hekla walked along the side of the bed, trailing the leather strap down the length of his body and along one leg to his ankle, where she stooped and planted a kiss on his instep.

"Have you been bad, Haraldur?"

"Yes, mistress," he responded dutifully.

"Then a little more correction might be needed."

Another scarf was swiftly tied around the ankle and secured to the bed frame.

"Bad, bad man," she growled in the deepest voice she could manage and the other ankle was quickly tied, leaving Haraldur spreadeagled across the king-sized bed.

Hekla sashayed back to the top of the bed and showed him the ball gag. "Since you've been such a bad, bad man, I'm going to show you what a bad, bad girl I can be," she said quietly.

"Please, mistress," Haraldur panted.

"You really want me to hurt you?"

"Yes, mistress."

"Then watch this, Haraldur."

Hekla pushed the ball into Haraldur's mouth and put her hands quickly behind his neck to clip the strap shut. As she stepped back, he immediately began to breathe heavily through his nose, struggling to draw breath and splaying his cheeks to get some air around the ball.

"Now you're going to be patient and wait right there and think about how bad you've been," she said, disappearing back into the bathroom.

After what seemed an age, she reappeared. The plastic suit had gone, replaced with a hooded sweater, jeans and trainers. The makeup had been scrubbed off and the golden hair was gone, replaced with dark curls that reached her shoulders. Hekla dropped a large holdall on the floor next to the door and, as his heart sank, she went over to where his clothes had been hastily discarded, systematically going through the pockets. She switched off his phone and put it on the dresser, before opening his wallet and removing the notes, stuffing them into the pocket of her pullover without counting them. Next she extracted all of the cards and brought them over to the bed.

Hekla looked down at Haraldur, lying mute and helpless in front of her. She sat down by his head and looked into his bewildered eyes, unclipping a ballpoint pen from the neckline of her sweater.

"Are you listening carefully, Haraldur?" The only response was a limited straining of his arms and legs against the scarves holding him down and a desperate growl from behind the rubber ball.

"You know that's not going to help, don't you?" she told him as he went limp. "Now, listen. I'm going to go shopping for an hour or so while you ponder the error of your ways and remember how much you love your wife. All right?"

Haraldur's eyes bulged.

"Your credit card. Tell me your pin number. Clench your right fist for the numbers. Once for one, twice for two, and so on. Four numbers. Go."

Haraldur's fists remained obstinately clenched and Hekla sighed. "Look. There's an easy way and a hard way. If you give me the number and it works, when I've been shopping I'll call the hotel's reception and tell them there's a man in room 406 who is in trouble and needs some help urgently. If the number doesn't work, then I won't and nobody will come in here until the chambermaid comes to clean your room tomorrow morning."

She looked at her watch.

"It's half past four now, so that's in about sixteen hours' time. You might be a bit cold and thirsty by then. It's up to you."

Haraldur's fist clenched and unclenched in a series of numbers.

"Two-five-two-seven. Good. Now we're getting somewhere. And your debit card? Same number, maybe?"

Haraldur nodded furiously as she wrote the number on the back of her hand.

She held up a second debit card. "And this one?"

Another series of nods.

"Good. It's been a pleasure doing business with you, Haraldur. Don't worry about your cards. The bank will give you new ones easily enough. I'll destroy them when I've been shopping and I won't sell them on to anyone else."

She dipped into her pocket and drew out a small digital camera, pointed it at the helpless, naked Haraldur in front of her and pressed the shutter. Haraldur strained against the scarves that were holding him down and his face went a deep red as she took several pictures. She looked him up and down, screwed up her face in sympathy and spat in her palm.

"The least I can do for you under the circumstances, I suppose," she said as she set to work. It didn't take long. A minute later Haraldur stiffened, arched his back as far as his bonds would allow him and relaxed, while Hekla looked at him indulgently. She went to the bathroom, washed her hands and came back with a fluffy towel, which she used to wipe the man's belly clean.

"Be careful in future, and no hard feelings, eh? Business is business," Hekla said with a cheerful smile, looking down at the forlorn man in front of her as she swung the holdall onto her shoulder. "Goodbye, Haraldur. Someone will be up to untie you in an hour."

A light lunch of salad, soup and bread full of so many seeds that they stuck between his teeth gave Jóel Ingi the energy to wake up, and half an hour later he was stripped down to shorts and a grey T-shirt as he pedalled his habitual ten kilometres at the gym, surrounded by like-minded professionals with the same aim in mind. There was a sharp aura of dedication in the air as Jóel Ingi passed the ten-kilometre mark in the time he usually took to do eight. He wondered if that might be enough, but forced himself to continue.

"Hi, how goes it?"

The question took him by surprise as he was emerging from the shower. He looked round and saw only the back of someone he didn't recognize until the face appeared from beneath the towel that was rubbing a mop of dark hair dry.

"Hi, not so bad. And you? How's things on your side? Not that you're allowed to tell me anything about what you guys do," he joked.

"I can tell you exactly what we do," Már Einarsson replied, opening the packaging around a new shirt and taking it out of its cellophane wrapper. He grinned. "But I'd have to send someone to kill you afterwards."

"And then you'd have to kill him after that, I suppose?"

"Yeah, probably," he said it dismissively. The humour had gone from his voice. "We have a minor problem. Can we have a quiet word later today?"

18

"Sure," Jóel Ingi agreed. He knotted his tie and looked at himself in the mirror. "Urgent?"

"Hmmm. Could be. Let's say it is, shall we?" Már continued. "Wait for me at the door, would you? We can talk there and it'll only take a minute."

The shower had been too hot and had left his pores wide open. In the warmth of the gym's lobby, Jóel Ingi found himself sweating uncomfortably. He considered taking off his coat, but that would only mean putting it back on as soon as Már appeared, so he decided to be too hot for a few minutes before plunging into the welcome chill of the cold afternoon.

By the time Már appeared silently at his side, Jóel Ingi was almost asleep, his eyelids drooping.

"Ready?"

He shook himself awake. "Sorry. I've not been sleeping well recently," he explained.

"You need more exercise. Or are you pushing yourself too hard?"

"Ach. I don't know. A bit of both, probably."

Már made for the door. "Walk with me. There are too many ears around here," he murmured.

The sun shone outside for the first time in days, a pallid sunlight with no warmth, but welcome all the same in the dead of winter.

"Problem," Már announced once they were clear of the gym and anyone who might overhear. "A whisper from the Brits, of all people. Three men and a woman who disappeared from Germany two years ago turned up in Libya. Dead, and not from old age."

"And what does this have to do with us?"

"Nothing at all, I hope. You tell me."

"This was the four who . . .?"

"So it would seem."

"Shit. What do you know? What do they know?"

Már slowed his pace; he obviously had no intention of reaching their destination too soon. "I'm not sure. But they decided to tell us this, which is what makes me wonder. You realize the implications, don't you? There could be heads on blocks all over, starting with yours and mine, and all the way up from there."

"But we did what —"

"What we were told? Come on. We can't use that excuse."

Chastened, Jóel Ingi nodded. "Does our guy know about this?"

"I doubt it. He'd have blown his stack by now if he did. Or he'd have blogged about it," Már said with a snigger. "But Ægir wants to be briefed."

"Give me an hour," he said as the back door of the ministry building loomed. Jóel Ingi turned to face Már. "I'll do a few discreet checks," he said, keeping his nerves under control, his hand on the door and his mind already focused uncomfortably on what had happened to his computer.

The expression on the minister's political adviser's face showed that the meeting was not going to be a happy one.

"Is there any link to these men?" Ægir Lárusson demanded in a tone caustic enough to strip paint from the wall.

"Not as such," Már Einarsson replied.

"And what does that mean, or is it just bullshit?"

Már winced. People with political rather than ministry backgrounds could be tiresomely rude. "It means that as far as we know, there are no links."

"As far as you know? So you mean there could be? What am I going to tell my boy in there when he's up on his hind legs and one of those hairy-legged lesbians asks him straight out if those four terrorists came to Iceland?"

"There was no evidence that they were terrorists," Már protested. The man was simply too crude.

"Or if the press get hold of even a whisper of this?" Ægir's voice was rough, with a scratched quality that reminded Már of fingernails scraping down a wall. His face was redder than Már had ever seen in a man who was seldom far from an angry outburst.

"Listen. There's one of those lesbians with hairy armpits in the office next to mine. She's the human rights and gender equality officer, and if she gets a sniff of this, even a hint, she'll raise the roof, and I personally will ensure that your pickled testicles are lovingly put in a jar for your wife to keep by her bed as a shrivelled memento of what could have been. Understand? Now, will you tell me just what 'as far as we know' means in plain language?"

Már took a deep breath. "There's nothing on paper. Not a scrap. I've checked records and been through the archives. There were phone conversations at the time. There are no notes and no memos here. I can't speak for the minister," he said in an attempt to hold his own.

"I'll speak for my boy. But?"

"But what?"

"I can see it in your face. You were about to say 'but . . .' weren't you? So, but what?"

Már took a deeper breath. "There were emails. I've already done some housekeeping on that score. There's nothing here. But . . ."

"You're doing it again," Ægir snapped.

"There's a laptop. It went missing."

"When?"

"Not long ago. A few days before Christmas."

The expected outburst didn't materialize. Instead, there was an even more disturbing silence while Ægir sat down and placed his hands together on the desk, intertwining his fingers. "Then I would suggest, Már, that you and your people set about finding that laptop with all due speed. That is, providing' your wife doesn't want to abandon every ambition she has of arranging the seating plans at ambassadorial dinners in Paris or Washington one day in the distant future. Because the alternative is that she might end up as a fishery officer's wife in Bolungarvík, possibly in the not-too-distant future."

"I have already . . ."

"Don't tell me what you've done," Ægir cut in. "Just let me know when it's fixed."

The girl looked uncomfortable in the shabby magnolia-painted canteen that contrasted with the opulence of the hotel's lobby and sumptuous rooms.

22

Gunna smiled and wished that Yngvi would stop fidgeting.

"*Hæ*, my name's Gunnhildur Gísladóttir and I'm a detective sergeant in the city police. What's your name?"

"Valeria Hákonarson," the girl replied uncertainly through dark eyes that flickered towards Yngvi in his suit, which was beginning to look a lot less smart than it had a few hours earlier.

"Where are you from, Valeria?" Gunna asked. "You speak Icelandic well enough, don't you?"

"I'm from Romania, but I've been here for a few years," she replied in passable Icelandic, but with a distinct accent. "My husband's Icelandic."

"Been working here long?"

"Two years," she said, her eyes flickering towards Yngvi again.

"All right, I'd like you simply to take me through what happened today. No pressure, I just want you to describe what you did and what you saw, that's all."

Valeria took a deep breath and collected her thoughts. "I knocked and there was no answer. So I knocked again. Still no answer, so I call out, 'Chambermaid', and open the door. I go into the corridor and the light is off, so I go into the room and the man is there on the bed," she explained with a curl of her lip.

"Did you touch anything?"

"Just the light switch in the hall, I think."

"You touched the body?"

"I touch here," Valeria said with a shudder and put a hand to her neck. "Check for heart. Nothing, then call for help."

"Who did you call?"

"Ástrós, the supervisor. She was in the linen cupboard down the hall and came straight away. She saw the guy on the bed and called Yngvi," she said, nodding at Yngvi as he sat gloomily twisting his fingers in knots.

Gunna nodded. "Apart from the man on the bed, was there anything that you noticed was out of place?"

"No, I don't think so," she said with a shrug. "I was only in there a few moments."

"All right, then. Thank you, Valeria, that'll do. My colleague will scan your fingerprints before you leave so that we can identify which are your prints in the room."

"Then I can go now?" Valeria asked, relieved.

"Yes, thank you. Just speak to my colleague, the tall youngish guy, and he'll do the fingerprint scan for you." Gunna turned to Yngvi as Valeria left the room. "Is Ástrós about anywhere?"

"I'll get her," Yngvi said, half-standing until Gunna waved him to sit down.

"No big hurry; I need a statement from you as well. I take it Ástrós alerted you?"

"She did. We have these bleep machines so the managers and supervisors can be located. Ástrós bleeped me and I was there a minute later."

"And you saw . . .?

He shrugged. "Just the same as Valeria described. The man was lying on the bed. I didn't really take much notice other than to do the same as she did and check for a pulse. I couldn't find one, so I made the 112 call from the front desk and noticed that Sveinn Ófeigsson was in the restaurant. So I asked him to come with me."

"Why didn't you call 112 from the room itself?"

"I, er," Yngvi floundered. "I, er, just didn't think of it. The man was dead, no doubt. I didn't think a few seconds would make a difference."

Alerted by Yngvi's obvious nervousness, Gunna instinctively pushed him harder. "This was at what time?"

"I don't remember. Around one, I think."

"The 112 call was made at 13.12," Gunna said, consulting her notes. "How long was it after finding the body before you called 112? Was it before or after Sveinn Ófeigsson went up to the room with you?"

"Er, before."

"I take it Jóhannes Karlsson was overdue checking out of his room?"

"He was. I had expected him to leave by twelve, as usual. He's a regular guest so it wasn't a problem that he was a little late. We try to be helpful here, you know," he said, bridling in defence.

"It's all right, I'm just trying to build up a picture of what went on here. He was supposed to check out around twelve. He didn't show up, so what's the normal procedure?"

"Reception would call the room's phone and ask if the guest has been delayed. If there's no reply, they call again ten minutes later — in case the guest is, er, indisposed."

"Yup, in the shower or taking a dump, you mean? Then what?"

"Then someone will knock and, if there's no reply, they'll enter the room. You understand, there have been cases of people sneaking out without paying, so it's general policy to keep an eye on these things."

"Understood. But surely Jóhannes Karlsson wouldn't do that?" Gunna said, tapping her teeth with her pen. "Who would normally enter a guest's room, in that case?"

Yngvi shifted uncomfortably in his chair. "Normally it would be the duty manager or a supervisor."

"And in this case it was a chambermaid?"

"I don't know what went wrong. I asked Ástrós to check the room at around one as Jóhannes Karlsson was due to check out and, as we're busy at the moment, the room was needed tonight. Maybe she asked Valeria to knock and check. She's been here for some time and is very competent and trustworthy. I haven't yet had a chance to check with Ástrós, but I imagine the management will expect an enquiry into this."

"And that's why you're so nervous? Because the right procedures weren't followed?" Gunna asked and was rewarded with a tight-lipped frown.

"You can draw your own conclusions," he snapped back and immediately apologized. "Sorry. It's been a difficult day. Is there anything more I can help you with?"

★　★　★

Hekla walked smartly past the trendy end of downtown Reykjavík and through the streets of the old western end of town. She had a spring in her step and cash in her pocket, her holdall slung over one shoulder as she enjoyed the crunch of the snow beneath her trainers.

Her Toyota was parked discreetly in a residential street in front of a rambling old house that had been converted into a warren of tiny apartments. She had reckoned that with so many people living in the house, residents would assume the car belonged to a visitor in one of the other flats. She put a huge carrier bag from one of Reykjavík's more expensive shops in the car's boot and dropped her holdall next to it; a couple of small gift-wrapped packets nestled reassuringly in her jacket pocket.

The car started with an effort. Giving it a minute for the engine to warm up and the fan to start circulating some warm air, she hunched low in the seat and looked around quickly. The street was deserted and as far as she could tell, nobody was looking out of the windows of the apartments she had parked by. The Toyota bumped along the street as Hekla headed through town, taking care not to drive too fast or too slowly but to look as if she were simply going home from the gym. In the queue of waiting traffic at the lights by Lækjargata, she turned the radio on, drumming the steering wheel with her thumbs in time to the music and trying not to peer towards the town centre.

It was with relief that she saw the lights change to green and the traffic begin to move. She decided to go with the flow of traffic and let it take her through the city and out the other side, with a stop at one of the big supermarkets at the busiest time of the day to shop for the week's groceries en route.

She wondered if the two men had been set free yet, and how long it would be before their cards stopped working. The first one would have been found by now, she thought. The older guy would be furious; there had been no mistaking the virulence of the hatred in his stare, which was only magnified by his naked helplessness. But he would just have to lick his wounds and get over it, she decided, certain that the man could easily afford the relatively modest shopping spree he'd unwillingly funded.

Fortunately she had already been to several cashpoints and had milked the cards of everything the machines would dispense after she had bought herself some expensive shoes and what she liked to think of as investments against a rainy day. The second guy's cards had resulted in a good deal of cash and some more of the same expensive, understated gold and silver, which would keep its value in a safe deposit box.

As the city centre disappeared behind her, Hekla relaxed at the wheel, feeling safer inside the cocoon of late afternoon traffic heading for the suburbs and listening to the wheels judder on the uneven road surface with its coat of gravel, thankful for the thick weather, which she wore like a disguise.

She shopped in Krónan, filling her trolley with as much as she could, including two heavy pork joints that the family wouldn't normally be able to afford, one for the weekend and one for the freezer for Pétur's birthday. She chose the checkout with the youngest cashier, a gawky youth who looked as if he should still be in school, with glasses and a fuzz of soft teenage beard on his cheeks. He looked stressed and tired, and seemed unlikely to look too closely at a credit card, Hekla decided.

He sneezed as she approached with the laden trolley.

"Bless you," she said cheerfully.

The young man blinked behind his thick glasses. "Thanks," he said, sniffing and swiping Hekla's purchases rapidly past the till as she tried to keep up, stowing things into bags.

"That's seventy-one thousand, six hundred and eighty," the young man said as if the number were a single word, sniffing again and kneading the bridge of his nose between finger and thumb as Hekla handed a card across as if it were her own while she continued stowing tins and boxes into bags.

"Sorry, it's been rejected," the young man said. There was an almost audible sigh of irritation from the queue for the till.

"What? It should be fine. I was paid yesterday and there's plenty in there. Can you try it again?"

He swiped it again and the queue, muffled in coats and hats against the New Year chill outdoors and steaming gently in the supermarket's heat, shuffled its feet with palpable impatience until the young man shook his head.

"Sorry."

"What?" Hekla said in anguish. "Hell, that useless bank must have been messing me about again. I promise there's more than enough in there to cover it. Could you try again, or charge it manually? Please?"

The young man shrugged and rubbed the card hard on his sleeve before swiping it through the machine a third time as the queue continued to fidget and sigh audibly.

"Shit," the young man muttered with a glance at the impatient line of shoppers behind Hekla and the lengthening queues for every till in the shop, which snaked their way into the spaces between the aisles. He reached beneath the counter, came up with old-fashioned card-swipe machine and quickly made an imprint of the number.

"Sign, please," he said as Hekla treated him to the most dazzling smile she could manage and the queue let out a collective sigh of relief. She threaded the trolley quickly through the throng and out into the darkness.

She was a tired woman with wisps of greying hair that floated around her face. She swept them back, and when she saw him the lines around her mouth became dimples and the fatigue vanished as a grin swept across her face. A second later Baddó's face was crushed into her shoulder and she hugged him with an unexpected ferocity.

"It's still a surprise to see you here," she sighed, hugging him close a second time. "It's so good to have you back after such a long time."

"I'm not sure yet if it's good to be back," he said uncertainly, his nose sending him warning signals as he sneezed violently. He could feel his eyes start to sting and water.

"What's the matter?" María asked.

"Nothing," Baddó said, shaking his head and sneezing a second time. "Where have you been?"

"Of course. Hell, I'm really sorry, it slipped my mind," she said as Baddó splashed his face with cold water from the kitchen tap. "I stopped to see old Nina on the way home and her cat was all over me. I'd forgotten they make you sneeze."

"It's all right, María," Baddó said, the sneezing fit over as she hung up her coat. "I'm wondering, how long do you think you can put up with me?"

"You know you can stay here as long as you need," she said, straightening up from stacking packets in the fridge. "As long as . . . you know," she finished, lips pursed in disapproval.

"Yeah, I know," he said morosely. "Just wondering what I'm going to do here. It's not as if there's a demand for my skills."

María dealt cutlery and crockery onto the table like a croupier. "There's work for those that want it."

"I'm not fussy, but my CV doesn't look great."

"You'll find something," María said, but Baddó caught the uncertain waver in her voice. "Sit down. I'm sure you're hungry, aren't you?"

He munched a sandwich made with the heavy bread and solid, bland cheese that he remembered from his youth, while María spooned fragrant herring fillets onto a plate and sliced black rye bread, as thick and soft as any rich cake.

"I expect you've missed this."

"María, I've been in prison for eight years," he said. "I've missed everything."

"Dad's not well," she added, clearly wanting to change the subject. "I go and see him a couple of times a week now. There's only so much he can do for himself these days."

Baddó nodded. Family matters were something he would have preferred to avoid discussing.

"He wrote to me once. Sent it through the Foreign Affairs Ministry, or some such government department."

"Really?"

"Aye. Just half a page to say that whatever situation I was in, it was nothing to do with him and that as far as he was concerned, I wasn't his son any more. Just what you need when you're looking at eight years of four concrete walls."

María said nothing, but Baddó could see that she was taken aback and the shadow of a tear slipped down her cheek.

"So that's that. How did they find you, then?"

"It was someone from the prisons department. He said that you were being released and deported home. They've been keeping tabs on you, mostly because several of us have badgered the government to make sure you weren't forgotten over there."

Baddó laid chunks of herring fillet on a slice of black bread and bit deep into it, lingering over the texture of the bread and revelling in the aroma of the pickled herring. He wondered if this was the most delicious thing he had ever tasted and thought that it might well be.

"How's Freyr?" he asked. "You hear from him?"

A spasm passed over María's face. "Sometimes. He said he doesn't want to see you right away and that he needs to square things in his mind that you're back first."

Baddó nodded. "That's more than I expected, I suppose. It's not as if I've seen much of him."

"He changed his name. He's Freyr Jónínuson now."

"Ach. Can't say I'm surprised. Jónína always was a prissy bitch and I suppose she didn't want him being Hróbjartsson after everything that happened back then. She found a new man, I suppose? Poor bastard, whoever he is."

"A word?" Már said to Jóel Ingi as he passed his office, smiling at Hugrún, the human rights and gender equality officer, as she bustled along the corridor with a smile for everyone.

"Hæ, Már, could you let me have yesterday's reports when they're ready, please?" she asked, her smile fading. "Absolutely terrible what's happened in Libya, don't you think? It could be such a wonderful place if it were run properly. It could be Norway in Africa with all that wealth," she said sadly, continuing past him and hurrying past Ægir Lárusson's lair.

With Hugrún having faded into the distance, Már hissed. "You have a handle on this, don't you?"

"Of course I do. Look, I've asked someone to help out, discreetly."

"You're not serious, surely? Who?"

"A friend," Jóel Ingi said uncertainly. "It's not as if we can expect the police to deal with this, can we? Or maybe we can? Just a friend. Someone who can be trusted."

"Jesus. I hope so. It had better be someone we can all trust. Otherwise . . ." he jerked his head in the direction of the minister's and his political adviser's end of the office. "Otherwise you can have your balls ripped off and pickled instead of me."

Helgi yawned in front of the screen. The hotel manager's office contained a computer that held all of the hotel's CCTV footage and a plump middle-aged man was sitting alongside Helgi as he ploughed repeatedly through the same scenes.

People scuttled across the screen at double their usual speed while Helgi's companion, one of the reception staff, kept up a relentless commentary.

"My dear, it's quite amazing some of the things a person gets to see in a place like this. Especially at night. The graveyard shift can be most entertaining," he said with satisfaction.

"You work nights as well, do you?" Helgi asked, just to say something.

"Oh, yes. I prefer the night porter's shift. I'm the lord of all I survey at night when all the stuffed shirts are asleep," he said with a wink that Helgi missed as his eyes were on the screen. He froze the picture.

He pointed at a figure standing at the reception desk. "Who's that?"

"That gentleman is a Russian businessman. He's something to do with herring, I believe. A regular winter visitor to these shores."

Helgi set the sequence to run again and watched the crowd around the reception desk, only looking up briefly as Gunna came into the room quietly and pulled up a chair behind them.

"Any joy, Helgi?"

"Nobody so far that . . . I'm sorry. Your name's slipped my mind . . ." he said apologetically.

"Gústav Freysteinn Bóasson, at your service. Known to his friends as Gústav and the staff and clientele of this place as Gussi," he replied grandly, waving a hand to indicate his surroundings. "And you are?"

"Me? I'm Gunna."

"Known as detective sergeant Gunnhildur to us food soldiers," Helgi added wryly. "Who's that character?"

Gussi hooked a pair of horn-rimmed spectacles onto one ear at a time and peered at the screen. "Ach," he said dismissively, "that's nobody."

"And what do you mean by 'nobody'?" Gunna asked sharply and saw Gussi flinch at her tone.

"He works in the bar. He's a rather silly young man by the name of Kolbeinn, I believe."

"Here," Helgi interrupted. "That's Jóhannes Karlsson, isn't it?" The black-and-white figure moved jerkily through the lobby, looked from side to side and disappeared from view. "Gussi, where does that door lead?"

"That leads to the bar. It's quiet at that time of the morning."

"You were on duty this morning. Didn't you notice him?" Helgi asked, pausing the replay.

"I may have," Gústav shrugged. "I was at the reception desk and we were quite busy. I can't keep tabs on every person who walks through the lobby," he said without hiding his impatience.

"Is there CCTV in the bar?"

"There most certainly is. In this city, Big Brother is everywhere."

"All right," Helgi said with immense patience. "How do I switch this machine here to the recording from the camera in the bar?"

"Choose number six from the menu at the top."

Glasses on the end of his nose as he switched camera, Helgi grunted with satisfaction as almost instantly Jóhannes Karlsson appeared in view. He was a tall, broad man with a deliberate way of walking. The camera caught him stalking across the empty restaurant and taking a seat at a low table where he opened a newspaper. A minute later a waiter appeared and spoke to him briefly.

"No sound on this, I don't suppose?" Gunna asked.

"It's just supposed to be good enough to recognize faces," Helgi said, eyes on the screen. "This is exciting, isn't it, watching someone reading the paper. Gussi, what's the waiter's name? The guy he spoke to just then?"

"As I told you only a minute ago, that young man is Kolbeinn, one of the lowly staff like myself who keep this ship on an even keel."

"Kolbeinn," Helgi wrote down. "Whose -son?"

"Ah, there I fear I fail you. Yngvi will be able to tell you his name, patronymic, his mother's name and his ancestry going back eight generations."

Helgi directed a sideways glance at Gunna and lifted his eyebrows with a despairing shake of the head.

"Ah, company," Gunna said, looking past Helgi to the screen. "Gussi, did you notice this?"

All three of them watched as Jóhannes Karlsson folded and put down his newspaper, standing up as a woman approached him. They shook hands and both sat down, Jóhannes Karlsson at ease in his chair, looking towards the camera, while the back of the woman's head faced the lens. All Gunna could see was a black coat with a high collar and fair hair that spilled over it. The two sat and talked for a few minutes before Jóhannes Karlsson beckoned the same waiter as before and sat back. As far as could be seen on the grainy footage, he was smiling.

"No ideas, Gussi?" Gunna asked.

Gústav spread his hands wide and his face was a picture of innocence. "Do you see me there anywhere? I was on the reception desk all morning. I didn't see what was going on in the restaurant. The bar is Kolbeinn's domain today, not mine."

The waiter returned with coffee. The pair at the table in the corner of the empty restaurant sipped and talked, although it seemed that Jóhannes Karlsson was doing most of the talking. The woman crossed and uncrossed her long legs several times, and leaned forward to sip from her cup.

Eventually the woman stood up, slipped the straps of a holdall over her shoulder and strode from the room. Jóhannes Karlsson could be seen admiring the expanse of long legs in knee-high boots reaching to a short skirt that peeped below the hem of her coat. She looked around her and gave the camera a quick glance, looking right into it.

"Stop right there," Gunna ordered. "Can you get that as a still picture, Helgi?"

"No idea. Gussi?"

His fingers tapped at the keyboard and Helgi inserted a flash stick into a slot. "Save it onto that, would you?" he instructed.

Gunna studied the face, blurred but with a piercing look directed straight at her from beneath an ash-blonde fringe. The lips were full and too dark to be anything other than painted. The woman's coat was open enough to show a pale-coloured dress or blouse underneath, while the hand that held the straps of the holdall on her shoulder sported a broad ring, which was distinct even on the grainy image.

"I wonder," Gunna muttered to herself.

"What, chief?"

"Nothing. This is someone we ought to have a word with sometime very soon. Roll the tape, would you? I'd like you to root around the other cameras and see if you can find out where the girl went, but first let's see what Jóhannes Karlsson decides to do."

They watched as he unfolded his newspaper unhurriedly, sipped his cup of coffee and read quietly, occasionally looking up. Gunna watched the clock ticking in the corner of the screen; five minutes passed before Jóhannes Karlsson stood up, refolded his copy of *Morgunbladid*, tucked it under his arm and strode from the room, looking neither to the right nor left. As soon as he had gone, the waiter appeared, cleared the table, wiped it carefully and retired, leaving the bar deserted.

"Baddó."

It was a familiar voice, and not a welcome one.

"I thought I'd be able to live the rest of my life without hearing you wheezing in my ear again. What the fuck do you want?" Baddó asked without turning round.

"That's not a nice thing to say to an old friend who has your best interests at heart, is it?"

Baddó wondered if the best move would be simply to abandon his beer and walk out, but a sneaking curiosity as to why Hinrik the Herb had made the unwelcome effort to find him held him back.

"Tell me what you're looking for. You have as long as it takes me to finish this beer, and then I'm out of here."

Hinrik beckoned to the barman, who scuttled over as quickly as his feet would carry him, ignoring the line of people already waiting to be served. "Vodka, neat, and not the piss you give the usual customers."

"You run this place, do you?" Baddó asked, curiosity getting the better of him. "Come up in the world, haven't you?"

A smile that made Hinrik's narrow face look even more menacing appeared briefly and then vanished. "Let's say I have an interest in this place, as well as a few others." He sipped the vodka that appeared at his elbow. "Insurance," he explained modestly.

"You mean you're running a protection racket?"

Hinrik shrugged. "Call it what you like. It works. The people who run this place don't get any trouble, and we get a cut of the profits. Pre-tax, of course," he said and the menacing smile reappeared.

Baddó drained his beer and banged the glass down on the bar. "Well, a pleasure to see you again, Hinrik. Let's leave it another ten years before we catch up again, shall we?" he suggested, turning to go.

Hinrik's hand descended on Baddó's forearm, and he made to shake it off impatiently as a second glass of beer appeared in front of him.

"What's the hurry, Baddó?" the silky voice asked. "It's not as if you have work to go to."

"And what the fuck does that have to do with you?"

Baddó looked at the beer in front of him and put a hand towards it. He knew that taking a sip would mean listening to whatever Hinrik the Herb had sought him out for. As he lifted the glass he had the feeling he was watching a mistake being made.

Hinrik looked into his eyes and raised his vodka. "Cheers. Welcome back," he said, and threw the spirit down his throat in a single fluid movement that saw the empty shot glass return to the bar before Baddó had even wet his lips.

40

"There are people around the city who don't like your face, Baddó, and they have long memories."

"Meaning what?" Baddó flashed back, the old fury rising inside him. "I've paid my debts. There's nothing I owe anyone."

"I didn't say there was, did I? Don't jump to conclusions." He paused. "Don't forget your beer," Hinrik reminded him. "A free beer doesn't come anyone's way too often."

"Like a free lunch?" Baddó sneered. "They say there's no such thing as a free lunch, and in your world there's no such thing as a free drink."

"Your world as well, Baddó. It's your world as well."

"Not any more," he said with decision, draining the glass and putting it back on the bar upside down. He glared at the barman, who was already at the pump, waiting to pour him another.

"That's where you might be wrong. There's some work for you if you want it, and I think you do."

"How much?" Baddó asked quickly, and immediately regretted it.

"That's more like it." Hinrik crooked a little finger towards the barman and down at the two empty glasses. "Six-fifty."

"And the job?"

"Find someone."

"Not for six hundred and fifty thousand."

Hinrik frowned. "Baddó, you're not in a position to negotiate. But for old times' sake, I reckon we could stretch it to a million."

"Yeah, that means you've already negotiated a couple of million from whoever it is who wants someone found," Baddó said and saw the first flash of anger on Hinrik's otherwise impassive features.

"Whatever. You know well enough how business works," Hinrik retorted and reached into the inside pocket of his leather jacket. He extracted an envelope and pushed it along the bar with one finger. "You might want to start your enquiries over there," Hinrik said, the cruel smile returning to his face as he jerked his head towards the bar's long window and the imposing bulk of the Gullfoss Hotel across the street. "It's part of a chain now. A customer of mine works there, name of Magnús; he drives a beaten-up old black Golf. Ask him. But don't ask him too hard, y'know. I don't want to lose any trade. Of course, a successful outcome could also wipe out any past misdeeds, don't forget."

"What are you looking for? Name, address, shoe size, bank accounts, or what?"

"A name will do nicely. An address would be worth a bonus."

"And an advance," Baddó decided just as two glasses appeared on the bar.

"Meet me here at the same time tomorrow and there'll be cash," Hinrik said, raising his vodka aloft. "Cheers. Welcome home."

On the main road she joined the stream of lights heading out of town at a steady pace through the falling sleet that had made the road treacherous. Once past Mosfellsbær, the traffic thinned and Hekla kept her speed to a manageable and unobtrusive seventy as she followed a truck rolling through the dark in front of her. As the truck slowed going up an incline, Hekla took the opportunity to signal to the less patient traffic on her tail and pulled onto a slip road leading to an unused roundabout with turnoffs heading to outlying districts of the city that so far existed only on plans.

She rolled down the window and lit a cigarette, with the car parked and ready to roll down the slip road and back onto the main road. It was a relief at last to have the cigarette she'd been denying herself all day and she savoured each drag as she hauled them deep into her lungs, flicking ash out of the open window as she thumbed a text message into her phone.

She looked carefully about her and, with a swift movement, her ink-black hair was pulled off to reveal a short mousy crop that nestled above the tips of her ears. She quickly ran a hand through it, relieved to be free of the day's second itchy wig.

The cigarette butt was dropped into the slush at the side of the road and she pulled away and joined the stream of traffic again, blindly following the car in front along the busy but unlit road, with cars bound for the city flashing past and wheels throwing up a constant barrage of wet spray that the wipers struggled to clear.

A few kilometres before Kjalarnes, Hekla wound down the window and looked in the mirror to see that the driver of the nearest car behind was too far away to notice anything falling from the vehicle in front. A handful of credit cards and receipts fluttered into the darkness to be crushed and lost in the frozen sleet on the road's surface.

It was still cold outside, but a miserable damp cold, as if winter were deciding whether to stick it out or give way to spring a few months early. It was the kind of insidious chill that ate its way into your bones, he felt, as he longed for summer and sunshine. Jóel Ingi huddled into his coat and turned up the collar. Then he turned it down as he felt it made him look ridiculously suspicious, especially as he had left the building to make a surreptitious phone call.

"*Hæ*. It's me," he said as the phone was answered. "Any news?"

"No, not yet. Look, you can't expect results just like that," the voice on the other end replied irritably.

"But you said you'd get onto this as quickly as you could, didn't you?"

"That was only a few days ago, pal. This stuff doesn't happen overnight."

"I've paid you a lot of money. You said you'd be as fast as you could."

"I work as fast as I can, but I don't have a magic wand," the voice replied dismissively. "That kind of stuff costs extra. A lot extra."

"But this has to be done quickly. You have to find it. You have no idea how important this is."

"Look, pal," the voice said, staccato. "You can have cheap, you can have fast, you can have discreet. No way can you have all three. If you want discretion, then it has to take time. You understand?"

"Yeah, I get you," Jóel Ingi replied resignedly.

"I'll be in touch," the voice said shortly and the line went dead.

Gunna stared at the image that Yngvi had printed out for her. The woman's eyes were shadows under heavy makeup, eyelashes unrealistically long and heavy, but the eyes still had a piercing quality that the camera had captured as she'd glanced directly into its lens. The hair seemed too perfect, elegantly coiffured in a deceptively complex cut that let the hair spread over her shoulders.

The face was long, with a distinctive bony nose that wasn't quite straight, and Gunna had little doubt that she would recognize the woman if she were to see her in person. She tapped the table as she thought things through. The woman had clearly arrived at the hotel with the intention of meeting Jóhannes Karlsson, and it was just as clear that he had been expecting her, but the handshake indicated that this was a formal meeting of some kind, or else the first time they had met.

"Here, chief," Helgi called softly, his finger on the mouse as he scrolled back through the digital recording.

"What do you have?"

"Look."

Gunna and Helgi watched as the woman emerged from the lift on the fourth floor and made her way around the corner towards the room where Jóhannes Karlsson's body was still spreadeagled on the bed as the forensic team examined every fibre in the place. She looked quickly left and right as she passed the camera, after which the camera recorded twenty seconds of blank corridor before it stopped.

"It's automatic," Helgi explained. "On the floors upstairs the cameras are fitted with motion sensors, so they start recording as soon as they sense someone moving."

"I got the gist of that, thanks, Helgi."

"So the next thing we see on the tape is this," he said, eyes still glued to the screen as Jóhannes Karlsson emerged from the lift with a swagger, and looked both ways along the plush corridor just as the young woman had done, before disappearing from view.

"That's it, is it? We don't get a view of the door to the room itself?"

"Nope, according to that weird night porter, the cameras record the lift and the door to the stairs, so that they only record who goes to each floor, not who goes to which rooms. It's a human rights violation, apparently, if they record who strays into someone else's room."

"And this is the kind of place lawyers can afford to stay in, so I suppose they have to be careful. Helgi, what's your take on all this?"

Helgi sat back; the recording was paused with Jóhannes Karlsson's back freeze-framed in the swing doors leading to the fourth-floor suites. "Simple. He orders a hooker, meets her in the bar downstairs. They go up to the room separately, although I'd bet the staff here knew exactly what was happening. She takes off her bra, his blood pressure goes through the roof when he gets an eyeful of her tits, he has a heart attack and she gets out as quick as she can."

Gunna held her chin in her hands as she looked at Jóhannes Karlsson's broad back on the screen, frozen in mid-stride. He had been a big man, and a muscular man in his youth, who walked with all the assurance that money or power can give.

"I reckon you're probably quite right. I'm sure this isn't a murder case, but we're going to have to talk to this woman and get her side of what happened. I doubt we'll even be able to pin an immoral earnings rap on her as it's her word against ours that they were anything other than just good friends," Gunna said thoughtfully. "Not that I expect Jóhannes Karlsson's wife will be too impressed."

"Right enough," Helgi agreed.

Gunna stood up. "But as this guy was a wealthy man, and I'd guess he has a few friends in high places, we'd best cover our backs and do it all by the book, otherwise it'll come back to haunt us later. I'm going to have a chat with some of the staff again. Go through the rest of the recordings, will you, and see if you can get a glimpse of her leaving the building so we can see when she left?"

María wasn't home and the flat echoed. Baddó's head buzzed after three beers and he reflected that a few years ago three beers would have been nothing more than the precursor to something better. Years of enforced abstinence had merely ensured that three beers made him want to spend the rest of the afternoon sleeping on his sister's sofa.

He made coffee, and made it strong enough to bring him back to reality with a jerk. A sandwich of cheese and cold peas mashed into the thick bread helped settle his stomach and, with a second mug of extra-strong coffee at his elbow, he looked at the envelope on the table in front of him.

Baddó reflected that he could return it to Hinrik the next day, unopened, and tell him that he couldn't do the job. But he knew that wouldn't be acceptable to the man in the leather jacket who made barmen jump with a wave of his little finger. He shook his head, disappointed in himself that his curiosity had got the better of him, instead of turning down Hinrik's job without asking any questions.

There were two photographs in the envelope. Printed on heavy gloss paper, but grainy and not as distinct as he would have liked. Looking at them carefully, Baddó decided that one at least was lifted from CCTV footage and showed a dark-haired woman in a tracksuit top zipped up under her chin and with the straps of a bag over her shoulder. The expression on her face was tight and determined, as if there were an insecurity or a tension about her. The ringlets of black hair fell past her eyebrows and around her head to her shoulders, as if she were hiding behind them.

The second photograph showed another woman. Taken in better light, this one was clearer, showing a woman in a pale dress, caught looking over her shoulder to give a three-quarter view of her face. Baddó admired the long legs that ended in surprisingly low-heeled court shoes.

Tall, he thought. She must be one-eighty, one-ninety if she can get away without heels.

He placed the two pictures side by side and tried to compare the dark-haired woman looking past the camera to the tall blonde smiling at someone or something to one side. He stood up and rooted in a kitchen drawer, eventually returning to the table with a cracked magnifying glass that had lost its handle. Any thought of sleep had gone and it wasn't because of the extra-strong coffee cooling in a mug at the corner of the kitchen table.

He pored over both pictures, starting with the backgrounds. The blonde was standing in a big room, and Baddó could make out tables and chairs in the distance. A restaurant, he guessed. Or maybe it could be a club of some kind. The dark-haired woman appeared to be in a corridor, with a blank wall over her shoulder and an indistinct sign tacked to the wall behind her, half cut off by the edge of the picture. He stared at it through the glass and finally made out "ncy Exit" picked out in large square letters.

"Emergency Exit", he decided with satisfaction. That means a restaurant, a club, a hotel, a school, an office even. Or some kind of government building, maybe, he mused.

Last, he turned to the two faces, as if to confirm his suspicion. The tall blonde in the slimline dress bore remarkably little comparison to the dumpy-looking girl in the tracksuit, but the blonde's bobbed hair accentuated her cheekbones, while the black curls made the other's face look broader and rounder. Placing one as close to the other as he could, Baddó went from one to the other and, within a minute or two, he was sure. The set of the jaw and the shape of the nose told him that the two were either sisters, or else the same person.

He sat back thoughtfully.

"So who are you, darling?" he asked himself, looking at the clock and slipping his jacket on. "And who have you upset so badly that they've paid that evil bastard Hinrik hard cash to find out who you are?"

Gunna left Helgi and Eiríkur to deal with the staff at Hotel Gullfoss while she went back to her desk at the Hverfisgata police station, where paperwork galore awaited her. A note on her desk asked her to look in on Ívar Laxdal, the senior officer in charge of what was nominally the serious crime unit, except that a general lack of serious crime in Reykjavík had ensured it remained part of the team of detectives working from the cramped office. The unit's chief inspector, Örlygur Sveinsson, had briefly returned to work to take up the post he'd been given, only to see a revival of the long-standing back problem that had already kept him off work for a long time. His three-week stint in charge had been blessed by nothing that could be classed as the sort of serious crimes the unit had been created to deal with, leaving Gunna and the others to handle the usual break-ins, "borrowed" cars and stolen mobile phones during a wonderfully peaceful hiatus. Word had already spread that Örlygur's departure for the couch at home seemed to have coincided with a spate of assaults, an attempted murder and a rape case that Gunna privately doubted would ever come to court.

She looked at the screenful of emails that needed to be dealt with, deleted half of them unread and immediately felt better, before looking at Ívar Laxdal's note, noticing that it had been written by the man himself, rather than a phone message relayed through someone else. She wondered if he was still at work, looked at the clock and decided to see if he could be found in person instead of calling his office.

"Ah, Gunnhildur," Ívar Laxdal's voice boomed behind her as she neared the canteen. "Coffee?"

His uncanny capacity to appear when needed, or when his presence was likely to be most awkward, never failed to unnerve his officers, although Gunna was starting to get used to it.

They had missed lunch by several hours and the canteen tables were being wiped down. Ívar Laxdal brought two cups of strong coffee and Gunna noticed her stomach complain. She felt the need for something solid and ruthlessly banished the thought.

"What happened at Hotel Gullfoss? Anything we need to worry about?"

"I don't think so. Looks like one of those jobs that's straightforward but takes some time. Helgi's on top of it at the moment. Why? Something you have in mind?"

"Just the usual," Ívar Laxdal said, a thumb rasping against the bristles under his chin as he scratched it while flipping through a list that Gunna could see had been written with an old-fashioned fountain pen on plain paper, rather than a computer printout. "We have a spate of break-ins in the western end of town. It looks like someone is targeting houses while the occupants are at work; every one has been carried out between two and four in the afternoon as far as the statements can tell us. There have been a dozen so far and it's getting serious."

"Is that one for me?"

"I think so. Read through the reports and let me know where you want to take it. Then we have a child abuse case, a boy of twelve who appears to have been not so much abused as ignored. He's been throwing out all kinds of stories after he was caught shoplifting for the twentieth time and social services want it investigated," he said with the bland air of a man reading a shopping list. "Then there are the usual stolen cars, one alleged rape and a mugging outside a nightclub on Friday night." He looked up suddenly with the innocent smile that Gunna knew to be wary of.

"Go on."

"I had a call from the Ministry of Foreign Affairs," he said. "Believe it or not, we have an African desk at the ministry and it seems that a departmental secretary has lost a computer they would rather like back. It's a MacBook, apparently, quite an old one."

Gunna tapped the side of her head in disbelief. "You are joking, aren't you? They want us to find a lost laptop?"

Ívar Laxdal looked impassive and broke into a smile as he handed the list over to her. "Gunnhildur, between ourselves, I don't care one way or the other. The ministry won't tell me much except that they lost a laptop and they want it back."

"If they want it back that badly, their best bet would be to go through the small ads until they find whoever's selling it."

"I know. All I want to be able to do is tell them that I've assigned it to someone. Go through the motions, would you? Talk to someone there and pretend that there's a hope in hell of finding their laptop. I'm a lot more interested in this fatality at Hotel Gullfoss. Tell me more, would you?"

"It looks like an old chap had booked himself a kinky escort and his blood pressure couldn't cope with the excitement. Name of Jóhannes Karlsson, in his mid-sixties and no featherweight."

"The shipowner?" Ívar Laxdal asked, an eyebrow turning into a questioning inverted V.

"No idea. Helgi's looking into his background and trying to get hold of the man's wife."

Ívar Laxdal nodded sagely. "Tread carefully. If it's him, then expect a few ructions. It's a prominent family, well connected. Just make sure all the boxes are ticked."

"You mean they donate heaps of money to one or other of the political parties?"

"Probably. They're the kind of people who will have influential friends, so be prepared. But that's not what I wanted to talk to you about," he said, depositing a file on the table. "This gentleman was released from prison in Lithuania and shipped home via Denmark. He arrived just before Christmas and the airport police had a chat with him. Hróbjartur Bjarnthórsson. Remember him?"

Gunna shook her head, trawling her memory for the tongue-twisting name.

"Better known as Bigfoot, maybe?" Ívar Laxdal prompted.

"Ah, yes. How could I forget him? Used to do a bit of debt collecting, didn't he? Haven't heard him mentioned for years."

"He upset someone in Lithuania eight or nine years ago and ended up serving his sentence without a single day's remission for good behaviour, or so I'm told. Anyway, he's back now and I'd like an eye kept on him."

Gunna frowned. "Has he done anything?"

Ívar Laxdal spread his arms questioningly. "Without a doubt. But are we looking out for anything specific? No. I'd be surprised if he didn't do something, though. It's not as if he's the type to get a job emptying the bins for Kópavogur council. More than likely some scores will need settling, so it would be no bad thing if he knows a friendly eye is being kept on him, and that others also know we're watching him." He stood up. "I'll leave the file with you and you can have a look through it when you have a chance, Gunnhildur. No pressure." He smiled. "But if you look back to 1994, I'd be interested to see what your take on that is. It's also interesting that he didn't want to be shipped home to sit out his sentence in the four-star hotels we have for prisons here. In fact, he fought *not* to be shipped home. Why, I wonder?"

He poured the last of his bitter coffee down his throat and was gone, leaving Gunna with a file that she knew, with a sinking feeling, was either going to eat up any chance of a lunch break, or at least half the evening.

"*Hæ*, Mum."

"Didn't expect to see you here, sweetheart," Gunna said in surprise. "Soffia's not with you?"

There was something about Gísli's bearing that instantly set Gunna's alarm bells ringing. He looked nervous, twisting the keys to his Pajero in his fingers and repeatedly checking his mobile phone.

"Going to sea tomorrow, are you?"

"Postponed. There's a problem with one of the fuel pumps, so we're not sailing until the weekend now."

Gunna reached for the coffee jar.

"Already made some, Mum. It's in the thermos," Gísli said quickly.

"What?"

"I made some coffee. I thought you'd be home about now and I wanted a word."

Gunna sat down at the little breakfast bar that Steini and Gísli between them had built, and poured herself a mug. "What's the matter, Gísli?"

"Ach . . . Nothing . . . Laufey's not home is she?"

"No, your sister's at Sigrún's and she's babysitting until about eight. Steini's doing a job in Akranes today and won't be back until tonight, so we have the place all to ourselves. Now, what's the matter? Soffía's all right, isn't she?"

She poured coffee into another mug and pushed it towards Gísli.

"Well, yeah. Sort of," he dithered, and Gunna looked at him with the silent tell-me-more expression she used on suspects but had to remind herself not to use on family.

"It's like this . . ." Gísli said, fumbling for words. "Soffía . . . she's great and I love her to bits . . ."

"She's a lovely girl," Gunna agreed. Her prospective daughter-in-law had been Gísli's girlfriend for more than a year, and while Gunna had been concerned they were too young to settle down, she was certain that Soffía, with her quick intelligence, sharp humour and red curls, would calm her son down into a responsible young man. The news of Soffía's pregnancy had been disturbing to start with, but it seemed that the young couple had everything organized. Gísli would take the winter off from the trawler he had been working on and use the time to study for his mate's certificates, while Soffía was confident that her teacher training could continue uninterrupted.

Gísli gulped. "It's like this . . ." he said while Gunna waited with growing concern.

"Soffía's chucked you out?"

"No. Nothing like that. Well, not yet, at any rate. Fuck . . . sorry, mum."

"Gísli! Calm down, will you? Take a deep breath and start from the beginning."

Gísli stood up and walked around the kitchen, car keys and phone rattling in his fingers. "It's like this. You know when we told you that you were going to be a . . ."

"A grandmother. Yes, I remember. That sort of thing doesn't happen every day."

"Look. You weren't very pleased, were you? Said we could have waited a year or two."

"I know. I still think you should both have finished college first. But these things happen, and considering I was sixteen when you came along, I'm in no position to preach."

"The thing is, Mum," Gísli continued, pausing again and sitting back down on a stool opposite her. "The thing is that you're going to be a granny twice over."

There was a long silence and the clock over the stove ticked to fill it. Even the radio burbling in next door's garage could be heard.

"Twins?" Gunna asked eventually. "Tell me Soffía's having twins."

Gísli shook his head in misery. "You know when we went to Vestureyri for Granny Árnína's funeral last year and you had to stay behind while I went south and Drífa got a lift with me to Reykjavík?"

"Your cousin Drífa?"

"Well, she's not really my cousin. She's uncle Svanur's stepdaughter."

Gunna thought back to the tall girl with the midnight hair and black clothes, who seemed to have gone from a gawky high-school adolescent to a stunning young university student in the space of a single summer.

"Soffía's having a baby in April and Drífa's having one in . . .?"

"May."

Gunna stood up and wondered what she could say that she wouldn't regret later. She stared out of the window at the grey slush on the road outside and the shadow of the distant mountains with moonlight glinting on their white slopes.

"Gísli . . ."

He sat with his head in his hands. "I'm really sorry, Mum."

Gunna reached for the kitchen cupboard and pulled out the bottle of cognac that was kept behind the packets of breakfast cereal.

"I think we both might need one of these," she decided, putting the bottle in front of Gísli and reaching for two shot glasses from the cupboard under the bar.

"You could have woken me up this morning," Agnes complained. Jóel Ingi checked his phone again and set the alarm for six. "What's the matter with you anyway? You've been like a cat on hot bricks the last few days."

She sat on her side of the bed and hauled her dress over her head, rolling it into a ball, which she threw clumsily towards the washing basket by the bedroom door, where it hit the wall and landed on the floor instead.

"I'm all right. Just tired."

He sat on the bed and lay back, trailing fingertips down the vertebrae studding Agnes's back as she unclipped her bra and sent it flying to land next to the dress. More curves than when they'd met all those years ago, but that's no bad thing, he thought.

"Shall we . . .?" Jóel Ingi asked invitingly. "It's not that late yet."

"A second ago you were tired." Agnes dropped her nightdress over her head without turning round. "Just get some sleep, will you?"

CHAPTER
TWO

Friday

It was dark, and the damp chill promised a miserable day, although the drizzle that had replaced the last few weeks of sporadic snowfall had started the long process of melting the hardened ice in the street outside Jóel Ingi's apartment. He swept the car out of the underground garage and into the street, where the tyres juddered on the ridges and troughs left in the packed snow. He swore quietly. Agnes had wanted to buy a 4x4, but he'd told her not to be ridiculous. Apart from the rare visit to the tourist attractions of Gullfoss or Thingvellir with visiting foreign friends requiring a fine summer's day, they never went further than the airport at Keflavík or the new shopping mall at Korputorg, and the grey Audi was more than good enough for that.

"It never snows in Reykjavík, or hadn't you noticed?" he had asked with a derisory laugh that Agnes hadn't failed to remind him of once the unseasonal snow began to fall.

He pushed the car cautiously along the city's main road. He could have walked easily enough, but today he felt like using the car and there was the chance that he might need it later. The roads were quiet, while the

60

carpark at the gym was already half full with 4x4s and a handful of cars.

Jóel Ingi ran for a few kilometres, cycled for six and did some bench presses for the sake of his abdominals, which he felt were starting to get a little too soft for comfort. A shower and an hour later, he plunged from the gym back into the morning darkness, the door swishing shut behind him. As the Audi hummed onto the road and into the wake of a slow-moving truck spreading grit, a tired Renault appeared in the mirror and he wondered if it had followed him from the gym.

He noticed the short-lived rain had turned to occasional flakes of snow spinning in his headlights and that the Renault stayed with him all the way along Sæbraut. He tried to see the driver in the darkness, stepping on the brake at intersections to throw a little light onto the face that had to be there. Eventually he simply told himself to stop being so stupid and that the car probably belonged to some deadbeat in a dead-end job who couldn't afford anything better. The Renault rolled past him, its nailed tyres rattling on the newly scraped road surface, and on along Snorrabraut as he turned off for the ministry. He still hadn't managed to catch sight of the driver, other than a glimpse of a bulky green coat and a baseball cap.

The moment Gunna woke, the previous day's news came flooding back to her and she arrived at the Gullfoss Hotel brooding over the frustration she had suppressed on the morning drive to Reykjavík. Usually driving for almost an hour to Reykjavík provided valuable thinking time but today it had been agonizing, with work driven from her mind. Deciding to start at the hotel rather than going to the station at Hverfisgata, where piles of paperwork and emails awaited her, she found Kolbeinn in the hotel's bar. He looked up from polishing a glass, put it on the rack on his side of the bar and let loose a winning smile.

"Good morning. What can I get you?"

"You can answer some questions," Gunna told him in a harsher voice than she had intended, and immediately reminded herself that while yesterday's news had kept her awake half the night and put her in a foul temper, work and personal life needed to be kept strictly separate. "I'd like a quiet chat, if you're not busy," she said, in a more gentle tone this time.

Kolbeinn shrugged and his smile remained unchanged. Gunna guessed that it was a requirement of the job. "It's quiet at the moment," he said, gesturing at the empty room. "Can I get you anything?"

"A coffee would do nicely. How long have you worked here?"

"A couple of years."

"And you were here yesterday?"

Kolbeinn nodded, concentrating on the coffee machine that steamed and spluttered. "I'm here most days."

"You work day shifts, do you? Or what's the arrangement?"

"Eight to four some days. Four to whenever the bar closes other days."

"Midnight?" Gunna asked, sipping the rather insipid coffee he had placed soundlessly in front of her.

"Midnight, two, four. Longer sometimes. It's all overtime so I don't mind."

Gunna tapped the bar with her finger, willing herself to be patient. She placed a series of grainy printouts from the hotel's CCTV on the bar in front of him. "You were here yesterday, so you served these two people, didn't you?" She asked, pointing at the woman sitting with Jóhannes Karlsson.

Kolbeinn's face was a bland mask. "That's right," he agreed. "Yesterday morning. It was around ten, eleven, I think."

Gunna rearranged the pictures. "I want you to look at the picture of this person. Any ideas?"

Kolbeinn shook his head, glancing from the statuesque blonde to the brunette with the curls and the tracksuit.

"No. I hardly spoke to her," he said, pointing at the blonde.

"But you spoke to the gentleman who was with her, didn't you?"

"Of course. He's a regular guest here," he said, clearly confused.

"You tell me. Have you seen either of these women before?"

Kolbeinn's voice was slow and unconvincing. "No, I don't think so. I'm not sure I've ever seen this one," he added, looking carefully at the picture of the woman with the curls.

"Who was here first yesterday?" Gunna asked, although she already knew the answer from the CCTV footage. "Him or her?"

"Like I told your colleague yesterday, the gentleman was here yesterday morning, reading the paper. Then the lady arrived and went over and sat next to him. I brought him a coffee and she asked for camomile tea."

"Hold on a second, which of my colleagues did you speak to yesterday?" Gunna asked in irritation, looking through her notes and wondering why Eiríkur and Helgi hadn't mentioned speaking to the barman.

"The one with the beard," Kolbeinn said, as if he felt sorry for the confused police officer speaking to him. "Nice guy," he added. "We went to Café 22 over the road and had a beer. He asked for my friend Magnús, but he's working over at the Harbourside Hotel these days."

"Really?" Gunna asked. "What did he ask you about? I'm sorry, but there seem to be a few crossed wires here."

"Everything you've been asking. Do I know this woman and all that." Kolbeinn was gabbling as Gunna glared. "He had a badge and everything."

Gunna took a deep breath. "All right. Now, tell me where you spoke to this man, will you?"

Kolbeinn looked frightened. "Here. He came in and had a coffee. There wasn't anyone about, so we got chatting and he told me he was a policeman who was looking for someone who had been reported missing and had I seen her? Then he showed me his badge and some pictures."

"These pictures?"

"I'm not sure if it was these," Kolbeinn floundered, "but it was definitely her. My shift was over and Gussi was supposed to take over, so we went for a beer and he asked a lot more questions."

"I don't suppose he gave you his name, did he?" Gunna asked and was rewarded with a shake of the head. "No, I don't suppose he did, and I don't imagine it was a police badge he showed you, either. Look, if you speak to anyone about this, it's either me or one of the two guys who are here with me today. Understand? Now, what time did this man appear and tell you he was one of us?" she asked, her anger cooling at the sight of the young man's crestfallen face.

Baddó was delicately sipping coffee when Hinrik appeared. He waved him to a seat, knowing that anywhere but propping up the bar wasn't the thin man's style.

Hinrik frowned at the sight of the cup in Baddó's hand. "You don't want a real drink?"

"Not this early. Sit down."

Hinrik lowered himself uncomfortably into a chair and looked about him until he caught the eye of the youth behind the bar, who scuttled over with a glass on a tray. "You look more wide awake today, Baddó."

"Well, you know, home cooking can do wonders for a man after eight years of cabbage."

"So. What're you thinking?"

Baddó sipped and put the cup down. He extracted the envelope containing the two photographs from an

65

inside pocket. "I'm thinking, why me, considering the cops are probably keeping an eye on me?"

Hinrik shrugged. "You're the right man for the job, and the police force has enough to do already without keeping tabs on a reformed character like yourself."

"Bullshit. You must have plenty of people you can call on to do some snooping and snap a few thumbs. Why pick this old fart?"

"Since you ask, I'll be honest with you." Hinrik laid a finger on the table next to his glass. "To start with, you're a new face who's not a new face, if you see what I mean. You've been out of circulation for long enough that most of the young fuckwits with their brains in their bollocks were still playing about on their skateboards when you were around."

Baddó nodded. "Fair enough."

"Two." Hinrik laid another finger on the table's edge, alongside the first. "This calls for discretion, so it had to be someone with something upstairs who wouldn't spill his guts after the first two shots on a Friday night."

"Agreed."

A third finger joined the other two.

Baddó nodded. "And three?"

"There isn't a third reason. Except maybe for old times' sake."

"Get away with you, Hinrik. You don't have a sentimental fibre in your entire body."

The thin man smiled, making it look like a facial muscle exercise. "True," he admitted, and took out a fat envelope, which he placed next to the one Baddó had already put on the table. "Down payment plus expenses."

Baddó stowed the fat envelope away in one smooth move and opened the other one. "I need something to go on here. Where's this taken? I'm not going to ask who she's upset, but what's this tart done that you're looking for her?"

Hinrik's smile disappeared. "I'm not sure what she's done," he admitted reluctantly. "But someone has been mightily pissed off."

Helgi was immersed again in the hotel's CCTV footage, alone this time as he pored over the blurry images fast-forwarding through the hotel's lobby and corridors.

"We've had some unwelcome company," Gunna said without preamble. "Can you put that thing on to the bar at around six yesterday?"

"Yesterday evening?"

"That's it. Some smart operator came in here masquerading as a copper and chatted up the bartender. He even took him across the street and bought him a beer."

Helgi grimaced as he fiddled with the computer to find the footage from the previous evening. "Buying anyone a beer would rule him out as one of us, wouldn't it? So what do you reckon that was all about?"

"Ach, I don't know," Gunna said, failing to hide her irritation. "Some nosy bastard. A journalist, I'd imagine."

"Are you all right, chief?" Helgi asked, looking around and peering over the reading glasses on the end of his nose.

"Fine, thanks," Gunna scowled. "What's on the screen?"

Helgi clicked and the figure of Kolbeinn in his white shirt and black waistcoat could be seen at the bar, polishing a glass. He served a couple of customers in rapid, jerky fast forward as Helgi scrolled through half an hour in a matter of minutes. As the clock rolled over to six precisely, a bearded man in a leather jacket approached the bar and Gunna could see him in conversation with Kolbeinn, their talk continuing over the cup of coffee the barman served him; she could see a wallet being flashed quickly.

"He could have showed that lad a library card at that speed and got away with it," Helgi grunted as the bearded man left the bar with a spring in his step. "That was pretty quick, wasn't it?"

"Remarkably so. Let's have a look at the lobby, shall we? He's admitted that this guy invited him over the road for a beer, so let's just see how fast that happened. Then you can get me a still of this deadbeat hack's face. I'll see if he can be tracked down and I'll have a quiet word in his ear."

"Enough to sow fear in any God-fearing man's heart," Helgi intoned.

"Any news?"

Jóel Ingi shook his head. "Tonight, I hope."

"I hope so. Ægir's not going to let this go easily."

"He's a bastard. A real bastard," Jóel Ingi announced in a whisper not quite discreet enough for comfort.

"Shhh. Someone could hear you," Már scolded, stepping back and taking a closer look at Jóel Ingi. "Are you all right?" he asked eventually. "Been overdoing it?"

"Not sleeping all that well, but I'm fine. I can handle this. You wait and see."

Yngvi was in his office, and as Gunna approached the open door she could hear his querulous protests in the face of a verbal onslaught. Stepping past the door, she was able to see through the narrow gap between it and the frame and catch a momentary glimpse of Yngvi behind his desk, leaning back in his leather office chair as a bulky man leaned with both hands on the desk.

"It's a damned disgrace and it shouldn't be allowed for you people to harass staff outside working hours . . ."

"I assure you . . ." Yngvi protested uselessly.

"Reprehensible," the broad-backed man complained. "If you want to carry out your damned investigations into the disgraceful things that happen in this place, then you should do them on the premises. You shouldn't be doing it in people's own time and invading their privacy. It's a damned scandal and I shall be taking this to the union. Have no fear."

"If I can say something," Yngvi finally managed to say as the bear of a man paused for breath — Gunna could almost hear Yngvi collecting his thoughts. "If I can say something. Look, Hákon. That's your name, isn't it? I'm sorry if your wife has been inconvenienced. She's an outstanding member of staff."

"And so damn what?" The big man wheezed. "Why's she getting this harassment? That's what it is," he said in triumph, as if he had been searching for the right word. "Damned harassment."

"Listen to me, will you? We will be carrying out an internal investigation, but that hasn't started yet and it probably won't be conducted until the police investigation is complete."

"So what are you trying to tell me?" The big man demanded and Gunna stayed out of sight, also interested to hear Yngvi's explanation.

"I'm telling you that if your wife has been harassed, it wasn't anything to do with the hotel management. It must have been the police. It wasn't anything I have authorized and any internal investigation here certainly wouldn't leave the building."

Gunna continued along the corridor slowly enough to hear Yngvi's final comment to the man. "I suggest you speak to the police. There are three officers here right now, and the one in charge is a woman called Gunnhildur. Maybe she'll be able to put your mind at rest."

The picture wasn't clear, but it was clear enough. A broad-faced man with a goatee beard worn distinctively long had been caught on CCTV footage in a screenshot that was blurred but showed him looking almost towards the camera. Shortish hair and a faded dark leather jacket completed the picture. Gunna wondered where she had seen that face before with its determined look beneath heavy brows.

When the man she had overheard in Yngvi's office hadn't found her half an hour later, Gunna zipped up her coat as high as it would go and strode out of the hotel's entrance, the door grinding as it closed automatically behind her. Grit in the mechanism, Gunna guessed, screwing up her face in distaste as the wind swept flakes of stinging snow into her face; she could feel that the slush under her feet had begun to harden again in the thickening frost.

There was no post-Christmas rush to the centre of Reykjavík. With earnings having remained static for those fortunate enough to still be employed, while prices had risen since the financial crash that now seemed to have receded practically to the Saga Age, shoppers were hardly spending much — at least not until the new credit card month began, Gunna reflected. A few years earlier she had been seriously considering leaving the police to earn more money in a new environment with private security work, but with the upheaval of the crash vivid in her memory, she had resigned herself to holding on to her state pay cheque, and the transfer to plain clothes in Reykjavík after her rural beat in Hvalvík had made life more stressful but considerably more interesting.

In the lee of a shop, she extracted her phone and punched in a quick SMS.

At the office?

She had hardly put her phone away when it buzzed in reply.

Slaving away
Coffee?
5 mins?
OK. Round the corner

The café was almost empty, and as the man behind the counter chewed his lip every time someone walked past, Gunna assumed he must be the proprietor. He brightened as she pushed the door open and stamped snow from her boots.

"I'm sick of winter already," she said. "Coffee, please, and one of those things."

"What coffee you like?"

"Just old-fashioned coffee-style coffee. My mate'll be here in a minute and he'll want something fancy with asparagus honey and organic goat's milk, I expect."

The man took Gunna's money and she had taken off her coat and was deep in the previous day's newspaper when Skúli pushed open the door and followed her route to the counter.

"How goes it at the rockface of contemporary journalism?"

"Chipping away," Skúli admitted, sitting down with a tall glass of coffee. "Still at *Reykjavík Voice* — four days a week now. They advertised for someone, couldn't get anyone they liked, so they offered me an extra two days."

"So now you're working eight days a week?" Gunna asked, biting into the something she'd blithely ordered and discovering it was covered in a sticky coating that clung to her teeth. "Shit, hell and damnation," she cursed quietly, taking a mouthful of coffee and dropping the remains of the biscuit onto her plate.

"Are you all right, Gunna?" Skúli asked with concern.

"Yeah. Just a bit stressed at the moment. This guy," she said, placing in front of him the screenshot Helgi had extracted from the hotel's system. "Any idea who he is?"

Skúli gave it a quick glance. "Is this some kind of test?" he asked as Gunna gave him a long stare. "You don't know?"

Gunna stifled the urge to snap back at him: No, I don't know who this is, otherwise I wouldn't be asking. "He's a hack, I reckon, and someone I'd like to have a quiet word with, or else a chat with his editor."

"He's not a journo."

"Sure?"

"Of course I'm sure. His name's Baddó. He was in prison somewhere in Eastern Europe and was only recently released. I did a story about him a while ago because he didn't want to be repatriated and finish his sentence in Iceland as people normally do. He fought quite hard not to be sent home and he also fought against being deported from wherever it was once he was released. I'm trying to remember what his real name is. I tried to get an interview with him once he was finally sent back to Iceland — before Christmas, I think — but he wouldn't have it."

"Hróbjartur," Gunna supplied, her memory jogged back into gear. "Hróbjartur Bjarnthórsson."

"Yeah. Isn't it a terrible name?" Skúli said with a smile. "It doesn't get much more nineteenth century than Hróbjartur Bjarnthórsson. It's like something out of Laxness. Now I'm wondering why you're interested in him and if there's anything you can tell me?"

"Not right away. He's been snooping around a case I'm working on and I want to know why."

"This is about the thing at the Gullfoss? The shipowner who was found strapped to the bed?"

Gunna gave him another hard stare. "You don't know anything about that, do you, Skúli? I'm not asking, by the way. I'm telling you that you haven't heard anything, especially from me."

Skúli shrugged. "Fair enough. It's not exactly something I can print in *Reykjavík Voice*. But I do shifts at *Dagurinn*, and they were knocking together Jóhannes Karlsson's obituary last night. Nothing to worry about," he said hurriedly. "Just the usual crap about which farm his grandparents came from and how many grandchildren he had."

Gunna started uncomfortably at the mention of grandchildren.

"Nothing about him paying a hooker to tie him to a bed in a smart hotel," Skúli added.

"There'd be hell to pay if you did."

"But there are rumours."

"Like what?"

Skúli scratched his nose and looked about him theatrically, reassuring himself that apart from the two of them, the only other person in the café was the proprietor, yawning behind his counter.

"There's nothing concrete, but you know what *Reykjavhík Voice* is like. It's seething with gossip. It seems that it's the latest scam. Man books a kinky escort, she ties him up and disappears with his wallet after taking a couple of compromising photos, presumably as insurance. Simple as that. It seems one guy wanted his fun in the wardrobe, but she locked him inside it and stole his wallet. It's been going on for a while and it's all 'somebody knows someone who heard something from . . .' You know?"

"Yeah. I know, Chinese whispers that don't stand up in court."

"I thought it was just an urban myth until this thing at Hotel Gullfoss happened yesterday. Not that we journos know any more than the police," he said with a sly smile. "Although now some of us know that Bigfoot Baddó is involved. Not that we'd say a word out of place."

At lunchtime Jóel Ingi went for sushi. It wasn't something he did often, nor did he like it particularly, but the others enthused about the delights of raw fish and he joined the group of four at a small, smart place on Laugarvegur that had yet to become popular. Once it did, they would probably abandon it and find somewhere else, Jóel Ingi thought, enjoying the unaccustomed slow pace of the meal, made slower by his lack of skill with chopsticks, which he did his best to disguise.

The two women in the group departed together for the restaurant's bathroom, leaving Jóel Ingi and Már with Sævar, a translator from the next floor. Jóel Ingi daydreamed as the other two talked British football, something he had never been able to muster interest in. Coffee arrived as the two women returned, and Katrín from the press office sat down opposite him and smiled. Jóel Ingi liked her. Katrín had a sense of humour that seemed irrepressible. A short, round woman who he decided had never seen the inside of a gym in her life, she didn't attract him in the same way that his wife's spare, bony frame drove him wild, but there was no denying that Katrín was fun in a way that Agnes could never be.

Jóel Ingi remained distant, answering the questions Katrín laughingly set him. Her friend, a wiry girl called Ursula, was definitely more his type, he felt. The only one of the group not from the ministry, she seemed reluctant to engage in conversation with him, apparently preferring to talk to Már. Although he noticed her stealing the occasional glance his way.

"Hey, Jóel Ingi," Katrín grinned as the waiter placed tiny cups of Icelandic coffee in front of them to smother the subtle sushi flavours. "Chelsea v Spurs on Saturday. I'm sure you'll be glued to that, won't you?" she joked. "Spurs to win, you think?"

Jóel Ingi lifted his eyes to smile back at her and shook his head, about to speak. But as he looked at her laughing eyes and past her through the restaurant windows, a familiar parka and baseball cap combination strolled along the opposite side of the street, stopped to look into a shop window and carried on.

"Shit! I was joking about the football," Katrín said in alarm as the colour drained from Jóel Ingi's face and the coffee cup stopped an inch from his lips.

Seconds after leaving Skúli so he could return to editing the next week's TV listings, Gunna had her phone to her ear. She was relieved that the continuing snow promised by the deep grey clouds brooding a scant few feet above the rooftops of downtown Reykjavík was holding off releasing its payload.

"Eiríkur? Hi, Gunna," she said needlessly, as if Eiríkur had not already seen her number appear on his phone. She was cursing herself for not having spent the previous evening looking through Hróbjartur Bjarnthórsson's file, but Gísli's bombshell had pushed everything else out of her mind, and she reminded herself that first Laufey would have to be told of her big brother's predicament, and then the rest of the family. She wondered if her elder brother Svanur had yet been told of his stepdaughter's pregnancy, and the circumstances.

"Chief? You there?" Eiríkur asked, concerned. Gunna realized that her phone was at her ear while her mind was elsewhere.

"Sorry, Eiríkur. Brain's gone to mashed potato today," she said, smothering her growing irritation at herself and trying to concentrate. "Look, priority. No messing about. Jóhannes Karlsson's wife must have been told by now. I want access to his bank details as soon as possible, preferably within an hour. Any unauthorized transactions and all that. You know the score."

"Anything suspicious?"

"Anything out of the ordinary, especially anything yesterday, considering he was probably dead around lunchtime. Understand?"

"Understood."

"But quick, Eiríkur. There are more people than just us sniffing around. OK?" Gunna instructed, putting her phone away and approaching the hotel, where a bulky man with a black frown on his face was huddled in a padded coat, smoking a cigarette under the "No Smoking" sign.

"This is a non-smoking zone," she snapped and the man glared back at her, took a final pull and flicked the butt into the slush in the gutter.

"How would you like to mind your own business?" he invited and quailed as Gunna opened her wallet in front of him.

"City police," she said in the same sharp tone as before. "I believe you wanted a word with me. You are?"

"Hákon Hákonarson," he said once they were inside the hotel's lobby. "My wife works here and she was questioned twice yesterday. I just wanted to make it plain that this is unjustified and it's not right for you people to harass her like this."

Gunna nodded in agreement, suppressing the dislike that she'd instinctively developed for this corpulent man and his pompous manner. "If she had been interviewed twice, then I might agree with you, but there was one short interview and that was all. Where's your wife right now?"

"At home with a headache," Hákon retorted in a sullen voice, like a child scolded for someone else's misdemeanour.

"And where do you live?"

"Vallarholt. Number 87."

"And you drove here, did you?"

"Of course."

"Gunna felt in her pocket for her keys. "Well, if you go now, you'll be there before me."

Hákon looked stunned. "You think you're going to interview her again?"

"Yup."

"She's had two interviews already," he protested.

"That's as maybe. But she's only spoken to a police officer once and I'd very much like to know who she spoke to after she left this place yesterday." She made to go. "So I'll see you in about half an hour, Hákon. All right?"

Valeria looked ill while Hákon fumed in a corner. The flat was spotless, with not a single one of the many china statues of ballerinas and puppies out of place. Gunna felt nervous about sitting down and ruining the careful arrangement of cushions on the sofa, so she perched on the edge instead.

"Not feeling well, Valeria?"

"It's OK. I don't have a shift today, so I'm not missing work."

"Let's track back, shall we? You found Jóhannes Karlsson's body in his room at the hotel, right? I understand that you shouldn't have done. According to the rules, your supervisor should have gone into the room first."

"That's right. Ástrós is worried about it. There will be an . . ." She floundered, searching for the right word.

"Investigation?" Gunna offered.

"Yes. Investigate. Soon."

"I've a good mind to take the damned hotel to court and demand damages," Hákon rumbled, unable to contain his indignation any longer. "It's a damned disgrace that their staff should have to put up with this kind of thing."

"Quite," Gunna said shortly, pointedly ignoring Hákon and concentrating on Valeria, who was sitting on a hard-backed chair.

"I'm not having it, you know," he continued, failing to take the hint. "The last time this happened —" he stopped suddenly. Gunna looked at Valeria, who was staring at her husband in horror.

"The last time this happened?" Gunna asked, breaking the long silence that followed his furious outburst. "Just what do you mean by that? Explain, will you?"

Valeria sighed. "At Gullfoss Hotel once. I only work there two months, the week I start there. Before that I was working at Harbourside Hotel. Two times at Harbourside."

"Owned by the same company," Hákon put in. "They asked her to switch because Gullfoss needed more reliable staff when they took it over."

"Ástrós also. She work for these hotels for twenty years. First Arctic Hotel, then Harbourside. Then to Gullfoss. Same company for a long time. Now there are mistakes, problems, and she is worried. Not easy to find work for fifty-year-old lady."

"What happened at the Harbourside Hotel? And how long ago?"

Magnús yawned. The doorbell chimed insistently for the third time and he hauled himself out of bed and shuffled towards the front door of the flat. He had only lived there for a few weeks and there were still boxes in the hall that needed to be unpacked.

He ran a hand through his hair, scowled at the boxes and reflected that if Sara had moved in with him instead of going back to her parents, all the crockery and ornaments would have been put in cupboards and on shelves weeks ago.

Peering through the spy hole, he could see a middle-aged man in blue overalls with his finger on the doorbell button again, as he yawned and scratched his beard with the other hand.

"Who is it?" he called through the door.

"Maintenance. There's a water leak somewhere in the building and we're checking all the bathrooms."

"There's no leak here," Magnús called irritably.

"What? I can't hear you?"

He could see the man on the other side cupping one ear and Magnús cursed at having had to move to a cheaper apartment with no intercom.

"Plumbing," the man called out again. "Got to check the valves. It'll take two minutes."

Magnús groaned and considered going right back to bed, but in the end he gave way and opened the door to let the man and his toolbox inside.

"Where's your bathroom, pal? Sorry to disturb you. It won't take long."

Magnús scratched under the baggy T-shirt he slept in and walked ahead of him along the passage. "In here. But there's nothing wrong here," he began, and yelped in surprise as the man pushed him forward into the bathroom, looked around quickly and put a hand firmly onto Magnús's shoulder. A second later he was lying in the bath, dazed and with blood running down his face, wondering how the rim of the bathtub had flown up and hit his nose. The man's hand felt huge as it descended on his face, stifling the howl of alarm that welled up inside him as his mouth was filled with a foul-tasting ball of cloth.

With a knee planted firmly in the small of Magnús's back, the man bound his hands together with swift movements and a roll of tape, completing the task before his victim had even realized what was happening. Magnús kicked out as the man grasped his feet to bind those as well, and was instantly rewarded with a merciless jab in the ribs that left him gasping and cross-eyed with a pain he could hardly have imagined.

The man smiled and nodded, as if satisfied with his own handiwork. He leaned over him and spun the taps; ice-cold water poured into the tub, blending with scalding water that reeked of sulphur. The bulky man sat on the edge of the tub and lit a cigarette, gazing down sadly like a father contemplating a naughty child. Magnús wondered what he had done and spluttered to mumble past the ball of cloth in his mouth.

"Not a word. Understood?" The man reached forward and gripped his shirt to spin him onto his back. He then delicately pulled from his mouth what Magnús recognized as a pair of his own underpants, taken from the washing basket by the door. He felt instantly sick and sour vomit cascaded down his chest as he retched while trying desperately to protest his innocence.

"Shhhh," the big man said. "Magnús. You're not going to cause any fuss, are you? Of course not. Because if you do . . ." A hand swept forward, gripped the hair of his fringe, shoved his head beneath the surface and held it there until bubbles began to appear, before hauling him back up. Magnús gasped and barely managed a lungful of air before he was back below the surface. He writhed and a maelstrom of bubbles broke the surface. The big man counted to three and hauled his head back up while Magnús gasped and retched, shuddering as he gulped down precious air.

"As you can see, Magnús, I'm not playing any games. You can see that, can't you?" The man asked in a warm, avuncular tone, as if regretting that things had come to this.

"I haven't done anything . . ." Magnús groaned, too drained of energy to offer resistance.

"Let's just say that you haven't done anything that you're aware of, shall we?" The man smiled. "A woman showed up at your hotel yesterday morning. Tall, blonde, grey dress. What's the scam and who's in on it? Talk."

Magnús hesitated. The man grasped a handful of hair and again propelled Magnús below the surface, to reappear what seemed like half a lifetime later with a gasp and the words tumbling out of his mouth.

"I don't know, I swear. It's nothing to do with me and I just saw her come in and go up to the room," he gabbled, the words tripping over each other in his desperate haste to explain before his head was thrust below the surface again.

"All right, Magnús. Now, you tell me when she left. How long did she stay in the hotel. Whose room did she go to?"

"It was 406. There was a businessman in there. There was a phone call at reception at about twelve o'clock to say that there was someone in 406 who was in trouble and would we send one of the staff to check, and that it was urgent. I went up there myself and there was a guy who had been tied to the bed. That's the truth, and I didn't see the girl again. She went in but I didn't see her leave."

"And the guy who was in the room?"

"He was packed and gone about ten minutes later."

"You checked CCTV to see if she had left, didn't you?"

"Yeah, of course. But I didn't see her anywhere. She disappeared."

The man stood up and Magnús could see him thinking. "The victim. Name?"

"Haraldur, I think."

"Whose -son?"

"I . . . I'm not sure."

Again his head disappeared below the surface of the water.

"Any ideas?" The man asked.

"Samúelsson, I think. From out of town somewhere."

"He settled his bill and left?"

"He'd paid for the room in advance."

The man nodded slowly. "You know, Magnús? You're working this afternoon, aren't you?" he asked and continued without waiting for a reply. "You're going to go to work as usual and you'll get a phone call a few minutes after four, which is when you're going to give me this guy's name, address, phone number and his credit card number as well. You can get all those off the computer system, can't you?"

Magnús nodded, prepared to agree to anything that involved not being drowned in the bathtub of a cheap rented flat.

"You'll also go into the phone records and get me the number of the phone that called to tell you this guy needed some help upstairs. Understood?"

"I'm not sure I can —"

"Do it," the man said in a cold, hard voice. "I'm not going to play games. I know where you work. I know where you live. I know where your girlfriend lives. You get my drift? And if anyone else asks you about this shit, you don't know anything."

He stood up and picked up his toolbox. Magnús strained against the tape holding his wrists as the man made for the door. "Can you . . .?" he pleaded.

"Use your teeth, can't you?" the man replied with a smile that was even more unnerving than his scowl. "It's only sticky tape. It'll give you something to do while you think through what we've been talking about."

It took Gunna an hour to tease just part of the story out of Valeria in a session that came to a halt halfway through when she ordered Hákon out of the room. Without her overbearing husband present, Valeria had spoken more freely, but Gunna could see that much of what she said was hearsay and gossip. A hard worker, she had only been at the Gullfoss for a few months after its new owners, who owned several hotels in and around Reykjavík, had acquired it and set about modernizing its systems and standards. One of the city's older and more respected hotels, the new owners wanted to smarten it up discreetly and make it more efficient, but without losing the patina of age and respectability that their more trendy hotels lacked. Staff from the other hotels had been brought in to start making those changes. Ástrós had been promoted to a supervisor's job when she was transferred from the Harbourside Hotel and chose Valeria as the hardest worker to go with her.

Gunna wanted to track down Ástrós and push her harder than she had the previous day now that it had virtually been confirmed that Jóhannes Karlsson's experience had not been a one-off — apart from its abrupt ending.

She stalked back into the lobby of Hotel Gullfoss at three, hoping that Ástrós would still be around. There she found her and two men struggling to remove the bed from the room that Jóhannes Karlsson had died in the previous morning.

"It has to go," she panted as she hauled the mattress out of the door. "Policy. Someone kicks the bucket in the hotel, everything in that room has to go. Just as well it doesn't happen too often. I'll be right back."

"It's just as well the forensic team had finished in there," Gunna said, half to herself, as Ástrós shuffled along the corridor with the mattress behind the two men carrying the bed's frame. There were a dozen black bin bags that Gunna presumed contained the curtains, bedding and anything else from the room, which now looked stripped. A shadow of clean red carpet marked out where the bed had been, and showed just how old the carpet was.

Gunna peered at her phone, found Albert's phone number and listened to it ring. To her surprise, it was answered after only a few buzzes.

"Albert."

"Hæ. Gunna. Any news? Sorry. I know it was only yesterday."

"I thought you'd seen the directive," Albert said caustically.

Suspicious, Gunna was immediately on her guard. "Directive? Who from?"

"Upstairs. Due to budgetary restrictions forensics are now only able to attempt to perform miracles on even dates between one and five, weather permitting."

"Sorry, Albert. Of course I saw that, but I didn't think it applied to you. Look, I'm in this room that you went over yesterday. It's been stripped so I hope you got everything you needed."

"Yup, and I can tell you the name of the person who left that hair in the wash basin."

Gunna was silent for a moment. "Already? I thought getting DNA analysis results took weeks? Go on, then. Make my day."

"Barbie."

"Barbie?"

"That's right," Albert laughed. "Barbie. It's not real hair. It's fake, from a wig. Plastic hair."

"I see."

"So we reckon it's either Barbie or Elton John. Take your pick," he said and paused. "Are you a bit slow today, Gunna? A blonde moment or a senior moment?"

"Ach. Sorry, Albert. No, just a bit preoccupied. There's a lot going on at the moment."

"I know. Knitting booties . . ."

"Get away with you," Gunna retorted, and found that the reminder was not a welcome one. She stifled the urge to yell at Albert. "Do you reckon you can get any more information from that hair, whatever it is?"

"I'm not sure. I'll have a stab at figuring out what the material is and you might be able to track down the supplier, that's assuming it was bought in Iceland and not abroad."

"Yeah, or through eBay or something. It could have come from anywhere."

"I suppose so," Albert said and she could hear the sound of voices behind him as his attention was no longer on what she was saying. "There can't be that many wig suppliers in Iceland, surely? But that's your department, something for the detectives to detect."

"That's as maybe. But we only perform miracles on special occasions these days, unlike you guys, who have to come up with them every other day."

Ástrós was nervous, frightened and reluctant to speak. Gunna pondered her words as she drove through the city centre, past the slipways and old whaling ships to where the square block of the Harbourside Hotel occupied what had once been a hardware shop with shipping companies on the floors above. The shipping companies had long ceased to exist, although a few of their crests were still displayed prominently high on the walls, and the hardware store had moved to shiny new premises in an industrial park on newly reclaimed land across the road.

Inside the building nothing remained of what had once been there, as if everything had been stripped from the shell of the building and replaced. Gunna guessed that this was roughly what had been done. A smooth tiled floor stretched into the distance to a reception desk where, not that many years earlier, there had been shelves of nails, shackles and cans of paint.

"I'm looking for the manager. Is he on duty today?" she asked, taking advantage of the empty lobby and bored receptionist.

"Uh. I think so."

Gunna waited. "Where can I find him, then?"

The receptionist shook herself from her reverie and tapped at the computer.

"He should be here."

"Right here?"

"Yeah. He's in charge of reception today."

"But he's not here?"

"No. Can I ask who wants him?"

The girl looked sharper having seen Gunna's ID and took a decision. "You need to see the operations manager," she said.

After some whispered phone calls, Gunna found herself in a plush office, an aromatic coffee at her elbow.

"Símon Arnarson," the short man with a grey-streaked goatee and a twinkle in his eye introduced himself, extending a hand to be shaken. "What can I do for you?"

"My name's Gunnhildur Gísladóttir and I'm with the city CID. We have an investigation in progress and I'm looking for someone who may or may not be involved with the death of a guest at the Gullfoss. I take it you've heard about that?"

"Símon nodded enthusiastically. "Nothing official, but I heard from my colleagues. Word gets around fast. You know both hotels are owned by the same company?

Part of the same group, not that we like to use that word too much these days."

Gunna put the pictures on the desk, next to the rapidly cooling coffee. "This is the person I'm looking for, and I have reason to believe there was a similar incident here as well yesterday?"

"I . . ." Símon hesitated. "I was away yesterday and Magnús was the duty manager. He didn't leave anything in the notes about an incident," he said, looking at the two pictures. "Which one?" Símon asked, looking from the elegant blonde to the track-suited brunette, clearly perplexed.

"I'm working on the theory that they're the same person. So either version."

"This was taken at the Gullfoss. I recognize the bar. So was this, on the back stairs."

"You know the Gullfoss well, do you?"

"There aren't that many hotels in Reykjavík, not smart ones, whatever the tourist industry likes to tell people. There are a few of us who have worked in most of the city hotels at one time or another," he said thoughtfully. "I was the bar manager at the Gullfoss Hotel a few years ago and came here when this place was opened. Then the company that owns this and several other hotels bought the Gullfoss as well. We tend to swap staff between hotels when it's convenient, so I could find myself back there."

"Why's that done? Any particular reason?"

"Not really. It's just easier to rotate staff to where they're needed rather than taking on new people temporarily and then having to lay them off. I like it because it keeps standards high across the group. Sorry," he apologized with a wry smile. "That 2007 word again."

"Seen this person?" Gunna asked, hauling Símon back to the here and now.

"No. It's not a face I recall seeing, and now that you mention it, once you disregard the different hair, they do look similar," he said, laying an envelope over the top of the head of the woman with the black wig. "Do you want me to ask the staff?"

"Actually I wanted to speak to one of your staff. Magnús Jóhann Sigmarsson. His name came up in conversation with staff at the Gullfoss and I understood that he'd be working here today."

Símon grimaced. "He's not here, unfortunately."

"Any idea why?"

"Well, let's say he's a decent enough member of staff when he's here and a pleasant young man . . ."

"But?"

"But he's not punctual. He likes to sleep," he said with a return of that wry smile. "He should have been here at twelve. He's not here and instead of trying to get hold of him, I asked someone else to take his shift. So if he shows up at three, which is quite possible, he'll be told he's not working today after all and he'll be given his first written warning."

"All right. In that case, you have his address, phone number and so forth?"

Símon hesitated. "I'm not supposed to give anyone outside the company personal details, you understand."

"It's up to you. I'll track him down anyway. Tell me where he lives and it just saves me an hour or so of enquiries elsewhere."

Símon clicked and tapped at his computer, and wrote on a sheet of headed notepaper. "It's in Hafnarfjördur. He's only lived there a couple of weeks, so I may have saved you more than an hour's enquiries," he said. "Is it only Magnús you wanted to talk to?"

"To start with," Gunna said, and Símon hid a rapid grimace. "I expect I'll need to speak to a few more of your staff, but not today."

"We're more than happy to help with enquiries, but of course we'd prefer them to be as discreet as possible. The last thing any hotel needs is its reputation damaged, and that can happen very easily."

"Not a problem. Kicking down doors isn't exactly my style," Gunna assured him. "Not unless it's absolutely necessary."

Gunna hammered at Magnús Sigmarsson's door, and it remained resolutely locked and silent. It was on the third floor of a fairly old block of flats that had seen better days. There was no lift, and while there were buzzers by the outside door at ground level, there was no intercom and the door had been wedged open. Gunna peered the wrong way through the peephole in the door, but could see only the blank walls of a shadowy interior distorted through the lens. She could sense that the flat was deserted.

Not wanting to leave empty-handed, she knocked smartly on the door of the flat next door, from which the smell of frying onions and the sound of a radio indicated that it was definitely occupied.

"Good day, I'm a police officer," Gunna began as the door opened a crack and a suspicious face peered out.

"No more trouble, please," a voice inside pleaded in a thick accent. "You here for the boy again?"

"I don't know which boy you have in mind, but it's your neighbour I'm enquiring about," she said and could sense the relief from the far side of the door as it opened and an olive-skinned woman surveyed her.

"You have . . .?" She asked, miming showing an identification card. Gunna opened her wallet for the woman to check. She stared at it for some time and nodded, apparently satisfied.

"Your neighbour, Magnús. Have you seen him today?"

"No, not seen him."

"When did you last see him? Was it long ago?"

"Two. Three days, maybe."

"Do you know him well? Speak to him at all?"

The woman shook her head in a way that made it clear she had little time for her neighbour.

"He hasn't lived here long, has he? When did he move in?"

"Three weeks."

"And you haven't seen him today or yesterday?"

"No. Not seen him."

Gunna gave up and fished in her pocket for a card. "This is important. You understand?" She asked, wondering if the woman was taking in everything she said. "If you see him, can you give me a call? Thanks for your time and apologies for disturbing your meal."

The woman took the card and nodded as Gunna turned to leave.

"Not see him today. But we hear him," she said suddenly.

"So he was there today?"

"This morning. Walls are this thin," she said, holding up a hand with a minuscule gap between her thumb and forefinger. "We hear plenty. Too much," she announced with evident disapproval.

"What did you hear and when was this?"

"Ten. Ten thirty. He have friend there. In the bath."

"They were in the bath together?"

"I don't know. Maybe. Noise from bathroom."

"Did this go on for long?"

"I close the door. Don't want to hear." The disgust in her voice was overwhelming and Gunna understood why there had been no neighbourly contact. "I hear the door bang. Half hour, maybe. Then nothing. Quiet."

"I see," Gunna said thoughtfully. "All right, thanks for your time," she repeated. "But please give me a call if you see him come back, won't you?"

Jóel Ingi found it impossible to concentrate during the afternoon; he found himself gazing blankly at the screen of his PC several times, with his hands idle on the desk in front of him. Már looked in on him a couple of times without saying anything and carried on towards the printer.

In the middle of the day his mobile hummed discreetly and he squinted at the picture on the screen, where an image of Agnes looked back at him with that stern expression he rather liked.

"*Hæ*, darling."

"What time will you be home? You're not working late again, are you?"

It was an instruction rather than a question.

"No. I'm not feeling great. I'll do another hour or so and then I'll be home. Do you need the car?"

"No. Why?"

"I thought I'd walk home if you don't need it."

"All right then." She sounded dubious. "I'm going to my sister's for an hour. Text me when you leave work and I'll be home at the same time as you. All right?" Agnes asked, sounding brighter.

"No problem, darling. Will do."

He did nothing but sit at his computer for the following hour, and at the end of it he stood up, knotted his white scarf around his neck and pulled on his coat.

"Not feeling well. Not sure I'll be in tomorrow," he said to the girl at reception and was gone before she could reply.

Outside on the street he looked around him, watching out for the parka and baseball cap. Neither could be seen so he set off uphill, slowly, stretching his legs with each step after his day in the cramped office. With the car left behind he hoped to have thrown off his pursuer, but it also meant that he would have to forgo his visit to the gym in the morning. Maybe a workout at lunchtime would be in order? His head was roaring and he felt slightly faint, but he carried on all the same, glancing to the left and right, occasionally stopping to look in the window of a shop so he had an opportunity to look behind him.

A blonde woman with a small backpack and a purposeful look about her strode smartly past him, stepping with one booted foot into the slush of the gutter as she passed. Once she had gone, Jóel Ingi seemed to have the street to himself. Relieved, he pushed open the door of a smart block of flats, where his apartment occupied the top floor, and waited for the lift to arrive, just as the woman with the backpack peered around the corner, nodded to herself and quickly thumbed a text message into her phone.

Eiríkur wrote down instructions as Gunna barked them out, his head down over his pad.

"Any questions?" she asked once Helgi and Eiríkur had been given their orders.

"Straight away?" Eiríkur asked.

"Straight away. You're on shift until tonight, so you can start with the hotels this afternoon. This isn't serious enough to warrant any overtime, so just do what you can. All right?"

"Do you think it could get that way?" Helgi asked.

Gunna ran her fingers through her hair and sat back. "You know, I'm really not sure. I'm trying to decide whether this is a bizarre one-off of the kind that we won't see again for twenty years, or if there's something bigger going on that we haven't had a sniff of until now.

That's why I want a few questions asked, quietly. I really don't want to ring any alarm bells."

"You mean you don't want to get hauled over the coals again for upsetting people with important friends?"

"It's not so much that. I don't want to get a roasting for something you two reprobates have done. Right. Tomorrow. Helgi and I are on an early shift, Eiríkur. If you're starting at twelve, I suggest we meet at the bus station for lunch, compare notes and move on from there. Show of hands?"

Helgi and Gunna put their hands up. Eiríkur sat on his. "Why do you two always want to meet up at places full of old people?"

"Because they serve sheep heads and mashed swede at the bus station," Helgi said, almost salivating at the thought. "Proper old-fashioned food. The kind I don't get at home any more."

"Plus you can park at the bus station. It's not far from here and it's not full of yuppies and terrible music. So, motion carried two to one. The bus station it is."

Baddó leafed through the phone book. There were a few Haraldur Samúelssons there, but only one outside Reykjavík. Using a mobile phone with a pay-as-you-go SIM card bought that morning at a petrol station, he dialled the mobile number next to Haraldur Samúelsson's phone book listing and waited. There was no answer and the number switched to voicemail and a pleasant avuncular voice. Baddó closed the connection.

Next he tried the landline and was rewarded with yet another voicemail, this time a pleasant female voice informing him that there was nobody home right now, and inviting him to leave a message for Halli or Svava.

So he's married, Baddó thought with delight, hoping that the repeated ducking had concentrated Magnús's mind enough to remember the name right. It was just as well, because when he called the hotel at four, an irritable woman had simply told him that Magnús had called in sick. He thought of using his usual trick of hinting at something official without saying outright that he was a police officer, but instead he thanked her politely and left it at that.

Wheels. I need to get some wheels, he thought. He had borrowed María's car that morning to pay Magnús's flat a visit, but he wouldn't be able to do that often as it could be traced back to him. Besides, María needed the car to get to her lousy minimum-wage job that just about paid the rent.

He took the bus, an unlikely passenger among the few elderly and very young people making their way home on a cold evening. It was just as well that Magnús's girlfriend only lived in Kópavogur. His guess was right. Outside her parents' house a shabby Golf had been badly parked between a Volvo and a bright yellow Toyota.

Baddó wondered how long he might have to wait. Waiting wasn't a problem after what must have added up to several years of solitary confinement; he generally preferred his own company. What could be a problem was to be observed waiting, especially if the weather turned even colder. As it happened, there was no need to wait for long. Baddó stood motionless in a bus shelter across the road for almost an hour watching the house. A corpulent man in a sheepskin coat emerged and kicked the tyre of the badly parked Golf before reversing the Volvo out into the street and driving away. Another half an hour and a light in one room clicked off. Then another, over the front door, clicked on before the door opened a crack.

Baddó left the shelter and was across the road in a few steps, squatting on the Golfs passenger side out of sight as he listened intently to two people arguing on the steps.

"Come on, Sara. We're adults now, aren't we?"

"You heard what my dad said. I'm sorry, Maggi."

Baddó wondered if Magnús had told his girlfriend about his uncomfortable experience that morning and waited.

"I've had a fucking shit day. Now you're chucking me out and I don't want to go home."

Baddó frowned in the shadows. Maybe he had told her.

"Oh, don't be so stupid, Maggi. I'll come and stay at your place over the weekend, but I'm not staying if you haven't cleared up all that stuff in the hall."

"Æi. It's not that simple. Look, I have to leave and find somewhere else. The landlord wants me out already."

Baddó heard Sara sniff dismissively. "Don't be so silly. He can't throw you out if you have a rental contract. He must know that."

100

"Yeah. It's not that easy ..." Magnús said plaintively.

"Call me tomorrow, will you? At work, not at home. I don't want to upset them any more. Come on. You'd best be gone before my dad comes back," Baddó heard her say and imagined her standing behind a half-closed door, ready to shut it.

"Oh, all right," Magnús finally said in a sulky tone that made Baddó want to laugh. The door closed with a click and he could hear footsteps descending the flight of steps down from the front door. He counted six steps across the frozen gravel of the drive. The Golfs central locking opened all the doors simultaneously, and as Magnús got into his car, he found himself staring incredulously at Baddó grinning at him from the passenger seat.

"*Hæ*, Magnús. Didn't expect to see me so soon?" Baddó greeted him and shot out a hand that grabbed Magnús by the throat as he turned to open the door. "Less of the hurry, young man. Let's go for a little drive, shall we? Nothing hasty, Magnús, or I might have to do something unpleasant."

As soon as Gunna left the city behind her and passed the aluminium plant at Hafnarfjördur, all the worries and concerns that had plagued her came flooding back. What was Gísli going to do, and how was she going to tell Svanur that her son had made his stepdaughter pregnant — assuming he didn't know already.

Reykjanesbraut was dark, and when Gunna saw the streetlights on either side of the road waving dolefully in the wind she realized she needed to concentrate, as a gust of wind hit the car and threatened to send it spinning into the central barrier.

With barely sixteen years between them, she and Gísli had almost grown up together. They had always been close, to Gunna's mind closer than her contemporaries were to their children, especially as Gísli's father had played no part in his son's life. The narrow age gap had forged a bond that others found difficult to understand, though it had been threatened several times. When Gunna had met and married Ragnar Sæmundsson, it was as if Gísli, then only eight, had drifted into his own little world, from where Raggi's attention and perseverance had eventually drawn him out. When Laufey was born, though, there was nothing to indicate that he resented the arrival of a little sister.

When they had been hit by Raggi's death only a few years later, Laufey remembered almost nothing of him, while Gísli had been left with fond and enduring memories of the stepfather who had only been with them a few years, but who had made a lasting impression on him. The shock had battered them all, but Gísli proved to be the pillar Gunna leaned on in order to get herself through those tough early months as well as, she reminded herself, the black moments that still returned occasionally.

Picking over the past and asking herself what had gone wrong, Gunna almost missed the turning to Grindavík that would take her across the lava fields to Hvalvík, the run-down coastal village where she had been the village copper until just recently.

She wondered if Gísli would appear that evening and hoped that he would. She worried that her reaction to his news the day before could have been taken the wrong way. The news a few months earlier that Gísli's long-term girlfriend Soffía was pregnant had been a surprise, but not an unwelcome one. It only took Gunna a week or two to get used to the idea of becoming a grandmother before her fortieth birthday. Soffía had been radiant, planning and looking forward to motherhood.

Skirting Grindavík, she saw that there was spray coming over the harbour walls and hoped there would be some time for the weather to abate before Gísli's next trip to sea, then she scolded herself for worrying unnecessarily about him. The ship he sailed on as a deckhand was big and modern enough to cope with the worst weather the North Atlantic could throw at it.

There were far more dangers for a young man on shore, she reflected bitterly, coasting down the road into Hvalvík and through the village, stopping outside the terraced houses in a row right on the edge of the lava fields. She sat in the car for ten minutes outside the darkened house. The absence of lights indicated that Laufey was either at some club or else with Sigrún, the friend who once used to babysit the precociously clever girl when police business called for Gunna to work awkward hours.

She wondered how Drífa must be feeling. She struggled to recall much about the stepdaughter her elder brother Svanur had taken on all those years ago when he'd moved in with a woman with three small children. Drífa was the eldest, a quiet, studious girl who had blossomed in her first year away from home at university in Reykjavík. A year later she had become unrecognizable as the same person. Still vivacious and outgoing, Drífa had started dressing in black, colouring her hair and wearing heavy silver jewellery, while her university course in accountancy had been abandoned as she switched to sociology and immersed herself in politics.

Gunna held her head in her hands. She wondered what Drífa saw in Gísli, a stolid young man with no radical views and who seemed to have a career path mapped out ahead of him. She wondered how Soffía had reacted when Gísli told her his news, imagining the anger and disappointment at what she would surely see as a betrayal of the worst kind. She couldn't help sympathizing with Soffía's situation, having parted company with Gísli's father long before the boy was born all those years ago. She was also certain that Soffía was her preferred choice of daughter-in-law, a fiery but level-headed girl with a mind of her own. Drífa was an unknown quantity, as she'd only encountered the girl on a few occasions and had to trawl her memory to dig up any details about her.

A tap at the window shook her from her reverie and she looked around to see Laufey's toothy smile beaming at her from underneath the hood of the parka that encircled her face.

"All right, Mum? Thought you were asleep there. Forgot your keys?"

"No. Sorry, sweetheart. Just miles away."

"OK. Sigrún says hi. What's for dinner?"

Gunna was hit by the realization that she hadn't even thought that far.

"I have no idea. Open the door and I'll be right with you, darling. There's something I need to tell you about," she said with a feeling of dread.

Magnús drove carefully through Kópavogur, wondering what the brooding man in the passenger seat had in mind. Baddó merely pointed in which direction he wanted to go as he thought what to do next. The wind buffeted the car as they drove through Gardabær and down the hill into Hafnarfjördur, keeping off the main roads and among the traffic.

As they cruised through Hafnarfjördur and joined the evening traffic leaving town, Baddó sighed.

"The tart at your hotel," he said suddenly. "Seen her before?"

Magnús was silent for a moment. "Where are we going?" he stammered finally.

"Never you mind. That woman at your hotel. You've seen her more than once, haven't you? Who does she work with?"

"I don't know what you mean."

"It must be a racket. Who's she working for? Or is she solo?"

Magnús shook his head wildly. "I'm telling you. I saw her a couple of times. I don't know what she was doing there. We're not supposed to ask."

Baddó grinned in satisfaction. "Ah. We're getting somewhere at last. So you have seen her?"

"Er. Occasionally. There was yesterday, and the time before that was months ago, last summer."

"This businessman, Haraldur. He was in a bad way, wasn't he?"

"He was very upset."

"Not too fast. Keep to eighty. Tell me what happened. Every detail," Baddó instructed as the lights of Reykjanesbraut flashed by, illuminating the beads of sweat running down Magnús's face.

"He booked the room, paid in advance. She came to the hotel and asked for him. They sat in the bar for a while. I didn't see them leave. I thought she'd left the building. About an hour and a half later there was a call to the front desk; said a man was in trouble in 406 and would we help him?"

"Was it a woman calling?"

"I don't know. Someone else took the call."

"And you went and untied him?" Baddó said delightedly.

"Yeah. I don't know what went on in there but I got housekeeping to clean the room and get it ready right away. The man, Haraldur, came down and checked out on the spot, even though he was due to stay for a few more days."

"So he left? What do you know about this guy?"

"Nothing. He's in some sort of business. I don't know what." They were past the lighted part of Reykjanesbraut and Magnús became increasingly nervous in the darkness as cars and trucks sped past them, throwing gritty slush in their wake. "Where are we going?"

"Not far. This woman, then, has she done this stunt before?"

"Stunt?"

"Fuck me, boy. It's obvious, isn't it? Promises these old farts a spanking, ties them up and then clears out with their wallets. It's not that hard to work out, is it?"

"Oh . . . I hadn't thought of that."

"Well, has she?"

"What?"

"Done this before?"

"Er . . . I don't know. Maybe. There was some talk a while ago, but we were all told not to say anything about it. Look, how far are we going? There's not much petrol left in the tank."

"In that case, you can come off at the next roundabout."

Magnús slowed and eased the car down a slip road to a small roundabout at the bottom, where he stopped the car. He tensed and Baddó extended a bear-like hand.

"Don't even think about it," he growled. "That way," he said, pointing to the right. "Into the car park. Kill the engine and switch the lights off."

Magnús obeyed. The car came to a standstill in a deserted car park large enough for only a dozen cars. A forlorn picnic table squatted on a raised area at the end, lit up by the passing beams of cars speeding along Reykjanesbraut. Rain pattered on the windscreen. Magnús shivered.

"This is where we get out and go for a little walk, young man," Baddó said with the sigh of a man with an unpleasant job ahead of him.

★ ★ ★

Jóel Ingi lounged on the sofa, practically sinking into it, fiddling with his phone while Agnes watched a movie. He hardly took in any of the film, while she sat entranced, her hand going to her mouth occasionally from the bowl of popcorn he had made and placed on her lap. The credits finally rolled and Agnes looked up.

"Are you all right?" she asked with a sideways look.

"Yeah. Me? I'm fine."

"Sure? You've been sulking all evening."

"I have not!" Jóel Ingi retorted.

Agnes let a trickle of popcorn slide into her mouth and crunched suggestively. "You are so sulking," she sniggered. "What's up with you?"

Jóel Ingi sighed. "*Æi.* Work shit, that's all." He yawned.

Agnes leaned forward to put the bowl, now containing nothing more than a few unpopped kernels and a layer of salt, onto the vast coffee table. She let herself fall sideways and her cheek rested against his shoulder. "What's the matter, big boy?" She whispered in a tone that normally had him eating out of her hand. "Done something you shouldn't have?"

Jóel Ingi frowned. For once there were things on his mind that drove his wife's sure-fire seduction techniques right out of his mind.

"Or not done something you should have?"

"*Æi*, Agnes, what's the matter with you tonight?" he snapped as his phone tinkled.

Agnes's face set like a rock and she sat bolt upright, straightening the cardigan that had begun to come adrift.

108

"There's nothing the matter with me," she said harshly. "I'm not theone who's grouchy and uptight. I'm not the one who's waiting for someone to call," she spat and stood up. Jóel Ingi heard her footsteps on the iron spiral staircase that led down to the flat from their cosy TV attic. Then the bathroom door slammed and he heard the sound of water running as his phone tinkled again. He scanned the message on the screen, frowned and sent a quick reply before sighing to himself and wondering how long it would be before Agnes deigned to speak to him again. Occasionally it was a relief to have her in a foul mood. At least that way Jóel Ingi knew where he stood.

He could hear the muffled roar of the shower running at full blast as he sprawled on the sofa, twisting his phone in his hands and wondering whether or not to call. He picked up the TV remote, flicked through a dozen channels and frowned at the lightweight satellite dross on offer everywhere, before scrolling through the list of numbers on his phone and selecting Hinrick. He pressed "call", then immediately cancelled it, frowning to himself with one eye on the TV before deciding to call after all.

"*Hæ*. It's me."

"So I see."

Jóel Ingi could hear music in the background that practically drowned out the voice. "Anything yet?" he asked.

"I told you yesterday," Hinrik drawled, and from the self-satisfied sound of his voice, Jóel Ingi imagined him lying on a leather sofa being administered to by

109

gangster's molls of every description. "I told you yesterday that my best guy is dealing with this. When there's something to tell, you'll be the first to hear it, my friend."

"All right. Just wanted to be sure. After all . . ."

"After all, this is costing you a lot of money and you want results. That's what you were going to say, wasn't it?" Hinrik asked, his tone suddenly harsh.

"No. Not at all." Jóel Ingi said, flustered by the change of direction.

"That's all right then," Hinrik said, softly this time. "The job's being done. Now leave me alone to get on with it, will you?"

Jóel Ingi found himself looking at his phone, the connection having been abruptly terminated. He tossed it onto the sofa and looked out of the small skylight that provided a view of city roofs, as long as you stood on tiptoe.

"I'm going to bed." He turned and saw Agnes, her pale shoulders bare above the towel wrapped around her and her hair dripping as she looked into the TV attic from halfway up the stairs. "You coming, or are you going to stay up there all night making secret phone calls?"

"Agnes, I'm just . . ." he fumbled, but she had already gone and this time the bedroom door slammed.

It had been too long, Baddó flexed his shoulders and surveyed the bar from a vantage point at one end that let him see the door and, more importantly, who came through it. The music throbbed and it irritated him, this poppy youngsters' music that was all computers and drum machines. There was no soul to it, no feeling. A bunch of sweaty guys with guitars in a smoky club, that's music, he thought, not this factory shit. But hell, the place was busy enough and it was time for a man to iron out the creases after a long time away.

He sipped his beer, determined to make it last. The fucking price of it these days! Not that the price of beer alone had prompted him to leave the country when he did. Baddó reflected that it had been the right thing to do, even though it hadn't ended well. He could have stayed, he thought, faced them down, and all that unpleasantness would have been ancient history by now.

A couple of likely looking women were positioned here and there, one not too far away. Baddó returned to his thoughts, not that he made a habit of picking over the past, but seeing María again brought so much back.

He looked over at the woman nearest to him; she was a few feet away along the bar, trying to get the barman's attention. Decent figure, he reckoned, not too tall and no stick insect. Blonde — a natural one as far as he could make out — although maybe a little faded as middle age approached. Nicely dressed but not flashy. A few miles on the clock, but that doesn't have to be a bad thing. He sensed that she was about to look his way and averted his eyes, looking back in her direction just as she frowned in irritation as the barman again served someone else.

"Hey, Andri!" Baddó called in a tone that was gruff but carried in spite of the hum of noise. It was a voice that commanded attention and the barman looked up smartly at the hard-looking character he'd seen drinking with Hinrik a few times, a questioning look on his face.

"Lady here needs serving," Baddó said sharply, and Andri was in front of her in a moment, his original customer angrily bewildered at being abandoned.

"Thanks for that. I feel I owe you a drink," the woman said, appearing at his side ten minutes later, her group of friends at a table in the far corner forgotten.

Don't be too keen, he told himself. "You're welcome. I don't like to see someone without a drink for too long."

She smiled. Strong teeth, lines at the corners of her mouth, sharp blue eyes. She put out a hand. "I'm Ebba. Pleased to meet you."

"Baddó."

"I'll get you that drink if you'll make sure the barman gets here."

This time Baddó didn't even have to call. Andri was there as Baddó raised a finger. He was pleased to see her ask for two beers, as he had never held with fancy drinks for women. "Cheers," she said, clinking her glass against his and looking him in the eyes over its rim as she drank.

CHAPTER
THREE

Saturday

Gunna had intended to make the most of a morning at home, but by the time she had washed and dried clothes and given the kitchen a birthday, she realized that there was precious little left of it.

"Laufey! Laufey Oddbjörg Ragnarsdóttir! Rise and shine, young lady," she called in a thoroughly cheerful but convincing tone into the darkness of Laufey's bedroom, clicking the light on and off again.

"What? What time is it?" Laufey moaned.

"It's ten thirty on this delightful, cold, wet Saturday morning, and as Steini's gone to Keflavík to drive a digger for the day and I have to go to work this afternoon, I took an executive decision that it's your turn to clean the bathroom."

There was an incoherent moan from under the bedclothes and Gunna hoped that it signalled agreement with no further argument.

"I'm going to the shop," she declared into the gloom. "Be up by the time I get back, would you?"

The village of Hvalvík's only shop was sparsely populated on a blustery morning and it was a windblown and red-cheeked Gunnhildur who returned home with two bags of shopping to find a black car parked diagonally across her drive.

Scowling to herself, she parked in the street instead, carried her bags through the widening puddles that had been ice the day before and let the front door bang as she let herself in.

"Laufey!"

"Yeah, Mum." The reply didn't come from the bathroom, where she'd hoped her daughter would be toiling with a brush and mop.

"Is that one of your friends who doesn't know how to park a car straight?" Gunna demanded, dropping her boots by the door and carrying in three shopping bags, which she heaved onto the worktop before turning to see Laufey sitting at the kitchen table, patting the hand of a tearful young woman with a flood of ink-black hair straggling over the collar of her coat.

Gunna's face fell.

"Drífa? What brings you here? Are you all right, sweetheart?"

Pregnancy had not been kind to Drífa and when she stood up to hug Gunna, she could see the prominent bulge around the girl's midriff. It was only a few months since Gunna had last seen her brother's stepdaughter and the change was a shock. Her normally slim face with its lopsided smile had changed to a pale plumpness that looked distinctly out of place.

"I'm sorry, Gunna. I had to get away from Reykjavík for a few days. It's so lonely in the place I'm in and I wanted to get out of that miserable city for a while," Drífa sniffed. "I hope you don't mind?"

114

"Of course I don't mind. You're always welcome here," Gunna said, shocked at the change in Drífa, not just in her spreading width but also in her transformation from a confident young woman to this tearful, lost child. "Are you hungry, Drífa? Do you want something to eat? I'm going to work soon so I was going to have something anyway."

"I don't want to put you to any trouble."

"It's no trouble, sweetheart," Gunna said. "Laufey," she added and needed to say no more as the girl opened the fridge and started piling food onto the table.

"I'm not sure I could eat anything," Drífa said, buttering a slice of bread and spreading it with cheese. "I keep bringing everything up; I can't see why I'm getting so chubby when I'm hardly eating," she wailed.

"It could be water retention, you know, Drífa. Once the baby's born . . ." she said and gulped. "Once the baby's born you'll probably lose a lot of it straight away. That's what happened to me when Laufey was born."

"Please, Mum. Not endless pregnancy stories," Laufey said darkly. "This isn't a sewing circle."

In the end Drífa put away half a dozen slices of bread with cold meat, cheese or herring, an apple and a carton of juice, finally sitting back with more colour in her cheeks than there had been half an hour earlier.

"I'll have to leave you to it, I'm afraid, girls. I have to go to work," Gunna said finally, after the table had been cleared and the usual family news had been exchanged. Nobody had mentioned Gísli, and she hoped that it would stay that way for a while.

"On a Saturday?" Drífa asked. "Really?"

"Sadly, there are criminals who need to be chased and locked up at weekends as well. It would be lovely if murderers and drug dealers could stick to office hours."

"Is that what you do?" Drífa asked, wide-eyed, while Laufey sniggered. "I mean, like, I knew you were in the police, but I didn't think you did stuff like that."

"OK. What did you think Mum did?" Laufey asked, trying not to laugh.

"Well, I thought you were in an office or something."

"Somehow I don't think I'm quite the office type," Gunna said stiffly and the two girls fell silent, Drífa a little crestfallen and Laufey smiling broadly. "Now I have to get myself changed."

She returned to find the two of them chattering over the table, but they fell silent as she appeared, pulling on her quilted jacket and wrapping a scarf around her neck.

"Cold out today," she said to break the silence.

"Er, Gunna?"

"Yes, Drífa?" Gunna asked absently as she tied her bootlaces.

"I was wondering. Do you mind if I stay for a couple of days?"

"Fine by me," Gunna said, her mind already elsewhere. "But you'll have to use Gísli's room."

"Gísli's room? All right," Drífa said doubtfully.

"That's all there is, I'm afraid. I think he's taken most of his stuff anyway. Laufey, would you sort out Gísli's room for Drífa? Sorry, but I have to rush."

"No problem, Mum," Laufey said, taking charge.

"Right. Look after the place, ladies. I'll be back tonight; Steini should be here around seven and he's in charge of food tonight."

"Who's Steini?" she heard Drífa whisper just before the door closed.

"Duh. He's Mum's squeeze," Gunna heard Laufey explain as the door shut behind her.

Jóel Ingi left the warmth of his bed with a heavy heart. Agnes was still pretending to be asleep as he showered and dressed. He felt restless and out of sorts and it was as well it wasn't a working day. The intention had been to stay at home and take it easy, maybe spend the morning in bed and suggest that Agnes do the same, but as she was in a foul temper he decided that he might as well go for a run, regardless of the miserable weather.

There was nothing to suggest he was being watched. There was nobody to be seen anywhere as he jogged the lightening streets, wondering if running in the wind and rain was a sign of insanity. He was angry with himself for being so paranoid as to imagine that someone would want to tail a lowly temporary officer, long passed over for promotion. The lost laptop haunted his thoughts, not that he could tell Agnes why he'd been so nervous and preoccupied these last few days.

Shit, what if someone were to stumble across the computer's contents, he thought to himself, turning a corner and crossing Sæbraut behind a line of cars queuing at the lights. The traffic moved off and gradually overtook him, cars and vans spitting black slush from beneath their wheels as snowflakes that were almost raindrops spun the glare of the streetlights, turning to water as soon as they landed and adding to the flow gurgling down the drains. Buffeted by a blustery wind, Jóel Ingi picked his way carefully between the worst of the rivulets trickling along the seafront, wondering why he bothered to live in Reykjavík 101 and telling himself that if it were to freeze later, it would be impossible to get around.

The miserable weather and his own bad temper momentarily eclipsed his worries about the lost laptop and its dangerous contents. He even forgot to look around him to check if he were being followed, but if he had done, it was unlikely he would have recognized the blonde woman he had almost walked into on the pavement the day before as the same one who passed him half a dozen times behind the wheel of a down-at-heel Renault while keeping a wary eye on his progress.

"I've found out something about hotels," Eiríkur announced.

Helgi didn't answer, enthralled by the sight of old-fashioned food of the kind his young wife wouldn't allow in their house.

"Go on, then," Gunna said, "what's that?"

"If you want to get an idea of what really goes on, then go in the evening. The managers work nine to five, and once they've gone home you're more likely to get some thwarted droid who's only too happy to drop the man in the shit."

"So you came away with some dirt, did you? Excellent. Let's hear it."

The bus station was quiet. The early buses were long gone and in the dead of winter, with difficult roads all around the country, only a skeleton service ran. The cafeteria, which buzzed with life during the tourist season, was all theirs as they sat beneath old photographs of buses that travelled the country back when there were no tarmac roads outside Reykjavík and timetables were little more than inspired guesswork.

Eiríkur dissected his pizza while Helgi looked up from his plate to glare at it with distaste. He munched a slice and washed it down with Coke.

"Hell, and you dare to lecture me about eating healthy food," Helgi grumbled.

"Boys," Gunna said, reining them in. "Eiríkur . . . hotels. Remember?"

"Yeah. I went round a few of the big ones. The Airline Hotel, Hotel Ocean, Hotel Glacier, and avoided the Harbourside and the Gullfoss like you said. It's the same story everywhere once you get someone lower down the pecking order talking. At every hotel there's been at least one instance of this scam. Normally there's a phone call to reception from an outside number and a request to help a gentleman in a certain room. The gentleman is untied, is deeply embarrassed and disappears. Nobody ever wants to complain, and the reasons are pretty obvious."

"So each of these hotels has had the same thing happen? That's half a dozen times to our knowledge, which includes the late Jóhannes Karlsson."

"Mmmmm, yes," Eiríkur said, hurriedly swallowing. "The bar manager at one of the hotels said the same thing had happened at Hotel Moon out near Borgarnes at least twice, as far as he knew, and it had happened at that cheap place up on Ármúli, whatever that's called."

"A regular epidemic, isn't it?" Helgi ventured, straightening his shoulders as he pulled a sheep's head apart, much to Eiríkur's disgust.

"That's not all," Eiríkur said, bubbling with enthusiasm. "I spoke to Jóhannes Karlsson's son last night, and he said that there were five transactions on one of his debit cards that morning. Details should be on my email when I get back to Hverfisgata."

Gunna tapped the tabletop with her fingernails, rattling an irregular tattoo that Helgi and Eiríkur both knew and recognized as a signal that ideas were called for on their part.

"So how do we crack this, chief?" Helgi asked, pre-empting the expected comment.

"Y'know," Gunna said slowly, "I reckon it's time to push hard and give someone a fright. Look, there must be a dozen or so men around Reykjavík who have fallen for this scam over how long?"

"About a year, I guess," Eiríkur said.

"So we have to find at least one of them and pull his fingernails out one by one until he spills the beans." Gunna smiled grimly. "So I suggest we take one hotel each and give the manager a hard time until they come up with some names. How does that sound, gentlemen?"

Gunna was back at the Harbourside Hotel and this time Símon's smile had disappeared into the depths of the carefully shaped beard that framed his mouth.

"It's simple enough," Gunna told him. "There's a scam that's been taking place in hotels all over the city and I'm sure you're aware of it. A man takes a room and goes up there with a lady. An hour or two later there's a phone call to the hotel asking for someone in a certain room to be assisted. You get the picture?"

Símon shifted uncomfortably in the chair that fitted snugly into his curved desk. "I've heard . . . rumours that this was more than a one-off," he admitted finally. "But it's not something I've had to deal with personally."

"All right, then. Tell me a few of these rumours, would you?"

He scowled and Gunna could see him wondering what to say.

"As you can imagine, this is terribly sensitive," he said finally, with an effort. "I'm not sure what I can tell you."

"I would suggest that you tell me everything you know, because if you don't and it comes out later that you withheld information, then you'll find yourself in a heap of trouble up to your eyeballs."

Gunna watched as Símon fought an internal struggle.

"I think you might have to speak to the managing director," he said finally. "This is something that affects the whole group."

121

"Right. So where's the managing director?"

"Er . . . she's in London at the moment but should be back after the weekend."

"Good grief!" Gunna exploded. "I don't have the time or patience to wait for someone who's on a jaunt overseas, especially as this concerns what could conceivably be a murder investigation at the Gullfoss, which is all part of the same group, isn't it?"

"I'm sorry," Símon replied, a querulous note in his voice. "I'm not sure that I have the authority to disclose this kind of information."

"Fair enough. If you don't want to make a decision, then I'll speak to your managing director and she can make it for you. Whichever way, it looks bad, doesn't it?"

"There have been . . ." Símon paused and Gunna waited expectantly. "There have been incidents. We obviously want to keep this as quiet as possible, as you can appreciate," he gulped. "I don't have details. We don't log this kind of thing. Instructions from higher up. It happens. Whoever is on duty deals with it and we don't encourage staff to tell management about it afterwards."

"So if something does go wrong, you can say, with a grain of truth, that you didn't know anything about it?"

Símon grimaced again, and while Gunna understood that he was in a difficult position, she found it hard to feel sympathy.

"Look. Nobody wants to make waves. It's a tough world out there," he said with a vague jerk of his head towards the window and the street outside. "Jobs don't grow on trees like they did a few years ago, so we keep quiet and don't make a fuss. And if the MD knew I'd

122

told you that, I'd be joining the dole queue tomorrow morning," he said bitterly.

"All right. Let's make it easy for all concerned, shall we? Tell me what you can and I didn't hear it from you."

Símon raised his hands helplessly. "I've already told you everything I know. The duty managers deal with these incidents. I only hear about them indirectly later. But I can tell you that Magnús dealt with such an incident recently."

"And he's not here?"

"No. Still off sick, apparently."

"How convenient."

"Don't be so idiotic. Who would want to keep tabs on you? Me, I can understand, being the handsome devil I am." Már Einarsson grinned, hoping to put Jóel Ingi at his ease, but the flinty expression stopped any attempt at humour.

"That fucking computer is dynamite," he hissed, flicking a glance around the coffee shop that was at the far end of his morning run. "Do they know that?"

"I'm not sure what they know. I don't think Ægir knows anything, but he suspects everyone of everything. It's a power game for him. Don't let him grind you down, because he'll jump down your neck if he senses weakness."

"Yes, yes, I know all that," Jóel Ingi said. "But you remember the Libyans. There were no memos, no notes, nothing."

"Of course. And that's only right. No paper trail to follow."

"Yeah. No paper trail," Jóel Ingi snapped. "But there's a fucking electronic trail. It's in that computer if someone can figure out how to hack their way into it."

Már stared at Jóel Ingi in disbelief. "You mean you didn't delete everything?"

"I thought I had," he said miserably. "I deleted all the incoming mails but not the outgoing ones. I just forgot," he added bleakly.

"And if that gets into the wrong hands" — Már breathed — "it'll destroy the man, and he'll take everyone he can with him, if I know him right. Ægir, you, me. We're all expendable as far as he's concerned."

"It's password protected," Jóel Ingi offered.

"Yeah. That's crackable for someone who knows what he's doing. But it's not easy, unless your password's 'password' or 'admin' or something obvious like your wife's name."

"Oh . . ."

"Shit, you didn't?" Már said, watching Jóel Ingi's face fall.

The phone rang cheerfully and Svava Gunnarsdóttir answered equally cheerfully.

"Hello! Svava."

"Good day," a gruff man's voice offered. "I'm looking for Haraldur Samúelsson. Do I have the right number?" he asked politely.

"Yes, you've come to the right place, but I'm afraid he's at work at the moment. Can I take a message or do you want to call his mobile?"

There was a pause.

"It's all right. I'll call back later. It's nothing urgent."

"Can I tell him who called?" she asked and there was a second pause.

"Could you just tell him that Jón called and it's about his stay at the Harbourside Hotel recently? Thanks," the voice said, and Svava found herself listening to a dialling tone as the call was terminated.

The sound of air bubbling through water confused her for a moment until Gunna remembered the new text message alert that Laufey had programmed into her phone.

Bingo, Eiríkur's message read.

Full house? She thumbed back, walking through the angrily sleeting rain towards the car parked on the street outside the Harbourside Hotel.

Got one for you. Want the juicy details?

OK. Back at H-Gata in 10, she texted back, getting into the car and noticing with dismay the stack of printouts on the passenger seat that she still hadn't found time to read. She remembered with a stab of discomfort that Hróbjartur Bjarnthórsson's file was there and that as the name had cropped up linked to the hotel case, she should have read it by now.

She fished out her phone and scrolled down to reply to Eiríkur's last message.

Make that 20, she thumbed in as a second reply and started the engine, switching on the heater to clear the windscreen and start warming her feet as she skimmed his file.

Hróbjartur Bjarnthórsson, born in Reykjavík in 1972, known as Baddó or Bigfoot, she read. Average height, weight and looks, no distinguishing marks. She read through a list of misdemeanours from extracting money with menaces to assault, along with several stretches in prison that included fights with other prisoners and on one occasion an extension of his sentence for knocking a warder's front teeth out.

In 1996 he had been involved with a shipment of ecstasy that had been intercepted on the basis of information received, questioned and then released when there was insufficient evidence to link him to the goods. But some weeks later a man had been badly beaten and Gunna's heavy eyebrows knitted in a frown when she saw the name. According to the file, Baddó had been identified as the attacker, but with no firm evidence, no prosecution had resulted. A few months later, Baddó disappeared from Iceland and the file was empty until a request from police in Lithuania for information had been logged. Baddó, it seemed, had been involved in an operation that shipped cars stolen in Denmark and Sweden through the Baltic States to destinations in the Middle East.

As a footnote, someone had added that Hróbjartur Bjarnthórsson had attended the police college in 1993–94 and had graduated with good marks, but had never applied for a position with the force, presumably having decided that the other side of law and order was more his style. Gunna noticed that prior to 1994 the man had a clean sheet; she wondered what had sent him down that particular path.

There was just one recent photograph, supplied by police in Lithuania. Gunna found herself looking into the deep, truculent eyes of a man with a bull neck and heavy shoulders, who was clearly having his picture taken against his will. His head was pitched slightly forward, showing an expanse of wide forehead and close-cropped hair, black eyes looking up at her from under heavy brows.

Gunna wondered if the Lithuanian police had methods that were less proscriptive, as a charge was made to stick and Baddó spent eight years in prison before being released and immediately arrested as an undesirable alien and flown home.

"At taxpayer's expense and in club class, I expect," Gunna grumbled to herself guiltily, knowing that the turmoil at home over the last few days had sapped her energy and stopped her from reading the files when she should have.

"I'm really sorry, but I have to take this," he apologized, snatching up his phone and hurrying out into the street as he saw the number Hinrik used appear on the screen.

"Any progress?" Jóel Ingi asked as soon as the door had shut behind him, leaving Már bemused at the coffee-shop table behind his tall latte.

"Hey, Jóel Ingi. How goes it? Not disturbing you, am I?"

"It's not exactly convenient, so I'll have to be quick. Any news?"

"Progress, but not enough to tell you much. My guy is definitely getting there, though."

"And?"

"That's the good news. He's on the trail."

"And there's some bad news?"

Hinrik chuckled. "Funds. My guy needs another payment to continue his work."

"So soon? But you've already had . . ."

"I told you at the start this wouldn't be cheap," Hinrik told him abruptly. "You want quality, you have to pay for it. Try someone else if you like, but they'll have the same costs as we do."

"OK, all right. How much?"

"One will do."

"One hundred thousand?"

"Don't play games. One million."

Jóel Ingi stifled a groan.

"Still there, are you?" Hinrik asked.

"Yeah. Give me your account details and I'll transfer it across."

"Come on. You think I pay tax? We deal in cash. Krónur, euros, or dollars. Let me know when it's ready and I'll tell my guy he can keep up the good work."

"What do we have, young man?" Gunna asked, knowing that Eiríkur intensely disliked being addressed as "young man".

"Arctic Hotel, and about three weeks ago. The manager didn't like it one bit, but I said the alternative was that there would be a heavy investigation that would mean lots of guests and staff being interviewed,

128

so he caved in and found some scared receptionist who had gone up to a room and untied a fat guy who'd been trussed up like a chicken and blindfolded."

"Excellent, Eiríkur. Good stuff. It's a step up from teenagers stealing mobile phones, isn't it? What's the guy's name?"

"Hermann Finnsson. He lives in Mosfellsbær and his phone number's here," he said, pointing as Gunna copied the details. "Oh, by the way, the transactions on Jóhannes Karlsson's debit card are here."

He passed Gunna a printout of an online bank statement.

"You got this from his son, right?"

"Yup. Seems he had access to one of his dad's accounts and this one has a transaction on it right around the time the old fellow was found. The son's pretty upset from what I can gather and is trying to shield his mother from the truth."

"What? That his dad paid a hooker to tie him up?"

"Exactly. He's trying to get access to the rest of his father's accounts and he said he'd pass the details on as soon as he has them."

"Odd shopping habits for a shipowner in his sixties, wouldn't you say?" Gunna asked, her finger running down the list of transactions. "Plenty of cash withdrawn as well, I see. Looks like there's more to this than meets the eye."

"That's a jeweller," Eiríkur said, looking over her shoulder. "And that's a clothes shop."

"Something for you to investigate, Eiríkur, first thing tomorrow before they get busy. Now, where's Helgi?

Leave Hermann Finnsson to me and you get yourself off home."

Hekla paused at the end of the pool and rested. Thirty lengths was respectable, she decided and hauled herself out onto the edge, not bothering to swim the few metres to the steps. It was cold and she instantly shivered, drops of cold rain that wanted to be snow landing on her back as she made for the hot tub at a brisk pace.

There was space alongside two chatting women and a man who appeared to be asleep in the scalding water as Hekla lowered herself gingerly into the tub, gasping at the sheer intensity of the heat after the chill air.

"Young Tommi's being confirmed this year, you know. I don't know where the time's gone," the larger of the two women said. "It seems like it was only yesterday he was being christened."

"You'll be a great-grandmother before you know it, if he takes after his father," the smaller one laughed.

Hekla relaxed and stretched her neck back to ease the stiffness that had accumulated across her shoulders over the last few days. It felt odd being in this pool. Normally she would have gone for a swim at the pool nearer home, but that only opened in the afternoons, which meant that she would have had to take at least one of the children with her. She reflected that there was no way she could take one twin and not the other, and with both in tow, there would be no thirty lengths for her. So a visit to the Grafarvogur pool it had to be, combining it with a couple of other errands in town while the children were at a neighbour's house for a few hours.

"We had wondered about the catering. My Muggi wants to use the masonic hall, of course, but I'm wondering about which caterer to use."

Hekla closed her eyes and let the sound of the two twittering women wash over her as she let the tension seep out of her legs and into the hot, sulphurous water.

"Did he really?" The smaller woman asked mischievously. "He never told me about that, the little devil."

"He did, my Muggi said he saw him at it."

Hekla came to with a sudden jerk, conscious that she had almost been asleep, and looked up to see the pale-blue eyes of the corpulent man with elegant grey hair she had hardly noticed looking into hers with a disturbing intensity. Flustered, she looked away and ran a hand through the short hair above her ears, massaging her scalp with her fingers while the man looked at her with a mixture of confusion and surprise. He opened his mouth to speak, and quickly shut it again, as if he'd thought better of it.

"What those boys don't get up to. But it's so much better for them than being cooped up inside in front of the television all day, don't you think. Are you going to Florida again this year?" The larger one asked, the pair unconscious of the tension brewing next to them.

"Oh, next month, I think. February's such a miserable time, isn't it?"

Hekla risked a glance back at the man and saw that without the two women chatting next to them, he would have said something to her. She forced a brief smile at him and stood up, hot water cascading from her arms as the chill air bit again, just as the man opened his mouth to speak. Before he could say anything, she had waded past him and was up the steps and trotting to the changing room.

He stared at faces in the street, hoping that eventually he would see the features of that blasted woman who had caused him so much grief. Jóel Ingi was furious, mostly with the woman he knew only as Sonja and who was still there on personal.is, where he had stumbled across her and so much else. He wondered what Hinrik had done and why he needed more money so soon. The man had promised results and so far he had the feeling that his cash had been wasted; nevertheless, he'd been left with no option but to dig into his savings.

Angry, he walked faster, as if the expended energy would make him feel better. He knew that he should have gone to the gym to work off a little of the aggression he could feel building up in his biceps. The urge to vent some of the pressure grew inside him and, without realizing it, he found that he was almost running along the street, with passers-by giving him quizzical looks.

He fought to control his breathing, which came in gasps, and to calm down he told himself over and over again that there was nothing he could do. He would have to wait. He conjured up a warm, soothing voice in his mind, which he tried to imagine guiding him when he felt this way, the dark brown, earthy female voice that normally reassured him. He slowed his pace and his heart gradually stopped pounding. The sensation of overwhelming pressure in the centre of his chest began to fade and he took deep breaths, great gulps of clean air, which he released as slowly as he could. Suddenly he felt exhausted; it was time to rest.

Hekla looked over her shoulder as she hurried from the changing room, through the turnstile and into the car park. Behind her a pall of steam continued to rise from the open-air pool; she hoped the man was still in the hot tub where she had left him. She had changed at a speed the bulky man could hardly hope to match, she thought, throwing her towel onto the back seat as she sat behind the Toyota's wheel and groaned as it whined and declined to start.

"No. Not now, you bitch," she whispered to the car, leaning forward and resting her forehead on the steering wheel while forcing herself to rest the starter for a few seconds. "Go on. Do it. Do it for me. Start," she muttered, gasping a sigh of relief as the engine coughed into unwilling life, leaving a cloud of black smoke behind it.

With a glance over her shoulder, she gunned the Toyota's complaining engine and the car slipped sideways as the wheels failed to grip on the frozen ground, finally finding a purchase as she eased the accelerator and the wheels stopped spinning. The car bounced across the car park just as a heavily built man jogged from the pool door, catching a glimpse of Hekla's cropped head behind the wheel of the battered

red Toyota as his own four-wheel-drive car started first time.

He sped onto the main road, narrowly avoiding a collision and waving his apologies to the driver of the bus that had managed to stop just in time. Not knowing which way the red car had gone, he hoped it had gone right and sped faster than was wise though the slush. He took the first roundabout at a dangerous pace and prayed that the police weren't out, putting his foot down along the road past Korpúlfsstadir and the course where he occasional played a few holes. He ignored the speed bumps and was finally rewarded with the sight of a down-at-heel red car in the distance. Resisting the temptation to put his foot down and close the distance, he kept it carefully in sight, and was able to see well in advance which way it went at the next roundabout.

The red car was making its way along Vesturlandsvegur, the main road that passed through the last suburbs of the city outskirts before the stretch to the Hvalfjördur tunnel and the countryside beyond.

He chewed his lip and wondered where the car was going. He was certain it was the same woman. The hair was different, cut very short and made spiky by the moisture and steam, but she looked so familiar. That figure was the same, with those heavy breasts that he'd last seen encased in electric-blue PVC. He told himself bitterly that he had seen more of them through the blasted woman's demure swimsuit than he had during the session at the Arctic Hotel that had cost him so dear. On top of that, her listing was still there on personal.is.

From under the lids of half-closed eyes he had watched her relax in the hot tub, concentrating on the face alone, certain that the strong jawline and narrow, slightly kinked nose in a long but shapely face belonged to the same woman. Watching the car from a distance and with time to think, his blood boiled with anger at the humiliation, as well as the fact that she had bled his account dry. Taking deep breaths and telling himself to be calm and maintain a steady speed as the red car passed through Mosfellsbær without stopping, he reminded himself that the bitch had at least kept her word. She had skinned his credit and debit cards, but had only used them once, plus he had been released from his bonds exactly when she had said he would be. That didn't detract from the fact that he'd had to borrow money for the first time in years to tide himself over that month.

Where was the red car going? he wondered. All the way to Akranes, maybe? Or further? He looked at the fuel gauge and was relieved to see he had more than half a tank. With the last of the Mosfellsbær roundabouts behind it, the red car picked up speed along the quiet road.

Agnes was painting when he came in. She sat at her easel in the wide-open living room with an absorbed look on her face, a fine brush crosswise in her mouth and another in her hand as she concentrated every ounce of her attention on the small canvas in front of her. Jóel Ingi wondered what the abstract image was supposed to be as she etched a swooping line in aquamarine across half of the canvas.

"Is it a bird?" he guessed.

"Nope," Agnes replied distractedly. "Not sure yet."

He admired her dedication, wishing he could do the same. The tiny pink point of her tongue protruded between her lips as she took the broader brush from her mouth and worked at a patch in a corner of the painting, lightening the tone. A wisp of her pale blonde hair had escaped from the band around her head and she absently pushed it out of her eyes, her otherwise clear forehead furrowed in concentration.

"I'm going for a shower," he said, slipping off his jacket and loosening his tie. "Coming?" he asked hopefully.

Agnes had her eyes focused on the inexplicable painting. "Hmm?"

"Nothing," he said, turning and making for the bathroom as Agnes's phone tinkled in the pocket of her artist's smock.

His phone rang in the breast pocket of his jacket. A traditional sort of man, he had set the ring tone to sound like the bell of an old-fashioned phone, the kind with the rotary dial that nowadays you only see in junk shops.

"Haraldur," he greeted the unknown caller with a warm voice.

"Good day to you, Halli. I hope you're keeping well."

"Fine, thanks. Sorry, but who is this?"

There was a chuckle from the other end and Haraldur was irritated. It had been a busy day and he had no time to play games.

"Look, should I know you?" he asked sharply, abandoning his urbane voice.

"No. But I know you. My name's Jón and I'm investigating an incident connected to your stay at the Harbourside Hotel recently."

Haraldur suddenly felt faint and looked around for somewhere to sit. Fortunately he was alone in the office and let himself sink into the comfortable chair he kept to put customers at ease.

"Still there, are you, Halli?"

"I'm not sure I can help you."

"I'm sure you can."

"Is this some kind of a joke?" he asked, angry now that he had started to collect his thoughts.

"Oh, no. Far from it. The lady you met at the Harbourside. The one who started off blonde and then wasn't. I'm looking for her, and I'm surprised you aren't as well, Halli. I'm after a name," the voice said. "To start with."

"Who the hell are you?"

"Hey, calm down, Halli. It's all right. A little information and everything will be fine."

"I don't have time for this," he said abruptly.

"Really?" the voice drawled. "Because if you don't, then the lovely Svava might. I'm sure she'll be interested to know what you were up to at the Harbourside, wouldn't she?"

137

Halli felt faint a second time. He had tried to put the incident out of his mind and he'd almost succeeded.

"Her name's Sonja," he said weakly. "That's all I know."

"How much did the bitch sting you for, then?"

"About half a million."

"In cash? She emptied your account, I suppose?"

"Look, I really don't want to talk about this."

"But I do, Halli, I do. And if you don't, then I'll ask Svava if she can give me copies of your bank statements. I suppose you have a joint account, don't you?"

"Yes," Haraldur said faintly, understanding that the man with the harsh voice held all the cards, and deciding that Jón was probably no more his name than that woman's name was Sonja.

"All right. Now, answers. She calls herself Sonja. How did you meet her?"

"Through an ad on the internet."

"Where?"

"Personal.is."

"Which is what?"

Haraldur looked round as the door opened and frantically waved the secretary out of the room as the door rapidly closed again.

"It's a site for people to meet. You can look at it yourself, can't you?"

"I most certainly will. Now, this Sonja. Age?"

Haraldur floundered. "I don't know. Around thirty, maybe."

"Height, weight?"

"Tall. One-eighty, something like that. Weight? I have no idea."

"OK. Skinny? Fat? Big tits or small?"

"Er . . . medium I guess. Around medium."

"Eyes?"

"Green, I think."

"Yeah," the voice chuckled. "I guess you had other things than her eyes on your mind, didn't you, Halli? Listen, I appreciate your help. If I find her and it all goes well, then you won't hear from me again, and neither will Svava. All right?"

"Please. Leave my wife out of this," Halli said, trying to stop himself from pleading.

"G'bye, Halli. And not a word to anyone, anyone at all. Understood?" the voice said sharply and the call ended, leaving Haraldur sitting in the office chair with his shirt sticking to the sweat that had collected on his back.

Hekla stole an occasional look in the mirror. There were cars overtaking her at intervals, and there was always a car somewhere in the distance behind her, but too far for her tell if it was the same one. Surely anyone following her would have wanted to stay closer? She regretted not having taken a more roundabout route through Grafarvogur after leaving the swimming pool, taking a few twists and turns that would at least have given her an idea if she were being followed, but such was her hurry that the thought hadn't crossed her mind until it was too late.

She struggled to remember the man with the pale eyes. It had been a good while ago that she had met him at some hotel in Reykjavík; she wasn't sure which one. He seemed a decent enough old boy and she had almost not wanted to take his money, but times had been hard and still were, and the man's cash had paid for the car to be fixed and insured, as well as covering the month's rent. Halfdán? Hermann? She struggled to remember the name, although she recalled clearly enough the vaguely sad, pale-blue eyes in the heavy face, and the look of disappointment rather than anger when he realized he was being robbed, even though she had been considerate enough to get him off before leaving him to wait it out.

As she approached the little settlement at Kjalarnes, she was assailed by doubt. How long had that grey car been following her, had it been behind her all the way? She thought back frantically and decided that it had been behind her in the distance all the way from Mosfellsbær; she told herself it had to be someone on the way to Akranes, or maybe further. Someone from out of town, she told herself, slowing the car and noticing that the car behind did the same, allowing a van to overtake, whose driver was pushing it to the limits of what could be considered safe on the slippery winter roads.

She stopped to turn left and the van hurtled past, spraying slush over the red car's windscreen as it passed. Hekla fumbled for the wipers to clear it, hoping to see the grey car follow the van, but instead she saw that it was still some way off and clearly moving slowly.

She crossed the road, and rather than driving straight through the village to the house she rented on the far side, she pulled into the petrol station beside the first pump. Hekla took her time pumping fuel, hoping to give the grey car a chance to drive past, but with the tank full and only a truck having gone past, her heart sank. It had to be him, Hermann or Halfdán or Heimir or whatever the damned man's name was — something that began with an H.

He sat in the car at the side of the road, spots of cold rain pattering on the roof as he wondered what to do. Should he follow the woman he believed was called Sonja and confront her when the opportunity arose? Or should he simply follow her discreetly, find out where she was going and then retire and think again? He stared through the windscreen at the grey landscape, the mountains obscured by cloud and the sea to the left — a monochrome mass blending seamlessly with the sky.

Finally he put the car into gear and started moving as a truck roared past, its horn blaring a warning as it hurtled northwards, throwing a spray of ice and water up behind its rear wheels. He cruised towards Kjalarnes and as he signalled and pulled into the middle of the road to turn left, he could see the red car at the petrol station. His hands trembling and sweaty with nerves on the wheel, he cruised past as slowly as he dared, but the red car's driver was nowhere to be seen. He stopped and looked at the old Toyota, the red paint on its wings flaking into rust spots, and quickly wrote down the registration number on the back of his hand before sedately driving away.

Hekla emerged from the petrol station's shop, having lingered there as long as she could, visiting the toilets and spending as long as she dared looking at the magazines on the racks before paying for her fuel, all the while darting glances out of the window to see if the grey car, or the grey man with the pale eyes, was anywhere in sight. She emerged nervously, looking about her and hoping there had been nothing at all to worry about. There was nothing but the wind whipping spray off the sea, giving the air a piercing tang of seaweed and a freshness that made her eyes smart.

Relieved, but still worried, Hekla drove slowly down the hill, reminding herself that she ought to collect the children from their friend's house and next Saturday morning she would have to return the favour and have a house full of toddlers for a couple of hours.

He liked the café by the harbour with its down-to-earth feel, but Hinrik clearly felt uncomfortable there, which was precisely why Baddó had wanted to meet in unfamiliar surroundings.

"I used to love this place before I went away. There was always someone I knew in here."

"Yeah. There's always a clientele hanging around here," Hinrik agreed.

"Why do you say that?"

"Just over that way, there's a hostel for junkies and pissheads. If you want to sell any gear, that's the place. Want a dirty job done? Cash in hand, no questions."

142

"Oh, right. I had no idea."

"Things have changed while you've been away, Baddó." Hinrik smiled, sipped and grimaced at the stale coffee. "What's this shit?"

"For fuck's sake, Hinrik. It's coffee. Don't be so damned fussy," Baddó scolded, and raised his voice to call across to the raw-boned woman behind the counter. "Hey, Sína, sweetheart. Any fresh coffee over there for my picky friend?"

The woman looked over and chewed her lip at the sight of Hinrik in his leather coat pouring the contents of his coffee mug out of the window and quickly closing it again.

"There's fresh here if he wants to come and get it."

"You don't do table service?" Hinrik asked, flashing her a smile.

Sína glared back at him. "Depends who it is."

"For crying out loud," Baddó swore, fetching Hinrik a fresh mug himself and banging it down in front of him so that it slopped onto the table.

"Hell. Why did you want to meet in this dump?"

"Because at this time of day it's quiet. That's why. Are you keeping tabs on me, or what?"

"Baddó, old friend," Hinrik said, sitting back and smiling unconvincingly. "Of course I'm keeping tabs on you. What do you expect? I've paid you a wedge of cash to do a job that I've been contracted to sort out by someone I'd like to keep on the right side of. Wouldn't you?"

Disarmed by Hinrik's honesty, Baddó had to agree.

"Yeah. Well, what is it you wanted to know, anyway?"

"Just a progress report. That'll do."

"Calls herself Sonja. Operates here and there at the better hotels, including that smart place up there," he said, jerking a thumb towards the harbour and the smart district above the slipways that had appeared during his years away.

"How did you find that out?"

"You don't really want to know, do you?"

"Probably not," Hinrik agreed. "Probably best if I don't know. What else?"

"I'm getting there. I'll have more for you tomorrow. But if there's no time to meet you, it'll be because I'm on top of this," Baddó said, tapping the table with a forefinger and leaning forward. "Listen. If your client, whoever he is, wants this done quickly and quietly, why doesn't he tell me what he knows so I can get it done a bit faster?"

"Discretion, Baddó, old friend," Hinrik said. "I told you, this is delicate stuff. I'm the only one who knows who this person is, and that's the way it has to stay, so there was no opportunity to pass details to you."

"You mean someone was skinned by this bitch, doesn't want anyone to know and is out for revenge?"

"Never you mind, Baddó. Never you mind. Just come up with a name and an address, and you won't need to worry your sweet head about it any more. We'll see to the rest."

Even Baddó felt a chill at the lopsided leer of a smile that revealed how Hinrik's row of broken teeth had been patched with a single gold replacement.

144

"This might be of some interest to you," Ívar Laxdal said, handing Gunna a folded printout.

He had been on his way down the back stairs at the central police station at Hverfisgata and Gunna had been on her way up. She wondered if he had known she was there; the man's uncanny ability to head people off at the pass when they would have preferred to avoid him was well known. She wondered idly if he had a crystal ball secreted in one of his office filing cabinets, and if so, could she put in a request for one as well? But instead of saying so, she skimmed through the sheet of paper.

"Links to your case, doesn't it?"

"You mean the Gullfoss Hotel thing? Yes. When did this come in?" she asked, wondering just how carefully Ívar Laxdal was following what should be a fairly mundane investigation.

"An hour ago. A young woman called in tears and wanted to report this fellow missing. It's early days. It's only yesterday since she saw him last, so there's a uniform around there now taking a statement. Just so you know," he said, continuing downwards and giving the impression that the conversation had taken place without his having stopped at all on the way to the ground floor.

Gunna read Magnús Jóhann Sigmarsson's name and her heart sank.

It was an evening session and the place was full. Normally Jóel Ingi preferred to train in the mornings before work, but the business with Hinrik had derailed his usual schedule. He had spent half the afternoon at home as Agnes daubed at her inexplicable canvas and he lounged with his iPod in his ears, ignoring the music as he ran events back and forth in his mind.

When Agnes finally stood up, smiled and announced that she had finished painting, he looked at the canvas, shook his head in incomprehension and decided to go to the gym for an hour.

The look on her face spoke volumes in terms of disapproval.

"I'll pick up a takeaway on the way back. Thai or Chinese?"

"Thai," Agnes instructed, hauling the smock over her head and dropping it by the bedroom door.

At the eight-kilometre mark, he realized that if he had cycled to the gym he would have covered the same distance but through the early evening traffic instead of under pounding heavy metal. He decided to do at least another two kilometres before he stopped, not least because a slender young woman had just mounted the machine in front of him and the view of her muscular buttocks immediately inspired him to complete the extra distance.

Már appeared as he approached eleven kilometres, a towel round his neck to soak up some of the sweat a session on the rowing machine had produced. He nodded at the girl on the exercise bike in front and winked. Jóel Ingi grinned back. Már made a drinking motion and he nodded back, holding up two fingers to signify two more minutes.

"Didn't expect to see you here," Már said, handing him a bottle of chilled water.

"Ach. I had to get out of the house, y'know. Agnes is . . ." he shook his head.

"Agnes is what? She's OK, isn't she?"

"Yeah, she's fine. She's just being a bit hard work at the moment."

"As long as she's OK," Már said doubtfully.

"I said, she's fine, all right?" Jóel Ingi snapped, and immediately regretted the sharp tone. Már had known Agnes since childhood and had introduced them. But still Jóel Ingi sometimes resented her affection for Már and that the friendship pre-dated his and Agnes's relationship, as well as the nagging curiosity that sometimes irked him. He wanted to know if Már's and Agnes's friendship had been anything more than that, but had never dared ask.

"Does she know?"

"About what?"

"About the computer you mislaid?"

As far as Már knew, the missing laptop in its bag had been lifted from Jóel Ingi's shoulder by a pair of teenagers, one on a mountain bike, who pedalled along Pósthússtræti into the evening darkness, while his friend had been the distraction. Only Hinrik knew what had really happened, and he knew only a fraction of the truth, just enough to allow him to get CCTV stills from the hotel. Jóel Ingi didn't even want to ask how he had obtained the pictures so rapidly, guessing that someone on the hotel staff had either been bribed or intimidated into extracting them from the surveillance system.

His mind elsewhere, Jóel Ingi realized that Már was speaking.

"Look, can't you take some time off? You're wandering around in a daze. Ægir's noticed you've gone off the boil and he'll rip you up if you put a foot wrong."

"I'm all right. I can hold my own against that overblown windbag."

"You think so? The minister hangs on his every word. He can blight your career like that," he said, snapping his fingers to illustrate the point. "You're like me. No friends or relatives upstairs to fight our corner. Be careful."

Jóel Ingi scowled and said nothing, sipping from his bottle of water and watching as a gaggle of toned teenagers strolled through the chairs scattered around the gym's health bar.

"So what are you doing about this?"

"Don't worry. I have someone looking after it."

"Police?"

"Hell, no! A friend. Well, a friend of a friend."

Már's eyes narrowed. "Explain, will you?"

"Look, it's all in hand," Jóel Ingi told him, breathing deeply to keep his temper intact. "It's a friend of someone my brother knows."

"Your brother's not the most reliable character, is he?"

"Junkies aren't normally the most reliable people."

"So is his friend trustworthy?"

"I don't suppose so. But there's money involved and he's being paid to do a job."

"I'm not going to ask who this person is, but wouldn't you be safer going to the police?"

"Yeah. The police already know, and I'll bet you anything they've filed it away and forgotten about it. If I thought they'd actually do something, I wouldn't have had to find someone else to do the job. Anyway, I don't know the guy who's doing this, and it's better if I don't."

He almost wanted to cry when he saw how much his stash of foreign currency had been depleted. Everyone had thought he was mad at the time, selling his shareholdings just as everything had been going up, and leaving the financial sector for a boring job with a bunch of grey-faced old men at the ministry. But as the currency tumbled and the banks tottered, Jóel Ingi quietly congratulated himself on his astuteness. Another six months and things would have been very different, painfully different, he reflected.

But the stacks of euro notes that he'd originally stored in a bank deposit box, having decided that a foreign exchange account wasn't the safest option, were now looking decidedly thinner, and the equivalent of another million krónur in Hinrik's pocket was painful.

This time they met at a bookshop; they were practically the only people there who weren't sitting behind laptops and tablets over their designer coffees. Hinrik sipped his coffee with distaste. A proper drink would have been preferable at this late hour of the afternoon. Jóel Ingi had a tall glass in front of him that Hinrik eyed with suspicion.

"What's that, then?"

"Latte. Try one."

Hinrik wrinkled his nose. "Nah. Not for me. Got it?"

"Half," he said and watched Hinrik's eyes narrow in suspicion. "No results yet. Half now, and half when there's a name and address." Jóel Ingi pushed a padded envelope across the table between the cups. "Cash. In euros," he added.

The sour expression across Hinrik's face lingered and then dissolved into a smile devoid of any warmth. "In that case, as you're a valued customer, leave it with me." The smile vanished as if it had been turned off at the mains. "But we're a little light on information and you haven't given us a lot to go on. What's going on here? You're complaining that this isn't moving fast enough, but you won't tell me what I need to get the job done fast."

Jóel Ingi stared back at him.

"I mean," Hinrik continued, almost disconcerted by Jóel Ingi's dispassionate look, which told him nothing about what was happening behind those grey eyes. "You want this done quick, so give me an idea what it's all about," he said, lowering his voice. "You know I offer a comprehensive service, don't you? No need to get your own hands dirty."

"I'll think about it."

Hekla was exhausted. The day since she had returned from the pool so abruptly had dragged by and she had been unable to settle into doing anything. She sat at the kitchen table, Alda happily colouring in a picture and

150

Alli spellbound by the TV as Hekla flipped through the newspapers she had picked up at the garage that morning. Without reading anything much, she took in the headlines and checked that her own advertisement was still among the classifieds, not that she'd be renewing it. The morning's scare had told her that line of business had to come to an end, and immediately.

She listened to the radio, punctuated by the whine of Pétur's lathe in the garage, where he sat propped on a stool as he carefully turned out dishes, cups and ornaments from the lengths of wood stacked on the bench next to him. The whine stopped but she only noticed as the click of Pétur's crutch told her he was on the way along the short corridor; she wondered how long he would be able to get in and out without help.

"There's coffee in the machine," she said without turning round as she heard the clicks that accompanied the shuffle of every step Pétur took. He stooped to kiss the back of her neck, wincing as he straightened up again and smiling as he watched Alda concentrating on the colouring book.

Hekla turned a page in the paper and felt a chill run through her as coffee gurgled into Pétur's mug. He turned to her. "D'you want some as well?"

She felt unable to speak, transfixed by the picture in front of her.

"Are you all right, love?" Pétur asked, bemused. "Something interesting?"

Hekla shook herself back to reality. "No, fine. Just someone I thought I knew, but it's not. Yes, please," she added, pushing a mug to the edge of the table.

Mug in hand, Pétur looked at her fondly and made for the door again. "I'll do another hour and then call it a day," he said.

"I'll come and get you. Don't overdo it. You know what the doc said."

Pétur snorted. "The doc. What the hell does he know?" he demanded and was gone, with his step-shuffle-click signalling his progress down the hall and back out to the garage, leaving Hekla to stare aghast at the photograph of a young and dynamic Jóhannes Karlsson staring back at her from the midst of his full-page obituary.

With Helgi dispatched to Kópavogur to speak to the tearful girlfriend who had reported Magnús Jóhann Sigmarsson's disappearance, Gunna parked outside the Harbourside Hotel for the second time that day. The building was an imposing one, giving the upper floors some fine views over the bay, and Esja beyond it, with the stiff wind whipping up white horses on Faxa Bay in what remained of the daylight. Not that Reykjavík's favourite mountain could be seen in the gloom, Gunna reflected as she slammed the leased car's door and made for the entrance. Darkness fell early at this time of year and January was a bleak month, with New Year over and people nervously awaiting the first post-Christmas credit card bill of the year.

"Looking for Símon," Gunna growled at the receptionist whose company-issue welcoming smile faded away quickly.

"I'm not sure if he's here right now," she said. "I can call his office if you like?"

"You do that. Call his office and if he's not there, call his mobile," Gunna told the young woman. "And if that doesn't work you can give me his address and I'll go and hammer on his front door."

She walked around the lobby inspecting the vast canvases hung on the high walls of what had once been a hardware store and guessed that to get walls that high, the ceiling must have been raised by a metre or more when the place had been rebuilt.

Símon arrived looking flustered. Bags had appeared under his eyes since they had spoken that morning and he looked a dozen years older without the flirtatious twinkle in his eyes.

"Gunnhildur," he greeted her with undeniable dismay. "What can I do for you? Any developments?"

"You remember this place when the old hardware store was here, don't you?"

"I do," he replied, puzzled.

"When it was turned into a hotel, how did they manage to make the ceiling higher down here? Or is it my imagination?"

"Er ... the whole place was gutted, floors and everything came out. The only thing that's original are the outside walls. They more or less built a new building inside the shell of the old one."

"Right. I thought so. I was wondering if my memory was playing tricks. Magnús Sigmarsson should have been here for a shift yesterday and didn't show up. Has he been seen since?"

Taken aback by the suddenness of Gunna's change of direction, Símon's face fell.

"I . . . er . . . I don't know. I need to check the rotas."

"Good. Let's do that."

Símon practically elbowed the receptionist from her position behind the desk and tapped at the computer. He sighed. "Twelve to eight. He should have been on a twelve to eight shift yesterday, today and again tomorrow. He's skating on thin ice now. I could easily have him dismissed for this."

Gunna looked over the computer screen, which was covered in blocks of colour.

"That's him there, is it?" she asked, pointing to a dark green block that stretched across four days of timetable.

"That's him. Or should have been. One of the restaurant supervisors covered his shift yesterday, but I don't know what today's arrangement is."

"I have a feeling you might want to get his shift covered tomorrow as well. Something tells me he won't be in."

Símon looked shocked. "Has something happened to him?"

"You tell me. Magnús was reported missing by his girlfriend. She hasn't seen him for twenty-four hours. He hasn't shown up for work and his car's missing. Does he have a history of being unreliable?"

"He's often late, but he's never not turned up."

Gunna heard her phone buzz and saw Helgi's number flashing. "Yes?"

154

"*Hæ*, chief. The drippy girlfriend saw him the night before last. He didn't turn up as expected yesterday. Phone's dead, and his car's gone."

"All right, Helgi, thanks. Can you get onto comms and see if his name's on any flights?"

"Already done it. He's not on any passenger lists, and his passport's expired anyway."

"You'd best circulate the registration and if it's on the move traffic will pick it up soon enough."

"Ahead of you on that one as well," Helgi said with satisfaction. "Next step, we have a look at his apartment?"

Gunna walked across the lobby of the hotel with her phone to her ear to give Símon and the receptionist less of an opportunity to eavesdrop. "I reckon so. Can you arrange for the door to be opened? I'll meet you there in an hour."

"Will do, chief. See you there," Helgi said cheerfully and rang off.

"That was about Magnús, wasn't it?" Símon asked immediately. "He's all right, surely?"

"No idea, but I would hope so. Now, carrying on from our conversation this morning," Gunna said grimly. "It's time you were a little more forthcoming, otherwise I'm going to be down here with a team at eight tomorrow morning to interview every single member of staff from the globetrotting managing director to the unemployed immigrant who washes dishes for cash. Do we understand each other?"

★ ★ ★

The landlord was an elderly man who wheezed up the stairs and had to stop for a breather on the landing.

"Had to move out, you see, can't cope with stairs any more," he explained. "Got a place with a lift now. So much easier," he prattled as he selected a key from a bunch. "This is on the level, isn't it?"

"How do you mean?" Helgi asked, smothering a yawn.

"Could get into all sorts of trouble, couldn't I? I know it's my flat, but it's let and I can't just go waltzing in there when I feel like it. Tenants have rights these days," he said sadly.

"Open it, will you? If you get a complaint I think we can back you up."

The landlord turned the key in the lock and Helgi put a hand on his arm as the door swung open.

"I think you'd best stay here. There's no knowing what we're going to find," he said, snapping on a pair of surgical gloves.

The smell of long unwashed laundry was overpowering and Gunna wrinkled her nose as the aroma brought Gísli to mind; suddenly all the thoughts that had been running through her mind in the evenings came flooding back. She briskly banished them, forcing herself to concentrate on the job in hand as they went through the flat but found no clue as to Magnús Sigmarsson's whereabouts.

"At least the bastard's not drowned in the bath," Helgi said with relief.

"No, but someone's had quite a time in here," Gunna said, lifting a sodden towel from the floor to reveal another below it, stained red with blood. "Water's been everywhere."

"And somebody cut a finger over there," Helgi said, squinting at the rim of the bathtub against the wall where a smear of blood could be seen against the pale-blue plastic and a handprint in blood could be seen on the wall by the door. "We'd best get that checked, I suppose."

"Arrange it with forensics, would you?" Gunna said absently, thinking back to the words of Magnús's disgusted neighbour. "I wonder. Helgi, what does this look like to you? Water and blood everywhere and towels all over the floor?"

"No idea, chief. But it seems weird. The rest of the flat's much as you'd expect. It's a bit grubby and he hasn't done his laundry as often as he might have. I get the feeling something energetic has been going on in here."

"And I'm wondering just what. Would you like to give Magnús's drippy girlfriend a call and ask if they made a habit of screwing in the bath? Because if not, then what went on here may not have been that friendly."

Haraldur jumped when his phone rang and Svava looked at him oddly over the dinner table as he answered it with a quaver in his voice.

"Haraldur."

"Good evening. Haraldur Samúelsson?"

"That's me."

"My name's Gunnhildur Gísladóttir and I'm with the Reykjavík city police," Gunna said. Svava wondered what had happened when Haraldur twitched with nervousness.

"I . . . er . . . what can I do for you?" he asked and Gunna immediately sensed the dread in his voice. It went deeper than that of the law-abiding citizen caught up in something beyond his understanding and told her instantly that Haraldur's conscience was troubled.

"It's to do with an investigation; your name has come up in connection with an incident at the Harbourside Hotel. You were staying there a few days ago, weren't you?"

"I was," Haraldur replied, his voice almost a squeak as Svava stood up and silently left the room.

"I would prefer it if we could meet to discuss this. First thing tomorrow, maybe?" Gunna said in a tone of voice that made the "maybe" redundant.

"Yes. I'll be at the office in the morning until twelve. You can find me there. Fiskitangi 42."

"Fiskitangi? Where's that?" Gunna asked with the sinking feeling that told her the man was out of town.

"It's in Akureyri."

"Ah, right. In that case I'll get a flight in the morning and I'll let you know when I'm on the way."

"I could meet you at the airport if you like," Haraldur offered.

"I'll come and find you if you don't mind. Since I have to go to Akureyri, there are a few other errands I can run at the same time," Gunna said. "But thanks for the offer. I'll see you in the morning."

Haraldur sat still on the kitchen chair for a few moments after the conversation had ended. Svava deliberately shut the door behind her and turned to face him, hands on hips.

"Halli. Will you please tell me what the hell is going on?"

"I'm not sure. First there was a policeman on the phone asking all kinds of questions about when I stayed at the Harbourside when I went to Reykjavík to meet the Daewoo guys from Denmark the other day. Now there's this policewoman who wants to come up here tomorrow and talk to me."

"What's all this about, Halli? You've been as nervous as a cat for two days and don't you dare tell me there's nothing to worry about."

"It might be about my wallet being stolen," he said vaguely, picking up his plate and carefully placing it in the dishwasher. Svava's pursed lips indicated that she found his explanation wanting.

"And how did whoever stole your wallet manage to get into our account?" she demanded, her voice increasingly shrill. "I'm telling you, Haraldur Samúelsson. We've been here before and we don't want to go there again, do we?" She stalked out of the kitchen and slammed the door so hard that the cups and glasses in the kitchen cupboards rattled in sympathy.

Agnes just looked at him as he collapsed into one of the pair of leather armchairs.

"Hard day, darling?" she asked in a slightly sardonic tone that set Jóel Ingi wondering what was behind it before he noticed that her face was carefully made up and her long frame was sheathed in a startling red dress that matched her scarlet lips.

"Going out?"

"Yup."

"Will you be back late?"

"It's Saturday night. Of course I will."

"All right. Have fun," he said bleakly as she stood up. He admired her without saying anything, from the supple black leather boots that encased her calves to the dress that showed nothing but hinted at everything.

"See you later, sugar," she said, blowing him a kiss from the door. "Don't wait up. Bye."

Hermann Finnsson was not happy to get a visit from the police. A heavily built, balding man with jowls that trembled as he shook his head, he radiated nerves and continually looked through the window of the living room of the overdecorated, overheated upstairs flat he occupied.

"I understand that you stayed at the Arctic Hotel last week. You live in Mosfellsbær, so why stay in a hotel so close to home?" Gunna asked, hoping to put the man at his ease and watching his fingers tremble with nerves.

"I . . . er, I decided to stay in town that night. I'd been out with some people and didn't want to drive."

"Really? A taxi home would have been cheaper, wouldn't it?"

"Maybe."

"So, why stay at such an expensive hotel?"

Hermann Finnsson shrugged, lost for words. "I don't know. Does there have to be a reason?"

It was Gunna's turn to shrug. "Of course not. You're married, Hermann?"

"Not any more. I was, a long time ago."

"So who did you go out with that night?"

"Some people."

Hermann thrust his hands into the pockets of his cardigan, Gunna guessed to stop them trembling.

"Look, Hermann. I'm not investigating you or anything you've done. But I have a very good idea of what happened and I need to find the person who took you for a ride. No names, no hassle afterwards. I just want some information."

"Nothing happened," he said in a thin voice and leaned against the wall, a bead of perspiration running from his thick hair down one temple. "Honestly."

"No. Nothing didn't happen. I have it on good authority that you checked into the hotel that morning and left that afternoon. You didn't spend the night there, even though you had paid for it. Why was that?"

"Am I a suspect or something?" he blurted out as the bead of perspiration became a rivulet.

"No. Not at all. But you could be an important witness."

Hermann's eyes flickered to the window and back. "No. I can't. I don't have anything to say."

Gunna could sense his terror, so sharp as to be an almost palpable presence in the room, and the intensity of it set her wondering what he was so frightened of.

161

Facing a blank refusal to cooperate, though, there was little she could do.

"All right. If that's the way you want it, I can't force you to say anything," Gunna said with a grim undertone, taking a card from her wallet. "But if you change your mind, please give me a call. I repeat, I'm not looking for any wrongdoing on your part — just information," she said, putting the card into his hand and noticing that the palm was damp with sweat.

Leaving the flat, Gunna felt its windows glaring at her back, certain that Hermann would be dropping her card into the bin and trying to forget that he had ever seen her.

Baddó found the internet confusing. Since the two mustachioed gorillas had delivered him to Kåstrup and a flight to Iceland, he had seen many differences. The world had changed. Reykjavík had gone from a wayward child with too much cash in its pockets to a surly, suspicious teenager wary of receiving another hiding like the last one, but slowly becoming bold again.

He had noticed how construction had stopped, although that shiny square box of an opera house where the fish market had once been took him by surprise. Unlike the boisterous city of the boom years when the place was awash with money and the nightlife continued past dawn and into the next day, Reykjavík had a brooding presence now, as if it were waiting patiently for the good times to roll again. Not that Baddó had much time for the suited yuppies who'd taken the cash and run; what amazed him was that so many of them were able to go about their lives without being assaulted.

Nothing had surprised him for long, although it was still a shock to see how little his money would buy these days and it hurt to see his sister struggling to put food on the table for the two of them, refusing to take his money while he wasn't earning anything. The internet had changed the most. After the years that he hadn't had access to it, it now seemed that half the world could be found online and much of the world seemed to have disappeared inside a computer screen.

He typed in the letters Haraldur had given him — a stupid-sounding name, he thought, but what the hell? Personal.is opened gradually on María's old computer, although as far as Baddó was concerned, it was impressively fast.

It was a simple enough format, like a dating website, he thought, while wondering how it paid for itself. Users were either pink or blue, for men and women, Baddó guessed, and he clicked on one at random. As the profile appeared, and with it a picture, he instinctively looked over his shoulder to check María wasn't watching, even though he knew she was at work. He read that Kitten70 had a passion for horses and the outdoors, and while she was looking for the "right one" to fill her tummy with butterflies, she wasn't there for the taking. The profile picture showed a three-quarter view of a well-built woman from chin to midriff in a flowery, low-cut dress that left little of her physique to the imagination. CityGirl's and RannaH's profiles told him that men old enough to be their granddads weren't tempting, while Baddó nodded appreciatively at HotXHot's profile, which told him she appreciated the charms of a financially secure older man or even a professional couple.

Getting somewhere now, Baddó decided.

Noticing a search box in one corner, he typed in "Sonja" and waited until four profiles appeared. Looking at the pictures accompanying the SonjaSoy and 92Sonja, he discounted them immediately as teenagers. TinySonja gave her age as 30 and, as there was no picture, he read through the profile that described a quiet lady who combined a love of literature and music with an adventurous side; he wondered just what she meant by adventurous. Sonja2 made him shiver as there was an out-of-focus picture showing a foot tied with a scarf and the bold statement that Sonja2 preferred to be in charge. He read through the additional information, which told him she would message on MSN and his picture would get hers. Then there was a string of lettering that Baddó finally figured out was a cleverly coded email address.

At the top of her profile, he also noticed that Sonja2 hadn't been online for several days. He wrote a quick message in the box that personal.is provided as he clicked on the "contact" button and filled in the brand-new email address that María had set up for him, creating a user profile of his own at the same time. Baddó sat back once the message had gone and scrolled down to the rest of Sonja2's profile, where at the bottom of the page he found a row of thumbnail pictures under a "similar to" banner.

Ten minutes of browsing showed him that Bella specialized in discipline, Portia also liked to be in charge, while Lolla made no bones about her preference for submissive men who "enjoy a little pain". Baddó winced at the idea. He thought of himself as an old-fashioned sort of character, and while he wasn't of the opinion that a woman's place was confined to the home, he drew the line at women having too much control and the thought of a woman delivering pain went against the grain. On the other hand, the porn that some of the better-connected prisoners at Kaunas had access to showed the strangest aberrations, and the fact that some of his fellow prisoners clearly relished aspects of the discipline was something that was alien to him. Like Portia, Bella, Sonja and Lolla, Baddó preferred to be in charge.

He closed personal.is without any curiosity about what else might be found there and checked his new email address, was not surprised to see no messages waiting for him, and he shut the computer down as he heard María's key scrape in the lock.

"Hæ," she greeted him, kicking off her shoes and sinking into the flat's only armchair. "Had a good day?"

"Not bad. You've been busy, though."

María groaned and released the bun that held her grey-shot hair in place at the back of her neck, allowing it to escape over her shoulders.

"That's so much better," she sighed, lifting one foot and then the other into her lap to massage her toes. "So what have you been up to? No joy on the job front, I don't suppose?"

"Well. A little job has come up."

"Legal?"

"Let's say it's not illegal, depending on how I go about it," Baddó said, casually pushing what had happened to Magnús Sigmarsson to the back of his mind.

"And you're doing it legally?" María asked, wide awake now, her tone sharp. "I don't want to be visiting you in prison again."

"Don't worry. I've just been asked to follow someone and keep an eye on their movements. It's OK, and it's cash, so I can contribute to the bills."

"That would be very welcome." She yawned as her defences dropped. "I'm starving and I can't be bothered to cook anything."

"That's all right. I had some cash up front, so I can treat you for once. Thai or Chinese?"

"It's the second shower she's had today," Laufey said quietly.

Something sizzled in the frying pan as Steini prepared dinner and a sudden aroma of spice filled the house as an extra ingredient was added to the pan.

"Really?" Gunna said, disappointed that the shower was already in use when that was just what she felt in need of. "How is she, do you think?"

Laufey changed the channel on the TV for the 19.19 news bulletin that Steini would want to see and turned the sound down.

"I can't tell. She seems happy enough, and then five minutes later she's in tears again. What's that all about?"

"Ach, I expect you'll find out one day, young lady. It's not easy with your body doing weird things and your hormones running wild."

"It can't be that hard, can it?" Laufey said, brows knitted.

"Like I said, you'll find out one day and I expect you'll come to me and tell me how tough it all is."

"Yeah. But not for a while," she said as the bathroom door opened and Drífa emerged, swathed in towels. "I mean, she's like, only twenty."

"So? I was sixteen when Gísli was born."

"Well, I knew that. But you're . . ."

Gunna laughed. "Well, I'm what?"

"You're tough. One of those people who just fights their way through, aren't you?"

Gunna thought back to the hard years following Laufey's father's fatal accident, when she'd found herself a single parent for the second time.

"Ladies!" Steini called from the stove. "Is she out of the shower yet?"

"Only just," Laufey called back.

"Five minutes. Lay the table, someone, please."

"Do I have time for a shower?" Gunna called.

"Only if you get in it right now and you're out in double quick time."

"In that case I'll eat first," she called to Steini and dropped her voice to continue the conversation with

Laufey. "Try not to be harsh on her. It's not easy and she's got herself into a real mess."

"You mean Gísli's got her into a mess, don't you?"

"Careful, sweetheart. It takes two to tango," she said, levering herself off the sofa. "If you call Drífa, I'll lay the table."

CHAPTER
FOUR

Sunday

After a half-hour delay, during which she tried to pretend a cheese roll and rough coffee were a worthy substitute for breakfast, the first flight of the day to Iceland's northern town of Akureyri swooped low over the long fjord leading to the town. Gunna wondered how it could be gloomy and wet in Reykjavík while the sky was clear and studded with stars north of the mountains.

A giant of a man in uniform met her at the airport's arrival gate with a grin on his face.

"*Hæ*. Remember me?"

"Andrés? I wondered if it was you when we spoke on the phone yesterday," Gunna said, looking up into the open face of a man who would never be able to keep a secret. For once, she had to lengthen her stride to keep up with him as he loped out of the terminal to the squad car outside.

"How have you been keeping, then? Been here in Akureyri since you graduated?"

"Yup," he said as the car juddered over the rutted track between piles of cleared snow a metre deep on each side. "Graduated the year after you, wasn't it? Came up here and been here ever since."

"It snows up here a bit, then?"

"Just a bit. But you're used to that, aren't you?"

"Was. It's been a while since I last saw any proper snow. We don't get much of it in Reykjavík."

"But the place still grinds to a halt when there's an inch of snow on the ground." Andrés laughed.

"This guy I'm meeting, do you know anything about him? Anything you can tell me in advance?"

Gunna admired what she could see of the scenery with an hour or two before there would be any real daylight. Akureyri wasn't a place she was familiar with, other than for a few camping holidays with the scouts, which had involved much car sickness on long-distance buses before flying became affordable, although she had always thought of the town as a peaceful place.

"There's not much I can tell you," Andrés said, slowing down to drive through the town and down to the dock area where Haraldur Samúelsson had his office. "He doesn't have a police record, not even a speeding ticket. From what I hear he's a decent character, runs a business importing forklift trucks and hydraulic equipment. There's a small workshop there as well and I suppose he employs half a dozen people. He does Lions Club, football club, all that kind of stuff. Never had to have any dealings with him at all. His wife's a teacher and my missus knows her slightly. Nice enough lady, she says. That's it. Nothing to tell, really."

"Very odd," Gunna said. "Most people have something or other, even if it's only a parking fine."

"Not this guy. Apparently the tax office put him through the wringer a year or two ago, and he came up

170

out of that smelling of roses. That's unusual, not even a bit of black money."

"Shame. Gives me not a lot to go on."

"There is one thing, though," Andrés said, his face darkening.

"His son's a piece of trouble, not that he lives here any more, I'm pleased to say. Sammi's a long-term addict, been in and out of rehab half a dozen times, but never lasts more than a few weeks before he's back on something. He has convictions for theft, breaking and entering, all that sort of stuff. Nothing violent, just quick money stuff. I don't know what you're after, but maybe it could have some bearing on it?"

Gunna yawned. The 5 a.m. start after spending too long talking through things with Drífa was taking its toll already.

"I'm not sure. I'm pretty sure that Haraldur Samúelsson hasn't done anything himself, at least, nothing serious enough for me to pry into his comings and goings. But he was robbed not long ago by someone who seems to have stiffed him pretty badly and that's who I'm trying to track down."

"He didn't report it?" Andrés asked in surprise, drawing up outside an industrial unit.

"Quite the opposite. He's anxious *not* to have it looked into, but as the person who robbed him may also be a witness to something more serious, he'd better tell me what he knows. By the way, do you think Haraldur Samúelsson would have known Jóhannes Karlsson? He's from here, isn't he?"

171

"The dead trawler-owner? Green Jói? He was from Húsavík. But I'd assume they'd have known each other."

"Why Green Jói?"

"Years ago he had two trawlers that went to Poland for refits. While they were there, the shipyard workers stole so much of the green engine-room paint that the story goes you could tell which houses in Gdansk the shipyard guys lived in because the roofs were painted engine-room green. He still had enough left over to paint the roof of his office and store, as well as the engine rooms of both trawlers."

"So, Green Jói," Gunna chuckled as she opened the car door, eyeing the anonymous industrial unit with a modest "HS ehf" in rust-red letters on its signboard.

"Give me a call when you're done here and I'll pick you up," Andrés said as she shut the door.

Haraldur Samúelsson was already sweating when Gunna rapped on the door and went in without waiting for an answer. He reminded her of the frightened reception she'd got at Hermann Finnsson's flat the day before; she hoped that Haraldur could be persuaded to be more forthcoming.

"G'day," she offered, extending a hand that Haraldur took and shook firmly. She could see instantly that he was nervous as he sat at his desk and began fiddling with the cable that connected his iPhone to the socket. "I appreciate your finding time on a Sunday."

"Not a problem. The managing director seems to work seven days a week anyway. What can I do for you? I'm afraid I really don't have anything to tell you."

Gunna sat opposite Haraldur and wondered how far she could push this man before he either cracked and told her everything he had ever done or else closed up and refused to say a word.

"Look, Haraldur. I know you stayed at the Harbourside Hotel and had an unfortunate experience there. I can understand that it's embarrassing and that you don't want anyone to know, but I'll be entirely straight with you. This is a delicate and increasingly serious investigation in which your part is probably very small. I'm not even slightly interested in prosecuting you for whatever minor indiscretions you may have committed. Is that clear?"

Haraldur stared back at her in virtual disbelief. "You mean . . .?" He began, fumbling for the right words. "Not a word to anyone?"

"More or less. Tell me the whole story."

"And you really are from the police?"

"I am," Gunna confirmed, laying her warrant card on the desk, with the two screen-grab printouts from Hotel Gullfoss next to them. "Do either of these look familiar?"

She saw a tremor pass through Haraldur as his eyes opened wide at the sight of the pictures, and she knew immediately that she was on the right track. He slumped into his chair once the initial shock had passed.

"That's her."

"Sonja?"

"That's what she calls herself."

"I've a fairly good idea what happened. You were tied up and then she disappeared with your wallet?" Gunna asked and Haraldur nodded.

"How come you were tied up?"

"Because I asked her to," he said in a small voice that sounded incongruous coming from a man in a suit; his face was bright red.

"And was there a payment involved?"

"No. No money. I paid for the room, that's all."

"So she ties you up, which I suppose had been arranged, and once you're unable to move, she takes your money and runs? Why didn't you shout?"

"Oh, God," Haraldur moaned. "There was a gag as well. It's a domination thing. There's a scene . . ." he said and his voice tailed off for a moment while he took a breath. "A few of us like to experiment sometimes."

"Pardon my asking, but your wife . . .?"

His expression stiffened. "A few years ago she liked to, er, experiment as well. After a while she stopped enjoying it, I suppose. I don't know. It's not something we talk about now." He sighed and caught his breath. "She's a teacher. It wouldn't do if . . . if someone were to recognize her, and Akureyri is a small town."

"Does she know that you still take part in this kind of activity?"

"She suspects."

"You make a habit of this?"

"It's rare. Once in a while if I have to go to Reykjavík. Not here. Like I said, it's a small town."

"There's no 'scene' here?" Gunna asked.

Haraldur squirmed in his seat and Gunna reminded herself that humiliating the man, however easy that might be, was something to be avoided.

"There are people in Akureyri who are part of the scene, some of them much more extreme than the stuff Svava and I used to dabble in," he finally admitted after an internal struggle. "But it's difficult."

"So this stuff gets taken out of town?"

"Exactly."

"And how much did Sonja sting you for?"

"Just over a million."

"A million? Good grief. How did she manage that?"

Haraldur sighed at the painful memory. "Two debit cards and a credit card. She must have milked the cards as hard as she could until they wouldn't dispense any more cash, and then she did some shopping as well, using the credit card. Jewellery, judging by what I could see when I checked my account online."

"I need to see that. But how did she get the PINs for your cards?"

"Simple, I guess. She wanted the PINs and said that if the cards worked, then she'd call the hotel after an hour and tell them that someone in such-and-such a room was in trouble. If the PINs didn't work, she wouldn't bother and probably nobody would go into the room until the next morning," he explained in a hollow voice. "And then there were the photos."

"Photos?"

"Yes. She took a couple of pictures."

"Of you tied up?"

"Yes. So you can understand why I wasn't keen to talk to you . . ." he said, his voice fading away again.

Gunna's phone buzzed and she looked at the screen, noticing to her surprise that she had spent almost half an hour in Haraldur's company.

"Excuse me, I have to take this," she apologized, stabbing the green button. "Helgi, a bit busy at the moment. Call you back?" She could hear the wind whipping Helgi's voice away as it roared and faded in her ear. "Where are you?"

"Near the quarter-mile race track. Give me a buzz back when you're free. It looks like we've got Magnús Sigmarsson."

Gunna sensed the tension from Helgi's end, and looked over at Haraldur, who had taken the opportunity to check his own phone.

"But not in a good way, I take it?"

"Nope. Stone dead. Broken neck's my guess."

"Hell and damnation. All right. I'll call you when I'm finished here. I'll be back this afternoon at any rate."

"Righto, chief," Helgi said, and Gunna could hear that his attention was elsewhere with another voice calling his name as the connection closed.

"Sorry about that," Gunna said, frowning, as Haraldur put his phone down on the desk. "Now, tell me how you made the connection with Sonja. I don't imagine that's her real name."

"I have no idea. That's definitely her, though," Haraldur said, tapping the pictures Gunna had left on his desk. "Where were those taken? At the Harbourside?"

"I can't tell you where they were taken, but they were taken the same day."

"She's an attractive woman," Haraldur said with a wistful look on his face.

"So how did you arrange to meet? Why the Harbourside?"

"There's an internet site, personal.is. That's where a lot of people on the scene make contact. She was on there. I sent her a message, got a reply and we arranged everything that way without having to speak. She decided when and where, told me to book a room at the Harbourside Hotel and instructions on where to be." He shrugged. "So that's what I did, and look where it's got me," he added with the first note of bitterness in his voice. "My wife doesn't need to know about this, does she? I mean, after the phone calls and everything . . ."

"What do you mean, calls? Gunna asked sharply. "I called you once yesterday. Has anyone else been in touch you about this? Sonja, maybe?"

"Er . . . no," Haraldur said, flustered. "No, it's just that . . ."

"Just what?"

"The Harbourside guy who called, he said I shouldn't speak to anyone else about this."

"Who was that? Símon?"

"He said his name was Jón, that's all, and that I shouldn't speak to anyone else about all this. But considering you're from the police, I thought I'd best not hide anything," he said, the confusion apparent on his broad face. "I hope I haven't done the wrong thing."

It was still a pleasant surprise not to wake up in a metal cot on a mattress that was too thin. Baddó stretched and yawned. María had already gone, leaving him with the flat to himself. He swung his legs out of bed, furrowed his eyebrows as he saw that there were two missed calls on his phone from a withheld number and wondered who it could be. Probably Hinrik, he reasoned, knowing that the man changed his business number every few weeks to another anonymous pay-as-you-go number.

Yawning, with the percolator spitting in the background and the radio on, he sat at María's computer and waited for it to start up. It hadn't taken him long to learn how to use it and he was already wondering about getting a faster model of his own. There was one message waiting in his inbox.

"Sorry. I'm retired. Good luck elsewhere. Sonja x"

He quickly typed a reply, his jaw set as he tapped with two fingers.

Hæ again. Could you call me, please? I'll make it worth your while, he wrote, adding his phone number, and hit the send button. As he cupped his chin in his hands and thought what to do next, the radio newsreader burst into his thoughts.

"Police have not yet commented on the person believed to have been found on wasteland south of Hafnarfjördur this morning. There is a strong police presence in the area following the discovery early this morning of a body, but no details are yet available," he heard, immediately furious. "The national women's handball squad returned

178

today from . . ." the newsreader continued until Baddó snapped the radio off. Shit, damn and blast, he thought, hardly believing that Magnús Sigmarsson's body could have been discovered quite so soon and realizing that the car now parked outside, which had been so useful yesterday, had become a liability that would have to be smartly disposed of.

Standing outside Haraldur Samúelsson's office, Gunna punched in the number that he had extracted from his phone and listened to it ring until finally the "number not available" tone began, by which time Andrés had bumped his squad car across the car park.

"How'd it go?" he asked as she gave up calling the number and dropped her phone into her lap. "Where to now?"

"Straight back to the airport, if you would be so kind. Something's come up and I need to get back quickly."

"Weren't you going to see someone else?"

"I was, but that'll have to wait until later," she said grimly. "We have a body out by the quarter-mile track, and it's to do with this case I came up here for; suddenly it's looking rather more serious than it was an hour or two ago."

Mercifully, the rain had held off. Under a plastic tent erected over a deep fissure in the lava rocks, Gunna looked at the remains of Magnús Sigmarsson lying twisted into an impossible position half out of sight, the visible part of him illuminated by harsh lights fed by a chattering generator.

"Who found him?"

"Someone out walking his dog this morning. The dog found him." Helgi sniffed, the beginnings of a cold thickening his voice. He shivered inside his thick coat, a woollen hat pulled down close to his bushy eyebrows, which dripped with moisture. "I sent the dog owner and his dog home," he added.

"What do the forensic gurus say?"

"Apart from moaning about being asked to come out here in this weather on a Sunday? Too early to say, but I'd bet anything you like his neck's broken. You just have to look at the way his head's twisted round."

Gunna shuffled her feet, aware that water was seeping into her shoes.

"What we need to know is if it was broken before he landed down there, or was it the fall that did it, and when?"

"Yup," Helgi agreed. "That'll do it. How was your morning in Akureyri?"

Gunna shook her head. "The poor guy was scared shitless, didn't know what was happening to him. I just had to write it all down and now I need a few hours of peace and quiet to sort this out."

"Does any of it make sense yet?" Helgi asked.

"You know," Gunna said, wondering what to say, "so far, no. Jóhannes Karlsson had a heart attack and died. That's simple enough to work out and there's no foul play involved as far as I can see. There's no evidence of any kind of violence, and the post-mortem confirmed it was a genuine heart attack, which wasn't exactly a surprise in an elderly man with a history of heart problems."

"And this guy?"

"I know. It's weird, isn't it? There's nothing to link the two. Elderly man croaks from natural causes under odd circumstances, while a young man looks like he's been murdered, and if he wasn't, how the hell did he get out here?"

"Not related?"

Gunna shrugged her collar higher. "They shouldn't be related. There's nothing to link the two, but there's so much else happening around these hotels that the whole thing stinks," she said as Helgi nodded gloomy agreement. "Now there's a body I reckon we'll be giving this priority and overtime shouldn't be a problem."

Gunna looked around, as if expecting to see the stocky form of Ívar Laxdal looking over her shoulder; she was almost surprised to see he wasn't there.

The problem was transport. Baddó decided that getting rid of the car somewhere out of the way would be no great problem, but there was no way he was going to ask for help from anyone, least of all from that thieving shyster Hinrik. He would have taken the chance of using Magnús's car for a few more days with its carefully switched number plates, but now the police would be looking at murder, driving the Golf was a risk he didn't want to take. Besides, he could hear that a wheel bearing was about to wear itself out, and being stranded somewhere in the broken-down car of a murder victim would be unfortunate, to say the least.

Already nervous about what he had in mind for it, he walked downtown, past the bars and eateries that had sprung up in the city centre during his years away. The Gullfoss Hotel looked inviting and the warmth of the lobby hit him like a fist planted in his chest.

"Good evening," the odd-looking man behind the desk greeted him.

"Hi," Baddó responded. "The bar's open, is it?"

"It is. But it's quiet tonight. It's still early."

"Quiet will do nicely," he grinned. "For the moment."

The man smiled and gestured with a hand to the hotel's bar with its long window looking out onto city life outside, not that there was much life so early on a weekday evening.

The odd-looking man with the heavy tortoiseshell glasses appeared behind the bar just as Baddó placed a hand on it, looking round at the small number of drinkers already sat at tables here and there.

"I didn't think it would be this quiet."

"It's a Sunday. Not much happens on a Sunday."

"I'll have a beer to start with," he said, peering at the man's name badge. "Gústav."

"A beer coming up."

Baddó watched as the receptionist stepped into the barman's role with aplomb. Gústav was in late middle age, he guessed, not your average low-paid hotel droid. He reminded himself not to overdo it. Magnús Sigmarsson's car, parked along with the crossover of

Reykjavík's early-evening revellers and late-afternoon shoppers, still needed to be dealt with and a clear head would be needed for that.

The beer appeared in a tall glass with a flourish. "*Voilà*."

"*Na zdrowie*," Baddó replied, taking a long pull that half emptied the glass. "It's been a while since I was here last," he said.

"Oh, yes? Years or months?"

"Years. A good few years," Baddó said, hoping that Gústav hadn't noticed him speaking to that dim-witted Kolbeinn a few days earlier.

"Been abroad, or out in the country, have you?"

"Overseas. Things have changed, and not for the better."

"You'd have been better off staying somewhere a little more prosperous," Gústav said with a sad dip at the corners of his mouth and Baddó noticed that the man wore a cravat inside his open-necked shirt instead of the regulation hotel tie that the other staff wore. "Business abroad, if you don't mind my asking?" he enquired, and Baddó recognized the professional barman's openness to conversation with a punter who wanted to talk.

"I've been in security, the Baltic States," Baddó answered shortly, reckoning that being too specific would lead to no good.

"An up-and-coming part of the world, I'm led to believe. Half of this place's staff come from that way and, between ourselves, if we could replace the other half with Polish boys and girls, the place would run a lot better."

"Present company excepted, I presume?" Baddó laughed, emptying his glass. "Another of those would go down well."

Gústav grinned and began pouring a second drink, which arrived with the same flourish. "Good health."

"And yours. I'd buy you a beer as well, but I guess that would be out of order in working hours, wouldn't it?"

"Sadly, the unenlightened health and safety fanatics who run Iceland these days have made it impossible for a hard-working man to slake a decent thirst with anything other than coffee while manning the barricades," he told Baddó, pouring himself a cup from a thermos behind the bar and raising it in a mock toast. "More's the pity."

"Things have changed," Baddó agreed, taking a sip of his second beer and warning himself to keep the pace slow. "But tell me, where does a man go for a little discreet action these days?" he asked, looking down his nose with the hint of a wink.

"I'm the soul of discretion. There's action to be had, but I'm afraid I prefer to turn a blind eye."

There was a change in his tone, more guarded, but still with a note of curiosity.

"Even if there might be something of a drink in it for a man forced to stick to coffee?"

"Life is nothing but a series of possibilities and everything has its price."

Gunna stared gloomily at the screen on Eiríkur's computer, replaying the footage from Hotel Gullfoss for the fifth time. She was tired and the early start had left her feeling drained. Eiríkur and Helgi were busy interviewing Magnús Sigmarsson's relatives, girlfriend and those of his friends who could be tracked down, while she yawned at her desk at the Hverfisgata station, watching the fashionable blonde woman stride purposefully across the lush carpet of the Gullfoss Hotel, then watching her dark-haired incarnation slouch down a dim corridor in baggy tracksuit bottoms and a hooded sweater.

She played the footage back again, then looked through the stills, including a couple of computer-enhanced versions of the same pictures, which showed what the woman could look like.

The darkness outside filled her with foreboding and she wondered for the first time if she ought to relocate somewhere closer to the city than her quiet village, which could be an hour or more's drive to work if the weather were unkind. Almost without thinking, she dismissed the thought, even with the wind whipping raindrops like bullets against the office windows from the blackness outside.

She stood up and looked along the row of mostly deserted desks, spying a head at the far end.

"Dísa, would you come and have a look at this? I could do with a second opinion."

The woman at the far end nodded, tapped briefly at her computer and stood up. "What can I do for you, Gunna? You need some help from the drug squad?"

"Just wondering if you recognize this face, that's all," she said, setting the first sequence to run.

Dísa stood with her chin cupped in one hand, nodding as the blonde woman with the dress that showed off long legs took a dozen steps across the Gullfoss Hotel's bar and disappeared through the doorway leading to the lifts.

"Familiar?"

"No. I don't think so," Dísa said slowly. "Is this someone new?"

"Your guess is as good as mine," Gunna said. "You know the old guy who died at the Gullfoss Hotel the other day? This is the woman we think was with him when he blew a gasket."

"For sale, you reckon?"

"I thought so, but now I'm not so sure. I was wondering if there might be a narcotics angle. Someone you might know, maybe?"

Dísa shook her head. "No, doesn't look like any of the regulars we get to see."

"Any progress, Gunnhildur?" Ivar Laxdal's voice startled them from behind and Gunna turned to see that his attention was focused on the screen as well.

"Nothing so far, I'm afraid," Gunna said, feeling foolish at being taken by surprise and wondering if Ívar Laxdal made a point of moving as silently as a cat so as to keep his staff on their toes. "There's this as well," Gunna said, starting the grainy sequence from the hotel's CCTV cameras in the corridor. They watched as the woman with the mass of black curls made her way quickly along the passage, avoiding the lift and

186

making for the stairs, providing a close view of her angular face with its strong nose and deep-set eyes under the fake fringe, before the cameras watched her walking away and disappearing around a corner.

"Nope. Sorry. That's not one of our regulars," Dísa said. "I don't think this is drugs-related, do you? There are some about who will screw for dope, a couple of regulars, but most of them just now and then as far as we know. Not that they work anywhere as classy as the Gullfoss."

"That woman has kids," Ívar Laxdal rumbled behind them.

"What?"

"Scroll that sequence back to where she walks under the camera."

They watched the woman walk away from them again, and then a third time.

"Look at her hips and the way she walks," Ívar Laxdal said. "I'd wager a month's salary that woman has a couple of children."

Gunna wanted to ask if he meant his salary or hers, but thought better of it as she switched back to the first sequence in the bar, this time paying attention to the woman's gait.

"It's not so obvious there, I suppose because she's dressed up and isn't wearing completely flat shoes," she mused, then went back to the corridor sequence. "What do you think, Dísa?"

"I agree with Ívar. There she's wearing trainers and she's in a hurry, you can see she walks like a horse pulling a cart. I'd reckon she's either had a car accident or something at some point that's damaged her hips, or else she's popped out a few kids. You can tell from her butt as well," she added. "Tracksuit bottoms aren't very forgiving, are they?"

"You're right," Ivar Laxdal agreed. "They don't do you ladies any favours, and they don't turn heads like that dress does. So, how does it look?"

"Not great. We've no idea yet who the woman is, or even if she had anything to do with Jóhannes Karlsson turning up dead."

"And the body out by the quarter-mile track? Is it anything to do with this?"

"There isn't a shred of evidence to link the two, but to my mind it's too close to be a coincidence."

"Definitely murder, not an accident?"

"I'd say so. We'll know when the post-mortem has been done. But I'd say he didn't wind up in that hole in the ground willingly."

"Good," Ívar Laxdal said. "You should be off soon, Gunna, considering you were at the airport at seven this morning and it's getting on for six now. But come and find me before you leave, would you?"

Baddó drained his glass with a flourish as theatrical as the barman's had been when he filled it.

"Another?" Gústav reached for the glass.

"Why not? One for the road," Baddó decided, scenting what he was looking for. "And how much do I owe you?"

A tall glass appeared at his elbow and Gústav tapped at the till behind the bar. "That'll be two thousand two hundred," he said, almost apologetically.

Baddó carefully placed a pair of 5000 krónur notes on the bar with one finger resting lightly on them, increasing the pressure to hold the cash in place as a hand was extended to take it. "I'm still wondering where a man can find a little enjoyment around here."

Gústav looked nonplussed behind his oversized glasses. "Doesn't it depend on who wants to know?" he said quietly.

Baddó made a tiny downward movement of his chin towards the 10,000 krónur still held firm under his finger. "Does it matter?"

"Well, if you put it like that, I suppose it doesn't." He smiled and Baddó released the notes, which vanished with practised speed.

"Had a bit of trouble here recently, haven't you? Word gets around."

"Æi, don't ask. It's been a nightmare these last few days. Police everywhere and management running around with their heads up their fundaments," Gústav said with gusto. Baddó nodded with satisfaction that the cash had done the trick.

"From what's whispered in my ear, this has been going on a while, hasn't it?"

Gústav cocked his head to one side, as if wondering what to make of Baddó's question. "That depends."

"Depends on what?"

Gústav shrugged. "On your point of view as much as anything. Sometimes it's not healthy to notice too much."

"Maybe," Baddó agreed, sipping his beer to make it last. "But sometimes keeping your eyes skinned can be profitable. There's a scam doing the rounds and I understand that it came unstuck the other day when the old guy on the receiving end of it conked out. Am I right?"

"That's about right," Gústav admitted, uncomfortable by now, glancing around the bar, and giving up any pretence. "Look, pal. What is it you're after?"

"A name," Baddó said quietly. "The price is right." He quickly scribbled on a beer mat and slid it across the bar. Gústav glanced at it and slipped it into a pocket. "Give me a call on that number when your shift's over."

He drained his glass and left it standing in front of Gústav, who was wondering just what he'd meant by "the price is right".

Sif could hear them talking in the other room with the burbling of the TV in the background. Dad wasn't a problem, his injured hip made him pretty slow on his feet and she could hear him coming, but Hekla was another matter. A good bit younger than Dad and faster on her feet, Hekla could appear without warning with that bony nose of hers wrinkled in disapproval.

The laptop bag that had been stashed carelessly under the workbench had intrigued her and she wanted to know why it was there. Her own laptop was struggling and there were no more tweaks or upgrades that would improve it. It was all right for schoolwork, but there were games that she found herself excluded from. Here was a computer hidden away under the bench that might be better than hers and she wondered why it was there.

Opening it in her room, Sif found herself facing a blank screen with a single blinking cursor and a row of blank spaces. The damned thing was password protected. She wondered where her stepmother had got it from, and assumed that it probably hadn't been acquired honestly.

She tried "password" and nothing happened. The computer's screen gazed patiently back at her, waiting for the magic word. A string of zeros also failed to work, and she wondered how many attempts she could make before the computer failed to cooperate.

Sif rooted through the bag the laptop had come in. It was a good one, she noticed, not new by any means, but classy leather rather than some cheap crap. She was wondering who Jóel Ingi Bragason might be when she found a little wallet of business cards. Peering closely at the tiny image on the cards of a man in glasses and a grey suit, and noticing the crest of some government department next to it, she immediately dismissed Jóel Ingi Bragason as being of no interest whatsoever. However, something about the man might yield a clue to his password, so Sif dug deeper into the laptop's case.

"I'm off home as well," Ívar Laxdal said, "so we can talk and walk."

He shoved open the door of his rarely used office and was on his way down the corridor, buttoning his coat as

191

he went, before Gunna had taken his words in. She hurried after him.

"Jóhannes Karlsson, the haddock baron from Húsavík. Shot his bolt at the glorious Gullfoss Hotel in more ways than one. How the hell is there a connection with this lad the dog walker found this morning?"

"There isn't one. Or at least so far there isn't one that's staring me in the face."

"But it smells that way, does it, Gunnhildur?"

"That's about it. It stinks."

A hint of a smile played around Ívar Laxdal's black-bristled face as he punched a button to summon the lift. "Well, you've been right once or twice before when the rest of us thought you were losing the plot, so the benefit of the doubt is yours," he said, and Gunna recognized that this was high praise from a man so sparing with his compliments.

"Thank you," she said finally. "There are links, of course, but they're tenuous so far. I have a feeling there's a whole racket going on that we haven't had a clue about, and it may be that the haddock baron giving up the ghost on the job is what brings it to our attention."

"Right. Good." He stepped into the lift with Gunna behind him. Standing close together, she was uncomfortably reminded that Ívar Laxdal was half a head shorter than her, putting his eyes in line with her chin. "I can authorize overtime," he said after they had travelled to the ground floor in silence. "But keep it within reasonable limits, would you?"

"I'll do my best."

"What do you need?"

"What do you mean?"

"More bodies, or what?"

"Nothing right now. Eiríkur and Helgi will do just fine for the moment. But it would be helpful if you could keep Sævaldur off my back."

Gunna had already clashed more than once with the force's newest chief inspector, Sævaldur Bogason, and while her team wasn't part of his immediate department, she suspected that he wanted it to be.

"Don't you worry about Sævaldur. I'm trying to persuade him to apply for a post in Afghanistan. He won't go for it, as the man hasn't a shred of imagination between his flapping ears," he said. Gunna was almost shocked to hear him speak so freely about another officer and wondered if he were joking. "I'll leave you to it as much as I can, but . . ." he said.

"Is this where you tell me that Jóhannes Karlsson has influential friends who don't want to see any dirty washing aired in public?"

Ívar Laxdal flashed a sharp look at Gunna as they stepped out into the cold of the car park, and she wondered if it had been a remark too far.

"No," he said with a chuckle in his baritone. "Not yet, at any rate. I know very little about the man, but I'd guess that as he owned quotas, he probably had some influential friends. I understand that he dabbled in politics, and that he was probably a mason, a councillor and a pillar of his community, so I'm already being given encouragement for this to be dealt with promptly. Nothing for you to worry about, but the quicker you can get this wrapped up, the better."

He clicked the fob of his car keys and a brooding black car on the far side flashed its lights in recognition. This time Ívar Laxdal really did laugh, albeit fleetingly. "I hear congratulations are in order. Is that right?"

"Why's that?" Gunna asked, nonplussed.

"Imminent grandparenthood, I'm told."

"Oh, that. Yes. Thanks. But I didn't have anything to do with it and wasn't asked if I wanted to become a grandmother."

"It's not so bad," Ívar Laxdal said almost wistfully. "It's rather enjoyable, in fact. I'll see you in the morning," he added, stalking across the car park in the dark and leaving Gunna with an incongruous mental image of Ívar Laxdal dandling an infant on his knee.

The car stank and Baddó was concerned that the reek of petrol would cling to him as well. He stood upwind as the flames began to lick at the car, waiting for the fire to catch properly. He backed away, expecting a sudden blaze, and was rewarded with a burst of flame and a roar of sound as the fire caught the petrol the seats had been soaked with, sucking in oxygen and illuminating the rusted containers and abandoned vehicles on what was left of the shrinking patch of wasteground near Reykjavík's harbour.

Baddó turned and walked quickly, making his way along the unlit path and around the next corner towards the new shops and, ironically, he thought, the Harbourside Hotel, where the car's owner had worked until his unfortunate accident. He was still cursing the interfering dog walker who'd found the boy's body out there in the lava fields, where he should have been able to lie for years without anyone stumbling across him. He was also cursing himself for not making the whimpering fool of a boy walk a few hundred metres further through the lava crags before wringing his miserable neck.

Leaving the darkness, Baddó went along the wall at his side; as far as anyone watching would be concerned, he was just another city dweller walking home from one of the new harbour-area shops.

He would have preferred to dispose of the car somewhere more discreet, preferably somewhere out of town that would take the fire brigade half an hour to reach, by which time there wouldn't be much of a fire left to put out. But with no other transport and no appetite for asking that boneheaded thug Hinrik to help him out, it had to be settled somewhere uncomfortably public. He just hoped that the intense heat generated by ten litres of unleaded splashed over the interior would be enough to make the car unidentifiable, at least until he had finished the job in hand and figured out how to make a little extra from it that Hinrik wouldn't expect or even need to know about.

This time he needed to run; he felt he had to exhaust himself physically to match the emotional turmoil within. He stared at the screens above the bank of running machines, the chainsaw heavy metal that accompanied him bearing no relation to the subtitled news footage on the screens as he felt his legs ache and complain, forcing himself to ignore the pain until he could run no further. He collapsed onto a bench and chugged a bottle of chilled water, the muscles in his legs trembling.

He closed his eyes, held his head in his hands and made himself stand up. Half an hour later, showered and clean, but no less tense, he shouldered his sports bag and made his way to the lobby, stopping short in abrupt amazement as a heavy figure in a parka and a baseball cap appeared in his field of vision.

Unable to restrain himself, he marched up to the figure leaning against the counter and grabbed a shoulder of the oversized parka, hauling its wearer around in an undignified half-circle.

"Hey, what the hell . . . ?"

"Why are you following me?" He yelled, trembling as his fingers clung to the slippery material, shaking it until the figure's baseball cap fell off to reveal blonde curls and an earring.

"What the hell are you talking about, you idiot?" the girl shot back. "I don't know who you are."

"You've been following me. Yesterday in town, and the day before. Why? Who are you? Who sent you?"

"Look, pal. I don't know what you're talking about. I just come here to train, the same as you," the girl protested and stood up to her full height, equalling his, as a pair of bulky young men in shorts and tight singlets appeared on either side of him.

"Anything the matter?" one of the two lifeguards asked politely.

"Yeah, this perv just came and grabbed my coat," the girl said quickly as the woman behind the counter nodded sadly in corroboration.

"I think you'd best leave, don't you?"

"No, you've got it wrong. She's been harassing me," Jóel Ingi protested.

The two men looked at each other.

"I don't think so," the second one said, looking at the blonde girl. "D'you want us to call the police?"

"No . . . it must be just a mistake."

"You'd best be leaving, pal, before someone does call the law," the first one said slowly.

The two men nodded and between them they marched him to the door by his arms, Jóel Ingi's feet half dragging on the floor until he found himself outside with the cold air rapidly clearing his head as he asked himself what he had done.

The two lifeguards stood inside the glass door and watched as Jóel Ingi got into his car and sped faster than was wise through the slush out of the car park towards the main road, his tyres kicking up a spray of grit and water as it passed. The last they saw of him was an upraised finger with a furious face behind it as he passed, and a battered Renault that bumped along in its wake and followed at a discreet distance.

Baddó's phone buzzed as he walked past Ellingsen's darkened windows. He looked at the screen and saw only "private number calling". Hoping that Sonja had decided to call after all, he replied.

"Hello?"

"Hello, whose phone is this?" a woman's voice asked. It was a strong voice, not deep, but a voice with a mind of its own, Baddó decided.

"This is Jón," Baddó said. "Is that Sonja?" he asked and immediately kicked himself for asking so quickly. There was a long silence and he wondered if she was still on the line.

"Could be. Why?"

"It's just that I'm looking for some information and I think you might be able to help me," Baddó said. "I could put a little business your way," he added with a cheerful chuckle just as two fire engines with howling sirens passed him on their way — surprisingly promptly, he noted — to the blazing car. He hoped they wouldn't put it out too fast, although he was sure that any fingerprints would have been scorched off by now.

"What sort of business?"

"Let's say I think you could operate more effectively as part of a team."

"What sort of team do you have in mind?"

"So you're not retired, then?" Baddó asked.

"Let's say I'm not tiring myself out."

"Well, if you're interested, there are opportunities for both of us." There was another long silence and Baddó again wondered if she was still on the line. "*Hæ*. Still there?"

"Yeah. Let me think it over."

"Up to you. No pressure," Baddó said. "Can you give me your number? I'll call you tomorrow and we can talk more."

198

"No. I don't think so," the voice said decisively. "Leave it with me. I'll think things through and get back to you," she said and Baddó found himself looking at a lost connection.

Gunna bounced her phone in her hand and wondered to whom she had been speaking. Jón was presumably not the man's real name any more than hers was Sonja. She was relieved that she had called herself; Eiríkur or Helgi would never have been able to carry off that kind of pretence.

She dialled quickly and there was an instant response from the police communications centre.

"*Hæ*, is that Siggi? It's Gunnhildur here."

"Hang on, I'll just get him."

She pondered whether or not to call "Jón" back. He seemed keen and interested to meet Sonja, as indeed was Gunna, but she wondered how to go about setting up a meeting without being identified as a police officer.

"Gunna, sweetheart, how have you been?" A robust voice boomed in her ear.

"Not so bad. Listen, did you have something going out with lights and bells just now? About three minutes ago?"

"Yeah. Two appliances went out in response to a fire down at Grandi. Sounds like some kids set fire to an abandoned car."

"At Grandi, you said?"

"That's it, the wasteground at the back of the harbour. It was too close to the oil tanks down there for comfort, so we got the engines down there quick."

"All right. All out now, is it?"

"Should be."

"Fair enough. Can you put a trace on a phone for me?"

"I'll do what I can. Give me the number will you? I'll get on to the phone company."

"Thanks. It's almost certainly an unregistered mobile," Gunna said, reading out the number of Baddó's phone. "It would be handy to know where this guy is, if you could do that."

She leaned forward and switched on the engine, yawning as she did so.

"Been a long day, has it?" Siggi asked, hearing the yawn.

"It has, I'm afraid, and I've had enough for today. I'll check in with you tomorrow about that number."

The front of the house was dark and Gunna's heart sank. Increasingly, these days she came home to an empty house, and although she would have welcomed the idea a few years ago when both Gísli and Laufey were still under her feet, now that there was a level of peace and quiet, she wasn't comfortable with it.

Once inside, a sliver of light and the muttering of a television coming from under Laufey's bedroom door told her that she wasn't alone after all. Gunna filled and switched on the coffee machine, started up the laptop Gísli had left behind when he bought himself a new one and wondered whether or not to knock on Laufey's door.

She decided against it, went to the bathroom to turn on the shower and was soon letting the scalding water untangle some of her knotted muscles as it pummelled her shoulders. When she emerged wrapped in a towel, the coffee maker had filled the kitchen with an aroma that made the place seem like home again, and the mutter from Laufey's room had become an insistent beat. Dried and dressed in the baggy, comfortable clothes she felt at home in, she poured herself a mug of coffee and sat in front of the laptop, feeling her stomach make its first complaints and wondering if she should suggest a takeaway to Laufey.

Gunna tapped at the laptop and watched as personal.is loaded, a nondescript website she had heard of but never looked at. Jokes about the desperate people looking there and on other similar sites for companionship, or something more basic, had been enough to extinguish any interest.

She browsed curiously through the registry of users, startled to see that the site had several thousand with a sidebar listing those online and ready to interact. Blue for men, she guessed, pink for women. She wondered what the purple indicators meant, until she explored a few of their profiles and realized they were couples, mostly looking for adventurous young singles or like-minded couples.

Gunna shook her head in disbelief at the idea that all these people were online on a Sunday at dinner time. The registry revealed several Sonjas, and she wondered if TinySonja or Sonja2 were who she was looking for. Frustrated at being told that a direct message could not be sent to either of them unless she set up a profile of her own, Gunna baulked at the idea. She read through both profiles a second time and saw that they had a coded email address within the details; she wrote a short message to each, asking for them to get in touch and including her mobile number.

The sheer variety of requirements and requests on the personal.is pages was bewildering, as Gunna read through the profiles and requests for men looking for women and vice versa, men looking for men, women seeking women and couples looking for discreet adventures. She had to resort to a search engine to decode some of the English language terms and unfamiliar acronyms, and in some cases she was still unsure of what they actually meant, although she looked approvingly at some of the tools available and decided that a fully adjustable spreader bar in black lacquered steel might make a useful addition to the police's armoury for dealing with difficult drunks.

The key clicked in the lock and there was a blast of cold air as the front door opened and quickly shut again. Gunna thankfully closed personal.is and opened her email page instead as the double thump of Steini's boots landing on the floor in the hall preceded him.

"Hæ," he said. "Home alone?"

"Don't think so. There's a light in Laufey's room but I don't know if she's in."

"And Drífa?"

"No idea. Her car's there so she may be in Gísli's room, or she might be watching the TV with Laufey, or they might have both walked down to Sigrún's place.

202

I've not been home long and I haven't seen either of them."

"Hungry?" He dropped a plastic bag in the sink, washed his hands and dried them on a cloth before bending down to look over her shoulder. "Not doing work stuff, are you?" he asked.

Gunna could feel the droplets of moisture clinging to his moustache, which was on her neck as he wrapped his arms around her and the chair at once, one hand sliding inside her T-shirt.

"Yes, unfortunately," she said. "What's going on here? Feeling lucky, are you?"

"Who knows? When a man arrives with a bag of fresh fish and is ready to cook it, there's no knowing how lucky he can get."

Gunna stretched, feeling the ache in her legs and shoulders, leaning back in the chair as his arms wrapped themselves a little further around her. "What sort of fish? Boiled haddock's not going to get you far, you know."

"Wouldn't dream of it," he assured her, withdrawing the exploring hand and standing up. "But it'll be something good, so stay hungry."

CHAPTER
FIVE

Monday

The feeling of being watched stayed with her and she was unable to shake it off. Hekla woke early and made her way silently to the kitchen while Pétur slept. The pain that prevented him from sleeping soundly had receded for a few days, kept at bay by painkillers, which he had finally and grudgingly resorted to. The last year had been a difficult one. Pétur's health problems had caused him to retreat increasingly into a world of his own, especially when the pain in his leg kept him awake at nights, and he would sleep much of the day. Sometimes Hekla felt as if she'd become a lone parent, missing Pétur's company and the activity and companionship they'd enjoyed before the accident had half crippled him.

They had been friends long before they'd become the unlikely couple their friends saw them as. Their long acquaintance and the disparity in their ages gave them a closeness but also a distance that Hekla valued. She knew Pétur worried that one day she'd leave with a man closer to her own age and interests. She had sometimes scolded him for what she felt was a lack of trust, but then had to remind herself that the lack of trust could be justified. She hoped he knew nothing of the occasional adventures she'd indulged in with like-minded people Pétur would never be able to connect with. Those erotic adventures had eventually become the lucrative sideline that kept the family on an even keel financially, and as domination had become work before desperation had driven her to rob a few clients, her own desire for it had faded, although, she reminded herself, her expertise was undiminished.

Hekla brewed coffee and enjoyed the silence. Normally the house echoed with the games and activities of her two robust younger children, while her stepdaughter Sif was the quiet one of the house, an intense, withdrawn girl who kept to her own strange hours. Hekla had tried to connect with her, but felt that she had failed to reach the girl who now spent most of her time either in her room or staying with friends closer to college in Reykjavík. Hekla wondered if Sif had a boyfriend among the circle of odd friends she occasionally mentioned. She felt hurt and disappointed that Sif hadn't allowed her well-meaning stepmother past her defences. Or maybe there were no defences? Perhaps there were things that Sif just didn't concern herself with.

In the early darkness she could see the lights of Reykjavík in the distance across the bay and her thoughts went back to the day before and the picture of Jóhannes Karlsson in the newspaper. She dug out the paper from the recycling box and smoothed it out on the table in front of her. The fold had creased across the man's face, a younger, smiling version of the man she had left angrily kicking at his bonds in one of the Gullfoss

Hotel's shabbier rooms. Angry, but very much alive, she recalled.

Jóhannes Karlsson had been sixty-six years old, according to the obituary that listed his parents, two brothers, a sister and several wives before going on to list his children from two marriages. The man had been wealthy, she assumed. He had sat briefly in Parliament, owned fishing vessels and a factory. According to the newspaper, he had been a wonderful father and grandfather, a much-respected employer and a pillar of the community.

Not such a wonderful character that he hadn't been averse to being tied up and whipped hard in a dark hotel room by a strange woman he had asked to talk as dirty as she could, she reflected, wondering what other skeletons might have been in Jóhannes Karlsson's closet but not made it into the newspaper obituary.

At any rate, it seemed, her lucrative sideline was at an end. She might have to seek out a proper job at a time when her usual line of work was thin on the ground; living so far from the city was always going to make a regular job in Reykjavík awkward.

Hekla munched her toast as her thoughts drifted back to the arrogant old man at the Gullfoss Hotel, and the uncomfortable thought occurred to her that his death might have been linked to their session in the hotel room as she groped desperately through her mind for any details. He had been angry enough, but helpless, and his credit and debit cards had been carefully harvested. The old man's eyes had blazed with fury when he realized he was being robbed rather than given the rough treatment he had asked for so specifically in his emails before the meeting. It had been a pretty good day. The second guy that afternoon had been just as lucrative and a decent enough old boy compared to the one whose obituary she was reading. He was polite enough at least for something of a happy finish before she emptied his wallet. Between them the two wealthy out-of-towners had been skinned for enough to keep the family afloat for several months if they were careful, and Hekla was inclined to keep her head down and stay out of sight.

She wondered if it was time to delete her listing on personal.is and allow Sonja to cease to exist completely. Hekla poured coffee into two mugs, added milk to both and sugar to one and carried them along the corridor. Alda and Alli were asleep in their bunk beds, and out of habit she listened to their breathing. There was a strip of light from around Sif's bedroom door, the faint rattle of a keyboard inside and a low rumbling sound. Hekla guessed the girl was playing another of those interminable online games she played with people in Japan or Spain. Pétur turned over in bed as she came into the room; she shrugged the dressing gown off one shoulder and handed him the two mugs.

"There's sugar in the blue one," she said, pleased to see him smile. "Sleep all right?" She asked.

"Yeah, fine. First time for a while."

"That's good. Don't forget your pills."

"No chance," he smiled, counting white tablets into the palm of his hand and washing them down with coffee. "Cold out, is it?"

Helgi had bags under his normally cheerful eyes. He was the kind of man who enjoyed practically any kind of work that was varied and interesting, so it was a surprise to Gunna to see him grumpy and answering questions in monosyllables.

"Can you find out about that car, Helgi?"

"Car?"

"The one that burned out at Grandi yesterday."

"Car? What does that have to do with the Gullfoss Hotel stuff, for crying out loud?"

Gunna's voice hardened. She had never had to pull rank on Helgi in the year they had worked together. "Look, just do it, will you? It may have nothing to do with anything, but I want it eliminated. All right?"

Eiríkur listened to the exchange in confusion, almost as if he had surprised his parents in the middle of an argument.

"And you, Eiríkur, first of all, I want you to start with the credit card statements you got from Jóhannes Karlsson's son — start looking up those places where his card was used on the day he died. They're all pricy establishments and hopefully they'll be able to remember something useful."

Eiríkur nodded. "All right. I'll let you know what I find out," he said and scuttled from the room without another word.

Helgi sighed. "And you, chief?" he asked. There was a fatigue in his eyes that hadn't been there the day before.

"Me? I'm off to meet Magnús Sigmarsson's girlfriend to start with, and then probably his next-door neighbour again."

"If you ask me, the key to all this is somewhere in these hotels," Helgi said abruptly. "I'd bet anything there are staff at these places who know just what's been going on. I'm not sure that this Sonja could have operated without someone on the inside to smooth the way for her."

"More than likely, but none of them are saying a word," Gunna agreed. "Are you all right, Helgi?"

"Yeah. Just had a rough night, that's all. I'll see you when I've found out about this car."

Gústav Freysteinn Bóasson was uneasy. There was something about the hard-faced man in the leather jacket that was both disturbing and intriguing, irresistible qualities that he knew he would later regret his interest in.

He turned the beermat over in his fingers, inspecting the hotel's logo on one side and the "250k" that the man had written on the reverse in neat letters, along with the seven digits of a mobile phone number. A quarter of a million krónur wasn't a lot of money, barely enough to cover the bills for a month in the tiny flat he occupied in the eaves of an old wooden house at the top of Reykjavík's Thingholt district. On the other hand, times weren't easy. The company that owned the hotel group had instituted a pay freeze, supposedly across the board, but it was rumoured to apply only to junior staff, and 250,000 tax-free krónur would sit happily in the piggy bank for a rainy day.

Gussi wondered idly if it would be worth asking for more, maybe enough for a weekend in London and a little culture: the Tate, the Globe, Drury Lane. He sat back and smiled weakly at his daydreams while his thoughts drifted to poor Hekla. A striking and thoroughly talented girl, he remembered. He had to hand it to her, she had worked a scam that anyone could be proud of. Sadly it was a scheme that couldn't last in a small place like Reykjavík. In London or even in Copenhagen, she would probably have been able to get away with robbing wealthy elderly men indefinitely, so long as she didn't do it too often, and as long as her looks lasted. But Gussi reflected that Reykjavík was a terribly provincial city and eventually she would undoubtedly be caught out.

He stood up and looked out of the narrow window with its view over a slice of the winter city in its shades of dull grey. If he stood with his face close to the window and craned his neck, a partial view of the spire of Hallgrímskirkja could just about be seen. He weighed things up in his mind. It was years since he had last seen the girl, back when she was young and green, before she disappeared from the business. He wasn't even sure if she had recognized him in his cheap polyester company suit behind the check-in desk on the couple of occasions he had noticed her at the hotel. Probably not, he thought. He was greyer and not as trim as he'd once been, and his heavy horn-framed spectacles were as good a disguise as any.

It went against the grain to give the girl away to a hoodlum like the hard-faced man who called himself

Jón. Jón, he thought, chuckling. The man was no thespian. Any name but the most commonplace one imaginable would have been more convincing. On the other hand, it wasn't as if he had any obligation to Hekla, apart from the fact that they shared a profession they'd both left, temporarily, he told himself, and the money would come in very useful if he could bargain the man into doubling his offer.

His mind still wasn't made up as he left the house huddled in a coat that had once been stylish. It was his day off. He'd meant to sleep late and give himself a few extra hours under the duvet before the switch from a few days of evening shifts to a week of nights. A coffee in town would settle his stomach, he felt, and he could think while he walked through the crisp frost that he hoped would wake him up properly.

Ægir Lárusson was fuming. There was no mistaking it, and Jóel Ingi could feel his heart pounding at the same time as he told himself not to be frightened of this ugly man with the bad hair and short legs.

"Explain, will you? How the fuck did this happen?"

"Well, it was back in 2009."

"Before my time, you mean?"

"Exactly."

"Before the minister's time?"

"Of course."

"So nobody thought to mention this, considering I've been sitting here for two long and miserable years surrounded by fuck-witted daddy's boys in poncy suits?"

"Er . . ." Jóel Ingi mumbled, remembering Már's adage as Ægir's face went even redder. Don't be scared of Ægir too much as long as he's shouting. It's when he goes quiet you should start to worry.

"You mean to tell me that that inquisitive journalist I just laughed at and told to go and screw himself was right on the money after all?" Ægir roared.

Jóel Ingi was thankful that the door was closed behind him for a change, although he was sure that every word could be heard in the corridor outside.

"Er, there may be some truth in what he said," he mumbled. "But there's nothing he can substantiate, I'm sure."

"Something about a stolen laptop?" Ægir asked in a silky voice. Jóel Ingi's blood ran cold suddenly and his fingers went numb.

"I . . . er, it was misplaced. I have someone working on locating it."

"The police, or someone else?"

"Someone else. It's a private investigation."

"Who?"

"I don't know," Jóel Ingi ventured. "I don't know who he is and he doesn't know me or where I work."

"Ah. That's the first sensible thing I've ever heard you say. Sometimes it's best not to know things. Such as I haven't the faintest idea that you lost a ministry laptop containing sensitive information that would crucify the government if it were to come out."

"It's secure; password protected."

"If it's so secure, how did this kind of crap get out? And when I tell the minister it's only hearsay when I speak to him in half an hour, can I be sure it's only a foul rumour put about by the opposition to discredit the government?"

"Yes, I'm sure it could be that."

"Well, I'm not," Ægir said, his voice dropping so low that Jóel Ingi strained to hear. "To start with, the former minister, your old boss, is a young guy who needs a job and he expects to be in this politics business for a good few years yet. God knows, that brain-dead piece of garbage needs to stay in politics because he sure as hell can't do anything else."

Ægir's face cracked into a smile and Jóel Ingi felt for a second that the man understood his predicament.

"But, that said, he's a cunning bastard who knows better than to shit in his own nest. You get my drift? Look, Jóel Ingi, you're a smart guy. Did well enough at the bank before you were clever enough to get out while the going was good. The government needs young men with good legal minds like yours," Ægir said and Jóel Ingi's brief warm feeling began to evaporate. "You're a civil servant and you people don't understand politics, do you? You just sit tight and wait for a new man in the job, don't you? Because that's the way the game is."

Jóel Ingi cleared his throat awkwardly, desperately wondering where this was leading.

"No, don't answer that, because I know you couldn't," Ægir said without pausing. "But what happens is this. If something goes wrong, what we do is blame someone else. First we blame the previous government, of course, for landing us in this mess. And if that doesn't work, we blame our officials," he said, smiling, and slowly pointed a finger at the centre of Jóel Ingi's fluttering chest.

"You've been to Ikea often enough, haven't you?" he asked, leaving Jóel Ingi mystified.

"Yes, why?"

"You've seen the guy in the paper hat behind the food counter, haven't you?"

"Yes, of course."

Ægir smiled his smooth smile again, transforming his ugly face into a visage of sincerity that any man would trust. "Because if you don't get this fixed quickly and quietly, before I get any more questions from nosy bastard journalists, then that's the only job that you'll be able to apply for once you've been made redundant. If your personal fuck-up brings down the government and the minister, and results in an international outcry, then I'll personally make sure that your future lies nowhere more glamorous than deep-frying fucking Swedish meatballs in the Ikea canteen. Clear?" he snarled, his voice rising once again to a menacing growl. He sat back and Jóel Ingi could see Ægir's thin lips were white, pressed together in fury as a single blow from one clenched fist landed like a hammer on the desk in front of him, sending a picture in an ornate frame flying so that it landed on its back. The pretty, dark-haired woman in the photograph smiled at the ceiling.

"Now get the fuck out, and I don't expect to see your stupid, smug face anywhere near me again until you come and tell me that information is safe."

* * *

Sara's mother sat tight-lipped, perched on a corner of the sofa while her daughter sobbed in an armchair, her face bloated. Her father stood behind her with his arms folded and a dour look on his face, as if he blamed Magnús for being stupid enough to get himself murdered.

"I have to say I didn't think much of the lad," he said, prompting a further outburst of sobbing from his daughter.

"Sara, I really need you to think back and tell me everything you can," Gunna said, certain that there was little the distraught girl would be able to say with her parents in the room.

"Not that I'd have wished anything like this on him," Sara's father continued. "A pleasant enough lad, but no energy, I thought."

"When did you last see Magnús Sigmarsson, Óskar?" Gunna asked. "You clearly didn't have much time for the man, did you? What were your movements the night before last? Were you here?"

"No. I, er . . . I went out for a couple of hours. I had a class," he floundered.

"And someone will confirm that, I hope?"

"Well, of course."

"In that case, I'd appreciate it if you two would leave me and Sara to talk in private."

Sara's mother stood up stiffly to leave the room and her father grudgingly followed. Gunna could hear them go into the kitchen and stood up herself to shut the door firmly behind them. Sara sobbed and immediately collected herself.

"I'm sorry. Really sorry. It's been such a shock," she gulped.

"I get the impression your parents didn't approve of Magnús?"

"They thought he wasn't good enough."

"So what was the state of your relationship?"

Sara dabbed her eyes and Gunna could hear a silence from the next room that told her the girl's parents probably had their ears to the door.

"We had finished," Sara said. "We had a flat in Grafarvogur, but then I lost my job a few months ago and we couldn't really afford it any more."

"So you moved back here? And Magnús?"

"Well. We were going to get a cheaper apartment."

"The place that Magnús was living in, I suppose. Why didn't you move in there with him?"

Sara twisted her fingers and looked down at them. "I was going to," she said in a small voice, "but my parents were really against it, and I didn't have any money, and they talked me into moving back home. So I did."

"So you split up with Magnús and moved in with Mum and Dad? How did Magnús take it? Did you continue a relationship with him, or did you break it off?"

"Well, we stayed together, sort of . . ." Sara said and her words tailed off as she looked at the closed kitchen door. "I'd go and stay with him a couple of nights sometimes, but it's a shitty place in a block full of immigrants, so I didn't really want to go over there too often. People stare at you."

"So Magnús came here?"

"Sometimes. My room's downstairs in the basement and it's self-contained. So sometimes I used to let him in through the back window and he'd stay until the olds had gone to work. But my parents really didn't like him. Dad thought he was an idiot with no future."

Gunna made notes; she was starting to wonder if Magnús Sigmarsson's death could be related to events at his workplace, or if Sara's father could be responsible. It was easy enough to pick up on the man's clearly intense dislike for his daughter's boyfriend, and she wondered if that dislike could have been enough to result in violence. Instinct whispered to her that Óskar was a normal enough citizen, but common sense also told her that there was an aspect of the case that needed to be checked.

"Sara, when was the last time you saw Magnús?"

"A couple of days ago. He came here in the evening while the old folks were out and we were watching TV when they came in. Dad went nuts and was about to throw him out, but Magnús left right away and we talked on the steps outside."

"What did you talk about?"

Sara sniffed and a new set of tears rolled down her plump red cheeks. "He wanted me to move in with him again. Or at least come and stay more often."

"And what was your answer?"

"I told him I'd come and stay if he cleared his flat up and unpacked all the boxes in the hall. He'd been there more than a month and still hadn't got round to unpacking."

"How was he? Was he worried about anything? Nervous?"

Sara shrugged and shook her head. "I don't know. He was upset because I didn't move in with him after we left the old flat."

"But not so angry that he didn't come round and sneak in the window sometimes?"

"Well, yeah."

"He didn't talk to you about his work, did he? Nothing he was concerned about there?"

"No, I don't think so. He was worried about money because he couldn't afford the flat on his own and his friend Kolbeinn was thinking of moving in with him."

"Kolbeinn? Who works at the Gullfoss Hotel?"

"Yeah. That's him."

"They worked together?"

"I guess so. That company moves people around all the time."

"And have you worked there as well?"

Sara nodded, still looking down at her fingers, which were twisted together in her lap. "That's where we met. I was in the kitchen at the Harbourside for a few months right after it opened."

"But you didn't stay long?"

"No, I didn't like it there."

"And are you working now?"

"I'm a rep at AquaIce."

"Which does what?"

"We supply water-cooler refills to offices, mostly. But it's pretty quiet at the moment, so I'm only working four days a week."

Gunna scanned her notes and listened to the silence from the kitchen, wondering if Sara realized that their conversation was probably being listened to.

"The last time you saw Magnús, what happened exactly?"

Sara took a deep breath and Gunna could see her collecting her thoughts. "Well," she began, "he called me and asked if he could come round and I said yes, because Mum and Dad were out. We were in here when they came home and Dad hit the roof, said he didn't want to see Magnús here again, and then Dad went out."

"And how long did Magnús stay?"

"Not long. We talked on the steps outside for a while and I said I'd go and stay with him over the weekend. Then he got in his car and drove away."

"You saw him drive away, did you? Which direction did he go in?"

Sara hesitated. "I don't know. I don't think I saw him get in the car."

"You didn't look out of the window?"

"The last thing I said to him was that he ought to leave before Dad came back," she said, dropping her head and howling.

Eiríkur smoothed out the credit card statement on the counter in the exclusive goldsmith's shop. There were five transactions on Jóhannes Karlsson's credit card, one a cash withdrawal for the maximum amount the ATM would dispense, followed by one at a clothes shop, one at a decidedly upmarket shoe shop and two at jewellery shops.

The elderly woman behind the counter eyed Eiríkur suspiciously and her disapproval could be seen behind a thick mask of makeup. She lifted a pair of glasses that hung on a chain around her neck and held them up in front of her eyes to examine the entry on the credit card statement.

"Well, that's here," she said dubiously. "But I don't see what this has to do with the police."

"We're investigating a stolen credit card, and this may be one of the transactions on that card."

"That's ridiculous," the woman snapped. "We would never serve anyone using a stolen card."

"Even if you didn't know the card had been stolen?" Eiríkur asked gently. "This transaction was only a few days ago. Do you know who served this person?"

"Of course not. This is a busy shop, you know."

Eiríkur looked out of the window past the display of rings and necklaces, the gold gleaming against black velvet, at the practically deserted street outside as a truck with a snow plough on the front went past, scraping a layer off the road and piling it into a neat strip at one side.

"It doesn't seem busy at the moment."

The woman sniffed. "It's early."

"Look, were you serving on that day?" he asked, his patience starting to wear thin. "If not, who was?"

"This kind of thing never happened before these damned credit cards were invented. It was cash or cheque, and we only dealt with respectable people."

"This may be awkward for you, but these things happen. Is there anyone else here? Can I speak to the manager?"

"I am the proprietor," the woman said in a voice as icy as the wind blowing along the street outside.

"In that case, you must have issued a receipt with this transaction, and it seems unlikely that you don't

220

remember it, considering there's no small amount of money involved — several hundred thousand krónur."

The door at the back of the shop creaked open and a younger face peered around the door.

"Is everything all right?"

"Actually, no." Eiríkur said, thankful to see a cheerful face that might be more cooperative, as his patience with the woman behind the counter finally evaporated. The younger face belonged to a middle-aged man in a pullover that looked as if it had been inherited. "This transaction," Eiríkur explained as the man lifted a pair of glasses to his eyes. "Anything you can tell me about it?"

"And you are?"

"He says he's from the police," the elderly woman said in a tone that dripped scorn.

"Eiríkur Thór Jónsson. I'm with the city force," Eiríkur said, placing his identification on the counter next to Jóhannes Karlsson's credit card statement.

"Áki Sandvík," the man in the pullover said, folding his glasses. "Let's go to the back room, shall we? It wouldn't do to have the police here if a customer were to come in, would it, mother?"

Jóel Ingi felt slightly sick, but hoped the nausea would pass as the morning progressed. He'd work through lunch and go home early, maybe. For the first time since before Christmas, he felt calm and more in control, as if a switch had been flipped inside his head. The buzzing in his ears had receded to an almost unnoticeable hum and the stinging pain deep in his belly that he treated with handfuls of painkillers and

221

which tended to sneak up on him unawares had so far failed to make an appearance.

He read through a draft report prepared for the department by an outside consultant, adding his own observations in the generous margins, answered dozens of emails, and felt he had earned his salary by clearing his in tray.

His heart lurched as Már appeared, frowning, in the doorway.

"It's all right, nothing to worry about," Már assured him as Jóel Ingi felt an immediate tell-tale tightening across his belly.

"Is there anything going on?"

"Our boy's in a foul temper. He's chewed out half a dozen people already this morning over that Korean millionaire applying to buy land in the east. He's dead set against it, but it's as clear as day the man has some friends somewhere."

"On a purely legal basis, he's quite right," Jóel Ingi said slowly. "There's no precedent for it and the minister has an obligation to be cautious."

Már winked. "There's cautious and there's deciding who to piss off the most, the voting public or the people who run the show."

"Who knows where he'll go next?" Jóel Ingi said with a thin smile. "Do you understand why politicians do the things they do?"

Már spread his arms in a wordless reply. "And until then, we selfless public servants are doomed to be the messengers who get shot for bringing bad news. Speaking of which, Ægir was talking about you earlier."

"What? Really?"

"Yes. And not in a bad way. So when you get a roasting next time, just batten down the hatches and let it blow over, will you?"

Jóel Ingi sighed. "I'll try. You'll be there tonight, won't you?"

"Tonight?"

"Gallerí 12. Agnes is expecting you."

"How could I forget?" Már slapped his own forehead in slow motion. "Duh. I'll be there."

He went through a batch of receipts held together with a clip that had hung on a peg over the desk.

"Here it is," he said. "This time of year's pretty quiet and there were only a couple of sales that day. An eighteen-carat white gold chain, sixty-five centimetres, three hundred and twenty thousand krónur. A good day for January."

Eiríkur nodded and agreed that the figure tallied with the credit card statement. "Who served this person, do you know?"

Áki gestured at the receipt. "My sister Stella, judging by the handwriting. She runs the shop a couple of mornings a week." He looked up as the door opened. "And right on time," he said.

A younger, better-made-up version of the elderly woman from the shop looked enquiringly down at Eiríkur.

"This gentleman's from the police, Stella," Áki explained. "Wants to know about the white gold necklace you sold the other day."

Stella settled herself on a stool and Eiríkur sensed that she was wondering what to say.

"Do you remember the person who bought it?" Eiríkur prompted, unfolding Jóhannes Karlsson's credit card statement again. "It cost three hundred and twenty thousand, according to this."

"It was a woman, not someone I've seen before. Why? Is there a problem?"

"There should be a problem considering there aren't many women around called Jóhannes Karlsson."

"Oh," Stella said, crestfallen. "I, er, I see. I can't have checked the name. We don't normally look at it."

"Any particular reason?"

"Well. These are exclusive items," she floundered. "You don't expect dishonest people to come in here."

Eiríkur sighed. "All right. Tell me what happened. What time was it? Morning?"

"Around eleven, I think."

Áki hunted through a sheaf of receipts held together by another clip. "Eleven forty-one," he said, holding up a receipt that the credit card had generated.

"That's right," Stella agreed. "She came in, looked for a few minutes and I supposed she must have decided what she wanted before she came in here as she just asked for the chain and bought it. She was only here for a few minutes."

"No small talk? She didn't say anything?"

"She said something about being in a hurry. She had a big bag and had to hunt in it for her purse to find the card, so it didn't occur to me that it wasn't genuine."

"Or that it would be worth looking at the name?" Eiríkur suggested; Stella looked down at the floor in dismay at the reminder. "All right, let's have a description of this person. Age? Height?"

"Mid-thirties, I'd guess. I'm one-seventy, and I think she was quite a bit taller than me, maybe one-eighty or eighty-five?"

"Not wearing heels?"

"I'm not sure, but I don't think so."

"You don't have CCTV in here, do you?"

"It's switched off at the moment," Áki put in, a morose look on his face. "It broke down before Christmas and they still haven't been along to fix it."

"So no pictures. What was she wearing?"

"A black coat. She didn't unbutton it, so I don't know what she was wearing underneath."

"Trousers?"

"I'm not sure, but I don't think so. The shop isn't big and when you stand behind the counter you don't tend to see anything below the waist."

"Hair?"

"Fair, nicely cut."

"Covering the ears? Above them?"

Stella paused. "You could see her ears, because I was admiring the pearl earrings she was wearing."

"Pierced ears, then?"

"Yes. Small earlobes as well, I think. You notice these things when it's your business. Small ears make the earrings look bigger."

Eiríkur scribbled notes as quickly as he could. "And the face? Anything special?"

"No. I don't think so. Just an ordinary face, but with quite a big nose. Well, not big, but not small either, if you get my meaning."

"I think so. Eyes?"

"Er. Green, I think."

"Sure?"

"No, not really."

Eiríkur stowed Jóhannes Karlsson's credit card statement away and took one of the CCTV screenshots of the mystery woman from his folder. "Look familiar?" he asked.

Stella stared at the two pictures.

"That's nothing like her," she declared finally.

"You're certain?" Eiríkur asked and carefully placed a piece of paper over the photograph, showing the woman with black hair, but covering the face from the eyebrows upwards.

"It could be," Stella said grudgingly.

Eiríkur placed a finger over it to mask the hair. "We've established that the hair is fake. And now?"

"Those are the same earrings," Stella said immediately. "No question."

"And the face?"

"Yes, I think so. That beaky nose looks about right."

He put the picture of the blonde in front of her. "And this one?"

"Yes," Stella said. "That's her."

"In that case, that's all I need from you," Eiríkur said, putting the photographs away and standing up. "I'll give you a crime reference number, as this was a stolen card so no doubt the insurance company will want to ask you a few questions as well."

He had to admit to himself that there was something magnetic about the man. Gussi looked through the window of the café and saw the hard-faced man whose real name he still didn't know sitting with a cup and saucer in front of him as he sat back reading the cultural supplement of last weekend's newspaper.

Flustered, Gussi walked around the block, which was quiet at this time, between morning rush hour and the lunch break that saw people reappearing on the streets. He thought about Hekla and how many years it had been since he'd seen her last in person. A good ten, twelve years, he decided, although it could be more and he had seen her several times on television in bit parts and recognized that soft voice more than once in adverts and radio drama. As a senior player at the theatre, he had a room of his own and didn't notice many of the bit-part players, but Hekla had attracted so much attention. It wasn't just her looks, he recalled. She hadn't been beautiful in any classical way, although the young men certainly appreciated those bouncing tits and long legs, judging by their crude jokes, he thought with distaste. There had been a quality to her bearing that simply clicked as she walked into and inhabited a part to become that person. The girl had a real, God-given talent, he admitted to himself, trying not to remind himself that his own skills had been the product of sweat and hard work, not something to be simply switched on and off at a whim.

Walking fast along the half-empty pavements that took him in a circle past the tourist shops and closed nightclubs and bars, Gussi wondered if Hekla had been aware of her own talent. It was a terrible shame that she hadn't been able to find work and had had to search elsewhere after such a promising start. But it's a tough business, he reminded himself bitterly. Upset someone high up in the cultural mafia and you're screwed; second chances are as rare as a blue moon, unless you have a foot in the door via someone with connections or a bit of clout.

He stopped outside the café, having walked a full circle; the fresh air had cleared his mind, or so he hoped. The man who called himself Jón spied him immediately over the top of his newspaper, closing and folding it with precision.

Gussi sat down and immediately felt uncomfortable under the steady gaze that was neither friendly nor hostile, but which made him feel that his innermost thoughts were being scanned.

"What can I get you?" A deferential voice asked and Gussi realized that Jón must have signalled to a waitress without his noticing.

"A coffee."

"Ordinary?"

"Yes," he said and looked at the man waiting for him. "Please. And you?"

"The same as before, Alma, please. Could you bring us a few pastries as well?"

On first name terms with the staff here, Gussi thought. That doesn't happen too often.

"Good morning, er, Jón," he finally greeted Baddó, extending a hand that was crushed for a second until the grip was released.

"So, you have something useful for me?"

"You don't waste time, do you?" Gussi grumbled and got a cruel smile in return.

"No. I assume you do, otherwise you wouldn't be here."

"Well, yes," Gussi allowed. "And no."

He raised an eyebrow and looked across the little table between them; Gussi had the feeling he was being played with.

"I, er . . . I would like to know just who it is you're working for, before I say too much," he said quickly. "I don't suppose you're a police officer, are you?"

The man smiled and his hard face lit up with a flash of humour this time. "No, Gussi," he said. "I'm certainly not a policeman. I like to get things done quickly and discreetly, if you get my drift."

He continued to smile in amusement as the waitress reappeared and loaded the table with crockery, a dish of petite Danish pastries and a coffee pot. Gussi waited with impatience for the girl to finish, noticing Jón, or whatever the hell he called himself, checking out the curves of the girl's legs as they emerged, clad in sheer black, from the short skirt that hugged her behind.

"Enjoy," she said, straightening up.

He's old enough to be her father, Gussi told himself crossly, as the girl simpered in a way that spoke volumes.

"I'm afraid I couldn't tell you who I'm working for."

"You're not allowed?"

"I don't know myself. It's a rather delicate operation and I'm just a small player in a bigger machine here."

"But you work in security?"

"I've been in secure operations for a long time now."

Gussi looked away, needing a pretext to escape the keen eyes across the table, and put too much cream in his coffee.

"Let's just say that something sensitive has gone astray and there are people who want it back," Baddó said smoothly, guessing that this was probably somewhere close to the truth and watching Gussi's broad forehead furrow.

"All right," he said finally after he'd chewed his lip for a long moment. "I can give you some information but there are two things first."

"Fire away."

Baddó lifted his coffee cup and sipped without taking his eyes off Gussi and his flushed cheeks.

"It's not enough money," he said suddenly.

"A quarter of a million for a whisper of information. Sounds reasonable to me."

"You're asking me to give someone away."

Baddó laughed inside at the thought of this pompous fool trying to bargain with him, but merely nodded sagely. "And your conscience is worth more than that?"

Gussi flushed even redder. "It is," he snapped, "if you want to put it like that."

"I find it's normally best to speak as I find instead of dressing things up. How much are you looking for?"

230

"Half a million," Gussi said, surprised when the hard-faced man nodded again.

"And the other thing?"

"An assurance that the person will come to no harm," he said in a shaky voice, unnerved by the indifferent reception his demand had elicited. "No violence."

"I'll pass the message on and see what my clients say."

"About the half million, or the no violence?"

"Both," Baddó said with a return of the cold smile that Gussi found both chilling and exciting.

Something didn't feel right. Hekla cleaned the kitchen more thoroughly than usual, glancing out of the windows at the sporadic snowfall from a grey sky that was filling the footprints at the back of the house, gradually wiping them out as if they'd never existed. The red Toyota outside had grown a white layer a hand's breadth deep as the snow fell evenly in the still, heavy air; it felt like the lull before a storm.

She tried to assuage her own tension by attacking the burned-on stains at the back of the oven with a scouring pad and increased vigour, hoping the activity would push the unease from her mind. An hour later the kitchen was spotless. The muted whine of Pétur's lathe could be heard from the workshop as she decided the bathroom was next. She opened the bathroom window to let in a blast of cold, fresh air and used the opportunity to spy on the outside world, all the while telling herself that there was no need.

By the time she had finished, the newly mopped kitchen floor was dry. She made coffee and stood staring out of the window at the greyness beyond as the horizon merged seamlessly into sky. The thickness of the weather that masked Reykjavík across the bay also muffled any sound from outside, rendering the noise of the traffic on the main road little more than a distant mutter.

She took two mugs of coffee with her to the workshop where Pétur stood half-perched on a stool on his bad side in front of the lathe. Strips of curled wood shavings lay like a deep carpet around his ankles and Hekla breathed in the sharp aroma of newly turned wood.

She put one mug on the bench where Pétur could reach it and cradled the other in her hands. "How's it going?" she asked, nodding at the stack of newly turned bowls on the bench.

"Not bad." He smiled. "A dozen so far and I'll do a few more before I start polishing them up."

Hekla picked up a bowl and admired the pattern of grain that swept across its broad base, lost in the twists and whorls.

"They're lovely, Pétur."

"I like to think so."

"It's just a shame that you can't get more for them."

"I know," he sighed. "But there's only so much people will pay for these things."

"I still reckon that wholesaler's ripping you off."

Pétur shrugged. "Probably. But he has overheads to pay as well."

"Come on. He pays you twelve hundred for each of these bowls or cups and he sells them for at least eight thousand. I've seen his website. We should be selling these ourselves, not giving them to someone else to make all the money on them."

"I know. But what can I do? I can either make these things or I can stand behind a counter and wait for someone to buy them. I can't do both."

"You could get a stall at the flea market."

"We could get a stall there, maybe."

Hekla decided to let it drop. The idea of standing behind a stall at the Kolaport flea market with half of Reykjavík walking past was not an idea that appealed to her, not that any of her former customers would be likely to recognize her without one or other of her wigs. Then the face of the corpulent man from the swimming pool came rushing back to her. He must have recognized her, or else made a mistake and thought she was someone else.

"We could get a stall, I said," Pétur repeated. "You're daydreaming again."

"Sorry. Yeah, I suppose we could try it and see what happens," she said dubiously. "I'll see if I can find out how much it costs."

"Even if we only sell a few ourselves, it would make a difference, I expect. Especially if we can charge gift-shop prices for them."

Hekla scanned the space under the bench on the far side of the workshop and wondered what was missing.

"Where's that laptop bag that was over there?"

"What laptop?"

"The one I picked up cheap before Christmas. I left it under the bench."

"I don't know," Pétur shrugged, his mind already on the lathe again as he clamped a section of wood into it. "You're sure it was there?"

"Gunnhildur," Ívar Laxdal told her, appearing in the doorway. "A word, if you don't mind."

Gunna wanted to laugh at the "if you don't mind" that was an instruction rather than a suggestion. Not sorry to leave the clutter on her desk, she joined him in the corridor, wondering why the man always liked to walk when he was talking.

"It's the ministry again," he said. "It's about this laptop they've managed to lose somewhere."

"They really think we're going to find a laptop that someone left in a taxi?" Gunna asked and was rewarded with a scowl.

"There's more to this than meets the eye, Gunnhildur, and I don't know what they're playing at either."

Gunna wondered if the scowl had been directed at her remark or at the ministry. "What do they expect, then?"

"They expect us to find the damned thing, that's what. I have the serial numbers and a description."

"That's something, I suppose. But who lost this computer, and where?"

Ívar Laxdal grimaced. "That's just what they don't want to tell me."

"This really is a needle in a haystack, in that case?"

234

"Exactly."

"Can I ask how this request came to you?"

"You can ask, but I'm not supposed to tell you. Between ourselves, it comes through a ministry official called Már Einarsson. I've checked him out as far as I can and he has, naturally, a clean record. He deals with foreign relations, apparently. He's listed simply as an adviser, whatever that means."

"And I can speak to him?"

"Hell, I don't know. Leave it with me for the moment and I'll have another word. I'll see if I can get these jokers to agree to a meeting this afternoon. The whole thing sounds fishy to me."

Gussi's head whirled. He was trying to work out how he had managed to end up with the hard-faced man who both frightened and fascinated him sitting in the only chair in his flat looking quizzically at him.

He looked around appreciatively. "Nice place."

"It'll do. It's a bolt-hole really."

"How come?"

Gussi didn't want to be reminded, but he had to come up with an answer. "I had a larger place. I still own it, actually, but I can't afford to live there and it's rented out."

"Came out of the crash badly, did you?"

"I did."

Gussi poured a little brandy into a tumbler and handed it across to his guest, the only guest the little apartment had ever seen.

"Sorry to hear that. I missed out on all that stuff."

"You were abroad?"

He nodded and smiled in a way that set Gussi's stomach doing somersaults. "Back to business. Four hundred thousand is on the table for the information I'm after. Cash, no comebacks, no questions. No reason to see me ever again as long as your information is accurate."

Gussi grimaced and started to shake his head as he sat down on the three-legged stool that belonged in the tiny kitchen.

"It's just a name you're looking for?"

"A name will do fine."

"I don't know," Gussi wavered. "Four hundred thousand doesn't go far these days. Can we stretch to half a million?"

"You drive a hard bargain."

Gussi sighed, reminding himself that he had been determined to ask for double that. "I have plenty of debts," he said finally. "If you could stretch a little further than that . . .?"

There was that enigmatic smile again, and Gussi felt unnerved as it vanished suddenly.

"I don't like to do things the hard way, but sometimes there's no alternative," Baddó said in a soft tone and delved into the inside pocket of his jacket to take out a fat envelope. He placed it on the chair's armrest. "Four hundred thousand. Take it or leave it." He looked at Gussi with an unwavering gaze that made it plain there was no more on offer. "I'd advise you to take it."

"I, er . . . I don't know."

Gussi stretched to pick up the envelope and, as he did so, Baddó shot out a hand that caught Gussi at the wrist in a solid grip that left him leaning forward with the stool about to collapse underneath him.

"The name."

"What the hell . . .?"

"The name. Before you pick up the cash. A name."

"Hekla," Gussi gasped.

"And the rest?"

"Hauksdóttir. Hekla Elín Hauksdóttir."

The grip relaxed. "You know where she lives?"

Gussi shook his head, his breath coming in gasps. The man's hand released his wrist so that the stool sat back on its three legs again with Gussi, red-faced, slumped on it with his back against the wall.

"How come you know this girl?"

"We were in *Othello* at the National Theatre. I played Iago," Gussi said with a pride in his voice that he couldn't conceal. "It was ten years ago, or more. She had a part in it as well. I remembered her, that's all."

"And is she going to remember who you are, Gussi?"

"I don't know. I doubt it." He could feel his chest heaving and took off his glasses to wipe the sweat from his forehead onto the sleeve of his shirt. "It was a long time ago."

"And you've come down in the world, haven't you? So this woman was an actress," Baddó mused. "That's interesting."

Gussi stuffed the envelope full of cash into his trouser pocket. "No harm will come to her, will it? You gave me your word."

237

"How long has she been pulling this stunt with rich old men? It's a smart idea."

"I've really no idea. I haven't been taking notes."

"No, but you've been able to put two and two together, haven't you?"

The gaze remained unflickering, and Gussi felt that the man sitting calmly in the chair was stripping him bare, fully aware of any lie he might try to tell. He shivered in spite of the warmth in the little apartment. "I've seen her once or twice," he admitted.

"And at a few other hotels as well? Word gets around, surely, and you people compare notes."

Gussi nodded glumly. "It happens. But it's not often."

"When did you last see Hekla Elín Hauksdóttir?" he asked, rolling the names slowly across his tongue, as if testing them for flavour.

"Last week."

Baddó thought rapidly without dropping his gaze from Gussi's eyes. Last week meant that the woman was still working, still pulling her stunts. "What day was that?"

"I don't know," Gussi said, flustered and hot, levering himself to his feet. "Four or five days ago."

"The same day that old guy was found dead at the hotel, was it? Anything to do with your friend?"

"I don't know anything about that," Gussi said quickly.

"Ah, but I think you do, my friend, and I think you may have told me more than you were going to," he said, standing up from the chair with a grace that Gussi

238

found beguiling in a man of his bulk. "You said anything to the police?"

"No. Not a word."

"Good. And you're not going to, are you? I assure you, it wouldn't be worth your while," Baddó said with soft menace. "Not if you want to keep your health."

Jóel Ingi threw two pills down his throat and washed them down with a cup of chilled water from the cooler. He rubbed his eyes with the heels of his palms until the lights behind his eyelids flickered red.

"All right, Jóel Ingi?"

He looked up to see the grinning face of Katrín, the plump press officer from the next floor.

"I don't know. Flu coming on, I think."

"Well, I'd prefer it if you don't give it to me. I'm on holiday in a couple of weeks, going to Dublin for a few days rest and a couple of nights on the town. Now that I'm single again, I'm allowed to start enjoying myself," she said. "That's what you need, to let your hair down for a few days."

"I'm OK," he assured her, refilling his plastic cup and draining it. "It's this place, I'm sure of it. Air conditioning all year round isn't healthy. What happened between you and Axel? I thought you were rock solid?"

Katrín lifted her shoulders in an unspoken question, hindered by the files she had hugged to her ample chest. "I don't know," she said with a sigh. "I guess I must have realized that deep down he was never going to grow up mentally to be more than fourteen. That's fine when you're young, but after a certain point enough is enough."

"I'm really sorry to hear it."

"I'm not," Katrín told him with an arch lift of her eyebrows. "I'm working out again as well now, so maybe I'll see you at the gym?" she suggested, looking over her shoulder as she left him at the water cooler in bemusement.

"All right, are you?" Már asked, finding him standing there with a dull look on his face.

Jóel Ingi shook his head. "I don't know. That fat Katrín just came on to me two minutes ago right here."

"In broad daylight?" Már laughed, his smile brought to a sudden death by the morose look on Jóel Ingi's face.

"That's about it."

"I'm shocked. I'll have a word with her line manager and see that she's given a written warning for flirting with the fourth floor," Már said, breaking into a laugh as he saw the serious look on Jóel Ingi's face. "Seriously, though. Be flattered. I mean, I always thought you were queer."

"Get away, you bastard," Jóel Ingi retorted, a smile finally appearing on his face.

"Listen, though. A quiet word."

Mar's suddenly serious tone switched off the laughter.

"What's the matter?"

"It's that laptop you had stolen before Christmas. Ægir's as nervous as hell. A human rights group in Holland has figured out that those four Arabs left

Germany and travelled to Amsterdam. That's where they lose track of them. They got hold of the same information as we did about those four being found shot in the back of the head in Tripoli, plus I don't know what else . . ."

"They were tortured?"

"I don't know. But they weren't being sent to a summer camp with four meals a day and team-building exercises. I'd be amazed if they hadn't been."

Jóel Ingi's pale face went a shade paler. He poured cold water from the cooler and drank it down fast, wiping away the sweat that had suddenly appeared on his forehead. "Good God, what have we done?"

"It doesn't matter. It's done. There's nothing we can do about it, except keep quiet. Listen, the do-gooders lose track of them in Amsterdam. They may know they came through Keflavík, but they don't have anything to prove it. Let's keep it that way, shall we?"

"Ægir knows all this?"

"Hell no. Not all of it. But he's a shrewd bastard and he can read you like a book. That's enough to tell him that something's up. He's been on to the police about it."

"I'm looking after it, all right? Isn't that good enough?"

"Hey, calm down, man. I know Ægir's an arsehole, but he has every right to be worried."

"It's in hand, I keep telling you."

"You're sure, Jóel Ingi? With one of your brother's mates looking after this?"

Jóel Ingi looked about quickly. "What the fuck else can I do?" he hissed furiously. "Tell Ægir that some bitch stole my laptop?"

"Bitch? You said it was a couple of lads."

"Ach, to hell with it. Forget it. Forget I said anything. I'll get it fixed and that'll be all."

"If you say so," Már said with doubt in his voice. "When? How long's this going to take?"

"Soon."

"Yeah, but how soon? I'm fending Ægir off here, but I can't do it for much longer. He wants you spilling your guts to some flat-footed detective who has no idea what's on your hard drive."

"A couple of days."

"Make it soon. Otherwise there are going to be some cops here asking you awkward questions."

It hadn't taken long to find the address. Ten minutes with the national registry confirmed for Baddó that Hekla Elín Hauksdóttir existed, gave him her national registration number and date of birth, as well as her address, not to mention the interesting information that Pétur Steinar Albertsson lived at the same address, along with Sif Pétursdóttir, Albert Haukur Pétursson and Alda Björk Pétursdóttir.

Baddó calculated and worked out that Albert and Alda must be Pétur and Hekla's children, but Sif was possibly too old at seventeen. Two small children with the same date of birth and a teenager? A stepdaughter, maybe, from Pétur's previous relationship. He smiled in satisfaction at how easy it was to find someone in Iceland once you had the name as a starting point, and how straightforward it could be to work out who is who.

242

Cross-referencing Pétur Steinar Albertsson's name with the online phone book even gave Baddó the home phone number and a mobile number; he wondered whether a phone call posing as a salesman of some kind would be a good way of spying out the land.

He switched on his mobile, called the landline number and let it ring a couple of times before he gave up and keyed in the mobile number instead.

"Hi. This is Hekla. I can't take your call right now. Leave a message and I'll get back to you," the voicemail intoned and he ended the call without saying anything. The voice was warm and soft, and listening to it almost put him at ease. In fact it was even vaguely familiar and he wondered where he might have heard it before. For a moment he toyed with the idea of calling again, just to hear the voice, but decided against it, telling himself not to be so soft.

Disappointingly, he had to drive all the way out to Kjalarnes, a little suburb beyond the fringes of the city that he'd forgotten even existed. That required wheels, which would mean either finding some or else borrowing María's car, but that would have to wait until the morning, he decided. He'd already worked hard enough today for Hinrik the Herb's money. He felt like an afternoon off and wondered if Ebba could be persuaded to take a few hours off as well.

"And what do we have, dear boy?" Gunna asked, seeing Eiríkur grinning, while Helgi looked morose and deep in his own thoughts.

"Three jewellers, three positives. Our mystery lady spent something like a million krónur on other people's credit cards in one morning, buying gold and silver necklaces, a few bangles, that sort of thing."

"Stuff that doesn't lose value," Gunna said. "Unlike cash."

"Someone's putting something aside for a rainy day, aren't they?" Helgi observed, shaking his head as if shaking off his private thoughts.

"You think so?"

"I do. This is stuff that can be sold, but not right away. It's all identifiable and can be traced, but the longer it stays in a biscuit tin under her bed, the less likely it is to be noticed."

"Or a safe deposit box," Gunna mused. "Someone with a long-term plan, you reckon?"

"But that's not all," Eiríkur broke in, unable to curb his excitement. "I went to half a dozen other jewellers around the city and several of them recognized her, said that she'd been in before. One chap said he'd sold her some jewellery about a year ago and thought he'd recognized the face then, but wasn't certain. That's why the picture rang a bell after such a long time."

"Really? In that case you'd best go back there and see if you can jog his memory."

"Now?"

"Absolutely. Right now."

"What about . . .?"

"No, if this jeweller can come up with a name or whatever, then go and browbeat him until he remembers."

244

Eiríkur shrugged his jacket back on and left, shaking his head at Gunna's obstinacy, while she turned to Helgi and sat down.

"What's the matter?" she asked as Eiríkur closed the door behind him.

"Ach, nothing important. Nothing to do with work."

"Helgi Svavarsson, it may be nothing to do with your work, but it's affecting your work. What's bugging you?"

Helgi sighed deeply. "It's Halla," he said finally. "Problems at home."

"The kids are all right, aren't they?"

"Yeah, the kids are fine. It's the P word. Again. You've a problem of your own in that department, don't you?"

"Hell, don't remind me," Gunna said grimly. "That boy of mine has really given himself a cross to bear for the rest of his life. And mine, I expect," she added.

"What's he going to do about it? Has he actually talked to you, other than just to admit his misdeeds?"

"I don't know what the hell he's thinking, and I don't suppose he knows either. Anyway, what P word were you thinking of? The same one as me?"

"P for pregnant," Helgi said grimly.

"Congratulations."

"It's not that simple, and Halla's not pregnant. Quite the opposite."

"So what's the problem?"

"Halla's sister had a baby about three months ago and Halla's going wild, wants another one. It's driving me nuts."

Startled, Gunna stifled a laugh. "And that's a problem?"

"We live in a four-room apartment. Halla has a child, I have two who'll be in their twenties soon, and we have two together. Wouldn't you say that's enough? I reckon it is. But she wants one more, like completing the set or something. I'm forty-two, Gunna. I've had my share of nappies and teething. It's the second time around for me, don't forget."

"I'd have thought so," Gunna agreed. "Twice was quite enough for me."

"Fair enough, but what would you do if Steini suddenly decided he needed an heir?"

"Steini already has children and grandchildren, so there's no chance of that."

Helgi ran a hand over his forehead. "Yeah. But *if*, Gunna?"

"I guess a year or two ago I'd have thought about it for five minutes and then said no. Twice is enough and another one's not on the agenda."

"Yeah, but Halla's not like you. She loves all that stuff, small babies, maternity things, playschool and all that. I just want to get past it all so I can play football with them."

"But does Halla understand how you feel? Really? Have you made it absolutely plain?"

"I've tried . . . but the flesh is weak, isn't it?" he said with a small smile. "You know, I've never used a condom in my life, but I swear I'm buying a pack on the way home tonight."

"And if Halla finds them before you whip them out at the crucial moment, she'll assume you've been playing away from home."

"You think so?" Helgi asked with panic in his voice.

"I do. Now. Work. Anything on that burned-out car? Was it Magnús Sigmarsson's?"

"We still don't know. We're trying to get the number off the chassis, but it wasn't the car it was supposed to be."

"How so?"

"We managed to get the rear number plate and the registration belongs to a van that's been outside a workshop in Kópavogur for weeks. It failed its inspection two months ago and the owner hadn't got round to fixing it so just parked it outside. When he showed it to me, he was more surprised than I was that the plates had been unscrewed."

"Someone wanted to disguise it."

"And there was a lot of petrol," Helgi added. "The firemen say there must have been petrol all over the seats and the whole interior for it to go up like a firework like that. Someone wanted it disposed of, and wanted to do a decent job of it."

Gunna rattled her fingernails on the desk. "The last sighting we have of Magnús is when he left his girlfriend's house. Nothing at all after that. So where did he go and why? And as he'd hardly drive out to the quarter-mile track and break his own neck, who was with him?"

"That's what we'd all like to know, isn't it? But he's nowhere on CCTV, and if he went direct from her place to the quarter-mile track, it isn't more than a twenty-minute drive."

"But if we have anything to tell us who that might be, it'll be in that car. So you'd best get down to forensics and pester them to go over it with a magnifying glass until they find something. If it's any consolation, as far as your problems with Halla are concerned, by the time you finish tonight, you'll be far too tired for anything in that department."

Helgi smiled weakly and Gunna sensed the return of the usual good-humoured Helgi she knew and preferred.

"And then it's Óskar Hjálmarsson for you."

"Who?"

"The father of Magnús Sigmarsson's girlfriend. I want him grilled properly about his movements on the night Magnús disappeared."

"You reckon it could have been him?"

Gunna scowled and rubbed her chin. "No," she said slowly. "My guts say it wasn't him. But the man has a motive and if it wasn't him, then we need to have him properly eliminated. So take your time and make sure. He's not a pleasant character so you can make him sweat if you like."

The round face of the blonde girl behind the desk at the Harbourside Hotel fell as Gunna walked in and smiled.

"Símon's not here at the moment. The MD's back and there's a management meeting over at the Gullfoss this afternoon."

"That's good," Gunna told her, "because this time it's you I want a quiet word with."

The girl's bottom lip protruded in a pout. "But I don't know anything."

"You don't know anything about what?" Gunna asked, her curiosity aroused by the instant denial.

"Anything," the girl replied after a few moments' thought.

"Are you on your own here, or is there a supervisor about?"

"I'm the reception supervisor."

"Is that since Magnús is no longer here? In that case, who are you supervising?"

She jerked her head towards a door behind the reception desk. "I've got a trainee with me."

Gunna looked past the girl and into the office where a young man with a fringe over his eyes was sitting at a computer screen.

"Hey, you."

The young man looked up cautiously and pointed a finger at his own chest. Gunna nodded back and beckoned. He stood up, clearly awkward in the smart hotel-issue trousers that he still managed to wear as low on the hips as decency would allow.

"What's your name, young man?"

"Eggert Thór."

"Listen, Eggert Thór. I need a quiet word with your colleague, so while she and I go over there and have a quiet talk . . ." Gunna said, jerking a thumb towards a set of armchairs in the hotel's echoing lobby. "You're a smart lad and you can manage to run things by yourself for ten minutes, can't you?"

"Er . . . yeah," he replied, with an uncertain look on his face.

"All you have to do is stand there and look like you know what you're doing. Any problems and we're right over there. All right?"

"Yeah!" the lad said, a happy smile stealing across his face as Gunna marched the girl to the set of armchairs and sat opposite her. "Magnús was murdered," she said bluntly and watched the shock register in her eyes.

"Why? Do you know who did it?"

"That's what I'm trying to pin down," Gunna said, catching sight of the girl's name badge. "Look, Eva. Something shady has been going on here and Símon hasn't exactly been helpful, any more than your colleagues at the Gullfoss have."

"I think Símon's really worried about something. Normally he's quite cheerful, but these last few days he's been mega-grumpy."

"There's a scam been going on here and at a few other hotels across Reykjavík. You have an idea of this, right?"

"A what?" Eva asked and Gunna inwardly cursed the girl's slow-wittedness.

"People being tied up in rooms. That's happened a few times, hasn't it?"

Eva chewed her lip and looked nervously over towards Eggert, standing like a sentry behind the reception desk. "We're not supposed to say anything."

"Says who?"

"Símon. And Magnús. They said that if anything about this got out and it affected business, we could find ourselves out of work, and it's not easy to find work at the moment."

"When did they tell you this? Recently?"

"It was before my birthday. I remember because it was the day before my party."

"And when was that?"

"August the ninth's my birthday."

Gunna was surprised that Sonja's scam went back so far; Eva twisted her fingers nervously.

"Am I going to get the sack if they find out I told you this?" she asked abruptly.

"I've no idea. I wouldn't think so. But if you don't tell them, I won't. This was Símon, right? And Magnús told you the same thing?"

"They told all of us. But not all together. Just in ones and twos."

"How did Magnús seem to you? Was he nervous or upset in any way?"

"Not that I noticed. His girlfriend threw him over because her parents didn't like him, or so he said. He tried to make out he didn't really care, but he was well pissed off," Eva said. "I mean, it's not as if Magnús was the kind of dreamboat who was going to find another girlfriend just like that."

The hostility in the air was unmistakable. Jóel Ingi Bragason and Már Einarsson sat on one side of the polished table, practically identical young men in suits that Gunna felt made them look like youngsters ready

251

for confirmation, while Ívar Laxdal sat at one end of the table and glowered.

"So this is a MacBook that has been mislaid and you want it back, or so Ívar tells me," Gunna opened.

"Who are you?" the slimmer and younger-looking of the pair demanded with outright distrust in his tone.

Gunna sighed and put her identification on the table for them both to see.

"As I'm sure smart gentlemen like you are already aware, I'm Gunnhildur Gísladóttir and I'm a sergeant with the serious crimes unit. I don't doubt that my colleague" — she nodded towards Ívar Laxdal — "has already told you exactly who I am, so let's stop wasting everyone's time, shall we?"

The younger man with the narrow face and the darting eyes — Jóel Ingi, according to the hurried briefing Ívar Laxdal had given her — sat back and pouted sulkily while his colleague Már smiled winningly and clasped his hands together in front of him.

"Jóel Ingi, would you like to explain exactly what happened?" Mar invited.

"Yes, well . . ." he floundered for a moment before regaining his footing. "It was a few days before Christmas, I think."

"You think? You don't know for certain?"

"Of course I do. I'll just have to check my diary," Jóel Ingi snapped back. "I was walking home and had my laptop in a bag on my shoulder, as usual. There were two boys in the street, and one of them had a bicycle. They were having an argument," he recited.

"So what happened?" Gunna prompted.

"One of them pushed the other quite hard in the chest, and he fell backwards against me. I stumbled and fell. The boy who had pushed the other grabbed my laptop case and made off on his bicycle."

"And the other boy?"

"I . . . er, I don't know. I ran after the one on the bicycle, but couldn't catch him. When I looked round, the other boy had gone as well."

"And where did all this happen?"

"Skipholt," Jóel Ingi replied. "The corner of Skipholt and Bolholt."

"Which way did the lad on the bike go?"

"Back along Skipholt."

"What time of day was this?"

"Around five, five-thirty."

"So it was dark. What was the weather like?"

Jóel Ingi stared back. "What?"

"Weather? Cold? Wet? Raining?"

"I don't remember."

Jóel Ingi's eyes widened in suspicion as Gunna glanced at Ívar Laxdal.

"I'll need descriptions of the two lads, anything that might distinguish them. What ages?"

"Around sixteen, I'd say."

"Tall? What sort of height? Fair hair, dark hair? Long? Short?"

"They were both wearing hooded sweaters and I didn't see their faces properly. It all happened so fast."

Gunna sat back and looked disapproving.

"Officer, do you expect that these two boys can be found?" Már Einarsson asked in a tone that was an attempt to defuse the tension.

"I'm sure they can, if we had the time and manpower to do it. But you're not giving me a great deal to work on."

"Jóel Ingi, is there anything more you can recall?" Már asked.

"No. It was dark. It was all over in a few seconds."

Gunna sat back and cracked her knuckles. "I can't help feeling that we're wasting our time here."

"You think so?" Már asked, a worried expression on his pleasant face.

"Two boys steal a laptop and run off. You've given me practically nothing to work on other than the serial numbers of the laptop. We have to look for two lads who may or may not be around sixteen, without knowing what they look like except that they wear hoodies, like every other teenager, and one of them rides a bike."

"I see what you mean," Már agreed.

"I'd say your best option would be to go through the small ads in the papers. If this laptop is going to surface, that's where it's most likely to turn up. On the other hand, it may well be under some teenager's bed by now, or it may have been reformatted, so anything on it will have been erased."

"That's what we need to know," Jóel Ingi broke in.

"So just what is it that's so sensitive? It would certainly give me something to work on if I had an idea of just why this four-year-old laptop is so important,"

Gunna said, and the two young men looked at her in silence.

Ívar Laxdal sighed audibly. "Let's not even go there, Gunnhildur," he rumbled, the irritation plain in his voice. "They won't tell me, let alone you."

The two police officers left the building together and Jóel Ingi breathed a sigh of relief, winding his scarf around his neck.

"Why didn't you tell me they were going to be here today?" he asked as Már waited for him.

"I didn't know. That ugly bastard, Ívar, called me about four minutes before they came through the door. I didn't have a chance to put him off."

"And who was that terrible woman who asked all those stupid questions?"

"It seems she's a detective, and a very good one, or so Ívar said. He reckons that if anyone's going to find your laptop, then she's the most likely candidate."

They stood in silence in the lift as it descended, checked out at the security gate and emerged into the street.

"Your friend," Már said, "the one you said your brother had lined up. Any progress?"

"I'm going to see him right now."

Már nodded as they set off along the street towards the corner where their paths would diverge.

"You know . . ." Már began, hesitating, "what you told the police about those two boys?"

"What about it?"

"Was that the truth? Was that what really happened?"

Jóel Ingi stopped at the corner and squared up to face Már, his face flushed in anger and frustration. "Are you saying you don't believe me?"

"It's not that," Már mumbled, stepping back to allow a young woman with a pushchair to pass between them. The blonde girl stood on the corner, waiting for the lights to change, but still looking to her left for a break in the traffic that would let her hurry across before they did so.

Már spoke as quietly as he could. "You just weren't convincing. I'm not saying I disbelieve you. But I don't suppose that fat policewoman believed you."

The lights bleeped and the young woman strode over the crossing, the pushchair swishing through the puddles that had collected in the melting snow.

"I don't care what the fuck they believe," Jóel Ingi said furiously.

Már watched as the young woman with the pushchair disappeared into a shop on the other side of the road and was shocked when he looked back at Jóel Ingi and saw a twitch under his left eye.

"Listen. Calm down, will you? If that laptop was stolen by some kids, as you say, it's probably been wiped and used as a games machine by now. Don't worry so much," he said.

"It's dynamite," Jóel Ingi retorted. "It doesn't matter if it turns up next week or in ten years. What's on there is going to destroy my career, and it's going to screw the minister. In fact, it's going to screw both of them."

"Both of them? What do you mean?"

"Shit, where have you been? You know what was in that information that came from the Brits. Those guys arrived here right after the election, or don't you remember? One minister in and one out, both of them were in the hot seat."

"But neither of them had anything to do with this, did they?"

"Of course not. But the buck stops somewhere. If this comes out and they try and blame me, then I'll blow the whistle on both of them."

Már looked shocked. "The minister wouldn't try to make you a scapegoat, surely?"

"Maybe not. But Ægir would, and he'd do it in a heartbeat." Jóel Ingi said, turning to walk uphill. Már frowned to himself and opened his mouth to call after him, but thought better of it and remained silent, watching Jóel Ingi trudge up the slope with his shoulders hunched against the cold wind as if the weight of the world were on them, while the young woman emerged from the shop opposite with a carrier bag slung over one of the handles of the pushchair in front of her.

Ívar Laxdal drove back to the station at Hverfisgata and Gunna let herself sit back and be enveloped in the softness of the leather seats of his car, which purred effortlessly between sets of traffic lights.

"So what did you make of that?"

"Jóel Ingi Bragason? Bullshit from start to finish."

"You think so?"

Gunna looked over at Ívar Laxdal in surprise. "Didn't you? You could see it in his eyes and hear it in his voice. That stuff about the two kids was something he made up beforehand and just spieled off. The rest of it was made up on the fly."

Ívar Laxdal nodded. "I'm glad you thought so as well," he confirmed.

"It was like watching a schoolboy caught with a bag of goodies. I'm really wondering what this lad's done wrong."

At the next corner, Jóel Ingi took an unexpected turn, went through an alley between two old houses and made his way almost back the way he had come, this time heading downhill, walking fast towards the centre of town.

The woman with the pram stopped, thought quickly, folded the pushchair into a compact flat arrangement and placed it behind some dustbins at the side of a shop. She quickly unrolled a thick quilted anorak from where the pushchair would normally have accommodated a child, shrugged it on and set off behind Jóel Ingi. She pulled a ski hat low over her eyes, keeping him in sight, but only just. She allowed him to go out of view as he rounded a street corner before increasing her speed to catch up and keep him in sight.

She was lucky to see him vanish, with a quick look over his shoulder and a smart sidestep, into a bar in a side street off Laugarvegur, a dark place that looked quiet on a weekday afternoon as people were making their way home from work. The Emperor was a bar she knew by reputation but had never been inside; she wondered if she should risk going in alone, and eventually decided to wait for Jóel Ingi to emerge.

In a music shop directly opposite, she flipped listlessly through the racks of CDs, wincing at the price of some of them, but always keeping an eye open through the floor-to-ceiling window for Jóel Ingi to leave the Emperor and hurry back along Laugarvegur towards home.

She had looked slowly through every rack of CDs, declined an offer of assistance from a startlingly pink-haired woman who proceeded to stare into space from behind the counter of the otherwise deserted shop, and finally gave up waiting.

The Emperor was gloomy inside and some muted heavy metal grumbled in the background. The dim walls and the dark brown wood of the tables conspired to make the place look stuffier and smaller than it really was. A few of the customers glanced up as she walked in, and she went straight to the bar instead of looking around for Jóel Ingi. The shaven-headed barman looked at her enquiringly.

"A beer."

"Small? Large?"

"A small one."

She looked around her as the barman poured and then sipped her beer appreciatively. It wasn't often that a drink on the job was acceptable, and she enjoyed the feeling, unzipping her quilted coat.

"Haven't seen you in here before, have I?" the barman asked, the light above the beer pump shining on the angled facets of his bristled head, giving him a sinister look.

"Don't expect so. I'm from out of town."

"Where from? I'm a country boy myself."

"Bíldudalur," she said, praying that the man was from some other part of the country and wouldn't want to embark on a conversation about small-town affairs that would immediately catch her out.

He shook his head. "I'm from Thórshöfn, me. Mind you, it's a dump and it's twenty years since I went there last. So what brings you to the bright lights?" he asked, a glint in his eye as he deliberately ignored a young man standing at the other end of the bar waiting to be served.

"Looking for a friend. Jóel Ingi," she said, deciding on the spur of the moment to take a wild chance. "Actually he's a cousin and I'm told he drinks in here sometimes."

The friendly smile vanished from the barman's face and he muttered something she didn't catch as he moved off to serve the man at the other end of the bar. She sipped her beer and wondered if mentioning Jóel Ingi had been a mistake. She waited for the barman to return and toyed with the thought of another beer before deciding against it.

The barman returned and nodded at her glass. "Another?"

"Not this time," she said, pretending to think about it for a moment. "Where are the toilets?"

The barman took the glass and jerked his head towards the bar's dark interior without a word.

She zipped her jeans and pulled on the anorak again before opening the cubicle door, then immediately froze.

"Curious about something, are we?"

One light was flickering as its fluorescent tube died a slow death and the intermittent glow flashed on the single metal tooth that showed as the thin man smiled.

She pushed the cubicle door back, knowing that it was a hopeless thing to do as the man put his shoulder to it and forced it inwards.

Helgi was back at his desk at Hverfisgata as Gunna arrived, the phone to his ear and a bemused frown on his face as he shook his head at her.

"No, that's fine. Not a problem. I'll drop by in the next few days and take a statement. Thanks," he said and left the phone propped under his chin as he used the butt end of a pencil to press the button on his desk phone to end the call.

"And?"

"He's not a happy man, Óskar Hjálmarsson."

"How come? Locked him up, did you?"

"He's in an interview room, and man has he been sweating. But he checks out. He had nothing to do with Magnús Sigmarsson's death, as far as I can see."

"Good. Then we can rule him out, can we?"

"Yup. He left the house at seven-thirty and was at his karate class until after ten. Half a dozen people have confirmed he was there, including Steingrímur from the special unit."

"And after ten?"

"He bought a takeaway at Ning's and the lad who was serving remembers him buying chop suey sometime after ten."

"Fair enough," Gunna decided. "Let the man go, but give him a stern warning, will you? He's not completely in the clear until we've a confirmed time of death for Magnús. All right?"

Helgi pushed his chair back and stood up, dropping the phone back into its cradle. "Suits me. He's not someone you'd want to spend a week in Spain with, but I'm pretty sure he didn't break Magnús's neck." He yawned and stretched. "Oh, and there was some guy who tried to call you a couple of times. Your mobile's switched on, isn't it?"

Gunna cursed and remembered that her mobile had been set to silent for the meeting at the ministry and she had forgotten to reset it. She hastily looked at the screen and saw three missed calls, all from withheld numbers.

"Well, if it's important, they'll call back, I suppose," she grumbled to herself as Helgi left the room to set an angry Óskar Hjálmarsson free, before calling him back. "Helgi! That car? Anything new?"

"Not from forensics. Eiríkur's down at Grandi now asking questions," Helgi replied, his head around the door. "It's cold out, so he'll be back soon, I expect."

In his haste, Jóel Ingi almost missed his footing on the stairs. At the top he paused outside his front door and took a couple of deep breaths before opening it and giving the door a kick for good measure.

"Agnes!"

There was no need to shout. The air was thick with the overpowering smell of grass, which told him she was home.

"*Hæ*," she said absently without looking round from the easel in front of her and the blocks of colour she was applying to the canvas with a flat brush. Jóel Ingi could see the joint smouldering in the ashtray and there was a faint tremor at the back of her alabaster neck below the wisps of fine hair as golden as summer straw that escaped a bun coming adrift at the back of her head.

He stood and fumed, waiting for her to turn round, still captivated by the porcelain beauty of one shoulder half exposed from her loose T-shirt. He took a deep breath and lunged closer.

"What the fuck have you been playing at?" he hissed into her ear, stepping forward, digging his fingers deep into the bun of cream hair and hauling Agnes's head sharply back so that her blue eyes stared into his.

"Let go of me," she ordered in a steady voice.

"No. You tell me what the fucking game is. Why have you been having me followed? What the hell's going on?"

"Get your fucking hands off me or you'll regret it, you animal," Agnes spat and tried to twist out of his grip.

Jóel Ingi's fury boiled over. The slap echoed against the bare walls. Agnes's eyes widened and she glared as Jóel Ingi released her hair and stepped back. He watched as she sat up, a red patch widening across one cheek.

"You bastard," she said, her tone matter-of-fact. "You'll pay for that."

"You tell me what the fuck's been going on. Why am I being tailed day and night?"

"You're insane. I don't know what you're talking about."

"Yeah. That's not what your detective said."

Agnes picked up the joint and relit it from a candle without taking her eyes off him. She took a long pull at it and moved across the room, keeping the white sofa between them.

"What detective? Jóel Ingi, I really don't know what the hell's got into you," she said in an ice-cold tone. "But I think I'm the one who's owed an explanation."

She lifted a hand to her red cheek. Jóel Ingi's stomach lurched and he felt sick seeing the outline of his hand etched in red on her cheek.

She still had her phone. They hadn't taken anything off her, not that there was a great deal to take as she'd been careful to leave anything important in the car. She adjusted the mirror and looked at the damage to her face. She would have a black eye in the morning, she thought, though she was more worried about the tooth that she sucked at and rolled her tongue around, wondering if it was likely to come out.

The nondescript Renault that had once been dark blue rolled out into the road. It was time to go home. Checking the mirrors carefully for anyone who might

264

be following her, and taking a couple of false turns that would take even a vigilant pursuer by surprise, she drove through the city, wondering if she really ought to tell Jóel Ingi's wife where he had been, and consoling herself with the thought of the domestic strife she had probably caused.

The weeks of tailing Jóel Ingi Bragason had finally been worth it. The confirmation of seeing him white with anger in the background while that oaf Hinrik and the bald barman went through their tough guy act with a woman who didn't even come up to their shoulders was something that would be worth passing on.

Gunna's phone buzzed; it was back to the usual ringtone after she had managed to persuade Laufey to remove the sound of bubbling water.

"Gunnhildur."

"*Hæ*. Siggi. Busy?"

Gunna laughed. "Next question, please."

"That phone you wanted tracked, with the number ending 017. You remember?"

"Yes. The unregistered number. Any sign of it?"

"Half an hour ago it was switched on for a couple of minutes and there was a ninety-second phone call. Then it was switched off again."

"Right. Where? And do you have the number called?"

She could hear the clicking of a keyboard on the other end of the phone as Siggi in the communications division went through his records.

"Sure it's him?"

"Yup. No doubt about it."

"OK, and the number called? Another unregistered mobile, I expect?"

Siggi laughed. "Just to make your day, it's a landline and it's in the phone book, and there's a mobile number registered to the same user. Ready with a pencil are you?"

Gunna wrote down the number quickly. "Thanks, Siggi. Can you keep an eye on this one for me? Call my mobile as soon as you have anything."

"Yep. Will do," Siggi agreed and rang off.

Eiríkur found her a few minutes later with a pencil between her lips and a frown on her face as she hunched over her computer.

"Chief?"

"Yeah?"

Eiríkur said nothing, knowing that the expression on Gunna's face meant she wasn't listening; he waited patiently.

"Where's Helgi?" she asked after a few minutes. "Been sitting there long, have you?"

"An old pisshead called Egill Skafta down at Grandi, lives in the hostel there and is supposed to be drying out, reckons he saw a man walking quickly just after that car burst into flames."

"OK, any more details?"

"I asked him if he was sure it wasn't just kids larking about, and he looked at me like I had two heads, told me that kids these days stay indoors and shoot each other on computer games but don't get up to stunts like that any more. He's something of a character and he's no fool — when he's sober, anyway. He reckons that car went up like a Roman candle, so it was more than just someone setting light to a bundle of rags."

Gunna nodded. "Promising. Go on."

"I bought him a coffee and a sandwich, and he opened up a bit more. Valdi reckons he saw a thickset man with a beard walking away quickly. He couldn't swear this guy had anything to do with the car, but it's a coincidence."

"Good. Excellent. I have a candidate in mind."

"You do?" Eiríkur asked, startled.

"I do. I have a few things to do for ten minutes, so I'd like you to check with forensics and see if there's anything on that car. If it's Magnús Sigmarsson's car, I want to know, and preferably yesterday. Think you can manage that?"

"Yeah, of course."

Gunna rummaged through a tray of papers on her desk and handed Eiríkur a file.

"Once you've done that, get yourself back down to Grandi, find Egill Skafta, and show him that picture."

Eiríkur looked at the photo of Hróbjartur Bjarnthórsson, looking into the lens as if the man behind the camera were beneath contempt. "You reckon this is him?"

"As usual, Eiríkur, I have no idea. But if it's not him, then we need to start looking for someone else."

"An old friend of the police?"

"You can read it later. But he's more than an old friend of ours. He's one of us, sort of."

"How come?" Eiríkur asked, perplexed.

"He was almost a police officer once, back in the nineties. What went wrong, I don't know, but he completed police college and then decided he didn't want to join the force after all."

"The phone's registered to Pétur Steinar Albertsson," Gunna told Ívar Laxdal without any explanation.

"Something to do with Magnús Sigmarsson, is it?" he asked in a grumpier tone than usual. "I have a press conference in half an hour and by rights you should be there as well, Gunnhildur. I've already had calls from two newspapers and TV today asking if there's any progress, and I'm going to have to give them something."

"I'm concerned about this character who's been shadowing everything we do."

"You have a stalker?"

"Someone who has an interest in Jóhannes Karlsson's death pumped some of the Gullfoss Hotel staff for information."

Ívar Laxdal's single thick eyebrow that stretched across his face thickened as he frowned. "Why didn't you tell me this before?"

"I wasn't sure. I'm still not sure, but it's becoming clearer."

"Jóhannes Karlsson and Magnús Sigmarsson's deaths are linked, you reckon?"

"There are too many links for comfort," Gunna said thoughtfully. "I didn't think so at first, and I was sure that his girlfriend's father had a hand in it. But now I'm

268

confident we can rule him out. He didn't like the lad, but not enough to want to kill him."

"So what the hell's going on?"

"My guess is that someone else has an interest in Jóhannes Karlsson's death, and in finding the woman who was with him, which is exactly what we've been trying to do. I have a suspicion who this person might be, and it's the first link to someone else who might be involved."

"What do you want to do?" Ívar Laxdal asked, looking at his watch.

"Ten minutes ago I was tempted to go charging in and haul this Pétur Steinar Albertsson into the station. But now I'm more inclined to sit back and watch."

Ívar Laxdal nodded. "Do that. Find out every last bit of information you can about the man first. But don't hang around. There's pressure from all sides to get this wrapped up."

"Where from, exactly?"

"The ministry; the commissioner; the press; Jóhannes Karlsson's family, who are discreetly pressuring the minister through their MP. You name it," he grumbled. "I'll see you in the morning, but you can see me on TV this evening. It'll probably be the fourth or fifth item, right after the city not being able to afford any more snow clearance until the year after next."

There was a spring in Baddó's step. He parked María's car carefully, as it would never do to have to admit that he'd scratched his sister's Ford's paintwork, even if it was an old wreck. He had celebrated his conversation with Hekla, or Sonja as he still thought of her, even though she was now a flesh-and-blood person, with a visit to Krónan on the way back to town, where he'd bought some pork that he was already looking forward to hearing sizzle under the grill. A bottle of wine would complete the evening, but he'd keep that for Ebba later.

He toyed with the idea of having a word with Hinrik to try and find out a little more about why someone found Sonja so interesting, and what it was that was so valuable, but he decided that a night owl like Hinrik needed to be approached first thing in the morning when his senses were dulled with vodka and homegrown grass, not with evening drawing on and his mind still relatively fresh.

Baddó locked the car, put the key in his pocket, zipped it up and hefted a carrier bag in each hand as he pushed open the door of the apartment block. Once he'd made a bit of money, he'd get María somewhere better, he thought, hearing the outside door click shut. He stiffened as a second click immediately alerted his senses.

"*Hæ*, Baddó. Long time since you've been seen around here."

He spun round to confront the soft voice, and as he looked into the shadow of the stairwell, a stocky figure emerged and a hand grabbed his collar from behind just as a swinging kick swept his feet from under him, sending him sprawled face down. The wine bottle smashed on the concrete floor and its aroma flooded the lobby as it soaked into the dust.

270

Baddó thrashed furiously as a knee was planted securely on his neck and one arm was wrenched high up his back.

"Stay still, Baddó. No point in arguing, is there?"

He thought fast. These weren't cops. The police would have cuffed him by now. He lay still for a second and could hear someone leaning over him. There had to be two of them. Or maybe three? With his cheek crushed to the floor in a rivulet of wasted Chilean merlot, it was hard to tell.

With a feeling of dread, he recognized again the metallic click that had alerted him to start with. It took him by surprise that the cut as it sliced into his cheek wasn't painful. It was only once the carpet knife's blade was clicked home again that he felt it begin to sting as drops of blood dribbled onto his lips and the floor, mingling with the rich red wine. He blinked sweat out of his eyes and screwed his head round as far as he could to get a sight of his attackers, but he saw only faded combats and black boots.

"This is payback from an old friend, Baddó," the soft voice hissed in his ear, cut short as a burst of cold air told him the outside door had opened. He could feel the pressure of the knee in his back relax as its owner was distracted. Baddó twisted with all his strength, taking the man by surprise as he rolled and kicked out. He took in the shocked face of the elderly woman from the flat below María's in the doorway, staring at the tableau in front of her.

"Shit —" the soft voice snarled, momentarily distracted and giving Baddó an opportunity to scrabble for the remains of the wine bottle, pulling himself onto all fours and catching hold of it by the neck just as the smaller of the two men barged the woman to one side and was gone. Baddó was fast enough to swipe with the smashed bottle at the heavier, slower man as he followed his friend out and was rewarded with a howl of pain and surprise as the glass slashed deep into fabric, skin and muscle.

Baddó leaned on the door frame and watched as a blue 4x4 that had seen better days skidded to a halt and the two men tumbled into it, one trailing drops of blood into the snow behind him, the leg of his trousers already soaked with blood, his face alight with agony and alarm.

The elderly woman picked up her shopping bags.

"Are you all right?" he asked once he'd managed to steady his breathing as his legs turned to jelly beneath him.

"I'll be all right, young man," she replied in a voice of schoolteacher severity, "but you aren't."

Gunna yawned and looked at her watch, startled to find that it was long past the end of her shift. Eiríkur and Helgi were already long gone, both of them only too happy to escape the office. Gunna cursed herself for being tempted to do just a few things that had since eaten up almost two hours of her own time.

Nevertheless, a stack of routine paperwork had been dealt with, either signed and sent on or returned, or else consigned ruthlessly to the bin overflowing behind her. On top of that, she had already identified the occupant of the house at Kjalarnes that the phone number belonged to. A quick call to the communications division confirmed that the mobile phone belonging to the man she knew of only as Jón had remained stubbornly silent. It had been switched off following that single call earlier in the day and it had stayed that way.

Gunna tapped her teeth with a pencil and wondered how Haraldur Samúelsson and the mysterious Jón were connected to Pétur Steinar Albertsson. A search through police records showed that Pétur Steinar had a criminal record with convictions for vehicle theft, drunkenness in a public place and a little housebreaking. Gunna looked at the dates and frowned to herself. His record had been clean for more than twenty years, which meant that she was most likely looking at a series of youthful indiscretions.

Moving to the vehicle register, she flashed up Pétur Steinar Albertsson's driving licence and saw a picture taken ten years earlier of a thickset man with heavy five o'clock shadow and laughing eyes. Gunna moved to the national registry and found Pétur Steinar Albertsson, Hekla Elín Hauksdóttir, a teenage girl and two toddlers with identical dates of birth. She compared dates of birth and decided that the teenager could, at a stretch, be Hekla Elín's child, but that it was more likely that Sif Pétursdóttir was the result of an earlier relationship on Pétur's part.

Looking back at the police records, she saw that Hekla Elín had a drugs conviction for a minimal amount of cannabis more than a dozen years ago;

Gunna calculated that the woman would have been nineteen at the time. There was nothing since, other than a solitary speeding ticket and a fine paid promptly. Neither he nor his wife had fallen foul of the law for a long time and there was no reason to expect that either of them had done anything wrong. Smiling humourlessly to herself, Gunna reflected that one of her colleagues in particular would have observed in his usual foghorn voice that once a criminal, always a criminal, and would advise her to drop down on the family in Kjalarnes from a great height and with maximum manpower.

Not that I'm inclined to take Sævaldur Bogason's advice on anything, she said to herself softly. Out of curiosity she went to the vehicle register and typed in Hekla Elín's name. The computer hesitated and a photograph of Hekla Elín finally appeared. Gunna frowned at the sight of the young woman, whose picture had presumably been taken when she was around twenty. A distinctive long face and toothy smile looked back at her; Gunna quickly rooted among the papers on her desk, lifting up the CCTV photo of blonde Sonja next to her monitor.

The face had filled out in Hekla's thirties, with cheekbones that gave it character, and the dark brown hair and fringe that framed her youthful face had to be taken out of the equation and replaced by the blonde version, but the line of the jaw and that distinctive nose with its slight kink were convincingly similar.

So there you are, Sonja, Gunna breathed to herself, sorry that she was alone in the office, with neither Eiríkur nor Helgi there to share her discovery. She wrote down the phone numbers that she'd extracted easily enough from the online phone book, and made notes of the registration numbers of the red Toyota and the antique Land Rover, both of which were registered to the address, before shutting down her computer.

It can wait until tomorrow, she decided, wondering whether or not it would be worth a quick drive out to Kjalarnes to check out the neighbourhood, but immediately telling herself not to be stupid. Half an hour or more to Kjalarnes, the same back, plus the hour's drive home to Hvalvík would see her arriving home close to ten o'clock, and as Steini had promised to be back from wherever he was working at a reasonable hour, it would be worth being home on time at least once in a week.

She pulled on her coat and zipped it up in the lift, preparing herself for the cold shock of the car park after the warmth of the office, and wondering if she would find time to read the records she had printed out.

Shoving open the door, she scrolled through the numbers on her mobile and dialled, listening to the phone on the other end buzz once.

"Comms."

"*Hæ*, Siggi. Gunnhildur."

"I know. I recognized the number. We are supposed to be the communications wizards, after all."

"Apologies for underestimating you, in that case. Listen, do me a favour, would you?"

"I never say yes without knowing what it is first," Siggi laughed.

"It's all right. It's not your body I'm after."

"That's a relief."

"You cheeky young pup. Just keep an eye out for that number, would you?"

"Yeah. Will do. I've been monitoring it, but it still hasn't been switched on."

"OK, thanks. Just send me a text it if it pops up, can you? All quiet, otherwise?"

She heard Siggi yawn on the other end of the phone as she opened the car door.

"Yeah. Not a lot happening on a night like this. There was a fight of some kind an hour ago and the victim's in casualty having his face sewn up. Quite nasty, I'm told."

"Not something for me to deal with? Not tonight, anyway?"

"Nope. Uniform are dealing with it. The guy'll be in hospital until tomorrow at least. Something for you to look forward to."

"Oh, joy. Hoodlums fighting over a bit of dope, I expect. I'll see about it tomorrow. G'night."

"Sleep well, Gunna," Siggi replied, yawning again. "Another four hours and I can go as well."

Steini put down his book and clicked off the television. Gunna lay on the sofa, her eyes closed and with the reports she had promised herself she'd read in disarray on her chest. The place was blissfully quiet for once after an awkward few days with Drífa among them.

Gunna knew that the girl felt uncomfortable there, but guessed that the flat she was sharing in Reykjavík with a gaggle of first-year university students had also become less comfortable as her pregnancy progressed. Gunna had tried to probe gently and find out if Drífa intended to return to her parents in the Westfjords town of Vestureyri, but understandably the fear of small-town gossip and notoriety meant she had no desire to go home to her mother and stepfather. She wondered if the girl were waiting for Gísli to come home, but there were still more than three weeks left before he returned from sea — the second to last trip he had planned before Soffía was due to give birth in April. Even more worryingly, Gunna wondered if Soffía would let Gísli back into the little flat they had rented in Kópavogur, raising the spectre that the lad might have to come home to his mother as an emergency measure.

Steini knelt next to her and lifted the papers, squaring them neatly and laying them on the table. Concern registered on his face as he saw Gunna frowning to herself in her sleep.

"Hey, sleepyhead."

When there was no response, he stroked the tip of one finger down her cheek and was rewarded with a bleary eye opening.

"What time is it?"

"It's tomorrow, and some of us have to get up in the morning."

"Tomorrow, as in after midnight?"

"Yup, coming to bed?"

Gunna yawned and lifted herself up on one elbow. "Can't you just bring me a duvet and I'll go back to sleep here?"

"You're telling me to sleep alone?"

"You should be so lucky," she said, swinging her feet to the ground. "It's a cold night and I don't want to freeze to death before morning." She yawned. "Where are the girls?"

"Laufey's babysitting for Sigrún while she has a date with some new man, and Drífa went with her."

"Steini, are you all right?" Gunna asked, noticing the more than usually serious expression on his face.

"Yeah, fine."

"That doesn't sound convincing to me. What's the problem?"

Steini shifted from squatting uncomfortably to sitting on the floor. "Well," he said in an awkward tone.

"Well, what?"

"I was just wondering if I'm, y'know, up to the mark?"

Gunna wrinkled her forehead in incomprehension. "What are you driving at?"

He cleared his throat awkwardly. "You see, it's like this," he said and paused, while Gunna looked expectant.

"For a man who normally gets straight to the point, you're not doing a great job."

"All right, then. I was using your computer yesterday and I saw your browser history."

"And what about it?"

"I couldn't help but see that you'd been looking through personal.is a lot. I'm just wondering if there's something going on that I should know about?"

Perplexed and still half asleep, Gunna realized Steini's predicament. "Ah, you mean you're wondering if I'm up for a threesome or looking for a like-minded, discreet couple, or if I fancy trying out riding crops and leather underwear with studs on the inside?"

Steini coughed, embarrassed for the first time since she'd known him. "Well. Yes, I suppose that's what I'm asking."

"In a good way or what?"

"You mean would I be interested in all that stuff? A threesome with a nineteen-year-old who waxes his chest or a horny housewife from down the street? Actually, no. I was just wondering if there might be something I wasn't doing right."

Gunna yawned, stretched and sat upright on the sofa. "That's good, because if you were expecting an interest in fluffy pink handcuffs, then I'm afraid you're going to be disappointed. My trawl through personal.is is purely work-related as that's where it seems a now-dead punter made his arrangements to meet a potential witness we're trying to track down. That's about it," Gunna said, yawning. "And that's about all I can tell you as well."

She studied his reaction and was relieved that he didn't seem visibly disappointed.

"So we'll just keep to the old-fashioned way, shall we?" he asked.

"Ten minutes every other Saturday night before I put my curlers in, you mean?"

"Yeah. Something like that," he said with a grin and Gunna could hear relief in his voice, which he tried to conceal.

She stood up and looked at her watch. "Well, as officially I don't have to be in at eight tomorrow, and Laufey's at Sigrún's place, we can give it a trial run if you feel like it."

Steini's grin spread across his face. "In ten minutes before the curlers go in? I should be able to manage that."

CHAPTER
SIX

Tuesday

It took hours for the doctor to clean up Baddó's wound as best he could, lips pursed in concentration and frustration.

"It's going to be painful," he said long after midnight when the job was done, pushing his glasses back up his nose with the back of his hand. The nurse who had assisted whispered in the doctor's ear and he nodded.

"It's going to leave you with something of a scar," he told Baddó sorrowfully, who wanted to snap back that the guys in the boots and combats had probably been paid a decent wedge of cash to do just that.

"I know, doctor," he sighed, his face stiff and numb with local anaesthetic. "Looks like my catwalk days might be over, doesn't it?"

The doctor ignored the quip, although Baddó could see that it had been registered and wasn't appreciated. He stood up and looked down at him disapprovingly. "I'd like to keep you in overnight for observation," he said. "And I believe there are a couple of police officers who would like a word with you."

"It was an accident, doc. Honestly," Baddó told him. "I had the knife in my hand and fell down. It caught my face as I tried to break my fall," he said.

"Yes," the doctor replied absently. "That's as may be," he said, making it clear that he didn't believe a word of what Baddó was saying, "but we have an obligation to report anything that could possibly be an injury with an edged weapon to the police and they'll be here to speak to you in a moment."

The doctor left the room and Baddó stood up to get a look in a mirror for the first time.

"Shit!"

The wound's ragged edges had been fixed together as well as possible with tape sutures and Baddó was shocked at how raw the cut looked, not least as part of his beard had been roughly shaved away to give access to it.

"If you'd like to come this way, Jón," the nurse suggested as she put her face around the door, beckoning him to follow. Baddó heard a blast of laughter from down the corridor as a door quickly opened and closed, cutting it off abruptly. "There are two police officers here to speak to you, but I'll get you bedded down and then I'll go and fetch them. All right?"

Baddó nodded, too numb and tired even to check out the nurse's figure as he followed her along the passage, his leather jacket over his arm. He sniffed the musty air of the small room she showed him into.

"You can take a shower, but you might want to be careful of your face. The sutures won't come off, but

282

you really don't want to get your face wet for a day or two," she said, disappearing behind the door as it shut behind her, leaving Baddó alone.

He sat down on the crisp white bed, wondering how long he would be able to pretend to be Jón Daníelsson, a name he had picked from the phone book, along with an address and a national ID number that he'd stored away, ready to reel off when needed. He quickly ran the ten digits over in his mind to ensure they were there, ready for use. Baddó wondered if he should just get into bed and be asleep before the cops arrived. He suddenly felt exhausted, as if he'd run a race, and the bed looked so inviting. But thinking back to the attack cleared his mind and the rekindled anger at being jumped by two thickheads made him want to punch the walls.

He took a final look in the mirror, grimaced at the sight of the ragged cut running along his jaw and made a decision. He slipped out of the room, being careful not to let the door slam. Baddó could hear the soles of his trainers squeaking on the floor, so he trod carefully as he pulled on his jacket. The place was quiet apart from a buzz of conversation from the staff room, from where he'd heard a gale of laughter earlier. He tiptoed past, catching sight of some police uniforms inside the half-open door.

He headed for where he reckoned the door should be, guided by instinct and a faint whiff of fresh air, but a rush of hurrying feet saw him smartly step to one side into a doorway as the doctor who'd treated him and two nurses hurried past in response to an unheard summons.

He emerged into a waiting area, which was empty but for two figures surrounded by white coats. Baddó watched and stopped himself from smiling. It hurt his face, but he couldn't help grinning at the sight of the heavy man in a blood-soaked pair of combat trousers being lifted onto a stretcher, clearly not far from losing consciousness, while his distraught friend looked on.

Baddó walked purposefully and quietly towards the entrance, where he turned and stood in the doorway. The victim's friend looked on helplessly as the big man was wheeled away at a smart pace. He sank into a seat where he buried his head in his hands for a moment. Baddó watched as the man looked up; he could see the tears in his eyes, followed by the shock of recognition as he saw Baddó looking at him with a malevolent gleam in his eye.

The man's eyes widened and he opened his mouth to shout, stopping only when he realized there was nobody present to shout to. He was unable to drop his eyes as Baddó put a finger to his throat, made a slow, deliberate cutting movement and pointed at the man transfixed in the plastic chair with shock all over his face.

Baddó turned and was gone into the night. As he walked quickly away from the hospital entrance and past a waiting taxi with its driver asleep behind the wheel, he felt a surge of fierce pleasure at having terrified one of the idiots who'd jumped him. He would have to take a taxi, but not somewhere so obvious, he thought, deciding to flag one down closer to town.

"What a beautiful morning," Helgi observed as the very first glimmerings of daylight appeared, mirrored in the national hospital's windows. "You weren't asleep when I called, were you?"

"Of course I was. What the hell do you expect me to be doing at six thirty when I'm not due on shift until ten. What's it all about, then?"

Helgi grunted as he pushed through a heavy pair of swing doors. "A dead stoner. Name of Ásmundur Ásuson. Record as long as your arm. A bit of strong-arm stuff, but mostly dope and petty thievery," he explained, walking fast to keep up with Gunna's pace.

"You realize I've been to this hospital to see dead people more times than living ones? That's not great, is it? I know where the morgue is, but I couldn't find much else here without having to ask. What happened to this character?"

Helgi opened a second set of doors and the temperature dropped as they stepped into the mortuary.

"It's not so much this guy as his friend you'll be wanting a word with," Helgi said, and turned as the doctor who'd been on duty that night came in. The fatigue in his face was plain.

"Not much to tell you, I'm afraid. You'll get the post-mortem results soon enough, but that's not my department," he said with resigned distaste.

"You treated this man when he was admitted? When was that?"

"Just after two this morning. He appeared in casualty out of the blue. His friend brought him in a taxi, not an ambulance."

"What happened to him?" Gunna asked.

The doctor jerked a thumb at a steel table with a sheet over it. He strode over to it and lifted one edge, exposing a thigh with a deep gash that extended out of sight behind the leg.

"That's the cause of death?"

The doctor shrugged. "He left it too late. It looks like this happened some hours before he turned up here. A combination of shock and blood loss, probably some self-administered medication as well, and lights out," he said, snapping his fingers. "If he'd come in right away, we'd have stitched him up, kept him in for a few days and he'd have had a limp but he'd still be alive."

Gunna moved to the end of the table and lifted the sheet covering the man's head. She looked carefully but quickly, and shook her head as she let the sheet fall. "Nope. Not someone I recognize. Helgi?"

"Ási Ásu? Yeah. I remember him from my days in uniform. Never out of trouble. I'd be amazed if the post-mortem doesn't tell us he was buzzing merrily when he went."

"And did anyone speak to him? Any idea of when and where this happened?"

"We got his name and ID number," the doctor said, frowning. "He wasn't properly conscious and we were more concerned with keeping him alive than getting his life history. Look, do you need me any more? I'd very much like to get out of here sooner rather than later."

"Of course. Sorry, I didn't mean to imply that you should have questioned him. There were some police officers here last night, weren't there?"

"There were," Helgi said. "Tinna Sigvalds and Big Geiri were on duty and were called in to interview another suspected knife wound."

"Then this gentleman turned up and things suddenly got very busy," the doctor said. "I saw to the other casualty as well and I gather the man in question discharged himself, even though we were going to keep him in for observation."

"Someone else was cut?" Gunna asked and looked sideways at Helgi with a frown. "Serious?"

The doctor scowled. "Said he tripped with a knife in his hand, but that's bullshit. Someone clearly cut the man's face with a double-loaded knife."

Helgi looked blank. "Double-loaded?"

"You've not heard of that? It's an ordinary carpet knife, but they put two blades in it instead of one. It's common enough in other countries, but it's the first time I've seen it here."

"Why do they do that?"

The doctor sighed, as if losing patience with a child who's slow on the uptake. "It means there are two cuts side by side. It's very difficult to stitch and it leaves a much nastier scar." A thin smile crossed his face. "I don't suppose you'll have much of a problem finding him. His face is covered in tape sutures and there's a cut along his jaw and cheek this long," he said, holding his thumb and forefinger to his face to indicate a four-inch gash.

"But I take it that as this guy wasn't in such a bad way you didn't get a name out of him?"

Jóel Ingi's neck was stiff. He had been awake for hours, lying on the white sofa underneath an old duvet he had found in a cupboard in the spare room. He could have slept in the single bed in there, but he'd felt that sleeping on the sofa instead would help emphasize his disgruntlement at being excluded from sleeping with his wife under their twin crisp eiderdown duvets.

He lay wrapped in the scratchy old duvet, a relic of happy student days, and stared at the ceiling, wondering how long Agnes would sleep. Eventually he gave up and made for the shower, emerging twenty minutes later fresher and ready to try and repair the damage of the day before.

He gently pushed open the bedroom door and saw Agnes was still hunched in bed in a posture that indicated she had no intention of being disturbed. Jóel Ingi dressed in silence, taking one of the sober suits he kept for the office. He could tell that Agnes was awake: the timbre of her breathing told him she was waiting for him to leave the room before she made a move herself.

He took his time, knowing it would irritate her, before taking a seat at the breakfast bar and putting a spoonful of honey into a mug of weak tea. His head felt heavy, as if the air were crackling with an approaching storm, and he thought back to the previous day.

What if he had been wrong? What if that nosy woman had lied? Maybe she wasn't being paid by Agnes to keep tabs on him? In that case, who had sent her? The horror of the idea flooded him and he found himself absently stirring his tea long after the honey had dissolved. He left his slices of toast, his appetite gone, reminding himself that the damned laptop still needed to be located before either his work or his marriage could be satisfactory again.

"Good morning." Her formal greeting was a rebuke in itself.

"Agnes. About yesterday," he began, and felt sick at his own words. "I'm sorry. It was a mistake. I've been under a lot of pressure."

She shrugged and he could see her porcelain features set in the same suppressed anger as yesterday.

"I'm going away," she said, dicing an apple with a razor of a kitchen knife. "With Sunna and the children. Just so you know."

"All right. When?"

"This afternoon."

"Going for long?"

Jóel Ingi watched, fascinated by the deft movements of the knife as a banana and slices of pineapple got the same treatment as the apple, before she replied.

"I'm not sure. I need a little space."

Jóel Ingi knew better than to argue and waited for the sudden screech of the blender to stop before saying anything more. He nodded as Agnes poured the thick pulp into a bowl and added a spoonful of yoghurt, stirring slowly.

"Will you text me when you get there? How long will you be staying?"

Agnes shrugged. "A few days, maybe," she said absently.

"Look, about yesterday . . ." Jóel Ingi said before Agnes cut him off.

"Shhhh. It's not important."

"Hólmgeir," Gunna read off the report in front of her.

"Yeah?" The sharp-faced little man with greasy hair which fell into his eyes responded.

"You're Hólmgeir Sigurjónsson and you have a record that stretches back to kindergarten as far as I can see. Your friend Ásmundur Ásuson's dead and you're going to tell me just what happened."

Hólmgeir's eyes shifted rapidly from side to side and he licked his dry lips. Gunna could sense the wheels turning in his mind as the man quickly considered how much he could get away with keeping back. He'd made no obvious reaction to the news of his friend's death and he reminded Gunna of a rat in a trap.

"Let's start from the beginning, shall we? You turned up with Ási at casualty in a taxi. How did he get cut like that, and why didn't he get to casualty earlier?"

"I don't know what happened. He just appeared at home like that."

"Where's 'at home'?"

"My place. Ási rents —" he stopped and corrected himself. "He rented a room from me."

"So you don't know what happened to him? You weren't with him when this happened?" Gunna asked. "Because I'm damn sure you know just what went on."

290

Hólmgeir licked his lips; even without the trembling of his fidgeting hands, his nerves were palpable. "I don't know anything. Ási turned up with blood all down his leg and I tried to get him to go to hospital but he wouldn't have it."

"You could have called an ambulance, couldn't you?"

"Well, yeah. There was that," he admitted.

"So why didn't you?"

"Ási wrapped it all up in a bandage and said he'd be all right. He had a spliff and went to sleep on the couch and I reckoned he knew what he was doing so I went out for a bit."

"And?"

"And when I came back he wouldn't wake up properly. He was spaced, woozy. So I got him in a taxi and took him to casualty."

"Who slashed Ási's leg, Hólmgeir? Who did he have a fight with?"

"I don't know! I wasn't there," he said, his voice rising in pitch with anger and excitement. "Look, where's my lawyer?"

Gunna sat back in her chair and folded her arms. "Why? You're not under arrest, not yet, at any rate. Why do you reckon you might need a lawyer?"

"I don't trust you bastards."

Gunna opened her mouth to speak and stopped as Helgi quietly came in. Hólmgeir's mouth shut like a door as Helgi leaned over Gunna's shoulder and murmured in her ear.

Hólmgeir's eyes swivelled from one to the other. His growing panic could not be mistaken and he struggled to hear the muttered conversation.

"Yeah. No problem," Gunna said finally and Helgi straightened, picked up Hólmgeir's file from the desk in front of her and left the room, shutting the door quietly behind him.

"What's he taken that for?"

"Just an administrative matter," Gunna said. "Hólmgeir, are you sure there isn't anything you want to tell me?" She asked, standing up and smiling in a way that she could see set his pulse pounding with nerves. "Don't go away."

She hurried across the lobby and reached the lift with only a second to spare.

"*Hæ*, Jóel Ingi," Katrín giggled, breathing hard after her headlong run for the lift. She opened her thick coat and fanned herself. "Phew . . . not used to exercise, I'm afraid," she said, slowly unwinding her scarf and smiling at him, a rosy glow in her plump cheeks.

"You're very smart today," she said, looking sideways at his suit while Jóel Ingi tried to stop himself looking down at her billowing chest, which seemed to be trying to escape from the low-slung blouse imprisoning it.

"Coming out for lunch with the rest of us today?" she asked. "Már was talking about a place by the harbour that does a lunchtime seafood buffet."

Jóel Ingi scowled and quickly adjusted his features into the best smile he could manage. "I'm not sure," he said. "I have a few meetings this morning and I might have to miss lunch if they overrun."

Katrín sighed. "I do like a man who's dedicated to his work," she said. "But not too dedicated. Bye!" She grinned, stepping out of the lift as the door hissed open on the third floor and leaving him alone in the steel box, wishing that he could stay there for the rest of the day.

He took a deep breath as the door shut and a moment later it slid back again to reveal Már looking at him.

"Stay there," he ordered, stepping quickly into the lift and stabbing the button for the ground floor. "You're in the shit. Ægir's had some journalist from *Reykjavík Voice* on the phone already this morning; he chewed him out and said no comment, but he's on the warpath right now."

"What's happened?" Jóel Ingi asked with dread in his voice. "What's this hack saying?"

Már took a deep breath. "He's asking if the minister can categorically deny that three Libyan men and one woman who were murdered in 2010 in Tripoli passed through Iceland the year before. He has names and dates."

"How?"

"How the fuck should I know? It was between us and the Yanks. If you remember, we didn't even have a minister then. One was leaving just as the new guy was having his office measured for carpets."

Jóel Ingi felt his fingers go numb. "But all this was nothing to do with the minister. He can deny having known anything about it."

"You know that and I know that, but we both know where the buck stops. Laughing boy was the minister. The fact that he'd been in the job five minutes means nothing."

"So what now?"

Már glared. "I don't know what information that greasy hack has, but without any proof, they're not going to get far on hearsay. So I'm hoping they don't have the laptop you've been insisting is about to be recovered."

"So what now? What am I going to tell Ægir?"

The lift stopped and Már stood in the door, stopping it from closing. "I'd recommend that you go home, phone in sick and then find that fucking laptop, even if it costs you money."

"It's cost me a fortune already!"

"That's your problem. You shouldn't have mislaid it to start with, should you?"

Baddó looked at himself in the bathroom mirror and didn't like what he saw. His rough-cut beard had been left lopsided and he grimaced with discomfort as he trimmed it back as far as he could with a pair of scissors he'd found at the back of María's bathroom cabinet.

He looked ruefully at his handiwork and scowled at the livid cut across his face. Pain was one thing — pain could be managed — but this was going to make him unmistakable. It was as bad as having an orange flashing light on top of his head, he thought furiously.

294

Deep in a cupboard he found an old hoodie that had belonged to María's son, a young man who had long flown the nest but had neglected to take many of his discarded belongings with him. It wasn't something that María had mentioned, but Baddó knew the boy was in prison after being caught at Keflavík airport with a bag of pills, a steady job in a bakery abandoned in the quest for a quick payday, Baddó guessed. He wondered if he'd be joining his nephew inside if he couldn't turn things around quickly. With the hood of the sweater shrouding his head and his chin tucked deep in a scarf, the cut could almost be hidden, and in this dark winter weather a man wrapped up warmly would be nothing remarkable.

Baddó scribbled a note for María and left it on the kitchen table. He made a quick sandwich and ate it in a few rapid mouthfuls, anxious to be away before his sister came home and started asking awkward questions. Worse still, the police could be on their way to pay him a visit as that ham-fisted thug he'd cut with the broken wine bottle would probably have spilled his guts by now.

He switched on his phone as he closed the door behind him, clicking it quietly shut. Money and transport were the main things on his mind as he slipped down the stairs and out into the street. Hinrik's mobile rang a dozen times before he gave up and stabbed the red button. He cursed under his breath and punched in another number from memory, marching along the street, hunched inside his coat to keep the bitter cold off his aching face.

"Hello," a pleasant voice answered.

"*Hæ*, Ebba, it's me. You all right?"

"I was expecting to see you yesterday," she answered, her voice cool.

"I'm sorry about yesterday. I had some trouble and I was in casualty until the early hours."

"Casualty? You're hurt?"

He was pleased to hear some alarm in her voice. "I had an accident and it needed some stitches. So I'm not a pretty sight right now."

"What sort of accident?"

"Someone decided he didn't like the colour of my eyes, I guess."

"But you're all right, though, aren't you?"

Baddó wondered what to say; he was far from Ebba's conception of all right.

"Listen, Ebba. I really need to get away for a few days." He paused, stifling an unexpected pang. "I'll be back in a week or so. OK?"

He heard Ebba sigh. "If you say so, Baddó. It was nice knowing you. But if you've better things to do, then just say so straight out."

"Really. Genuinely, Ebba. I've had a problem. Someone wants to cut my throat and last night he almost managed it. I'm not a teenager who has to make up excuses," he started harshly and immediately thought better of it. "I keep my word. I said I'd be back in a week or two and I will. But first I need to make myself scarce."

"Fair enough. Give me a call when you're back in town, won't you?" she said, and Baddó tried to figure out if she meant it or if she was telling him to get lost.

Hinrik rolled himself an early-morning joint from the little bag of grass that he kept in the coffee jar. He puffed and rolled his eyes as a tapping at the unbroken pane of glass in the front door echoed through the apartment. He put the spliff down, tied the towel securely around his waist and went to the door, picking up a baseball bat on the way and holding it behind his back.

"Who's there?" he called to the indistinct figure outside.

"It's me. Jóel Ingi."

Relieved, Hinrik propped the bat in the corner behind the door and opened it a crack. "What the fuck are you doing here?"

"I need to talk to you. Let me in."

Hinrik scowled. He found it hard to see Jóel Ingi as anything but a tiresome youngster with soft hands. Anyone who parted with money so easily had to be simple, he reckoned.

"Look, I'm not even dressed yet. What's the hurry?"

Jóel Ingi's agitation was infectious and Hinrik found himself suddenly on edge.

"Let me in, will you? This is important."

"Come on, man. It's the middle of the night."

"It's almost noon, for fuck's sake! Open the bastard door, will you? I can't hang around outside here."

Unwillingly, and against his better judgement, Hinrik eased the door open and padded down the corridor. He pointed towards the kitchen. "Go in there. I'm going to get some clothes."

Jóel Ingi sat on a chair and crossed his legs, then uncrossed them and stood up. The flat was quiet apart from a rumbling snore that came from somewhere close by. Unable to stay still, Jóel Ingi sat down again and took a deep breath, trying to recall the relaxation classes Agnes had dragged him to when she'd been into yoga, but which he had spent ogling the teacher's hourglass figure rather than listening to what she had to say.

Hinrik appeared, sour-faced, wearing black jeans and buttoning a black shirt. "What's your problem, then?"

"Results? You've had plenty of time."

"This stuff doesn't happen overnight, y'know."

Hinrik lit the joint that had gone out in the ashtray and hauled the fragrant smoke deep into his lungs before letting it go with a series of regretful coughs that set his narrow shoulders shaking.

"I've paid you a stack of money and you haven't come up with anything."

"So? Sue me," Hinrik offered with a lopsided smile. "Go to the police and see what they say."

"You don't understand —"

"I reckon I do understand. You get rolled by some tart and you want it sorted out discreetly. But you didn't tell me you liked rough stuff, did you?"

Hinrik grinned, but his triumph faded at the sight of the fury etched on Jóel Ingi's face.

"You really don't understand, do you? You have no idea how deep this goes, you stupid bastard," he snarled.

"Hey, look. It's nothing to do with me, man. You asked me to do a job and I've done what I can."

Jóel Ingi's palm smacked the table with a crack and his lip trembled. Hinrik stopped with the joint halfway to his mouth in surprise. "You idiot," he whispered. "You don't understand. If you don't come up with the name and address you were paid to find, then I'm going to be in the shit up to my neck, and anyone who had anything to do with that computer is going to be right there with me."

"Ah," Hinrik said with a slow smile. "So what's this computer you're talking about now?"

Jóel Ingi's stomach lurched as he realized he'd said too much in the heat of the moment. "You fool. You fucking idiot. Forget that stupid laptop. I've been tailed and watched for the last month, and do you imagine for a second that you haven't been as well? This is poisonous, you stupid thug. Anyone who's had anything to do with me is going to get hauled in and you can take it from me that none of us will get a slap on the wrist and few months in an open prison."

"Get away, will you? Don't try and sell me this kind of crap. This is Iceland, not some fucking stupid mafia country."

Jóel Ingi's hand, still on the table where it had landed, began to tremble. "You think so? I'm telling you. This goes way beyond anything you might think, and there are people with reputations and influence to protect who aren't going to let anything stand in their way, least of all a deadbeat pusher who thinks he's some kind of big shot." He sneered. "When you wind

299

up dead in a ditch, d'you really think anyone's going to shed a tear, or even look too hard for whoever did it?"

"Wha — ? What's going on?"

A heavy-faced woman appeared at the kitchen door, her eyes puffy and her hair tousled. Jóel Ingi eyed her with alarm as she shuffled into the kitchen and let water gush from the tap into a grubby glass. As she drank he saw with alarm a lurid home-made tattoo across her shoulder, emerging from the gaping arm hole of the vast sleeveless shirt that was obviously the only thing she was wearing.

"Why don't you go back to bed, Ragga?" Hinrik suggested.

She belched and sat down on a stool as she rummaged through a drawer. "Pills," she said. "My head feels like it's been under a truck."

Hinrik put his hand up to a shelf and picked up a packet of painkillers, which he tossed to her, his mind ticking over at the possibilities that Jóel Ingi had unwittingly revealed. He had assumed the man had wanted to find someone so he could administer a beating, but it seemed there was more to it, maybe something that could turn out to be profitable. Ragga caught the packet and snapped four pills from it, throwing them down her throat and gulping the glass of water to wash them down.

"Shit," she moaned, holding her head in her hands. "Must have been a good time last night. I don't remember a thing."

"You had a good time, I assure you," Hinrik said. "Ragga, we're talking business here."

300

"Yeah, yeah."

"Leave us to it for a while, will you?"

"I know, I know. I'm going to take myself back to bed like a good girl."

She hauled herself to her feet and padded out of the room. Jóel Ingi felt a flickering of excitement in spite of himself at the sight of heavy legs and muscular shoulders as Ragga scratched and yawned on her way out. She stopped in the doorway, blew a kiss and belched before vanishing. Jóel Ingi could hear the sofa in the next room creak and a mutter of sound as the TV clicked on.

Ragga's arrival had broken Jóel Ingi's concentration. He could feel anger dissipating and being replaced by a wave of fatigue. He dug his fingernails into the palm of his hands and thought of everything he had worked towards; it was all about to be lost because of a stupid indiscretion.

"I want that woman's address," he snarled, feeling the anger return. "Otherwise I'll have some really unpleasant people coming after me, and I'll make damn sure they come after you as well."

The bakery was full. Baddó stood in the queue with his hood down and a scarf swathed around as much of his lower face as he could manage. The bakery wasn't big, but the quality of its Danish pastries and the easy parking outside meant the place did a roaring trade in the mornings.

Not in any hurry, he watched from one of the tall tables at one side, sipping coffee and idly flipping through yesterday's *DV* newspaper. He watched people lining up to get to the counter, tracking them as they left their cars outside and made their way in through the doors to buy their lunchtime sandwiches or a mid-morning snack.

It's just as well Iceland's such a safe place, Baddó thought. In mainland Europe, or practically anywhere else, people would be careful about the wallets and phones hanging out of their pockets.

He moved into the queue at the counter, one eye on the array of pastries on display but another on a young man in a knitted jacket with gaping pockets. He stood there deciding what to buy, a bunch of keys clearly visible in his cavernous pocket.

An orange-faced girl standing next to him looked blankly at the same display, a handbag slung over her shoulder, popping gum as she waited in the queue. He could sense her impatience growing behind the incongruous midwinter tan as her gum popped rapidly three times.

"In a hurry, are you?" Baddó asked and was rewarded with a blank stare and a nod. The rattle of something cheerful breezed out of the iPod earpieces in sharp contrast to the bored look on her round face as she shuffled past him. Baddó took a short half-step to one side, letting her brush against his coat as he smartly dipped into the handbag and came out with a set of keys that vanished into his parka's sleeve.

He slipped out of the bakery and clicked the fob. Looking around for flashes, he saw the hazard lights of an anonymous mud-brown Hyundai wink as he pressed the button a second time to make sure. As he drove away, Baddó caught a glimpse of the girl emerging from the bakery with a bag of Danish pastries in one hand, rummaging in her capacious handbag for keys that were no longer there.

The old lady had sat stiffly on one of the plastic chairs in reception for half an hour before a uniformed officer showed her into the interview room.

"Have I done something wrong?" she asked as Gunna sat down opposite her. "I don't want to waste anyone's time?"

"Not at all. Quite the opposite," Gunna assured her and turned in her chair to call back the uniformed young man who was just about to close the door behind him.

"Hey, before you go," she called after him, "since we kept this lady waiting for so long, how about you bring her a cup of coffee?"

"We don't normally . . ." he began before Gunna cut him off firmly.

"It's not every day that someone takes the trouble to come down here and give us information. So two coffees, please," she instructed. "Milk?" she asked the elderly lady who sat with her handbag clutched in her grasp.

"Yes, please," she said and finally let slip a glimmer of a nervous smile.

The door shut, although the young officer's disgruntlement could be felt through it.

"My name's Gunnhildur Gísladóttir and I'm a CID officer. My colleague has given me the gist of what you came in here to tell us, so now I need you to tell me the story again," Gunna said. "But first, could you tell me your name?"

"I'm Sigurlín Egilsdóttir but everyone calls me Lína. I live at Háaleitisbraut 80. It's a block of flats and I'm on the ground floor on the right."

"Thank you, Lína. My colleague who should be bringing us a cup of coffee told me you saw an incident last night. Could you tell me what happened?"

"Well. I came in and there were some men fighting in the entrance. Three of them. Two of them were hurt, I think."

"And when was this?"

"It was just before seven yesterday evening. I'd been shopping and took a taxi home as it's too far to walk in this weather."

"And what happened?" Gunna coaxed.

"I opened the door to go in the entrance, as usual, and I was surprised that it wasn't locked. But as soon as I opened the inside door I could see what was happening. There was one man on the floor and two others trying to beat him up. He had a cut on his face and there was blood."

"Did you recognize these men?" Gunna asked, opening a folder and putting a picture of a rather fresher-faced Ásmundur Ásuson in front of her. She stared at it.

"He looks like the young man who ran away," she said slowly.

"And this one?"

A fatter Hólmgeir Sigurjónsson than the one waiting in a cell glared out of his mugshot.

Lína nodded. "Yes, I saw that man as well. Those are the two who ran out of the door past me."

The door opened and the uniformed officer appeared with two mugs of coffee and a small carton of milk.

"Thanks," Gunna said, giving him an approving smile as he sidled out. "Now, Lína. These two, they were attacking a third man?"

"I think so but I'm not really sure," the old lady said, and Gunna could see her marshalling her thoughts. "The man who was on the floor, the one who's face had been hurt, was María's brother. But this young man was injured as well," she said, pointing at Ásmundur's deadpan portrait. "There was a puddle of blood all along the floor. I could see him bleeding as they ran past me. He was limping and making a lot of noise."

"Who is María?"

"She's the girl on the top floor. When I say girl, she must be your age, but she looks young to me. She said her brother had been overseas for a long time and had come back to Iceland after many years; he's staying with her while he looks for work."

"Top floor on the right? Do you know the brother's name?"

The old lady shook her head. "No. He did tell me, but I've forgotten. He was hurt, too. He had his hand over his face. He said he was all right, but I could see it was bleeding."

The door creaked open again and Gunna looked round to see Eiríkur's face peering round.

"Chief. Can I have a word?"

"Excuse me a moment." Gunna pushed her chair back and went outside. "What is it?"

"The number you wanted tracked," Eiríkur said quietly. "Siggi said it popped up ten minutes ago, made one call that wasn't answered and another that was, then switched off."

"To unregistered numbers, I expect?"

"Got it in one."

"Any location? Háaleitisbraut, maybe?"

Eiríkur looked at Gunna with a new admiration. "How did you know?"

"Looked in my crystal ball before I came to work this morning. I want you to get in a squad car and take three beefy uniformed people with you. Háaleitisbraut 80, top floor on the right. But first find out who lives there. It should be a lady called María, but we're after whoever's there with her," Gunna rattled off.

"OK, chief," Eiríkur said, keen to get out of the building.

"Eiríkur."

"Yeah?"

"Be careful. By rights we should get the special unit out for this, but I want it done quietly and without any more fuss than is necessary. Don't go being a hero. This guy might be nasty. Understood?"

"Gotcha."

"Good. Let me know."

Back in the interview room Lína sipped her coffee. She looked at the picture on the desk and then at Gunna. "Have you found him?"

"Who?"

"The young man," she said, pointing to Ásmundur Ásuson gazing blankly from the ten-year-old police mugshot. "And is he all right?"

"We'll find him and I'm sure he'll be fine," Gunna assured her, not wanting to tell Lína that Ásmundur Ásuson's remains were cooling in the National Hospital's mortuary.

She sucked the loose tooth and gingerly placed a finger against it. It shifted slightly under pressure. Although it felt awkward, like a foreign body, the tooth felt firmer than when the dentist had pushed it back into position, tutting his disapproval.

The van was cold and there was something living in the back amongst all the boxes of junk with a familiar smell that she had no intention of looking into, but it seemed a better place to sit than in the Renault. She had cleared a tiny patch of snow from the windscreen to get a better view of the house, an old one clad with sheets of steel that had faded from a cheerful blue to match the colour of the winter sky that was starting to appear.

Opening the passenger window, she listened for noise and watched for movement. She pulled off her woollen ski hat and ran fingers through her thick fair hair, stopping gingerly to finger the bruise on the side of her head. The black eye hadn't turned out to be as bad as she'd expected, just a shadow under one eye instead of the discoloured patch she had expected to see and which would have taken weeks to fade.

She admitted to herself that yesterday had been a mistake. Following Jóel Ingi into that bar had been the right thing to do, but asking after him had been a wrong move. As for asking for the toilet and using that as a pretext to scout around the Emperor's dark inner recesses, well, that had been a real lapse of judgement.

A smile appeared on her face as she watched a light click on in one window of the flat where she knew Hinrik lived. Maybe it hadn't been a mistake after all? It had been a painful and unpleasant experience, but at least it had prompted the man into making a mistake. It had showed her without a doubt that Hinrik Sørensen and Jóel Ingi Bragason had something in common, and she wondered which of them owed a debt to the other.

It was a while before Jóel Ingi left the apartment, pacing across the car park to the smart Audi that stood out like a sore thumb amongst all the parked wrecks. She shrank back in the van's passenger seat, hoping he wouldn't see into the shadows beyond the windscreen's coat of grime and snow. As he walked along the side of the van and hammered at it with one fist, setting off a dull echo inside, she managed to get a clear look at him in the van's wing mirror, which had been angled carefully for just that reason. She wasn't surprised to see a look of furious tension across his otherwise handsome face.

She had no choice but to stay in the van until the Audi had gone. She had parked her own car out of sight and couldn't risk letting Jóel Ingi see her, even fleetingly in the mirror. She stayed still in the van, the door cracked open to let in some air and dispel the thick smell inside. Ready to step out, she quickly pulled the door closed again as a mud-coloured car rattled to a halt, watching the driver get out with a mobile phone to his ear and talk as he walked slowly towards Hinrik's door. She wondered what had happened to the man's face to require all those stitches.

Breakfast was over, the twins had been deposited at playgroup and Hekla felt that at last she could relax for a few minutes. She listened to the washing machine whirr and mutter as it finished its cycle and wondered whether or not to open it straight away. The sound of Pétur's lathe could be heard faintly through the wall.

She thought back to the fat man with the mournful eyes in the swimming pool, the one she was sure she had shaken off before he could follow her. The nagging feeling returned to her that this was something to do with the angry old man at Hotel Gullfoss, the one whose obituary she'd been startled to see in the paper, or maybe one of the others?

Hekla got up from the stool she'd been sitting on while brooding and banged on Sif's door.

"Are you awake?" she called and was rewarded with noise that wasn't quite human speech but indicated that the room was occupied.

The door opened and Sif appeared wrapped in a dressing gown and with her long brown hair in disarray over her face. She shambled to the bathroom and Hekla heard the lock snap to. She carefully pushed open the door of Sif's room and peered into the gloom inside. The curtains were drawn tight and had probably been that way since they'd moved in a year ago. Hekla wrinkled her nose at the musty smell and clicked on the light. The bed was strewn with books and papers, and she could see where Sif had lain in bed surrounded by the collection. On the desk the light on a large flatscreen monitor gleamed, while two laptops were also open on the desk on either side of it.

A flush sounded and a tap could be heard running. Hekla switched off the light and retreated, noticing as she did so the vaguely familiar laptop bag open on the floor behind the door. She closed the door and went back to the kitchen.

"Y'all right?" Sif yawned, her hair not brushed, but gathered untidily behind her head. Her eyes were red behind her round glasses and she yawned again, wider this time, revealing multi-coloured braces on her teeth.

"Fine, thanks. Sleep well?" Hekla asked, trying not to sound sarcastic and remembering what it was like to be a teenager. "Can you sort your washing out, please? The machine's finished and I need to do a wash myself."

Sif rustled through a cupboard and came up with a jar. She carefully spread butter on a slice of bread, followed by jam from the jar, and folded the bread into a makeshift sandwich.

"Yeah," she said, through a mouthful of bread and jam. "I'll get dressed first."

"Make it quick, would you?"

Sif shambled back to her room and Hekla wondered how someone with such outstanding grades at college could be so disorganized. She sighed to herself and hauled the pile of damp clothes from the washing machine before reloading it. She pointedly left the basket of damp clothes where Sif would have to step over it, certain that it would still be in the same place by evening, but hoping to be proved wrong.

It was half an hour before Sif emerged from her room again, dressed in the baggy clothes she preferred, but with her hair still awry. As if performing a vital service to mankind she loaded her damp clothes piece by piece into the dryer.

"Sif," Hekla called as the dryer started to hum.

"Yeah?"

"Do you have that laptop I was given before Christmas? The one that was in your dad's workshop?"

"Er, yeah. Why?"

"I'd like it back."

"But you don't use it."

"I know, but I'd still like it back."

"Why?"

Hekla fought to control her temper and smothered the urge to snap back. "Because it was given to me and I might need it. Is it in your room?"

"Yeah. It's a piece of crap anyway. Really old and slow."

"You managed to start it up?" Hekla asked in surprise. "I tried and it was locked. I was going to get the password for it."

Sif looked at her suspiciously. "Where did you get it from, then?"

"Someone I used to work with. Why?"

Sif laughed. "Unless it was a guy called Jóel Ingi Bragason who gave it to you, then that's a stolen computer," she announced, turning to disappear back into her room.

"So how did you get into it?" Hekla asked.

Sif turned back. "Easy. I cracked the password."

"OK, fine. Well, I want it back now, thanks."

"You're not using it and I don't know where I put it."

"It's on your desk. And the case is on the floor."

"The case, yeah. But the laptop's at Hilmar's house. It's been there for weeks."

Hekla called on new reserves of patience. "But it's in there on your desk."

"That's an old one that belongs to college. What's the problem? It's not as if you were using it," Sif retorted. "Or even if you had a password for it."

Baddó parked the Hyundai out of sight behind a van that had been on blocks for long enough to let a summer's worth of grime accumulate on it while snow surrounded it in shallow drifts. He preferred to deal with people in comfortable blocks of flats, not in these old houses with cubbyhole apartments and creaky doors that could take a man by surprise.

312

He switched on his phone and keyed in a number, leaning against the abandoned van, eyes on the house as he listened to the ringing tone.

"Baddó," Hinrik wheezed, and he could hear the click of his lighter. "Got something for me?"

"Could be," he said. Hinrik was no early bird and he hadn't expected him to be awake. "Let's say we need to do a little negotiation."

"How come? Negotiate over what? I gave you a job and a good rate. Either you've come up with the goods or you haven't."

Baddó walked quickly towards the house, looking it over as he spoke. "I had a rough time last night. You wouldn't know anything about that, would you?"

"What the fuck? Are you playing games, or what?"

Baddó nodded to himself. Thirty-six hours with practically no sleep meant that he was wide awake on energy alone, but he knew that at some point exhaustion would set in, and quickly. He eased open the back door of the old house and stepped inside, letting the hood of the parka drop back.

"Where the hell are you, Baddó?" Hinrik demanded. "And why are you talking in that stupid voice?"

"Never you mind. It's not as if I'm fit to be seen at the moment."

"What's this crap you're talking?"

Baddó heard Hinrik yawn as he spoke and stood still, listening to the creak of old floorboards above his head. He smiled as much as the numbness down one side of his face would allow. He put a cautious foot on the bottom step of the narrow stairs and gingerly made his way up, keeping close to the wall to avoid making the steps creak as loudly as the floorboards above his head.

"All right, you mad bastard. What's this negotiation bullshit you're talking about?"

Another step, around the corner and the door to Hinrik's flat was in sight. "Somebody tried to tell me to keep my nose clean last night, and I don't take kindly to a lesson in manners from deadbeats like those two fuckwits."

"I'm telling you, man. I don't know what you're talking about. I want you to do the job I gave you."

Baddó heard shuffling feet. Standing at Hinrik's door, he peered through the single remaining frosted glass panel next to a broken one that had been badly repaired with tape and cardboard.

"I'm not happy, Hinrik," he growled, his jaw aching now that the painkillers were starting to wear off.

"What the fuck happened to you, man?" Hinrik asked and Baddó could hear him yawn just as he could see an indistinct figure shuffle across the hallway and disappear into another room. Hinrik's breathing suddenly magnified in his ear, together with the sound of running water. Baddó pushed though the cardboard taped over the broken window pane, thankful that he wasn't going to have to kick the door down, and eased a hand through it to unclick the catch. He padded down the hall, his phone now in his pocket, and turned to stand behind Hinrik as he urinated carelessly in fits and starts in the flat's tiny toilet.

"You still there, Baddó?" he heard Hinrik say into the phone jammed under his chin.

314

"Right here," Baddó snarled, placing a foot in the small of Hinrik's back and pushing, sending him staggering forward, the yellow stream spattering his feet as he fell and one hand desperately reaching out to stop his face hitting the cistern, while his phone fell with a clatter and a splash into the toilet bowl.

"What . . .?" He roared. "Get off me, you mad bastard!"

"I'm mad, right enough," Baddó hissed, one hand in Hinrik's lank hair and the other wrenching his arm up high behind his back. "Who were those two dipshits who tried to turn me over last night?"

Hinrik twisted, forcing his head around. As he saw the livid cut and stitches on Baddó's face, his eyes bulged. "Shit, man. Who did that to you?"

"You tell me. Or you're going down there until you think of something."

Hinrik thrashed as his face was pushed into the toilet bowl. Baddó hauled his face back out after a few seconds and Hinrik gasped for air, retching between each deep lungful, which was cut short as his head was thrust into the bowl again. Hinrik's free hand stretched out, desperately scrabbling for a hold on anything, while his legs kicked feebly.

Baddó wrenched Hinrik's head clear of the foul water and gave him a few seconds to haul some air deep into his heaving chest. His sparse locks of dark hair lay over his face and he made to push them away as he spluttered and fought for breath.

"Shit . . ." he moaned, retching yet again. "Baddó, man. I swear. It was nothing to do with me. Hell," he moaned, his breathing starting to slow.

"Talk, Hinrik," Baddó ordered, nodding towards the foul-smelling toilet. "Spill the fucking beans, or you're going back down there and you're not coming out."

Hinrik lay collapsed against the wall, one arm behind him and the other across his chest. He stared into Baddó's hard, dark eyes and didn't like what he saw.

"They made a real mess of you, Baddó man," he said. "Who were they? What did they look like?"

"You tell me."

"Why would I have you rolled? You're working for me, remember? Why would I have you turned over before the job's done? Are you going to let me get up? I reckon you've made your point."

Baddó allowed Hinrik to get shakily to his feet, one hand on the wall as he supported himself. He closed the lid of the toilet and sat down heavily on it, groaning. He took a better look at Baddó's face. "They did a job on you, didn't they?"

"Who did?"

"Hell, Baddó. I don't know," Hinrik snarled. "It's none of my doing and it's not as if you're, short of enemies who owe you a bad turn."

"I need some cash. Right now."

"You have a fucking weird way of asking to be paid for a job," Hinrik said, the shadow of a smile appearing at one corner of his thin mouth.

"But it's more than just money, Hinrik," Baddó snarled, pointing at his face. "This changes everything. There's some information I'm after as well."

★　★　★

Wondering if she was wasting her time, Gunna signed an unmarked car out of the pool and took it through town, pleased for a change to see clear skies after a dark night and more than a week of incessant snow, punctuated by spells of rain every time the temperature hauled itself above zero. Twice Gunna braked and swore as cars pulled across lanes without warning. The mid-morning traffic was fast and too close for comfort, with the road covered by a film of water quickening in the thin sunshine.

Past the half-empty car park at the Korputorg shopping centre the traffic thinned to trucks and a few cars heading out of town and by Mosfellsbær the city receded into the distance. Esja's white slopes gleamed in the sun and the road became a black scar lying across a landscape the colour of a grubby bandage at ground level, rising to pristine white pierced with jagged black rock outcrops on the higher slopes.

The warmth of the sunshine was a welcome change, but Gunna wondered what the night would bring. The forecast was for clear weather and a northerly breeze, conditions bound to bring a chill with them, and she remembered how that morning's sparkling air had nipped at unprotected ears and noses, as if to provide a reminder that winter was still here.

She found herself enjoying the drive through less familiar scenery. The daily commute from Hvalvík into the city had become a routine chore on most days, especially the night-time drive both ways during the winter months. But driving this way out of town, in the opposite direction to the one that would take her to

Hvalvík, was also fraught with memories of travel from her childhood home to Reykjavík in the days when roads were gravel and it was a long day's travel to the westfjords. She wondered idly how long it would take for people to miss her if she were to continue to the Hvalfjördur tunnel and keep driving north and then west, when her question was answered by her phone buzzing.

"Gunnhildur," she answered.

"Driving, are you?" Helgi asked.

"Yeah. But it's all right. There are no cops about here."

"You know Johnny Depp's waiting for you in reception?" Helgi asked, and Gunna could hear the grin on his round face. "Refuses to speak to anyone else."

"Can't be," Gunna retorted. "I left him at home, exhausted and strapped to the bed."

"Like that guy at the Gullfoss?"

Gunna shuddered at the thought. "Nice idea, but I'm afraid not. Is there really someone for me in reception?"

"No, just wanted to see what you'd say. But I'm finished with Hólmgeir, and he sang like a bird eventually."

"Good. Explain, if you would be so kind."

"Right, the bones of it is that Hólmgeir and Ási were paid a bag of grass and their debts written off to beat someone up, and no, he absolutely won't say who paid them; says it's more than his life's worth. He also swears blind he has no idea who the victim is and that they were just given an address and a picture, which he dropped in a bin afterwards."

"So they beat this person up, or tried to?"

"So Hólmgeir says. But he said their victim lashed out with a broken bottle, which is what gashed Ási's leg. That's a fatal wound, so I guess we could be looking at a murder charge there."

"Not sure the legal eagles would swallow that," Gunna mused. "Manslaughter, certainly, I'd say. Anything from Eiríkur?"

Helgi laughed. "Yep. The lady in the top flat is María Helga Sturlaugsdóttir. She's mystified and hadn't seen her brother for a few days until she came home and found a note saying he'd left town for a bit. She does shift work so it's not unusual for her not to see him for days at a time, she told Eiríkur."

"So who's the brother? Anyone we know?" Gunna asked, slowing down and checking her mirror for the Kjalarnes turnoff. She could hear Helgi's hollow laugh echo down the phone.

"He's her younger half-brother and goes by the name of Hróbjartur Bjarnthórsson. So, yes. Our elusive victim who sneaked out of hospital this morning is Bigfoot Baddó, and he's definitely someone we know."

"What the hell's going on, Helgi?" Gunna fumed. "First he's shadowing us at the Gullfoss and then his description fits the character who was spotted after that car burned out at Grandi. Any news on that yet, by the way? Do we know if it was Magnús's car?"

"I don't know. Haven't had time to pester forensics."

"Right. Do it now. Kick them, bribe them, buy them doughnuts, whatever. If we can tie this to Bigfoot Baddó we'll have made real progress. But circulate his description anyway. If Hólmgeir doesn't fall apart in the witness box, we'll have the bastard for manslaughter as well as Magnús's murder."

Jóel Ingi almost wanted to shed bitter tears of frustration. Agnes hummed in the bathroom, and hadn't even asked why he was back from work so early. His distress was evident, and she seemed to be ignoring him, acting as if he wasn't even there, sitting and staring into space as she casually piled clothes into a suitcase on the bed.

He sat on the sofa, his fingers twitching nervously as he felt his phone vibrate in his pocket. Glancing at it, he saw "private number calling" and decided that it was best left unanswered. Hinrik had told him nothing of any use and he had come away from the flat where Hinrik lived with that bruiser of a woman as frustrated as he had been when he'd arrived.

His phone buzzed a second time and he gulped as he saw the text message displayed.

One hour. Be here. Ægir L

A minute later the house phone began to chirp. Surprised that anyone would call his landline, Jóel Ingi hunted for the handset and found it behind a pile of magazines just as Agnes padded in from the bathroom in a cloud of steam, towelling her hair and giving him a dazzling smile that confused him even more.

"Jóel Ingi?" An unfamiliar, brisk voice asked.

"I'm not buying anything —"

"That's a shame, because I have something you need."

"Who is this?"

"My name's Jón. Our mutual friend Hinrik mentioned that we ought to talk, so answer your mobile in half an hour."

Agnes listened to Jóel Ingi's side of the conversation, her head cocked to one side, watching as the conversation was abruptly terminated and Jóel Ingi was left holding a buzzing phone. "You're going out," she said, sitting down in an armchair and opening a drawer in a table next to it to bring out the makings of a joint.

"Do you have to smoke that fucking stuff in the house?" Jóel Ingi snapped, his irritation boiling over.

Agnes shrugged. "It's my house as well."

"I'm a public official. If you get caught —"

Agnes's laughter tinkled. "Who's going to catch me? Anyway, I like it. It helps me think," she said. "It helps me relax and it makes me horny. Not that you complain about that."

"I have to go."

"Shame," Agnes said coolly, rolling with practised ease. "Going to be long? My flight's at six."

"Hello! Pétur Steinar Albertsson?" Gunna asked, recognizing from his driving-licence photo the tall man with a lined but fresh face who looked round from his workbench. "I knocked on the front door, but nobody answered."

"Yeah, I'm Pétur. What are you selling?"

"I'm not selling anything," Gunna said and held open her police ID as the man stood up and a cloud of concern descended on what looked like a normally cheerful face.

"Anything wrong? The children . . . ?"

"Nothing like that," she assured him. "But I need a few questions answered."

Pétur wiped his hands on a rag and limped towards her. "That sounds ominous, and we have enough problems as it is. But what can I do for you?"

Wondering how far she should go, Gunna looked around the workshop with interest. "What do you make here?"

"These," Pétur said, tossing up and catching a wooden bowl from the top of a stack. "I'm disabled and can't work a full day any more, so I make these for a tourist shop. They sell pretty well once they've been polished up."

"Who lives here?"

"Me. My wife. Three children."

"I know your name already. What's your wife's name?"

"Hekla. Hekla Elín Hauksdóttir. Why?"

"Just wondering who lives here."

Pétur shifted his weight uncomfortably, leaning on a stick. "We're renting this place month by month. We thought we were only going to be here for a few months, but now it looks like we might all be here for a while."

"All?

"There's me and Hekla. My daughter Sif, and mine and Hekla's children, Albert and Alda. You still haven't told me what this is about."

"To be straight with you, I'm not entirely sure myself," Gunna told him. "In any case, there's only so much I can tell you. But this address has come up in connection with an investigation and I need to decide whether or not it has anything to do with you, or maybe whoever lived here before you. How long have you been here?"

"About a year. Just over. We moved in a few days before Christmas last year."

"And who lived here before you?"

Pétur smiled grimly. "Hard to tell. The place had been empty for about two years. It was owned by a big shot at one of the banks, who was going to tear the place down and have a summer house built on the site. But he didn't get planning permission and by the time it looked like he might, the bank had gone tits-up and the gentleman in question left the country in a hurry."

"So who's the owner now?"

"It went to one of the pension funds in the fallout. One of Hekla's uncles is involved with the bank's winding-up committee and he put in a word. We can stay until it sells, however long that takes."

"So there's been nobody here but you?"

"I don't really know. There's a scout troop that camps on the meadow in the summer, and there were some squatters here for a while when the big shot owned the place, but that was before our time. I gather he got them out pretty quick. It was something of a pigsty when we moved in. Part of our agreement with the winding-up committee is that we fix the place up and make it habitable, not that there was much that needed doing. The house itself was fine. It just needed a massive amount of cleaning."

"So you fell on your feet. Your wife at home, is she?"

"She has a day's work today."

"What does she do?"

Pétur smiled fondly. "She trained as an actress, but times are tight these days. Mostly she does voice-overs and things like that. She's reading something for a radio ad today, as far as I know."

Gunna nodded. "Mind if I take a look around?"

Pétur looked surprised. "Sure. Anything in particular you're looking for?" he asked, suspicion etched across his face.

"I don't know, to be quite honest. But as this address has come up as part of the investigation, I'd like to get a feel for the place and an idea of the layout in case things go any further."

"And you can't tell me what all this is about?"

"I'm afraid not," Gunna smiled, seeing the disappointment on his face as Pétur made for the workshop door, swinging his stiff right leg with each step.

The house was small but warm, she thought, imagining what it had been like after a few empty years. Pétur had sanded and varnished the floor of the living room and a large window provided a view over the sea, with Reykjavík in the distance across the bay. Unconsciously, Gunna compared the warmth of what was clearly an old building against her own modern concrete terraced house. Somehow wood gave a house a friendly feeling, she thought, scanning a line of pictures on the living-room wall and stopping herself from doing a double take.

"Is that your daughter?" Gunna asked, pointing to a teenage girl in a low-key monochrome print, who looked to be hiding behind long dark hair that covered half of her face as she sat cross-legged, flanked by a gap-toothed, light-haired boy and girl.

"That's my Sif with the twins," Pétur told her, pride unmistakable in his gruff voice.

"And you and your wife behind them?" Gunna asked, leaning forward to peer at the print and the slightly out-of-focus background figures. "Any idea when she'll be back?"

"This evening sometime, I expect."

"Do you know where she's doing this reading?"

"Nope. There are a couple of studios where they do that kind of thing. I don't bother asking which one any more."

Baddó swore and dropped the phone on the car seat. Fatigue was starting to catch up with him and the painkillers were making him drowsy. It was taking every ounce of his mental energy to concentrate on the road and he desperately wanted to close his eyes and rest for a few hours. He felt exhausted, staring at the road in front of him without knowing quite where he was going, but certain that if he were to relax for a second, the car would be off the road. He was also sure that the police would be looking for the mud-coloured Hyundai by now, so it would have to be either dumped or disguised somehow.

He stopped just as it was becoming fully dark. The wind had dropped and it looked like it would be a cold night with no low cloud to help keep the day's warmth close to the ground. An endless stream of cars and trucks swished past in the growing darkness and Baddó squinted at his phone to punch in the numbers.

It rang only once before it was answered, and there was a moment's silence before anyone spoke.

"Hello?"

"Jóel Ingi? This is Jón and we need to speak. I have something you want but it's going to cost you."

There was a moment's silence as the passing traffic roared in his ears and rocked the car.

"What for? Why are you calling me?"

"I know Sonja and I can retrieve what you're looking for — at a price."

"How do I know you're not stringing me along? How do I know this isn't bullshit?"

Baddó sighed. "I know about Sonja, and I know about personal.is. Hinrik contracted me to do some investigation on your behalf, but you can forget Hinrik. I'm the professional; you deal with me now."

"But I'd already paid Hinrik," Jóel Ingi protested, a plaintive tone in his voice.

Baddó wanted to laugh. "That's between you and Hinrik, but I have a feeling Hinrik will be busy elsewhere for a while."

"What do you want?"

326

"I want five million, right now."

"Cash? I can't get that much money in cash."

"You can get it in euros, so do it. Five million is thirty-two thousand euros. Let's call it thirty thousand for cash, shall we?"

"Twenty thousand is the best I can do. But you have the . . . ?" Jóel Ingi asked and Baddó wanted to punch the air with glee.

"Make it twenty-five thousand and I'll make sure that what you don't want seen doesn't see the light of day. Understood?"

There was another long silence as the roar of the wind died down.

"You have the computer, then? I want that laptop handed back to me."

Baddó thought fast and wondered what was so special about the computer. "It stays with me. You pay for it to stay safe — and for me to stay safe as well. You shit on me and I'll do the same to you. It works both ways."

"I'll need to get the money together. I can't do it straight away. And I need to see the laptop."

"Of course," Baddó said coldly. "You wouldn't want anyone to rip you off, would you? Give me an hour. Call me on this number then," Baddó ordered, and stabbed the red button.

Ívar Laxdal seemed to fill the whole of the detectives' coffee room. Gunna, Eiríkur and Helgi sat around the table as Ívar waited expectantly.

"Gísladóttir, Eiríkur and Helgi. Well, Gunnhildur?" he invited.

"The woman who was pulling the stunts at the Gullfoss and a few other hotels is Hekla Elín Hauksdóttir. She calls herself Sonja as her business name and advertises on personal.is and a few other places, as far as I've been able to find out, such as classified ads in the press. She's thirty-three years old and lives out at Kjalarnes with her husband and three children. One's his, the younger two are theirs. She's an actress, it seems, or was. Until a year or so ago they were living in Akranes; they lost their house when the bank foreclosed and managed to swing this old place instead. The husband is a decent enough character, a good bit older, disabled in an accident a few years ago when he lost his job."

Ívar Laxdal nodded. "And she's in an interview room right now, is she?"

"No, we haven't tracked her down yet, but as we have her address, phone numbers and the number of her car, I don't expect it'll be long. According to her husband, she was out today recording an advert at a studio somewhere. That's what seems to be left of her theatrical career: dubbing voices onto cartoons and reading ads for the radio."

"Fine. What else? You didn't bring me down here just for that, did you?"

"Far from it. What did you get from Siggi at comms, Eiríkur?"

"Mister 017, who we are certain is Hróbjartur Bjarnthórsson, has been in touch with these numbers

328

so far and we're keeping a watch on his phone," he said, passing across a sheet of paper. "He's been pretty quiet most of the time. It seems he switches on his phone, makes a call, and then switches it off again, mostly from around the same area. But today the phone has been switched on all morning and these are the numbers called."

Eiríkur tapped the sheet of paper and circled a group of numbers in red.

"This is an unknown mobile that Dísa over there at the drug squad believes is one of several used by a dealer called Hinrik Sørensen," Gunna said. "These two here are the mobile and home phone number of Jóel Ingi Bragason," she said, her finger on the paper. "Both calls were made less than an hour ago."

Ívar Laxdal's mighty eyebrows knitted. "Jóel Ingi? That snot-nosed young pup who lost his laptop and expected us to find it for him?"

"That's the one. Either Baddó has been shadowing our investigation of what happened at Hotel Gullfoss when Jóhannes Karlsson kicked the bucket, or else he'd already been digging into it. Wherever we look, someone has been there first or right after us, normally calling himself Jón and telling people he's in security."

"He has been in security," Helgi laughed and the smile disappeared from his face. "He spent seven years in prison in Kaunas, so he should know a thing or two about security."

"You're sure about this?" Ívar Laxdal growled.

"When I visit Sonja's victim in Akureyri, who's already been in touch? The mysterious Jón, who we have identified from CCTV at the Gullfoss as being Hróbjartur Bjarnthórsson, aka, Bigfoot Baddó," Gunna continued. "We grill Magnús Sigmarsson, then he vanishes. That points to the mysterious Jón, who it seems had already pumped other hotel staff members for information. We start to get close to Jóel Ingi and, hey presto, Jón/Baddó again. He is now, without doubt, our prime suspect for Magnús Sigmarsson's murder, as well as the manslaughter of Ásmundur Ásuson."

"And now we have Jóel Ingi implicated in the mix as well," Ívar Laxdal mused, elbows on the table and his chin resting on his hands as one stubby forefinger tapped out a slow rhythm against the other hand. "What do you want to do, Gunnhildur?" he asked suddenly.

"Probably what you won't let me do."

"Which is?"

"Haul Jóel Ingi Bragason down here and make him sweat. There's something very suspicious about that young man."

Ívar Laxdal smiled in a way that made his features light up under those heavy black brows. "You can do what you feel necessary, Gunnhildur, as far as I'm concerned. It's a serious case and we can't pussyfoot around with half measures. But there's one piece of advice I'd like to give you before you approach the ministry."

"And that is?"

"There'll be an election soon. This year, or next at the latest. As they'll be back out in the cold soon enough anyway, you can piss off the politicians as much you like. But don't upset too many officials without good reason, as they'll still be running things when we have new people in charge."

A phone call to a friend in the car trade told her the mud-coloured Hyundai was more than likely a stolen vehicle. The man with the scarred face was certainly not the Elma Líf Sævarsdóttir the car was registered to, and she guessed that there was something shady that linked Jóel Ingi, Hinrik the Herb and the desperate-looking man with his face covered in stitches.

With Jóel Ingi's trail gone cold, she told herself that she could pick it up later, either from his home or the ministry, and the tracker she'd discreetly stuck inside a wheel arch meant that his trail could be picked up whenever she felt like it. The instinct developed during years spent in uniform told her the Hyundai would be worth tailing in the meantime. This time she was ready. The brown car toiled up the slope and the venerable Renault, sharp and well looked after in spite of its age, was quick enough to keep up at a respectable distance.

She followed it through the thickening afternoon traffic as it seemed to go aimlessly through the city and out the far side towards Kópavogur before joining the main road to Hafnarfjördur. She watched the Hyundai make a slow circuit of the harbour area, encountering locked dock gates several times before it occurred to her that the driver was lost.

Finally it stopped at the side of the road in an industrial area, parking between a couple of trucks outside a row of small fish-processing plants. The little factories were deserted, the day's work over by mid-afternoon and the staff long gone, but leaving tubs of waste outside for the gulls to peck and gnaw at. She wrinkled her nose at the aroma of stale fish that the breeze brought and closed the car window as she parked a hundred metres behind the Hyundai and waited.

After a while it occurred to her that she might be in for a long wait, telling herself it could be uncomfortable sooner rather than later. There were no lights to be seen in the Hyundai and she wondered what the driver was doing. She slipped out of the car, zipped her parka up to the neck and pulled on a baseball cap that she hoped would hide her face, walking away from the Hyundai and taking a short cut between two buildings into the street higher up, conscious that this could be a mistake. The man could decide to move off at any moment, leaving her unable to follow quickly enough.

Walking briskly around the corner, she completed a circuit by striding back towards her car, taking care to stay on the opposite side of the road, thereby giving her the opportunity for only a very quick view of the Hyundai, where she was relieved to see its occupant with closed eyes, the seat laid back as far as it would go.

Satisfied for the moment, she walked smartly back to the Renault, looking about her rapidly to see if she'd been observed, and side-stepped between two shipping containers. Dubious about the cold, but left with no choice, out of the wind and out of sight, she unzipped, squatted quickly and emerged relieved a moment later to take her place in the Renault, where she switched on the radio, told herself that she was now good for the rest of the day, and waited for the Hyundai's occupant to wake up and move off.

Ægir Lárusson was unamused and Már Einarsson was visibly agitated at his side.

"Jóel Ingi Bragason is on sick leave. He was taken ill last night."

"So he's in hospital, is he?" Gunna asked. "Which one?"

"I don't know," Már said stiffly. "As far as I'm aware, he's at home."

"What's his address?"

"I can't tell you that. It's confidential."

"Oh, come on. It's not going to be that hard to find out where the man lives. You may as well tell me and save me going through the national register."

Már looked at Ægir, who gave the tiniest nod of assent. Már wrote a few lines on a notepad and tore the top sheet off, handing it to her.

"Classy address," Gunna said. Standing behind her, Helgi heard his phone chime and she registered him raising an eyebrow as he read the text message. "I'm wondering what does Jóel Ingi's sudden illness have to do with this mysterious laptop that you were so anxious about a few days ago?"

Már looked anxious and flashed a glance at Ægir, who forced a smile. "Officer, I don't know exactly why you are suddenly so interested in a matter you were asked to investigate some time ago. It's not as if the police were particularly enthusiastic then."

Gunna held his gaze as he tried to stare her down. "I don't know either. But I'm not a great believer in coincidences. I get the impression that Jóel Ingi is out of his depth and that neither of us has the full story. I certainly don't believe the ministry has been entirely open on this. Far from it, in fact. I'd say that we've been asked to clear up your mess, but without being given the correct information."

Ægir frowned. "There are things I'm not at liberty to divulge."

"That's up to you. But without the facts, there's not a lot we can do. On the other hand, it may well be that the ministry's security is compromised. Tell me, what does Jóel Ingi do here, exactly?"

Már coughed. "He works with me. We're part of a team that carries out analysis and prepares digests for policy development."

"Tell me that's more than watching foreign TV news reports?"

"Of course it is," Már snapped.

"So he, and you, are dealing with sensitive or confidential data?"

"Naturally."

"Like what?"

Már looked at Ægir, who pursed his lips and shook his head. "Where is this going, officer?" he asked wearily.

"What I'm after is some kind of background information that could tell me if Jóel Ingi is being pressured or even blackmailed. What kind of information is he working with?"

"Trade figures, mainly. Analysis of exports from countries that compete with our industries. That's his main role at present."

"What about his personal life? He's married? Children?"

"He's married, no children."

"Hobbies? Activities? Clubs? Politics? Friends?"

Ægir sat back and his eyebrows twitched. Már looked blank. "He works out a lot. Fitness is important to him. When I go to the gym, he's normally either there already or on the way. Politics? I don't think he takes an interest. At least, not an active one. He doesn't have many friends, as far as I know, not after he left the bank."

"What? Explain, will you?"

"He used to be a legal adviser at one of the main banks before the crash. He left the bank about six months before everything went wrong, so I don't know if he'd seen it coming or what, but he got out and applied for a post here instead. I gather most of his friends were in the banking sector and pretty much cut him off after the crash."

Gunna looked squarely at him without saying anything until Már's hands fluttered. "I really don't know why. I suppose they resented the fact that he'd managed to get out with clean hands and a few million stashed away. There were never any questions about his role at the bank. He wasn't called in by the winding-up committee. As far as I'm aware, he came away from it with his hands clean."

"And his personal life?"

Már shrugged. "I really don't know. He doesn't have close friends. I suppose I'm the closest thing he has to one," he said haltingly. "Although . . ." he tailed off and paused.

"Although what?" Gunna prompted.

"I'm not sure his marriage is all that stable. He's devoted to Agnes, but it's quite a stormy relationship. They can both be pretty volatile and I've seen them practically fighting one minute and in each others' arms the next."

"Understood," Gunna said, making notes before turning to Ægir Lárusson. "This laptop you're so keen to retrieve. What's on it that's so important?"

"You're not security cleared. All I can say is that it contains sensitive data."

"Just who is going to be inconvenienced if this sensitive stuff leaks out? Jóel Ingi? You? Someone higher up?"

Ægir scowled and his face flushed. "I'm not at liberty to say. All I can say is that we consider it important that this information doesn't fall into the wrong hands."

"And whose hands would those be? The press? Another ministry? The opposition?"

Ægir shoved his chair back. "That's all I have to say," he said abruptly.

As he put the phone down and the panic started to rise again, Jóel Ingi saw his phone flash a second time. While he hoped that it was Agnes calling to heal the rift between them, he knew deep inside that an apology would have to come from him first.

"Hello," he said, answering the call even though his instinct had been to ignore it.

"*Hæ*, my name's Skúli Snædal and I'm a journalist at the *Reykjavík Voice*," he heard and froze. "Hello?" the voice continued. "Hello, is that Jóel Ingi Bragason? Are you there?"

"I'm here," he said after a long pause. Fatigue seemed to have eaten its way deep into his bones as he closed the car door. "I'm sorry. This isn't a good moment. Can it wait until tomorrow?"

"I have an allegation from a foreign human rights group that four asylum seekers arrived in Iceland in 2009, but that they weren't processed in the usual way and were instead immediately put on a flight leaving the country. Can you confirm that this was the case?"

Jóel Ingi heard a buzzing in his ears that almost drowned out the sound of the man's voice. He felt a sense of removal, as if he were looking down on himself from above.

"It's not something I can comment on," he said.

"That's a shame, as we have been given copies of emails that appear to have been sent from your ministry email address, implicating several officials and confirming that a transfer could take place at Keflavík airport, where these four people were placed on a military flight leaving that same evening. Are you telling me this didn't happen?"

He sighed. "I'm sorry. I really can't comment."

"Was the minister aware of this?"

"I told you, I can't comment. Listen, I'm not well. I'm on sick leave right now. You need to contact the ministry about this, not me."

"I'll have to say that you declined to comment, and that you're implicated personally."

"You need to speak to Ægir Lárusson. Do you want his personal numbers?"

She almost missed the Hyundai move off and had to accelerate hard to keep it in sight as it rounded the corner. She bullied her way into the road, ahead of a pickup truck whose driver flashed his lights angrily at her, and put her foot down in spite of the icy road, praying that the nails in the tyres would keep her from sliding. As darkness fell, the frost accompanied it. The air was so cold that her first breaths almost hurt and the road under the Renault's wheels crackled as the water on it became glassy ice.

Her eyes were glued to the Hyundai's lights as she watched it drive along the Hafnarfjördur seafront before taking the road back towards Reykjavík. With two cars between them, she waited at the lights, pulling away fast and taking note as the mud-coloured car swung sharply right and drove through yet another industrial area, this one a series of workshops and offices. As the car stopped on the forecourt of an empty workshop, she cruised past to the end of the road, did a quick U-turn and came slowly back, stopping outside a pizza place in the middle of an untidy knot of badly parked cars.

She reached down and picked up a small pair of binoculars from the pocket in the door, confident that she couldn't be made out by the Hyundai's driver as she focused them on the brown car and its occupant, his elbow resting on the wide-open driver's window as he scanned the road. Her heart beat faster as a second car pulled up alongside it, and she recognized the black Audi, and Jóel Ingi getting out of it to walk towards the Hyundai.

She desperately wanted to know what words passed between them, as well as what was in the package that went from Jóel Ingi's hand and disappeared inside the brown car. A moment later Jóel Ingi was gone. The Audi was speeding away, too fast for her to follow, but his trail could be picked up later.

She wondered what was going on as the Hyundai headed out of town in the steady stream of rush-hour traffic, northwards past Mosfellsbær, and she decided that anything north of the tunnel under Hvalfjördur would be far enough.

Staying just far enough behind to keep the mud-brown car in sight and trying to keep at least one car between the two of them, she saw it overtaken by a grey van as it slowed and pulled off the road into a lay-by occupied only by a dormant roads-department bulldozer. She slowed down as well, dropping her speed low enough to see the driver hunched over the wheel, his phone to his ear.

She kept her speed as low as she could, watching the mirror for the brown car's reappearance, but she saw nothing. She decided to give up, and at the Kjalarnes turnoff she slowed down and pulled into the middle lane, disappointed that she'd wasted the best part of an hour on a futile trip out of town and determined to get back to the job of tailing Jóel Ingi, which had now been made more difficult by the fact that she would have to remain out of sight.

She stopped at the Kjalarnes petrol station, pulling up by the pump and taking the opportunity to fill the car's tank. Inside the shop she bought a newspaper, a sandwich and a bottle of water as a belated lunch, deciding to take a break, but was surprised to see the mud-brown Hyundai appear on the forecourt. Instead of coming into the shop, the car nosed up to the drive-by service window, where the driver, his face partly hidden by a hood, ordered a hot dog and a bottle of fizz, which were handed to him by the bored boy behind the counter.

As the car pulled away, she dropped her sandwich onto the seat beside her and followed, trying to keep the same discreet distance as before. This time the man with the scarred face took a detour around Kjalarnes, stopping for a few minutes at the far end of the village with the engine running as the driver stared at an old house a little way outside the settlement. After a few minutes, he turned back the way he had come to the main road and, worryingly, again headed north. With the tunnel entrance approaching, she decided the chase had to be cut short, and slowed down in order to use the turnoff for the old Hvalfjördur road the tunnel had replaced for a U-turn. The Hyundai did the same. Keeping it as far ahead as she could without losing sight, she watched it slow down and turn off.

She wondered why he was going along a road that was only occasionally cleared of snow and which would lead to nowhere but a few isolated farms and summer cottages. Deciding that the Hvalfjördur road would be too much for the Renault, she watched the Hyundai's lights disappear into the distance, before turning back to town, and the job in hand, wondering about the significance of the old house at Kjalarnes.

Gunna rubbed her eyes with the heel of each hand. She shook herself and went through a list of numbers. Frustrated, she called a number and was rewarded with a "this number is not available" message, with no invitation to leave a message of her own. She drummed the desktop with her fingertips and instead dialled Pétur Steinar Albertsson's home number, listening to it ring a dozen times. She was about to put the phone down when there was a click.

"Er . . . hello?"

"Hello, my name's Gunnhildur and I'm with the city police force. I'd like to speak to either Pétur or Hekla, if either of them are home."

"There's nobody here. Just me."

"That's a shame. Are they going to be long, do you know?"

"I dunno."

"Is that Sif I'm speaking to?"

"Yeah, that's me," was the surprised response. "Who are you?"

"I'm Gunnhildur. I really need to speak to your dad or to Hekla. It's important."

"I don't know where they are. Why don't you call the mobile?"

"I would if I had the number."

"Wait . . ."

Gunna drummed the desk with growing impatience as a muffled conversation could be heard in the distance before Sif returned.

"You there?"

"I'm here."

Sif reeled off seven digits and Gunna wrote them down and repeated them.

"Is that your dad's phone or Hekla's number?"

"It's hers. Dad never goes anywhere, so he says he doesn't need one."

"Who's there with you, Sif? You said you were alone."

"My friend," she retorted. "What's it to do with you, anyway?"

"No reason. Just wondering. Thanks, bye."

She quickly dialled the number Sif had given her, comparing it to the communications division's list as it rang, nodding as she recognized it as one of the numbers Baddó had called that afternoon.

"*Hæ*. This is Hekla. I can't take your call right now, so leave a message. Thanks."

Gunna put the phone down in disgust.

"Helgi, why the hell do people never answer their mobile phones?" she demanded.

"Beats me. My kids tried that for a while, not answering when I called."

"Do they still do it?"

"Nope. I told them that as I was paying for their phones, if they didn't answer when I called they could pay for their own airtime. Why? Laufey being awkward?"

"Not at all. It's Hekla Elín that I'm trying to get hold of. No reply, blast her. Are you off?"

"I am, and so should you be, chief. It's getting late."

"I've a good mind to drive out to Kjalarnes and sit by her front door until she turns up."

"You should be going home." Helgi said firmly, snapping his glasses into their case. "It's late and we've been here since we were called to the hospital at some ungodly hour of the morning. Remember?"

"Was that really today? It feels like it was weeks ago."

"It feels like I've spent a week on that idiot Hólmgeir Sigurjónsson's paperwork, and I have to say I feel I've done the community a service having locked that waste of skin up."

"Yeah. Until a magistrate pats him on the back and tells him not to do it again."

"Well, there is that, I grant you. But if you're going out to Kjalarnes, then I'll go with you."

Gunna shook her head. "Go home, Helgi. Let's pack it in for the day. I've asked for a uniformed patrol to run out to Kjalarnes a couple of times tonight to check there's nothing untoward going on there."

"Why's that?"

"I don't know. I've been trying to track the bloody woman down all day and haven't been able to get hold of her, and I can't help feeling there's some part of all this that we haven't figured out yet."

Helgi pulled on his coat. "Come on then," he prompted.

"Come on, what?"

"I'm not going home until you're out of the building, so will you get a move on, please?"

Gunna stood up and stretched, knotting her fingers and cracking her knuckles. "All right. You sound like my dad," she said. "In at seven?"

"Yeah. That'll do me."

"You can be early and go with Eiríkur if you want."

"Why?"

"He's tagging along with the drug squad tomorrow for an early start. Rather him than me."

Jóel Ingi parked the Audi behind Katrín's Saab and looked across the snow-filled garden at the basement flat's windows. A dim light was shining from one window and he could see the flickering of a television behind the curtains. Still nervous about being followed, he locked the car and looked about him before making his way past the garden gate, which was permanently open in a drift of snow, and knocking at the door.

He had left his coat in the car and it was cold. He shivered, rubbing his hands to warm them, and was about to go back to the car when the door opened a crack. An indistinct face and some dark hair that didn't belong to Katrín could be seen in the narrow opening.

"Hello?"

"*Hæ*. I'm looking for Katrín. This is her place, isn't it?"

"Yeah, but she's not here at the moment. I'm not sure when she'll be back."

"Her car's there."

344

"She can't have gone far if she's not driving. D'you want to give her a call?"

"I don't have a number. I work with her, I was just wondering if she was going to be long?"

The door opened a little wider. "You're Jóel Ingi, aren't you?"

"I am."

This time the door opened fully and a petite girl with a sharp nose and inquisitive eyes looked him up and down.

"You must be Ursula. I saw you at the sushi place we went to the other day."

"You'd best come in. It's freezing out. You want a coffee? Or a beer? You know Katrín talks about you all the time?"

He sat down in the flat's tiny living room and stretched out his legs while Ursula clattered in the kitchen.

"Lived here long?" he asked.

"No. Katrín split up with her guy about the same time as I did with mine, so we're renting this place together for the time being. How long have you known Katrín?"

"I don't know. I've been at the ministry since 2008 and she's been there at least as long. But she's on another floor so it's only recently that I've got to know her."

"At the lunch club?"

Jóel Ingi grinned. "Yeah. Már Einarsson's famous lunch club."

Ursula looked at her watch. "I called her but she's not answering. She'll ring me back when she sees there's been a missed call. She's organized is our Katrín."

The coffee was thick and fragrant, giving him a new rush of alertness.

"Where do you work?"

Ursula looked sour. "I was the accounts manager for a building company until last week."

"New job?"

"I've been made redundant."

"That's a shame."

Ursula shrugged. "That's the way it goes. Last in, first out. Business hasn't been great and they were optimistic when they took me on."

"No other job to go to?"

"Some freelance work, doing people's tax returns and stuff, but not a lot."

"That's a shame," Jóel Ingi repeated, at a loss for anything else to say.

In spite of the coffee having given him a momentary rush, he felt inexplicably drowsy, blaming the heat of the little flat.

"I'd like to go away for a while. I've been in boring jobs for years now and I want to see a little colour, so I might go travelling for a few months, and maybe go back to university in the autumn. That'd be nice." She glanced down to check her phone. "Katrín normally calls back right away."

"Maybe she's busy?"

"Could be . . ."

"Where would you go if you wanted to do some travelling?"

"I don't know. Spain, maybe. Or France."

Jóel Ingi smiled broadly. He liked her already, solid arms and legs in spite of her petite figure, nothing like Agnes's willowy frame.

"Then this could be your lucky day."

Ursula looked at him sharply. "How so?"

"I'm flying to Paris tonight." Jóel Ingi pulled a package out of his coat pocket, put it on the table and spread the notes in a fan. "If we don't go too wild, I reckon that should keep us for at least a year."

She had picked up his trail easily enough, and now she watched Jóel Ingi disappear up the stairs and into departures with the woman on his arm. They were travelling light, hand baggage only. She shrugged. There was nothing more that she could do other than report back. Under the street lamps that lit the car park outside with their harsh glare, she keyed a message into her phone, looking pensively out of the window as the Renault's heater whined and fought to disperse the thin film of frost on the windscreen.

She pulled off her ski hat, massaging her scalp, then prodded gently at the tender part of her face, relieved that it was no more painful than it was. It was close to midnight on a dark, cold night, and she asked herself yet again why she had given up a stable but frustrating job for this life of anti-social hours, awkward clients and unreliable payments. She wasn't expecting a reply until the morning, but the phone on the seat flashed once and hummed briefly.

She read the message, nodded briefly and punched in a one-word reply before putting the car into gear. It was rolling forward when the phone flashed a second time and she stopped to look at the message. Her eyebrows rose as she read it, before heading for the main road back to Reykjavík.

CHAPTER
SEVEN

Wednesday

Gunna slept badly and was on her feet long before the alarm started to buzz to the muffled sound of Drífa retching in the bathroom, the faint but unmistakable sound carrying along the corridor of the silent house. Her thoughts immediately went back to Gísli as she looked at the ceiling in the darkness, and how — or if — he would resolve things with his two expectant mothers when he came home in a few weeks' time.

Laufey was asleep and Gunna decided to trust her to get up on time and head off to school. She listened for a second at the door of what had once been Gísli's room, where Drífa had settled herself like a nesting hen.

She pulled on her coat and padded into the bedroom, where Steini lay on his side with one hand under his head and the other stretched out as if looking for her. Gunna sat on the edge of the bed and put out a hand to tickle his neck, her fingernail rasping briefly against his bristles. He muttered and shifted, his eyes still closed. She leaned forward and planted a gentle kiss on his cheek.

"Wakey, wakey, big boy," she whispered.

Steini's eyes opened wide in a flash. There was a brief look of disappointment as he took her in, sitting next to him fully dressed and with her coat on.

"You're up early."

"I know. Couldn't sleep, so I decided to get up."

"You could have given me a poke. I'd have told you stories until you fell asleep." He yawned, sitting up and sliding one hand under her coat.

"But that would have ended up being more than a story, wouldn't it? And then you wouldn't have got much sleep either."

"It's a tough call, but I'd have done it for you."

"You're a saint." Gunna grinned. "There's fresh coffee. The girls are still asleep. All right?"

Steini nodded and flexed his shoulders. "Any idea how long Drífa's going to be staying?"

"None at all. She's a pain, but I don't have the heart to send her home."

"You're all heart," Steini grunted. "Beneath that tough exterior . . ."

"Hides a woman who eats broken glass for breakfast. Yeah, I know. Even Helgi and Eiríkur have started saying that now."

"I'm doing a job in Keflavík today. Nothing difficult, but it'll take a while and I'll probably be back late. How about you?"

Gunna sighed and Hekla, Baddó and Jóel Ingi all came back to her. "No idea. This is a tough one and I've no idea how long it'll take, not that there isn't pressure to get it sorted out quickly. It doesn't help that there's a government department involved, but I shouldn't have told you that."

"I didn't hear a word." Steini swung his legs out of bed as Gunna stood up. "I'll see you when I see you, then?"

"That's about it." She blew him a kiss from the doorway. "See you tonight."

The cold north wind had strengthened overnight, bringing with it cold air that was almost painful to breathe and which stung her face as she hurried to the car. The car's wheels jerked and initially refused to move, held in place by the ice that had formed around them as the ground froze. A healthy foot on the pedal broke the grip with a crack, and the car crunched through puddles and pools that had formed overnight. Fortunately the road had already been gritted, as Gunna could feel the brittle hardness of the road surface instead of the slush of the past week.

Being early was a way of beating the rush hour and Gunna found the usual hour's drive pleasantly shortened as she parked in the yard behind Hverfisgata police station, next to Ívar Laxdal's hulking black Volvo. She wondered just how early she would have to be to get to work before the boss. The chance to ask the question came and went as she encountered him on the stairs.

"Were you planning to bring that insolent yuppie in for questioning today?" he asked.

"That was the plan, although there's other stuff that's closer to the top of the priority pile, like getting hold of Hróbjartur Bjarnthórsson before he does any more damage."

"Just as well, because Jóel Ingi skipped the country last night."

"What? Where did he go?"

"Initially, Paris. Where he's gone from there, who knows?"

Gunna fumed. "Hell and damnation. I should have had him headed off"

Ívar Laxdal dropped one of his rare smiles. "Don't worry about that. He was travelling on a service passport, so it's unlikely that anyone at Keflavík would have even checked someone like that. He'll be in trouble if he tries to use it again, though. Jóel Ingi may be an abrasive young man, but he's no fool. He'll know better than to do that."

"So what the hell can we do about him?"

Ívar Laxdal stopped on the top step and paused before heading along the passage to the office he rarely seemed to use. "Nothing for the moment, Gunnhildur. Nothing at all. He's not our problem any more. I have a feeling he'll show up sooner or later, and his absence may turn out to be for the best," he said, turning and walking away with one finger in the air. "Keep me informed, would you?"

She was awake early, munching toast and looking out of the window to check the weather. The laptop open in front of her showed the old house at Kjalarnes that the man with the scarred face had been so interested in, and after a few false starts going between the online phone book, mapping websites and the national registry, she managed to tie the address to names.

"Pétur Steinar Albertsson. Who the hell are you?" she wondered. "Or Hekla Elín Hauksdóttir? Which one of you nice people has done something to warrant being watched by that nasty piece of work?"

A search engine drew a blank when presented with Pétur Steinar's name. But Hekla Elín Hauksdóttir showed a handful of results and she trawled slowly through them. Amazed at what the internet could store by way of obscure information, from sources as far apart as a school reunion page to the TV and radio listings guide, she quickly built up a picture of Hekla Elín Hauksdóttir and her patchy career as an actress and more recently as a voice-over artist. The only photograph she could find of Hekla Elín was one showing a young actress as part of the cast of *Othello*, standing between a well-known actor made up for the title role and a short man in a doublet and hose.

". . . as Othello, Gústav Freysteinn Bóasson as Iago and Hekla Elín Hauksdóttir played Desdemona in her first leading role," the caption read.

Looks like her only leading role, she thought, moving on to Facebook, where she was presented with a complete blank for Pétur Steinar, as there was no entry for that name. Hekla Elín's name showed up, but with an anonymous avatar and an almost blank page. She saw that Hekla Elín had a relatively small number of friends, with an accessible list. She clicked and scrolled through them, looking for potential family members and alighting on Sif Pétursdóttir as a candidate. Her phone began to hum a discreet, insistent tune and she looked at the display and answered quickly.

"Yes?"

"Can you talk?"

"Sure."

"Where are you?"

"At home. It's not even seven yet," she said. "Job done. It's not as if I could have followed your man into the departure lounge," she said. The man on the other end of the line sounded harassed. His usual manner, a combination of abrasive and jovial, peppered with off-colour jokes, had disappeared. "Problems?" she asked.

"And how," he replied. "Listen. This has to finish today. It's of paramount importance that you finish the brief today, as quickly as possible. That machine has to disappear. You get my meaning?"

"This isn't the same brief," she said doubtfully. "This isn't about who goes where and who they talk to, is it?"

"Call it what you will. Just put in your invoice as soon as the job is done and I'll square it."

"I'll do what I can," she said, listening to the laboured breathing that gave away his impatience. "But I don't have a lot to work on and I'm not promising anything."

"Just get it done. I don't care how. All right?" the voice said sharply and the phone went dead in her hand, leaving her to finish her toast and replay the conversation back in her mind, mulling over the option of simply sending in an invoice and calling an end to an

354

impossible job before she went back to the computer screen and Sif Pétursdóttir's family pictures.

"Ah," she said to herself, clicking through them. "So that's what you look like now."

The tapping on the window of a bare branch of one of the stunted trees outside roused Baddó from a deep sleep. He was awake instantly and a hand went to his face as he awoke, fingering the drying scabs that had hardened overnight. His jaw still ached and he washed painkillers down with a gulp of water so cold it was practically ice.

He had slept soundly, a relief after two days of running on adrenaline and keeping himself out of sight. Peering in the tiny mirror over the kitchen sink, he could see that his face looked no worse. The cut had lost some of its livid colour and wasn't quite so obvious, not that anyone looking him in the face was going to miss it. He wondered if his beard would grow back where the cut had sliced his cheek into ribbons.

Baddó stretched and looked out of the window at the snow-covered valley beyond. Although barely more than a few kilometres from the new main road, the summer house hadn't been easy to reach. The Hyundai had been left by the side of the road on a bare stretch of ground where the driven snow would be carried off by the wind, although he was certain that a drift would now have collected in its lee. The hard part had been struggling through the snow, which had been untouched since the last person had been there in the autumn. He had been on the point of giving up and returning to the car when he finally found the place with the key hanging on a string inside the outer of the two doors, exactly where it had been kept the last time he'd been there more than twenty years earlier.

He had been exhausted and realized that hypothermia had been setting in as he fought through the snow. It had been bitterly cold, clear weather, while a stately dance was played out by the green and white bands of the northern lights shining on the crust of snow, undisturbed but for the tracks of a fox that had sniffed at the deserted cottage and gone elsewhere to hunt for food.

The microwave pinged and Baddó again privately thanked a God he had no belief in that the electricity supply hadn't been cut off. The instant meal from the freezer was a welcome first hot meal in a couple of frantic days, and he flipped through a six-month-old newspaper as he forked up what the packet claimed were Cantonese-style noodles with chicken. Looking out of the window, he wondered whether to stay for another day to recuperate, admitting to himself that he was deeply tired. The attack and everything after it had taken its toll and his whole body ached, from his head to his feet.

He wondered about the men who had attacked him and if the one he had bottled had been badly hurt. He sincerely hoped so and his thoughts turned to whoever had sent those slack-jawed lowlifes to teach him a lesson. Turning things over in his mind, he decided there were a few candidates: people he had upset in the past who had long memories and harboured grudges.

He smiled to himself, feeling the stiffness in his face. He could be patient and nurture a grudge as well as anyone.

With a start he remembered the fat envelope that Jóel Ingi had unwillingly handed over, and with his mouth still full of Cantonese-style noodles, he hunted through the zipped-up inside pocket of his coat and placed the package on the table in front of him, smiling to himself. He swallowed, pushed the remainder of the instant meal aside and tugged at the flap, pulling out a wad of notes. He thumbed the end of the first fat wad and froze.

He snapped off the rubber bands and lifted the 100-euro note on the top. Beneath it was a blank piece of paper, and beneath that was another. Apart from one note on top and another at the bottom, the whole of both wads of notes, the agreed 20,000 euros, was worthless, neatly guillotined paper.

Baddó sat back. One eyelid twitched violently. His instinct was to hammer the table with his fist and turn it into matchwood, but instead he took one deep breath after another. Jóel Ingi was a fool if he thought he could cheat Baddó. Bigfoot had a reputation and he would live up to it. Revenge would be administered and it would be harsh, but it would have to wait. He forced himself to think straight. The laptop that both Jóel Ingi and Hinrik had been anxious to find had to be valuable. It was time to pay Sonja a visit.

The man who hammered on the broken door looked like he would hardly fit through it, and Eiríkur was happy for him to go in front.

"Hinni! Open the door, man! It's the law come for a chat," he yelled through the letterbox, then went back to rapping on the door's complaining timbers with a heavy set of knuckles. Behind him two more officers waited for the door to open, while Eiríkur brought up the rear.

A shadow appeared behind the single remaining glass panel and Hinrik's bony form opened the door an inch, letting it stop on the safety chain.

"What?"

"Hinrik Sørensen? City police, as you well know, you being an old friend of ours."

"What do the police want with us law-abiding citizens at this ungodly hour of the day?"

"Don't talk shit, Hinrik. Open the door," the first officer repeated, as Hinrik obediently closed the door, rattled the chain inside and opened the door wide.

The three drug squad officers, two bulky men and a woman with a healthy outdoors look to her red cheeks, swept past and the first one in secured Hinrik against the wall and kept him there.

"Any company, Hinrik?"

He smiled as the sound of the toilet flushing loudly reverberated through the apartment. The bathroom door opened and Ragga appeared in the doorway, eyes bleary but with a look of quiet satisfaction on her face.

"Good grief, cover it all up will you?" the first officer told her as the checked shirt loosely wrapped around her flapped open. He looked back at his colleague and shook his head, knowing that anything incriminating they might have found in the flat had just been consigned to the sewer, while Ragga grinned in delight.

"Sorry, boys," she crowed, looking over her shoulder as she strode towards the bedroom. "I was caught short. Couldn't wait a second longer. You know how it is."

Two of the drug squad officers set about searching the living room, while one of them sat with Ragga and Hinrik, feigning nonchalance as he stared from under his heavy eyelids at Eiríkur, who watched the professionals make a thorough job of it, even though they already knew there was nothing to be found.

"Clean as you like," one of them grudgingly admitted once the search was complete. "Right, then, Ragga, my darling," the senior man decided. "You can come with us while we take a look around the bedroom and my colleague can search your knicker drawer. You'd best stay here, Hinrik, so my friend here can have a quiet word with you."

Hinrik looked taken aback, confused at the change of direction.

"What's going on . . . ?" he asked, surprised at the departure from the usual routine as the drug squad officers left the room and closed the door behind them.

"Where's Baddó, Hinrik?" Eiríkur asked without any preamble.

"Hey, mate. I don't know anyone called Baddó," he protested.

Eiríkur took out his phone and punched in a number. "It's ringing," he said, leaving the phone on the table with the loudspeaker on.

"Where's your phone, Hinrik?" Eiríkur asked.

"I don't know. It's somewhere."

"It's somewhere here, but where?"

Hinrik shrugged and spread his arms wide, as if to demonstrate his innocence, until the door creaked open and one of the searchers came in with a grin on his face. A cheap mobile phone buzzed and flashed in his gloved hand. "Is that one of you sneaky bastards calling our boy's phone?"

"Could be," Eiríkur said, taking the vibrating phone and dropping it in an evidence bag before placing it on the table, where it continued to demand attention until he ended the call on his own phone. A "missed call" message and a sad-faced smiley icon appeared on the phone in the bag.

"That must be Ragga's phone. She's a sloppy cow and she was looking for it last night."

"That's your phone. It's going from here to the lab and don't think for a second that your dabs aren't all over it. Now, back to business. Where's Baddó?"

"Honestly, mate," Hinrik said. "I don't know any Baddó."

"Firstly, I'm not your mate. Secondly, Hróbjartur Bjarnthórsson. He used to go by the name of Bigfoot, and you know him well enough. He's called that phone of yours half a dozen times in the last week. So don't give me bullshit, Hinrik, and don't imagine that this is about a few bags of grass. Baddó's facing a murder charge when we catch up with him and you've a good chance of winding up in the next cell."

Any remaining colour drained from Hinrik's face, which his nocturnal lifestyle had already endowed with a pasty pallor.

"What's he done?" Hinrik croaked, his throat left dry by the rapidly rising stakes.

"All in good time, Hinrik. All in good time," Eiríkur assured him. "I think you'll be safe cancelling all your appointments for the rest of the day. You and Ragga are both going to Hverfisgata with us for a very detailed chat. But first you'd best tell us where your old pal Baddó has got to."

"I don't know," Hinrik said miserably and Eiríkur could see that for once Hinrik would be happy to talk. "I reckon he's been living with his sister these last few months, since he turned up all of a sudden from the Baltic. But he's been keeping his head down. There are people who have unfinished business with Baddó and he doesn't have too many friends."

"Like Ási Ásu?"

"Don't make me laugh. Ási's a brain-dead dopehead who was still in short trousers when Baddó left the country. There are bigger fish who want to see Baddó's knees broken."

"Such as?"

"Mundi."

"Mundi Grétars, you mean?"

"Among others. Mundi has a long memory."

"Go on," Eiríkur prompted. "A quick history lesson."

Hinrik sighed and grimaced, glancing towards the door. "Mundi had a big deal going on. This was years ago, you remember. You lot busted Mundi's courier.

Mundi lost a ton of cash that went up in smoke and he reckoned Baddó had grassed. Like I said, Mundi never forgets."

"So where is he now?"

"Mundi?" Hinrik cackled. "Mundi's somewhere warm, I reckon. He doesn't get his hands dirty."

"No. Where's Baddó?"

"I guess you've been to María's place. If he's not there, then don't ask me. He's been seeing a woman these last few days, so maybe he's with her? I don't know."

"Name?"

"She's called Ebba. Lives somewhere up the top end of Kleppsvegur. That's all I know."

Eiríkur picked up the phone in its bag from the table and scrolled through the memory.

"Not clever, Hinrik. Just as well you didn't erase the call log," he told him. "Not that it matters much. Ah, here it is. Ten thirty-six yesterday morning you had a call that lasted just over four minutes. What did you and Baddó have to talk about?"

"Don't know, mate."

"If you call me 'mate' one more time, I'm going to ram this phone so far up your arse, sideways, that your eyes will light up every time it rings. Now stop giving me this bullshit and come clean, unless you want an extra five years on your sentence for obstructing a murder investigation."

Baddó had stopped at Kjalarnes the night before for a quick look around and knew where the house was. This

362

time he stopped at the shop, filled the mud-coloured Hyundai's tank and drank a paper cupful of bitter liquid that tried unconvincingly to pass for coffee. Refreshed by the caffeine and the cold, still morning air, he rolled slowly through the little settlement at Kjalarnes, past the rows of ordered houses to the single old wooden house beyond. An old farm building, he guessed, which had probably been there for years before the rows of silver-grey concrete terraced houses and the new school were built.

Baddó stopped the Hyundai behind a grey 4x4 that looked as if it had been there for a while, using it as a shield while he checked his phone for missed calls.

He punched in Jóel Ingi's number, but ended the call as the voicemail message began. Any message to that miserable young fool would be delivered in person, he decided.

The thought gave him a warm feeling, so much so that he found himself dreaming and almost missed the thickset man emerging from the house. Baddó sat up and paid attention, watching the place keenly. The man limped over to an old blue Land Rover by the door and started it with a cloud of white smoke before making his way back indoors. A minute later the man re-emerged, shepherding two small children into the back of the car, strapping them in carefully and putting a crutch inside with them.

Baddó hunched forward, pretending to be engrossed in his phone as the Land Rover chugged up the slope past him and into the distance.

* * *

"I've had the ministry on the phone twice already, and the National Commissioner wanting to know what the hell's going on," he said, making his way across the car park as Gunna strode along at his side, trying to match his pace. She had left Eiríkur with Hinrik in an interview room, with instructions to be as tough on him as the law would allow.

"I have the closest links I've been able to find to Hróbjartur Bjarnthórsson so far being booked in right now. Either that skinny deadbeat knows where he is, or else he knows someone who does, and we need to beat it out of him," Gunna said. "Is the ministry getting its knickers in a twist over Jóel Ingi Bragason?"

Ívar Laxdal double-clicked the fob of his car key and the black Volvo on the other side of the yard flashed its lights obediently.

"I'm not sure, to be honest with you, but we're going to find out," he said, his jaw set pugnaciously forward. "Get in," he instructed as the engine whispered into life and Gunna felt herself sink deep into the soft leather of the seats as Ívar Laxdal accelerated out of the yard and into the street.

She wondered why they had driven the few hundred metres to the ministry when walking would have been quicker, but Ívar Laxdal slotted the car into a space marked clearly for the minister's personal use and was halfway up the steps before Gunna was even out of the car.

A pale-faced Már Einarsson was in the lobby, in earnest conversation with a buxom young woman. He looked up as they came through the main entrance, bypassing the reception desk. He hurried over and shook Ívar Laxdal's hand.

"This way, please. Ægir's waiting for us upstairs," he said, ushering them into the lift. Gunna wondered if the drama was being overdone for their benefit, and as the lift closed, she wondered why the plump girl Már had been speaking to so intently a few moments earlier appeared to be so tearful.

Ægir Lárusson didn't keep them waiting. In his own office rather than a meeting room, he glared at Ívar Laxdal, who outstared him back until Ægir's gaze dropped to the desk in front of him.

"I hardly think your missing young man is our problem," Ívar Laxdal said. "Has he done anything illegal that we should know about?"

Ægir's voice was a rasp that almost struck sparks off the stylish steel-framed furniture. "You knew this was important. We requested the highest priority weeks ago, and you did nothing."

"I take it you're referring to this hopeless idea that we might be able to retrieve a computer that some overpaid clown mislaid? It hardly helped that you wouldn't tell us what was so remarkable about this laptop, and it helps even less that the clown who lost it lied about how and where he last saw it."

Ægir's eyes bulged for a moment and he took several deep breaths.

"You need to understand that there has been a considerable escalation in the urgency of the situation," Már said in a business like voice that he clearly hoped would defuse the explosive atmosphere. "We appreciate

365

that you have a heavy workload and that you have devoted resources to this, but the urgency of the situation has become an extremely serious issue, and there have been some rather sudden developments."

Ívar Laxdal leaned back in the fashionable chair, causing the brushed steel tubing to flex alarmingly as his bulk was rearranged.

"Explain," he ordered. "What's gone wrong to make things so urgent? The whole affair is as clear as mud anyway."

Már looked sideways at Ægir, who nodded almost imperceptibly.

"My colleague Jóel Ingi Bragason has disappeared."

"We know that. Has he been reported as a missing person? Or do you mean that you just don't know where he is?"

Már sighed. "Unfortunately we have a very good idea where he is. He's in France, as far as we're aware. At least, he boarded a flight to Paris late last night."

"You couldn't have stopped him?"

"He left without any notice. As he's travelling on a service passport, French immigration had no reason to ask any questions."

"And we didn't know he'd left the country until this morning," Ægir Lárusson said, speaking for the first time and with an expression on his ugly face sour enough to curdle milk at a hundred paces.

"How come?" Gunna broke in, deciding to get between Ívar Laxdal and the two ministry men in their identical suits.

"How come what?"

"I'm wondering why it took you so long to figure out he'd left the country. Why didn't you know last night when he boarded his flight? And how come he was able to travel on a service passport?"

"To start with, the ministry doesn't keep tabs on its staff outside of working hours," Ægir said in an acid voice. "In the second place, Jóel Ingi Bragason was part of the minister's entourage several times last year and as such he was issued with a service passport."

"This story about Jóel Ingi's computer being stolen by a pair of kids," Gunna said. "That's bullshit, right?"

"I couldn't comment," Ægir said, startled at her bluntness, while behind him Már's face told her everything she needed to know.

"So how did he lose it?" Gunna continued. "Did he leave it in a taxi or a bar somewhere? Staked it at cards? Come on, tell me, will you? That way we might be able to find it for you."

Ægir simply shook his head and said nothing. Már opened his mouth to speak and then closed it.

"All right," Gunna went on, watching the pair of them for reactions. "This morning we picked up a lowlife who it seems your precious Jóel Ingi used as a go-between to commission an old friend of ours to track down guess what? A mislaid MacBook and the person who stole it from him, more than likely under some rather startling circumstances. We also have two deaths on our hands that this character is responsible for so far. Am I making myself clear?"

"Abundantly so, Gunnhildur," Ívar Laxdal rumbled. "Maybe now it would be worth your while explaining what's behind all this, and just why the disappearance of a clapped-out laptop has so far resulted in two corpses. Just so you're aware, neither of them went happily."

Ægir opened his mouth but no sound came out, apart from a belated cough, while his face had begun to change from its usual ruddy complexion to something approaching beetroot.

"I think what my colleague is trying to say is that we are not at liberty to tell you any more than we already have, but this is a very serious matter and one that could cause the government a great deal of embarrassment internationally," Már said in a diplomatic tone, graced with a smile that conveyed apology, but no flexibility.

His face stung as he stepped out into the cold air and loped down the slope towards the solitary house along the tracks left by the Land Rover. It was still half dark and there was a single light to be seen in one window. He thought about knocking on the door, but decided against it. This would have to be quick and it would have to be brutal if necessary.

A strip of plastic was enough to deal with the worn lock on the back door, after which he found himself in a workshop with his feet swishing through wood shavings as he made for an outline of light leaking through an ill-fitting door. The moment he opened it, he felt his eyes itch and he swore quietly to himself as he stepped into the hall and went towards the sound of a radio and clattering dishes.

The woman's back was to him as she stood at the sink. Baddó looked at the tall figure with the spiky hair and surveyed the old house's kitchen. He leaned across one of the worktops and clicked a switch, shutting off the radio.

"Æi, Sif, what did you do that for?" The woman said in irritation without looking round.

"Hello, Sonja," Baddó said quietly. "We meet at last."

Hekla spun around and her mouth dropped open. Baddó looked her up and down, appreciating what he saw, a strong young woman with long legs hidden in baggy tracksuit bottoms and a man's white shirt covering plenty in the chest department. A shame to slap her about, he thought. But it has to be done, he reflected with a pang of regret. Business is business.

"Who —?"

He stepped forward rapidly, taking her by surprise, delivering a swift punch to the stomach that knocked the breath out of her and made her gasp for air, while a slap with the back of his hand left her dazed. As she doubled up in shock, he buried a hand in her thick, short hair, pulled her head back and growled. "Not a word. Not a fucking word. Understand?"

Hekla nodded mutely, desperately fighting for breath, which came slowly as she began to pant in panic.

Unexpectedly, Baddó sneezed, swore and glared at the woman in front of him.

"I know who you are, I know what you've been up to. I know where you live and I know where your kids go to school. So don't fuck about. Understood?" Baddó rasped, his eyes watering, and Hekla nodded mutely. "You have something I want. Where is it?"

"The pictures? They're in the camera," Hekla gasped.

Pictures? Baddó wondered, quickly realizing this could be a bonus. "Where are they?"

"In the other room," Hekla said, regaining her breath, and Baddó saw her eyes widen as she looked past him.

"What's going on here?" A cross, youthful voice demanded, and Baddó spun round to see a gawky teenage girl standing in the doorway.

"Sif, don't ask any questions and do as the man says," Hekla instructed, her voice husky and faltering. "Go to the desk in the living room and get the small camera from the bottom drawer, right at the back. Now."

The girl disappeared and Baddó stared into Hekla's eyes, seeing nothing but terror as they listened to Sif rummage in the other room. It seemed like an age before she returned, her hand held out. He took the camera from her and pressed the recall button, scrolling through the pictures with a grin on his face.

"You have been a busy girl, haven't you," he said and Hekla flushed.

"What's this about?" Sif asked, peering through the untidy hair that framed her face.

"Never you mind. Now where's the computer?"

"What computer?" Hekla asked and Baddó grasped a fistful of her white shirt, dragging her face to within a few inches of the ugly cut that ran down his cheek.

"I said, don't mess me about. The one you took off one of your punters a few weeks ago."

"I don't know where it went," Hekla said, desperately trying to avoid telling him that Sif had taken it.

"Stop, will you?" Sif squeaked, stepping forward and stopping as Baddó raised a hand. "It's in Dad's workshop. I put it back yesterday."

"Show me."

Baddó spun Hekla around, twisted one hand hard up behind her back until she gasped in pain, and marched her out of the kitchen and along the passage, bumping against the walls as she stumbled in front of him. In the dimly lit workshop, Sif fumbled among piles of boxes for the laptop case she knew should be there.

"Come on, will you? I don't have all day," Baddó growled, wiping his running nose on the sleeve of his free arm as the other hand held Hekla over a workbench, her face in the sawdust and shavings. "For fuck's sake, there it is," he said in disgust as Sif held out the laptop case, and at the same moment a fat black and white cat emerged from under the bench, purring and calling as it saw people in its domain.

Slackening his grip on Hekla's arm, he reached for the laptop case and aimed a vicious kick at the cat as it stalked amiably towards him, its tail in the air.

"Æi, no, Perla!" Sif screeched, dropping the case and sweeping up the nearest thing she could grab on the bench. Hekla stumbled, steadied herself, and heaved with all her strength just as Baddó let fly with his boot, missing the cat and losing his balance so that he stumbled against the bench.

"You stupid cow," Baddó snarled, snorting through his half-blocked nose, the laptop case clutched in one fist while he raised the other and moved towards the girl. Sif squealed in fright, flung one arm up to cover her face and lashed out wildly with the other hand as Baddó swung, just as he was shaken by another thunderous sneeze.

In his own rarely used office, Ívar Laxdal hunched over a sleek laptop, reading from the screen.

"'According to information that has reached *Reykjavík Voice*, four asylum seekers who arrived in Iceland in May 2009 promptly disappeared and their whereabouts remained unknown until a Dutch human rights group uncovered evidence that all four were executed in Libya later that same year. Following the Libyan revolution, a great deal of documentation from the former regime has come to light, including evidence that the three men and one woman were rendered to Libya in contravention of the United Nations Convention Relating to the Status of Refugees'," he read out.

"What's that about?" Gunna asked, peering at the laptop screen and continuing to read over Ívar Laxdal's shoulder. "'*Reykjavík Voice* has copies of emails purported to have been sent by senior Icelandic officials sanctioning the immediate transfer, without passing through formal immigration channels, of four Libyan nationals who arrived on a scheduled flight from Amsterdam to a military aircraft that departed from Keflavík airport later that night to an unknown destination.' Ívar, is there any truth in this?" Gunna asked. "Is this anything to do with Jóel Ingi and why he's skipped the country?"

"I don't know, Gunnhildur," he said, his face grey and set like rock. "If it's true, there'll be hell to pay in all kinds of ways."

"If it's true, then we should be able to find out, surely. Immigration is part of the force, so can't you demand the truth about it from the airport police?"

"I could. But I'm not sure that I should."

"Come on, surely . . ."

Ívar Laxdal's deep-set dark eyes looked back at her with no visible expression, but his face, sagging and exhausted, told her everything.

"I daren't," he admitted. "This needs to go upstairs. But in the meantime, I have to deal with the ministry, and there's going to be some serious trouble later today if, or rather when, there are questions in Parliament. I have a feeling that this is what that damned lost laptop is all about."

"If this is all public, is there any reason to worry about it? It's not as if we've been looking all that hard for it anyway."

"There hasn't been much to look for," Ívar Laxdal snorted. "If that pompous fool Ægir Lárusson had the sense to tell us the truth at the start, we might have got somewhere. It was always going to be a hopeless task and that's not something I'm going to worry about. The ministry can sort out its own dirty laundry. I'm more interested in you catching up with this hoodlum who's responsible for two murders in our back yard."

Gunna sat on the bone-hard chair that Ívar Laxdal kept in his office, designed to encourage visiting dignitaries not to linger.

"If this is what the droids at the ministry are shitting themselves over, then it's out in the open now. *Reykjavík Voice* is a bit off-centre, and not that many people read it, but all the same, this can't be hushed up now, surely? They even published this on their website in English, so it isn't just a local thing that can be contained."

"If this is the same thing, then you're quite right," Ívar Laxdal agreed. "On the other hand, the ways of civil servants are not to be understood by mere low-grade jobsworths such as ourselves."

"We're civil servants as well," Gunna pointed out, amused by his description of himself as "low grade".

"We are," he agreed. "But we're the kind of civil servants who actually achieve something, as opposed to the type who build themselves little empires and attend conferences while they wait for their pensions to kick in."

His thumbnail scratched at the stubble under the point of his chin as he thought.

"Leave it with me, will you?" he said finally. "I need to talk to upstairs. You have a pet journalist at *Reykjavík Voice*, don't you?"

"I wouldn't call him that, exactly."

"Maybe not, but if you could sound him out discreetly, it wouldn't go amiss."

"It'll have to wait. I can't put off a visit to Sonja any longer."

★   ★   ★

The place seemed deserted. She watched and waited. The mud-brown Hyundai, its sides caked with snow that the driver had barely bothered to brush from the windows, squatted unhappily a hundred metres from the solitary house.

She patted her pockets for her phone and took a can of pepper spray from the glove compartment before walking cautiously down towards the house. She listened for the slightest sound that would tell her that the man with the scarred face was on the move. She gently eased open the back door, the spray can held out in front of her, then slowly dropped it down as she took in Pétur's wrecked workshop.

Sif and Hekla were collapsed against the bench by the wall, while the big man was sitting with his back to the other workbench that filled the middle of the workshop, legs splayed out in front of him and his eyes staring, focused on nothing as a rivulet of saliva leaked down his chin. He was still hugging the laptop case, and it was only when she stepped closer and squatted down in front of him to tug it out of his grasp that she took in the rusty end of the narrow file protruding from the man's temple an inch behind his left eye. A ring of red surrounded it, gradually seeping along the tiny grooves in its surface and staining the metal dull red.

She instinctively put out a hand to touch it, then drew back before looking first from one shocked face to the other, and then to the bench where an assortment of files and chisels with and without their wooden handles had been scattered as Sif had snatched one up in panic.

375

"Are either of you hurt?"

"I don't think so," Hekla said, shakily getting to her feet. "Sif, are you all right, sweetheart?" she asked, stroking the girl's face.

"Is the man dead?"

"I don't know. Come on, let's get out of here."

Hekla put out her hands and pulled Sif to her feet, wrapping an arm around her shoulders as she supported her out of the workshop and back into the house. Back in the workshop the woman knelt in front of the man with the cut face and felt for a pulse in his neck. Satisfied, she pulled out her phone and dialled 112.

"Police and ambulance. I'm at Strandargrund 30 in Kjalarnes," she said in a measured voice. "It's an old house on its own at the far end of the street. There's one casualty with a serious head injury and two people in shock," she said, answering the police operator's questions.

"And your name?"

"Bára Kristinsdóttir," she answered and listened to the moment's pause.

"Bára who used to be in the force at Keflavík?"

She smiled grimly. "Yes, Siggi. That's me."

"All right. In that case you know what to do, don't you? There's an ambulance on its way, but it'll be a while before it gets there."

"I reckon you might need to get the air ambulance out for this one. It's not pretty."

"Fair enough. I'll alert them, but it's the ambulance crew's decision when they get there."

"OK, thanks. I'd best get back to the casualties. You can reach me on this number if you need to between now and the cavalry getting here."

"Fine. Thanks, Bára. It's an F2, so fifteen minutes."

Helgi's communicator buzzed and he looked over at Gunna, his finger on the earpiece.

"You'd better step on it, chief," he said. "F2, and guess where?"

"Kjalarnes? Hell and damnation. I knew I should have got out there last night."

"And there's no siren on this thing, is there?"

"Nope," Gunna said. "You'd better tell them we'll be there in ten."

"Control, zero-two-sixty. Heading for Kjalarnes, estimated ten minutes."

"Thank you, zero-two-sixty. There's a patrol car from the Krókháls station five minutes behind you and the ambulance is right behind that."

Gunna pushed the pedal to the floor, flashed the headlights on and off high beam and left drivers tapping their heads in disgust as they trailed in her wake. She could sense the tension in Helgi's voice: "Any idea what the problem is, control?"

"One serious head injury, two in shock. The helicopter's alerted and the local rescue squad should be there ahead of you."

"Thanks, control. We'll keep you informed," Helgi said, pretending not to be scared as Gunna slowed hard for the turnoff to Kjalarnes, the car's brakes complaining and its rear wheels struggling to grip the icy road.

They bumped down the road to the solitary house, where they found a diminutive blonde woman speaking to an animated figure next to a blue Land Rover. Gunna walked smartly across just as the wail of sirens on the main road was heard in the distance. A heavy 4x4 was already parked by the door.

"Afternoon, Pétur," Gunna said smartly. "Looks like the rescue squad's here. Helgi, check inside, would you? Bára, good to see you. You can tell me later just why you're here. What's happened?"

"One man in the workshop with a stab wound to the left side of the head; two women in shock. They're both in the main bedroom. Looks like one of them grabbed a file and lashed out with it."

"A file?"

"You know. A metalwork file."

"And nobody else has been in or out?"

"No, chief," Bára said, instinctively falling back on habit.

"Will somebody tell me what the hell's been happening?" Pétur said, his frustration boiling over. "I've just come home and been told by this person that I can't go into my own house."

"Well, you heard what the lady said, didn't you?"

Pétur leaned on his crutch and limped towards the door. "I won't be kept out of my own home, damn it," he roared.

"Gunna, the action's at the back of the place. Just get him to go in through the front door and he'll be clear of the crime scene," Bára said quickly as Gunna trotted to catch up with Pétur, taking his arm to steer him towards the front door.

"We'll go in this way, if you don't mind," she said.

Pétur grunted an answer that was neither one thing nor another and pushed his way through the front door, his crutch clattering to the floor.

"Sif! Hekla! Where are you?" he yelled and there was a call in reply from the bedroom. Gunna followed him and watched as he enveloped the girl in his arms, while the woman who was with her clung to him. The puffy, tear-streaked face was unmistakably that of the woman on the Gullfoss Hotel's CCTV, and Gunna felt a surge of relief at having finally found her.

A patrol car bumped down the road and two officers stepped out. Behind them the blue lights of an ambulance flashed and were reflected from the windows of houses further up as doors began to open and people stared at the sudden flurry of activity in the normally quiet village.

"Chopper job, this is," the paramedic said, shaking his head as his colleague monitored Baddó's pulse and breathing. "We need a doctor here before we even try to move this character. What the hell happened, anyway? I've never seen an injury like this," he muttered to Gunna out of the casualty's earshot. "I'm amazed the bastard's even alive."

"That's what I'm hoping to find out," Gunna told him. "It's a first for me as well."

The paramedic muttered into his communicator, looking anxiously at Baddó, whose expression had remained unchanged, his unfocused eyes staring into the distance. Gunna took in the livid cut down his cheek, some of the sutures having come adrift, leaving bloodless gaps in the line of ragged skin.

Gunna cornered Bára outside. "I'm not saying it isn't good to see you, but what the hell's happened? You've got quite a bit of explaining to do. Start by telling me how come you're here, will you?"

"I've been working as an investigator since I left the force. Not long before Christmas I had a request to shadow someone and report back. That person had a meeting last night with the man who's in there with a lump of metal in his head. I'm not sure how it works, or who was blackmailing who, but one thing led to another and, as far as I can make out, I turned up here just as this had happened."

"All right, so who's this mysterious person you've been tailing?"

"I'm not sure I can tell you."

"Come on. You were in the force for long enough to know that doesn't wash."

Bára frowned. "A guy called Jóel Ingi Bragason."

"Who skipped the country last night."

"That's right. I saw him go through departures at Keflavík last night."

"Did you? So who are you working for?"

"That's what I don't think I should tell you."

"Really?"

"Actually I'm not sure who the client is," Bára said. "You may not believe it, but we've only spoken on the phone a couple of times. To start with I thought Jóel Ingi's wife was behind it and that this was a straightforward divorce thing. The client wanted to know where he went and who he met, times and places. Everything was done by email and text, with a report every few days. It was only this last week that I had a couple of calls from the client and found out it was a man; he wanted a closer tail and reports by text four or five times a day."

Gunna nodded slowly. "And where's this famous laptop?"

"Laptop?"

"That's your car there, is it?" Gunna asked, jerking her head towards the Renault. "You want me to look in the boot?"

"You can't do that."

"I can, and we'd better be quick about it," Gunna said, shading her eyes as a black 4x4 with tinted windows sped down the street towards them, sliding to a halt in the snow next to the Land Rover. Two figures in suits tumbled out of it and hurried in through the front door.

Bára clicked the fob of her car key and the lights flashed for a moment. "Go on, then."

Gunna had the case tucked under her arm when the two suits reappeared, chased away from the house and the crime scene by a furious Pétur shaking his fist. They were ushered discreetly past a line of fluttering tape by one of two uniformed officers, who pointed them towards Gunna and Bára.

"Officer, will you hand over that laptop?" Ægir Lárusson demanded, puffing with effort and excitement. "It's government property," he added for good measure, and Bára blanched at the expression on Gunna's face.

"I don't think that's going to be possible, Ægir," she said, keeping her voice calm.

"That laptop is government property," Ægir repeated, this time spluttering with fury.

"As far as I'm aware, this laptop is the personal property of Jóel Ingi Bragason, and right now it's also evidence, so the answer's no. I'm not prepared to hand it over. If you feel it's your department's affair, then you'd best go through the proper channels."

Ægir's fury boiled over. "Hand that fucking thing over, you stupid woman."

That was rich coming from a man half a head shorter than her, Gunna thought, looking down on Ægir Lárusson and wondering if his wife cut his hair especially to emphasize the shining bald spot on top of his head.

Approaching from behind, Már Einarsson whispered in Ægir's ear.

"That woman there," he pointed at Bára. "That woman has been working on the ministry's behalf to recover that laptop, after you and your people couldn't do it."

"Interesting you should say that, as I was about to formally arrest this person for being in possession of

382

stolen goods, plus a few other things for good measure, and I'll be expecting her to explain all the circumstances surrounding this case in quite some detail," Gunna said, pleased to see that Bára looked suitably crestfallen.

Ægir Lárusson's face went even redder and Már muttered in his ear a second time.

"Gentlemen, this is a crime scene," she reminded them. "I have a serious assault to deal with here and every second counts. If you have a problem, I'd appreciate it if you take it up with Ívar Laxdal. All right?" she said, taking Bára by the arm. "And you're coming with me. Behave yourself or you'll be in handcuffs."

The helicopter fluttered overhead, silhouetted for a moment against the pure white of the mountains behind, before it thrashed away southwards through the cold, still air.

"Not a fucking hope," the paramedic said.

"What?"

"I reckon that guy's going to be a vegetable for the rest of his natural," he explained with a sour shake of his head. "I've seen plenty of road traffic accidents, fights, you name it. A head injury like that? I'd put money on it that he won't last the night."

Ívar Laxdal, resplendent in a short military-style coat and with his beret smartly perched on his head, narrowed his eyes at Gunna.

"If you'd been here ten minutes earlier . . .?" he ventured.

"If I'd had a crystal ball," she said. "If I hadn't gone to the ministry with you this morning, then Helgi and I would have been here an hour earlier. Of course, if we'd have turned up in the middle of it all, who knows what the result might have been? In my opinion, it doesn't pay to speculate after the event. You might be interested to know that Baddó had a gun in his pocket, which he'd probably borrowed or stolen from Hinrik the Herb, which is great for Hinrik as that means we can't pin possession of a handgun on him."

"What's this country coming to, Gunnhildur?"

"You tell me. This isn't about the people we're used to dealing with breaking the law. There's something much meaner and nastier behind it all. Now, if you'll excuse me, I have a crime scene that needs attending to, and there are two gentlemen over there who might want to speak to you."

Ívar Laxdal had the unaccustomed feeling that he was being told what to do; he opened his mouth to speak and then thought better of it before making his way to where Ægir Lárusson and Már Einarsson had parked their black 4x4 further up the street.

Inside the house Gunna sat on Sif's bed and looked at the accumulated teenage junk that reminded her of Laufey's bedroom. Sif sat stiffly next to her, looking overwhelmed as Gunna inspected the pictures of thrash metal bands pinned haphazardly on the walls.

"You know, I have a daughter who's just about your age, Sif," she said quietly.

"I expect she's a good girl, isn't she?" the girl said with a hint of a sneer in her tone.

384

"Far from it," Gunna said. "She's a pain in the backside and she drives me nuts a lot of the time."

"Oh."

"I want a quiet word with you before we all have to go to the station in Hverfisgata. It's going to be a long day, I'm afraid, and there are endless questions that you're going to have to answer. So between ourselves, before there are any formal interviews and anything is recorded, I just wanted to advise you to be upfront and tell it like it is. Understand?"

"Because you'll force it out anyway?"

"No, because unless you're smarter than even the most experienced criminals we've had to deal with, you'll trip over yourself and get found out sooner or later. It's nothing more sinister than that. Now, while it's just us, tell me about this laptop that all the fuss has been about."

Sif sighed and looked at Gunna with a new respect.

"What's going to happen?"

"Hospital to start with, then there'll be a lot of questions. Make it as straightforward as you can and it'll be fairly painless for all concerned."

"Am I going to be arrested?"

Sif's eyes were wide and there was fear behind her round glasses. "Maybe as a formality. You're certainly part of a large and rather complex investigation. Now, what's so special about this laptop?"

"It was in Dad's workshop. Hekla said she'd been given it by someone, but I didn't believe her. So I started it up; you need a password to get it to work."

"And?" Gunna asked as Sif paused.

"It was easy, really. The guy's business card was in the case as well. The password was his name."

"Jóel Ingi?"

"Bragason. That was like, really obvious. I was bored over Christmas and I tried to read some of the guy's reports, but they were really dull. So I went through his emails instead and found all that stuff in the outbox, all those emails between him and the people he works with about those four asylum seekers."

"You knew about that?"

"Duh," Sif said. "We're not all brain-dead dweebs who are only interested in music and partying."

"Sorry, I didn't mean to imply that you were. What are you doing at college, by the way?"

"Journalism and political science."

"Ah. That explains a few things. So who did you pass this information on to?"

"One of the guys on my course, and my tutor," Sif said in a small voice. "Will they get in trouble now?"

Gunna thought quickly. "No, I shouldn't think so. Is all this information still on the computer? How did you pass it on? Electronically or on paper?"

"There's nothing on that laptop. I reformatted it."

"What? You erased everything?"

Sif nodded and swept her hair out of her eyes. "The emails are copied to a dropbox on the internet as well, and I backed up the whole hard drive onto a portable HD."

She knelt on the floor and pushed a hand under the mattress, producing a small black box with two USB cables coming out of it. Gunna took it from her hand and put it in the pocket of her coat.

"That can stay safe with me, Sif," she said and looked towards the door. "Listen," she added quietly, looking into Sif's face and watching her eyes go wide. "What I said before about telling it like it is, do that. But as far as anyone's concerned, you didn't have a password, and you never got into that laptop. Is that clear? You just put it back where it was and forgot about it."

Sif nodded. "Yeah," she said. "I can do that."

Ívar Laxdal and Gunna watched as the first ambulance drove away sedately with Hekla and Sif on board, closely followed by Pétur in the old Land Rover and the black ministry 4x4 bringing up the rear, all of them heading for the National Hospital.

"Are they hurt badly?" Ívar Laxdal asked.

"No, I don't think so. Hekla had been slapped a few times, but no bones broken. The girl is the one I'd be concerned about. Seventeen is an impressionable age and this could haunt her for evermore."

"We still don't know which one of them stuck that thing into Bigfoot's head, do we?"

Gunna shrugged. "Does it matter? It'll be a self-defence plea whatever happens. As for Baddó, who knows? The ambulance guy reckoned he wouldn't make it to tomorrow."

"This needs to be kept discreet, Gunnhildur, as I'm sure you're aware."

"Is that what our friends in that black car told you?"

"I'm sure you'll do your work with your usual thoroughness and we'll see what rises to the surface, won't we?" Ívar Laxdal let fall one of his rare smiles and extinguished it just as quickly. "I have a feeling that one or both of them will be out of a job soon. Tomorrow, maybe."

Gunna did a double take and stared at Ívar Laxdal. "As quickly as that?"

"A fuck-up at that level, especially a potentially embarrassing one like this, isn't something that's easily forgiven, you know. Using a freelance private investigator to keep tabs on the ministry's own staff, even if they have screwed up, doesn't look good. The minister will find it easier to lay blame on people who aren't there any more if, or when, this becomes public knowledge."

"Jóel Ingi and one or both of those other clowns will be convenient scapegoats a month before the next election?"

This time Ívar Laxdal dropped a muffled laugh, an even rarer event. "You're turning into an old cynic, Gunnhildur," he said, almost jovially, and Gunna realized she was seeing a new side to the man, one in which he admitted taking delight in the tribulations facing the men from the ministry.

"You know that Már Einarsson knew that Jóel Ingi was leaving the country last night, but didn't tell anyone. He deliberately chose not to have him stopped? Bára was tracking the poor bastard and reporting his every movement to Már."

"And to Ægir, or further?"

"Who knows?"

"Anyway, Gunnhildur, would you like a ride back to town?" he asked, swinging his keys on one finger.

"Why not? Helgi can stay here with the forensics team to finish up. I'll just let him know, so he doesn't think I'm a missing person as well," she said, heading towards the house while Ívar Laxdal climbed into his car and the engine whispered into life.

"Long day, Mum?" Laufey said as Gunna groaned, dropped her shoes by the door and her coat over the back of a chair.

"Long isn't the word for it, and don't even ask what I've been up to," she said, wondering whether or not she dared to collapse onto the sofa, where Steini watched her over the top of his glasses and patted the seat next to him. "I mustn't," she said. "I wouldn't stand up again. Where's . . . our guest?"

Laufey jerked her head towards the hall. "In the shower, I guess. I reckon she was a bit put out."

"All right, who's upset her now?"

"Me, I'm afraid," Steini admitted. "She was hungry and I told her we wouldn't be having dinner until you got here, so she went out — I suppose she's been to the shop for a burger."

"She's in the shower, though? Again? Damn. Bang on the door, would you, sweetheart, and ask her if she's going to be long?"

Laufey pulled a long face, but got up all the same, while Gunna gave in to temptation and sank onto the sofa next to Steini, leaning against him, grateful for the arm he curled around her shoulders.

"Tough day?"

"You could say that. Exhausting, stressful, but there's a light at the end of a long tunnel."

"And another long day tomorrow, I suppose?"

"I'd be surprised if it wasn't. But the overtime won't do any harm if I'm going to replace that old car anytime soon," Gunna said with a yawn that left her gaping. "How about you?"

"I got in an hour ago to find Laufey and Drífa talking about men. They stopped as soon as I came in, thankfully. Those two are getting on like a house on fire."

"That's good." Gunna rubbed her eyes. "Are you cooking or am I?"

"I think it'll be me, don't you? And if Drífa has already filled up on junk food, that means more spaghetti for us."

Laufey reappeared and dropped back onto her seat as a vaguely familiar voice was heard. Gunna twisted to see the television and saw Ægir Lárusson's bald head and heavy features on the screen.

"Laufey, turn it up would you?"

". . . Not in a position to comment at the present moment," she heard him say, the wind blowing wisps of hair from the sides of his head as he stood in front of the ministry building. Gunna sat up and watched intently. Már Einarsson could be seen indistinctly as the camera panned back and a microphone was thrust under Ægir Lárusson's chin.

390

"Is this something you will be investigating as a matter of urgency?" an unseen interviewer asked.

"Absolutely. Definitely," Ægir Lárusson said with emphasis, smacking two fingers of one hand into the palm of the other. "If there is any truth behind these allegations, which I hasten to add have yet to be substantiated, then the ministry will do its utmost to examine the circumstances behind this deeply regrettable situation."

"That man lies like a cheap watch," Gunna said, lying back against Steini.

Steini frowned. "You know this guy?"

"And is the minister aware of what the implications could be for the government if these allegations are based on verifiable facts?" the interviewer asked.

Ægir Lárusson smiled, and Gunna saw Már Einarsson in the background, flanked by the plump young woman Gunna had seen him with that morning. Ægir Lárusson's smile looked sinister in the harsh lights behind the camera.

"I am confident that this matter can be resolved and that there are no skeletons in the ministry's cupboards," he said, stiffening and adjusting the collar of the same thick coat Gunna had seen him wearing only a few hours earlier, making it plain that the interview should be over.

"So can we expect a statement from the minister shortly?"

"That's up to the minister himself, and as you know he's taking part in a Nordic regional conference in

Riga. I'll raise it with him at the first available opportunity."

"But —"

"That is all I have to say for now," Ægir Lárusson said with a brief return of that wintry smile before he stepped smartly out of shot and the TV picture returned to a serious presenter behind a desk.

"Shrimp quotas for next year . . ." he began as Laufey turned the sound down.

"Loathsome, revolting man," Gunna grumbled, getting to her feet as the bathroom door opened and banged shut. "How long until dinner? What I really want to know is, are you doing garlic bread?"

"You're sure? Aren't you on shift tomorrow?"

"Oh, yes. A bit of garlic breath should make me even more feared an interrogator."

"They'll tell all just to escape your dragon breath."

"The lying bastards will be lining up to confess and I'll be a chief inspector before you know it. So pile it on, my good man."